The Great Twain Robbery

A Comedy Caper

by

Robert R. Guntrum

A Write Way Publishing Book

For S.

Copyright© 1994 by Robert R. Guntrum

Write Way Publishing
3806 S. Fraser
Aurora, Colroado 80014

First Edition; 1995

All rights reserved. No part of this book may be reproduced in any form, except by a newspaper or magazine reviewer who wishes to quote brief passages in connection with a review.

Queries regarding rights and permissions should be addressed to Write Way Publishing, 3806 S. Fraser, Aurora, Colorado, 80014

ISBN 1-885173-02-4

1 2 3 4 5 6 7 8 9 10

PUBLISHER'S NOTE:

When we first determined that we would publish this work of fiction, we assumed it was just that: fiction. Then the most amazing thing happened: a real manuscript by Mark Twain was discovered in a trunk in California!

From *Publishers Weekly*, June 19, 1995:

hot deals
by Maureen O'Brien

SYNERGY IN ACTON
"...Later this year, Random [House] will release a new, comprehensive edition of Mark Twain's *The Adventures of Huckleberry Finn*, based on a recently found manuscript of the 1884 classic that includes previously unpublished material ... after the manuscript was discovered in a trunk in California ..."

We all know the old saw about fact is stranger than fiction, but in this case, fiction came before the fact! Now, we're not saying that Robert Guntrum's scenario will play out the same way, of course...

Sunday through Friday

December 4-9

The Actors

Chapter 1
Sunday

THE ARTICLE IN THE NEWSPAPER said that the recently discovered, handwritten, unpublished, manuscript by Mark Twain would be on display from 9:00 AM to 11:00 AM, and from 2:00 PM to 5:00 PM, Monday through Saturday, at the Winslow Addison Museum and Gallery on North Lake Avenue in New Brighten, Connecticut.

It went on to say:

Discovered in an old trunk bought at an estate sale, the owner, Mrs. Louise Ann Bridges of Morrison Road, West Middlesex, Connecticut, said, "It was filled with all these folders stuffed full of papers. We found them when we opened it—after we broke the lock, of course; we had to, as old as it was, who knew where the key might be?—but we didn't know what it was. We just figured it was a bunch of junk we were going to have to throw away. We had no idea it would turn out like this. I only bought it for the trunk, didn't really care what was in it. I was going to use it for a coffee table."

Every collector in the country is expected to bid for possession of this amazing find. Richard Merriman, of Dorchester Publishing, the New York publishing house founded by Mr. Merriman's grandfather and now owned by an electronics and consumer products conglomerate out of Stuttgart, West Germany, said, "The intrinsic value of something handwritten by Mark Twain might prove to be worth many millions of dollars."

Experts agree. To date, except for Huckleberry Finn (the first half of which was just uncovered a few years ago—the last half was found in 1940) and a few letters of correspondence to various business associates, nothing else in the master's hand has ever been discovered. Even though it was common knowledge at the time that Twain wrote in longhand, according to reports—some confirmed by the author, himself—he usually destroyed those copies after publication. With the exception of Huckleberry Finn, no others were known to exist. The fact that this manuscript was never published was offered as one explanation as to why it was never destroyed.

"In my opinion," Mr. Merriman said, "something this rare, something that may very well be one of a kind, can only be defined as priceless." In addition, the publisher said, as with Mr. Twain's other works, once published with permission from the Twain heirs, a novel of this stature is bound to have "legs" [the publishing term for a novel that continues selling for a long period of time].

Possibly years?

Possibly forever, Mr. Merriman said. "For instance, if it were to become required reading in high schools and colleges, it could sell as many as a couple hundred thousand copies every year, which is," he explained, "one of the reasons why everyone's so interested. A manuscript like that would be a guaranteed revenue-producer, generating a high net for years and years. Needless to say, there's not a publisher in the world who's not interested in an asset of that magnitude. A manuscript that can generate those kinds of numbers year in and year out can cover an awful lot of fixed overhead."

A spokesperson for the Addison Gallery said that since the work is a valuable artifact—possibly even of greater value in an intrinsic sense than it is in terms of its tremendous publishing potential—rather than have a literary agent represent the property, Mrs. Bridges has decided to contract the gallery to act on her behalf. When asked what that value might be, the gallery would only comment, "We'll find that out on Sunday."

Sunday, December 10th, is the scheduled date of the auction at the Carneby-Glenn Auction House in Manhattan. Experts in the field estimate the total value of the entire package at a minimum of ten million dollars, adding, that if a collector wants it badly enough, who knows how high the bidding might go? The sky's the limit ...

The sky's the limit.

Henry Nash folded up the newspaper and tossed it angrily on the coffee table, the same coffee table that also supported his Sunday morning slippered feet, then let out with a sigh. Some people have all the luck, he grumbled to himself. Some old biddy in Connecticut buys a piece of junk for thirty bucks and before you know it she's a millionaire.

Talk about falling into it!

Didn't do squat for it, didn't do squat to deserve it, that's what irritated Henry.

Some people—like present company, for instance; like Henry J. Nash, for instance—worked their tails off week after week, year after year, and didn't have diddly dingle to show for it. One house, one—make that two—mortgages, one wife and two kids. And no future. Those most deserving got calluses and sore backs for their efforts, while others, like some old bat outta Who Knows Where, Connecticut, for instance, just happen to be in the right place at the right time and bingo, Big Bucks!

And this wasn't the first time it had happened, not by a long shot. Just the other day Henry remembered reading about some guy who found a copy of the constitution of the United States behind a two-dollar picture frame that had been in the bozo's garage for years. He said he didn't know how it got there or where it came from. And then another ding dong comes along with more money than sense and offers him a big fat five mil for it. Can you believe it? What I could do with five million, Henry thought to himself.

Henry huffed and puffed. The whole thing was beginning to get under his skin. Always the other guy; always somebody else. When was it going to be his turn?

Henry looked down at the newspaper—*the sky's the limit*.

And she says she isn't going to change her lifestyle at all, Henry recalled.

When Henry'd first read that he'd fumed. And as he thought about it now he fumed again.

"'Still going to bag groceries at the local Foodtown,'" Henry mimicked the article. "'Still going to live in the same old two-bedroom house.' 'May go see the kids in Ohio more often, but that's about it.'"

Whoopee! No Cadillac. No condo on the Riviera. No mink, no diamond, no big screen TV.

More than anything, that grabbed Henry the most. If you have it and don't use it, why have it? If you don't use it, you don't deserve it, that was Henry's motto. If you don't use it, what the hell good is it?

Henry pounded a right fist on the arm of his six-year-old easy chair in disgust. Dust clouds puffed. Probably wasn't even planning on buying her poor old husband a new easy chair, Henry thought. Even if it was loaded with dust, like you-know-who's.

Henry let out with another sigh, grumbled a few more indistinguishable syllables under his breath and then leaned back in his chair to ponder his lot in life. He hadn't done that in a while. He hadn't made a thorough appraisal of his position lately. Maybe something had changed.

Nothing had.

He pondered some more.

Nothing surfaced.

He gave up. So much for appraising his position. It was no use; all it did was make him feel bad. Destiny had dealt him a lousy hand and there was nothing he could do about it.

Except there was one thing he could do; he could escape now and then. He couldn't hide, not forever, but he could run away for a little while.

Henry reached into the magazine pocket on the side of his chair and pulled out the paperback novel he'd been working on for the past two weeks. He could count on Jesse to get his mind off the fact that it was always somebody else who fell into the outhouse and walked away with the new suit. He could count on his friends to help him forget it was always the other guy's smiling kisser on the front page of the newspaper or the magazine or on TV, always other people grinning The Big Grin, holding up their check for winning the Lotto, or winning The Publisher's Sweepstakes All-you-have-to-do-is-send-it-in First Prize. Lucky stiffs. It wasn't fair. Life wasn't fair. Henry put on his reading glasses and grumbled some more as he opened the book to the dog-eared page, and began to read.

"Rio Grande Escape," another story about the adventures of Jesse and Frank James, quickly absorbed Henry's mind, and before he realized it the adventures of one Louise Ann Bridges were swept out of his thoughts for the first time that morning.

Henry Nash was a big fan of Western novels. No, he was more than a fan—he was a fanatic. Maybe, some would say, psychotic. He read every one he could get his hands on. Some, his favorites, he read twice. Louis L'Amour, Zane Grey, The James Brothers, The Dalton Gang. Give Henry a good story about the Old West and he was a happy man. Deliriously happy. Let Henry lose himself in a saga about the life and times of bank robbers and gun fighters and cattle rustlers and range wars and stampedes and wagon trains and Indian uprisings and dying with your boots on, and Henry was in heaven. Life in the Old West, where men were men, and women thanked their lucky stars for them and vowed eternal gratitude. Those were the days. Not like today, Henry observed to himself, when women seemed to prefer a guy with a high voice and a low wrist. Give Henry a time where he could strap on his six-shooter, saddle-up Old Paint, and then ride away from the problems of the world: "go west young man" to *those glorious days of yesteryear*. That's right, Henry thought, *where the Lone Ranger rides again*. Just once, Henry Nash wanted to be the one who rode off into the sunset.

But Henry Nash had been born in the wrong century; he was a hundred years too late. Henry was a man of today, not a man of yesterday. Most definitely not a man of yester-year. For Henry Nash, it was too late to be a cowboy. For Henry Nash it was too late to be Jesse James.

But he could dream.

Lilith Bright didn't have time to dream. Lilith was too busy. Lilith was pissed.

That was the one thing you learned quickly about Lilith Bright: No matter how busy she got, she always allowed plenty of time to be pissed.

"Did you see this article in *Time* magazine?" she asked.

Her husband, Ralph, answered with a curious look.

Lilith was standing by his chair looking down at him, breathing hard, out of breath, puffing for no reason. Anger had that effect on Lilith. She held the magazine out for Ralph to see.

"Some woman in Connecticut bought an old trunk at an estate sale and guess what she found in it? Just guess."

Ralph lowered the Sunday comics he'd been enjoying onto his lap and looked up at his wife of twenty-seven years. Ralph didn't want to guess. Ralph didn't like guessing. Every time Ralph guessed, Ralph guessed wrong, and that made Lilith angry. Ralph knew from experience, however, that if he waited long enough he wouldn't have to guess.

Ralph waited.

And Ralph was right. Lilith and Ralph Bright had been married for over a quarter of a century and in that time Lilith usually supplied the answers, as well as the questions. This time was no exception.

"An unpublished work by Mark Twain, that's what," Lilith said. "*Handwritten*, no less. In his own hand. Can you believe it?"

Ralph mumbled something that sounded like: *Well, I'll be darned*. The expression on his face was flat and empty.

Ralph's lack of interest seemed to irritate Lilith even more than the article. "Jesus Christ, Ralph! Don't just sit there looking stupid. Don't you get it? I said, 'A woman in Connecticut found an *unpublished, handwritten* manuscript by Mark Twain'..?"

"Yes, dear. I heard you."

Irritation changed to disgust. "Ralph, wake up and smell the coffee. You know something like that has got to be worth a damned fortune."

It was obvious Lilith was searching for something.

"Yes, dear," Ralph repeated. "I'm sure it is."

Ralph was trying not to be patronizing, trying not to irritate Lilith any more than he already had, although for the life of him he wasn't exactly sure how to accomplish that feat.

Sometimes not irritating Lilith Bright was easier said than done. Especially since there were a lot of times when Ralph wasn't certain why his dear wife was irritated to begin with. Like this time, for instance. Sometimes Lilith just flew off the handle and Ralph was darned if he knew why.

Like this time, for instance.

After twenty-seven years of marriage you'd think you'd understand a person more, Ralph told himself. It stood to reason, after that long you should know your spouse pretty well, right?

Wrong. Not if your spouse was Lilith Bright. It was no use; when it came to Lilith Bright, *reason* had very little to do with *understanding*. There was a lot about his one-and-only that remained a mystery to Ralph Bright, even after all these years.

As in the past, Ralph's attempt at not irritating Lilith went for naught. Lilith stared down at him like an angry bull. Her eyes were two black holes that seemed to devour everything in sight. Her jaw jutted out from her face at a right angle and the corners of her mouth pointed straight down. She's gritting her teeth, Ralph thought. Not a good sign.

Even when she wasn't gritting her teeth, even when calm, even when sedate (Ralph recalled that just last month the periodontist had given Lilith a couple of little blue pills before he operated on her gingivitis, and even sedated she looked mean and ornery, as though she might open her eyes at any minute and bite your head off) Lilith Bright was a dark, foreboding woman, with deep-set eyes and thick, jet-black hair (aided in recent years by her friend, Miss Clairol). Endowed with an exceptionally large head for her gender, it did not, however, make her look top-heavy, but seemed to work well with the rest of her physique. Chiseled high atop her frame in the very center of two massive shoulders it blended perfectly with the structure below—much like Mount Rushmore blended perfectly with South Dakota.

Lilith was big, to say the least. She had a Mother Earth bosom, hips that screamed hippopotamus, and a caboose that could have hauled enough freight to have kept the Baltimore and Ohio profitable into the twenty-first century. She was a coarse, unwieldy woman, in tone as well as action; she didn't talk, she snorted; she didn't walk, she lumbered ... a female bull, if ever there was such a thing. Her words were cannonballs that she tossed around freely and eagerly, in a voice as gruff as a fog horn that not only penetrated the fog but diffused it. Heavy eyebrows grew together to form one solid ridge at the base of her forehead. They stuck out over her eyes and reminded Ralph of one of those sunvisors they used to put on all the cars back in the fifties. (It was an analogy that Ralph never bothered to point out to Lilith.) The advantage, if any, was the fact that they (it) shaded her eyes on bright sunny days. The disadvantage: when she didn't look like a '53 Mercury, she looked like one of her prehistoric ancestors. (Another metaphor Ralph chose not to share over the years.)

As Lilith stared down at him along her (rather lengthy) nose, Ralph wished he had a rock to crawl under. He'd seen that look many times throughout their twenty-seven *happy* years together; it spelled trouble. Clenched fists resting on ample hips attested to the fact that Lilith Bright was ready to do battle. It would not be a fair fight; she outweighed Ralph by fifty pounds.

"Ralph." Her voice said *Ralph*, but her tone said *dummy*. "Mark Twain? Samuel Clemens?" She raised an eyebrow. "Doesn't that ring a bell?"

Oh-oh, that's what Ralph was afraid of. He'd played dumb in front of Lilith on purpose, knowing the consequences, knowing it would irritate her and she'd be mad at him and he'd have to bear the brunt of that anger. But he had to because that's exactly what her comment had done—it had rung a bell. It had rung a very familiar bell. It had rung a bell that Ralph wasn't all that keen on listening to. It played a song that was not music to Ralph's ears. Ralph had feared that he knew what Lilith was getting at but had prayed with all his might that he was wrong.

Apparently he wasn't. Apparently, to Ralph's regret, he was right as rain.

Ralph found no joy in being right. Ralph had been here before. He took a deep breath and let some carefully chosen words tiptoe out of his mouth one step at a time, slowly, meticulously, testing the water as they came, making certain there wasn't a "word killer" out there with a big club waiting to bash their brains in. Like before, like always, the little voice in his brain sent out a warning: tread softly, Ralph.

"Oh, ah, yes, dear, I know. Samuel Clemens was a distant relative of yours, on your—what was it? Your great-grandmother's side?"

"Distant relative!" Lilith shouted. Ralph flinched. "He was my great-grandmother's brother-in-law, for Chrissake! That's not distant; that's *family*."

Ralph smiled and nodded. He wanted to say he understood all that. He wanted to say he'd heard the story so many times he was sick of it. He wanted to say it was her hostility, her obsession that he didn't understand. But Ralph knew better; Ralph was well-trained. Ralph had learned. Ralph chose to say nothing.

Of course, that didn't always work either. Silence was the coward's way out. She explained her hostility, with both barrels: "That manuscript belongs to me, Ralph! That's what I'm saying. Can you follow that? If you weren't so dense you'd have figured it out for yourself."

Ralph exhaled as if it were his last breath. Here we go again.

Although they started late in life (they were both in their thirties when love finally blossomed and they decided to tie the knot), throughout the ever-stormy marriage of Mr. Ralph Nathan and Mrs. Lilith Elaine Bright, Lilith had always felt that she'd never been properly recognized (maybe *compensated* was a better word) for the fact that she was related to the famous Mark Twain. They were "family," next of kin. Blood relatives. Ralph had heard the complaints over and over. Where was the fame? Where was the fortune? As Twain's only living relative (as far as Lilith knew, *as far as Lilith cared*), you'd think she'd be entitled to something. Wouldn't you?

Recognition? Reward? *Royalties?* At least *one* of the three Rs.

Damn straight!

But it never came. Her birthright—her "right" to fame and fortune—had never blossomed the way Lilith felt that it should have. It had never born the fruit of her labors. And it was certainly not for lack of trying.

Nor money spent. Lilith had squandered every extra penny she could squeeze out of Ralph's meager earnings—collected every other Friday over the past twenty-seven years at Clancy's Lumber and Tile—fighting with publishers about who *owned*, who had the *rights to*, who should get *royalties for*, the works of her dear, departed, great-great-uncle-in-law ... an uncle through marriage ... once removed.

Whatever.

It had never been completely clear to Ralph just "what" exactly Lilith considered this relationship to be. It seemed to change to fit the circumstances. One day he was her great-great-uncle, the next he was her great-grandfather on her mother's side. He'd even heard her tell someone on the phone one time that Mark Twain was her grandfather's twin brother. Ralph suspected that Lilith didn't really know "what" Mark Twain was, she simply knew that as far as she was concerned he was all "hers."

Her success up to this point was easily defined. She had, or rather *they* had, *one* two-bedroom, one-bath cottage that they'd lived in for the last twenty-five years (they'd lived with Lilith's parents for the first two years of their marriage); *one* seven-year-old Ford station wagon that managed somehow to get them to wherever they wanted to go, though certainly not in style; and *one* savings account at the Orchard Hill Savings and Loan that contained $2,437.37 *exactly* ... as of the beginning of the month.

That's what they had. But what had it cost them?

It had cost them a bigger house, a newer car, and a fatter savings account. And a lot of sleepless nights.

And for Ralph, those nights were the worst. How many hours had he spent lying awake staring up at the ceiling wondering how they'd make ends meet, how they'd pay their bills. How they'd survive in their retirement, while Lilith had spent her days shoveling that retirement, *their* financial future, down a rat hole? Clancy's wasn't General Motors; it offered no pension plan. Social Security would be all they'd have to live on. Social Security—and whatever they managed to save, which was, as of now, $2,437.37.

And what would they do if they had a medical emergency? Ralph shivered at the thought. A thought he'd had before. Every night for the last twenty-seven years.

And the days were not much better. Ralph spent many of those days watching in horror as his life, like their financial security, sailed away. First his youth, then middle-age. And now, what was left? There was nothing Ralph could do now but lie there and groan helplessly as the face of old-age peered at him over the horizon, smiling a toothless smile, winking a bloodshot eye. Retirement was not that far away—Ralph was sixty years old. He wasn't getting any younger. And neither was Lilith. They should be saving for the future, not chasing rainbows.

But more than the failure to achieve riches, more than the glory that was never theirs, more than the fame that never manifested itself, it was the loss of dignity that bothered Ralph the most. Each new escapade made him feel like a man on his knees with his hand out, a beggar in a bazaar of thieves. With the loss of his dignity came the destruction of his will and the death of his spirit. Time's foreclosure of his youth—wasted days, and wasted nights, wasted lives—that was a much greater loss than the bankruptcy that had overtaken his body. His mind, his desire, had aged even faster than his physical being. He was once a strong, vital man, in body and spirit. A man with purpose; a man with dreams. But not any more. The dreams had died when the spirit died, and only emptiness remained. A hollow man is far worse off than a dead man, Ralph told himself.

And he was right. A dead man felt no pain.

But Ralph felt it. The always fighting and always losing, that's what twisted him inside out. That, and what it had done to Lilith. What had started out as a simple voyage quickly turned into a pilgrimage, and then into a crusade. Over the years Lilith had become more and more obsessed with the whole idea. The older she got the harder she got, and the more determined she became. Nothing else mattered. The only thing that counted was The Quest, getting what (she thought) rightfully belonged to her. At any cost.

And it was all so useless: Ralph and Lilith Bright against the world. Just the two of them. The mismatch of the century.

Not that they didn't have a little help along the way. Sometimes they had more help than they knew what to do with. There seemed to be a neverending supply of people out there more than willing to help them collect and spend "the spoils of victory." Every year or so a brand new, bright-eyed, eager beaver let's-go-get-'em attorney—an attorney (shyster, really) who thought he smelled the potential for a quick killing—would crawl from the slime and volunteer his services. He'd read or heard about Lilith's claim, and through the gates he'd charge, beating on his chest, waving his banner, guaranteeing victory. He'd jump on board the bandwagon and promise the world. But the world is a place long on promise and short on delivery, a mean and wicked place. Most lasted no more than a month or two. Invariably they always beat a hasty retreat once the heavy artillery arrived—why get bloody if you can't win? They'd slink away, looking for easier battles. Shysters were no match for the pin-striped suited, pink-tied, manicured-nailed corporate attorneys the publishers kept shoving in their faces one after another, as though they were being manufactured by every law school in the country specifically for the purpose of pounding the living daylights out of the Bright aggregate. They came in droves, hordes, legions. The Phi Beta Kappas from Harvard and Yale were nothing more than mercenaries in Brooks Brothers' suits, shielded with leather briefcases and armed with injunctions and writs and disclaimers and precedent, and whereas upon whereas upon whereas ...

The Bright Team was outnumbered and outfinanced—overeager but outgunned. The weight of all the losing battles had piled up and eventually become too much for Ralph to bear. After a while the only course, the only alternative, was to surrender to it. At age sixty he was a tired, defeated puppy who just wanted to crawl into a corner and lick his wounds. Let them have it, he argued. It wasn't worth it. It wasn't worth the pain. He didn't need all this.

But all the battles had had the opposite effect on Lilith. Lilith became more determined with each defeat. Losing just added kindling to an already raging fire. All the more reason to get those bastards, she countered. They deserved it. It's them against us, Ralph.

Unfortunately, in addition to the anger, each failure added something else to an already numb human being, something new to the uncaring, the unfeeling, the it's-me-against-the-world mutant that the struggle had created: it added another layer of scar tissue to Lilith Bright. It put just that much more distance between her and rest of humanity. Lilith's coat of armor did nothing to protect, only to separate. The more Lilith lost, the more she was willing to lose and the more she was willing to sacrifice. She became a psychotic gambler who couldn't quit, a crapshooter who couldn't walk away from the table until everything was gone. An alcoholic who had to have one more drink. Lilith was a drug addict whose fix was the endless struggle, and whose high was the remote, baseless belief that one day she'd win. If she could just hold on long enough. It was just a matter of time. She'd get those bastards. She'd get them all.

And it was about to happen all over again. Ralph knew the look.

Lilith stood there staring at the magazine. Fire burned in her eyes. She spoke to Ralph, but it was to the entire world that she declared her determination and made her vow, "Well, by God, we'll just see about this!" Lilith said, each word a spike struck with sledgehammer resolve. "We will indeed."

She threw the magazine onto the coffee table. The glass-covered candy dish—a gift from her parents last Christmas—rattled under the wake.

Ralph took a deep breath. He wondered in silence: Could he ready himself one more time for the coming battle? Was there any fight left?

Chapter 2
Monday

6:52 AM

Henry stuck his time card into the slot. The automatic triggering mechanism in the time clock kicked in and gave out with a big CA-CHUNG! and automatically punched MO 6:52 AM under the IN column.

Monday morning, the worst space on the card. The whole week in front of me, Henry thought, letting out a sigh as he stepped forward and put his card into the brown metal holder hanging on the wall beside the time clock. Directly behind him his best friend, Roger Muldowney, repeated the process.

"So, Henry, how was the weekend?" Roger asked.

Henry grunted. "Glad it's over. Nice to get those lousy weekends out of the way, you know, so I can get back here and put in a solid eight for good old GM. I live for my job, you know that, Rog."

Roger laughed. "Yeah, me too. I love this company."

Henry's face showed no expression when he said, "I love my job. I love my company. I love my country. I love hot dogs and apple pie and Chevrolets."

The two men went directly to their lockers. Henry opened the combination lock hanging on door #1254. Roger did the same on #1253. They put their aluminum lunch buckets on the top shelf—Roger's was black, Henry's was gray—took out their aprons, closed the doors, snapped the padlocks shut and marched out the door and into the assembly plant.

Three minutes later they were at their stations. Roger put on the right tires and Henry put on the left. They had shared the same pit under the FINAL STAGING AREA of the Chevrolet Assembly Plant in Fort Lee, New Jersey, for the past sixteen years. The tires were the last things to go on. After that, it was up to one of the guys up above to get in and drive it away. Assuming the damn thing started, of course. Sometimes it didn't. That really pissed off the Quality guys. Henry and Roger usually snickered to themselves when that happened.

The job paid sixteen-fifty an hour and was boring as hell. And neverending. They felt like soldiers in a trench, fighting a war that would go on forever because nobody ever got killed. They just retired at age sixty-five and somebody else took their place. Boredom and complacency were the only killers here. Stagnant men in stagnant jobs leading stagnant lives. At precisely 7:00 AM a buzzer went off and the conveyor line overhead started to move. Roger and Henry went to work.

"Sure glad we got that buzzer," Roger said. "I'm too damn stupid to figure out when to start all by myself."

Henry said, "Yeah, me too. If it wasn't for that buzzer I'd probably never go home, either. Duh, I just wouldn't know when to leave, you know? Duh, life is awful comp-lee-cated."

"Yeah it is." Roger agreed.

Ten minutes passed.

Roger said, "Do anything exciting this weekend, Henry?"

"Naw," Henry said, sliding a whitewall onto a blue, four-door Citation. "Watched the Jets get their asses kicked on TV again. You?"

Roger made a face. "Nope. Liz Taylor called and wanted me to come over. But I figured I'd better not encourage the bitch. She might start expecting me to shit every time she said 'crap'."

"I think that was smart, Rog. You gotta keep broads like that in their place, you know?"

"Yeah."

Another ten minutes of life disappeared.

Then Henry said, "You happen to see that article in yesterday's paper? 'Bout that broad in Connecticut that found the Mark Twain stuff in an old trunk?"

Roger shook his head no.

Henry went on. "Yeah. Bought an old trunk at an estate sale and found a manuscript by Mark Twain in it."

"No kidding?"

"Yep. A handwritten job, no less. Never been published."

"What's the name of it?"

Henry's look was questioning. "What's the name of what?"

"What's the name of the book?"

Henry shook his head. "How the hell should I know?"

"Hey, you read the damn article, not me."

"It didn't give the name, Rog. Okay? Besides, what the hell difference does that make?"

Roger stopped working, leaned down and looked at Henry under the gold Camaro that had just moved into their section. "Might make a lot of difference. I may not buy it if I don't like the title."

Henry looked back. "Hey, dipshit, it's not for sale. It hasn't even been published yet."

"Yeah, but one day it will be. Right?"

Henry shrugged his shoulders. "I guess."

"Well, when it is, I better like the title, or I'm not going to buy it."

Henry was stunned. "You're shittin' me. You buy books based on the title?"

"Hell yes," Roger said. "Everybody does." Roger nodded to himself. "Damned straight."

"Didn't you ever hear 'you can't judge a book by the cover'?"

"Yeah."

"And?"

"Horseshit."

"Horseshit on horseshit. That's the dumbest thing I ever heard. What's the stupid cover have to do with it?" Henry shook his head, disgusted.

"It has everything to do with it." Roger slid a blackwall onto the gold Camaro. It wouldn't go on. He reached into his apron, pulled out a rubber-headed mallet and gave it a whack. It went on. He put the mallet away. "I've never read one book with a lousy cover that was worth a shit."

"You're kidding."

"No, that's the God's truth."

"Rog, I don't believe what you're telling me here. You're gonna make me think I've been working with a moron all these years. The cover doesn't mean shit and neither does the title."

"*El wrongo!* Take my word for it. You buy a book with a shit cover or a shit title and you're gonna get a shit book." Roger nodded and winked knowingly.

Henry turned around and reached into the barrel behind him and re-loaded his apron with lugnuts. When he turned back he said, "Okay, wiseass, gimme an example."

Roger busied himself in thought, then finally blurted out, "*Hitler and the Vampire of Berlin*. There. Lousy cover, lousy book."

Henry shook his head. "*Hitler and the Vampire of Berlin?* Jesus Christ, Rog. You're jerkin' me off, right? I'm sure the cover really had a hell of a lot to do with that winner, not to mention the title. You know, you'd think with a title like that, the book had to win at least the Pulitzer Prize, wouldn't you?"

No response.

For the next twenty minutes neither man spoke. In that time, Sal Vacossi, President of UAW Local 214, was paged three times.

Finally, Henry said, "So, I take it you didn't read the article?"

"No. Didn't see it. What about it?"

"Paper said it might have been in that trunk for over a hundred years."

Roger slid the right front wheel onto the gray Lumina that moved slowly over his head. "You don't say."

Henry wiped his mouth with the sleeve of his shirt. "It was in the paper. Says it's probably worth a fortune."

After tightening the front wheel in place, Roger moved to the rear wheel. "You mean the people who owned the trunk never looked in it?"

Once again, over the PA system: "*Sal Vacossi, call three-one-three-one.*"

"It was an estate sale, Rog. Some old biddy died and everything went up for auction. Only relatives she had were a couple of cousins who lived way out in Kansas who didn't want to be bothered, so they just told the attorney to hire an auctioneer and sell everything—'as is, where is'—and send them the proceeds. Paper said the trunk was locked and nobody bothered to look for the key. Said the woman didn't have two nickels to rub together. Nothin'. Nothin' worth nothin'. So," he shrugged his shoulders, "nobody figured there'd be anything in the trunk worth wasting their time for."

"No shit? Sounds kinda dumb to me."

"Yeah, me, too." Henry shook his head. "They say it's probably worth millions, according to the papers."

"No shit?"

"Yep."

"How do you suppose the trunk got all the way to Connecticut? Twain lived on the Mississippi, right?"

"See, there you go again, Rog. Proving you don't know shit about shit."

"What's that supposed to mean?"

Henry said, "Twain lived in Connecticut. Hartford, to be exact. He wrote about the Mississippi because that's where he spent most of his childhood."

"No shit?"

Henry tossed his head forward. "That's right."

Roger was impressed and said so. "I'm impressed. I didn't know I was working with a real live historian. How come you know all that stuff?"

"Hey, I make it my business to know. Don't want people accusing me of being a dumb ass."

"Henry? I got news for you: It ain't workin'."

Henry laughed. "You could be right."

Roger smiled. "Henry, take my word for it, I am right."

Henry nodded, "You could be," and squeezed the trigger on his nut-runner, screwing the last bolt into place on the left rear wheel of a black Corsica.

Carneby-Glenn's biggest sale to date had been a Picasso that went for six and a half million dollars. Carneby-Glenn was not as big a hitter as Sothebys, but when it came to auction houses, it wasn't minor league either.

Founded in 1920, the founders (John Jacob Carneby the third, and Joseph Sinclair Glenn, the first, and last—it was said no woman would have him; he was so ornery many questioned why his shadow had not deserted him) had, over the years, built the establishment into a solid business venture. It was well respected, unquestionably forthright, soundly scrupulous, exceedingly ethical, and, maybe, just a tad bit stodgy (which was considered by many to be a plus when it came to auction houses), and, even through the war years, had been able to generate an acceptable (although meager by Sothebys' standards) return to its investors.

It was Victor Romaine's job to "keep the coffers singing." Victor Romaine, Executive Director of Carneby-Glenn.

Victor Romaine had no fear of that. He was certain the auction of the Twain manuscript would top a Picasso by a couple of million, at least. As Victor proudly told his wife, that should make the current board of directors (minus the founders, who died within two days of each other in 1976, each at the ripe old age of eighty-eight, and, as the one remaining board member who knew them personally attested to, "cantankerous as all get out") sit up and take notice. Phyllis Romaine was thrilled with the news.

"Oh, Victor, that's wonderful. I'm so proud of you," she exclaimed into the telephone.

Victor leaned back in the black leather swivel-back chair and propped his feet up on the mahogany desk. The shine on his two-year-old cordovan Florsheims caught his eye. He thought to himself: No more Florsheims for this kid, from here on out it's Lorenzo Banfi of Italy all the way. Victor sighed, a contented man. "Yes, dear," he said. "This will make Carneby-Glenn financially solvent for the next five years."

And, he calculated, with his commission (one percent as far as his dear wife, Phyllis, was aware, but, in reality, one-point-five according to the latest contract he'd just signed—a little bonus from the board in recognition of his past service that he failed to mention to his extremely giddy-at-the-moment spouse) he'd also be able to pay off the twenty-five grand he owed Carmine Rico, too.

But that was a private debt. A debt the Missus was not privy to. The truth of the matter was: Carneby-Glenn would be in sound shape financially either way, regardless of outcome of the Twain auction; it was Victor Romaine who had the cash flow problem.

"I'm so happy for you," Phyllis Romaine told her husband. "You've worked so hard. You deserve this success."

Victor glowed in the light of the compliment. Hell, yes, he'd worked hard. Harder than she'd ever know. Harder than she'd ever guess. Executive Directors of auction houses were expected to work hard. That was their job. The long hours, the time away from home, that was all part of it. And for the last eight years, ever since he'd left that little dump in Chicago and taken the promotion to the Big Apple, Victor Romaine had been busting his butt. Victor knew that you couldn't survive in New York City any other way. New York City was the epitome of survival of the fittest. New York City was a jungle. It ate incompetents alive.

But it wouldn't get its fangs into Victor Romaine. He'd never slow down long enough for it to catch up. He was on a fast track and he was staying there. The Mark Twain manuscript would see to that. His dear wife was absolutely right: Victor Romaine deserved everything he got. He'd put in his hours, paid his dues, and now it was reward time. What she didn't know was that the long hours he'd so willingly absorbed were split just about evenly between two very different activities: one, entertaining clients of Carneby-Glenn, and two, watching very big ponies run around in very small circles.

Ah, the Sport of Kings. Horse racing—that was Victor Romaine's lot in life. *Betting his money on a bob-tailed nag*, that's what he was born to do. That was the plan.

But it never seemed to turn out the way Victor planned. The certain winners, the sure things, somehow always managed to turn into inevitable losers. Up to now the thrill of victory was buried up to its bridle in the agony of defeat. Standing at the cashier's cage counting fifty-dollar-bills was the glorious dream; but standing in the men's room tearing up worthless tickets was the cruel reality. *That*, and explaining to Carmine Rico's men that he'd have Mr. Rico's money by next week for sure. Honest. If they'd just give him a little more time.

Of course, he could have all the time he wanted. Mr. Rico understood. Sometimes things got a little tight. No problem, take another week. Just pay the vig (ten points—ten points equals ten percent, that's *per* week, which is only five-hundred-and-twenty percent *per* year, not counting a little item called *compounding*, which means, when you add it all up, it's only five hundred points higher than the rate Chase Manhattan advertised in yesterday's *Wall Street Journal*) and we'll see you next week. If you can't pay the ten, well, that's okay, too. But then we gotta add it to the principle, you see, and then charge you interest on the whole thing. You understand; it's business. The smile that always followed was bone-chilling.

Beads of sweat popped out on Victor's forehead when he thought about it. He felt light-headed; the room started to spin. The question was: Just how long would Carmine Rico be patient? He said he'd wait, but would he? Did he mean it? Could he be trusted? *Was there honor among thieves?* Victor had said he'd pay last week, too, but he hadn't paid. Why should Rico keep his word any more than Victor had kept his? Is that what Rico was thinking right now, Victor wondered; was Rico thinking about sending someone over to "teach him a lesson?" Victor fidgeted in his chair. Was Rico smiling out of one side of his mouth when he promised Victor he'd wait, and out of the other side issuing a contract? Carmine Rico was a lot of things, but there was one thing he wasn't: Carmine Rico wasn't a bank. And he didn't live by banking rules. He didn't foreclose; he broke bones. He didn't send sheriffs to evict; he sent no-neck gorillas with instructions to apply just enough pressure (to no joint, appendage or muscle group in particular) to make the veins on his forehead pop out. No long-term damage, just short-term pain. A reminder that Carmine Rico could do anything he wanted, when he wanted, to whomever he wanted. Sooner or later the man would get tired of waiting and smiling and understanding. Victor prayed with all his might that that time had not yet come.

Victor took out his handkerchief and wiped his brow. Why was he sweating? Everything was going to be fine. His problems were all behind him, now. There was a light at the end of the tunnel and it was the light of salvation. It didn't go by the name of Jesus Christ, it was called Mark Twain. The Mark Twain manuscript was Victor Romaine's savior, curing him of all ills, delivering him from evil, forgiving his sins—past, present *and* future. Victor Romaine was one auction away from being born again, healthy, wealthy and wise. And free. Free to start over. Free to make it really big this time. He'd gotten a couple of tips recently that he knew were bound to pay off big. He just needed a little more time and everything would be fine.

He took two deep breaths, put his handkerchief away and said, "We'll even make enough to buy you that little green Jag you've been talking about."

A piece of meat for his hungry lioness.

"Oh, honey. Really?" Phyllis bit into it without thinking.

"That's right. Hey, you deserve something, too." Butter the little lady up. Keep her thinking about her little toys and Victor would be free to play with his. "You've stuck with me through this whole thing, from the very beginning, right by my side. If you can't get a little reward now and then, what the hell good is it?"

"Oh, Victor, you're so wonderful. I can't believe it. You're too good to me. You know how much I love that car, don't you? It's so neat. Have you seen it? Do you know the one I'm talking about? It's—"

Victor let his wife ramble on about her dream car while he thought about other things. Cars didn't light his fire. He didn't want four hundred horses under a hood, he wanted just one, under a jockey. On a fast track. On a sunny day. With a handful of tickets in his tightly clenched fist, screaming like a maniac for the son of a bitch to get the lead out of his or her sorry ass and get to the head of the pack for a change, instead of always bringing up the damned rear. Didn't the horses he picked ever get tired of staring at the assholes of all those other horses for chrissake?

Phyllis kept speaking, tossing out thank-you's and declarations of gratitude and bones of praise one right after another, never realizing it was all to deaf ears, because it was now Victor's office that captured all his attention. To redecorate or not to redecorate, that was the question. Victor never flinched: redecorate, of course. Hell yes. And his desk, where his soon-to-be-replaced Florsheims were parked, would be the first thing to go. When his Mark Twain Ship came in, this sorry piece of timber would have a new home—Goodwill Industries was about to find one slightly-used executive desk under its Christmas tree this year. Victor needed something more apropos, something more fitting, something more suited to his new stature. After all, establishments of high caliber—the kind that Carneby-Glenn was about to become—had an image to uphold. Chippendale, that's what he'd be resting his Florsh—*Lorenzo Banfis*—on in the future. Once the manuscript was sold, Victor was certain he'd have no problem at all convincing the board to spring for a new piece of furniture or two.

His eyes stopped at the love seats, the ones Phyllis had picked out. Those gawd-awful love seats. Phyllis had insisted upon them: "They'll be marvelous," she'd promised.

They were atrocious.

They were history. Out! Gone!

Victor never did like them. But he let Phyllis decorate his office just to keep her busy—busy hands are happy hands. But now was the time to make a statement, and corduroy just didn't speak eloquently enough. Ultra-suede, that was the "in" voice this year.

And paneling. A soft oak, or rich cherry, something dark and heavy—like Sothebys. He looked down at his pin-striped jacket—maybe a couple new Georgio Armani's would be nice, too. After all, he should look as spiffy as his office, shouldn't he?

" ... and it has real wood on the dash, and ..."

God, the woman could ramble. Victor looked at the calendar on his desk, five more days to go. That hick museum in Connecticut had it for five more days, and then it would be on its merry way to Carneby-Glenn. And it would all be his. On Sunday afternoon at precisely 2:00 PM the gavel would fall, and one hundred of the most carefully selected invitees Victor could round up would bid the price of the Mark Twain manuscript all the way up to the Heavens' door—*the sky's the limit*, the *New York Times* had said—and Victor Romaine would begin his glorious journey. Life in the fast lane was about to become even faster, supersonic. New York City would grovel at Victor Romaine's feet. He would be a king, royalty. He'd have everything he ever wanted. In six more days he'd have it all. In six more lousy days Victor Romaine could tell Carmine Rico to go piss up a rope.

"Are you sure their security system's adequate? We can't afford to lose this son of a bitch. You know that, don't you? You know that."

Parker Gorman had been grilling Scotty Hunter for the past forty minutes. Gorman was president of The Jefferson National Insurance Company, which made him Scotty's boss. Jefferson was the primary carrier on the Mark Twain manuscript, meaning that although it had dropped off pieces of the pie to other carriers, it had the biggest chunk of the coverage on its books, meaning the president was nervous; if anything happened to the manuscript, the whole company would go down the proverbial dumper, which explained the reason for the third-degree.

"No problem," Scotty said.

"You're sure?"

"Guaranteed."

"You checked it out yourself?"

"I checked it out myself."

Parker wasn't convinced. "Don't let me down on this one, Scotty. I need to be sure. This is not just another policy."

"Park, Jesus Christ, quit worrying, will you?" Scotty's look, as well as his tone, was intentionally reassuring. His boss was nervous, and that made Scotty nervous, but he couldn't let it show. "Everything's fine. I checked it. Aetna checked it. The Rock checked it. Even though it's a small museum, they have state-of-the-art stuff. They're covered for fire, burglary, flood. Feast, famine. Locusts. Boils. *Everything*. If the Nile turns to blood and catches on fire, a buzzer goes off. If a mouse farts within three city blocks of the place, the cavalry's there in seconds. Take my word for it, everything's okay."

Scotty Hunter was Chief Security Advisor for Jefferson National. He'd served in Viet Nam with Gorman and then begun his career with Gorman at Prudential. While Gorman's career at Prudential took off like a rocket, Scotty's hovered at ground level. In less than ten years Gorman was Regional Vice President. He'd probably have made president one day if Jefferson hadn't come along and made him an offer he couldn't refuse: a piece of the pie, part ownership in the company.

Part owner, how could anyone turn that down?

Scotty could have been a VP, too—at least that's what he told himself— but he preferred field work to sitting on his butt behind a desk all day. And meetings put him to sleep. He needed physical activity, excitement. Scotty Hunter was a physical kind of guy, a man's man. He held a third degree black belt in both judo and kendo, could bench press five-hundred pounds, preferred his steaks well done, and didn't give a rat's ass whether you went to Yale or Mississippi Valley State. Scotty was a loner and unmarried. Gorman had only been at Jefferson National thirty days when he stole Scotty away from Prudential. Scotty didn't get a piece of the company, but he got a contract that bridged him all the way to age sixty-five: health insurance, pension, the works. *Security*, that's what lit Scotty Hunter's fire.

Scotty's self-assurance didn't relax Gorman. "I'm just telling you, pal, we're in this one up to our Y chromosomes. If everything goes okay, I get rich and your contract stays fat, dumb and happy. If not, it's Shit City for both of us."

Scotty looked at him, confused. "What the hell are you talking about? What do you mean, Shit City?"

"Just what I said. If anything happens to that manuscript we're both history."

"Bullshit; I got a contract, pal."

Parker laughed. "Join the crowd."

"Hey, my contract is tight, iron-clad," Scotty responded. "I had an attorney check that sucker out from top to bottom before I signed it. He said it was solid granite. Nobody can rip me off for nothin'. Even if I quit, I collect."

Gorman stuck a cigarette in his mouth. Once a confident man, his hand trembled uncontrollably as he tried to guide the butane lighter to the tip of his Winston. "Right. I agree. So's mine—as long as there's a company to collect from. That's the catch. You're golden as long as the company's golden. But, if the company goes belly-up, then," Gorman ran his finger across his throat, "bye, bye birdie."

Suddenly Scotty Hunter wasn't so calm. "Hey, wait a minute. Nobody told me that. What the hell are you giving me? What kind of company is this?"

"Calm down. There's nothing wrong with the company. It's no different than any other company. The Rock's the same way. If they'd have gone under when we were there, we'd have gone under right with them. It's the same at General Electric, Sears, AT&T, all of them. If the company goes down, everybody goes down."

"But I'm vested; my contract says so."

"So am I. We all are. All God's chillen are vested. But that and a quarter will buy you a cup of coffee if the company has to bite the green weenie."

"Are you telling me my pension isn't protected? Isn't guaranteed? I thought the government got into that a while back, and forced companies to make sure that kind of thing couldn't happen."

Gorman nodded his head yes. "They did. It's protected all right. But only for—" Gorman held up both hands in the Richard Nixon V-For-Victory sign, then curled his fingers two times rapidly, indicating quotes, "*past service*. You only get what you've earned up to the point where the company goes under. No future earnings. In other words: You only get what you already got." He raised his eyebrows. Surprise. "You're thirty-eight years old, right? That means your big earnings years are still ahead of you. As your salary grows, and as your years of service accumulate, the money that goes into your pension gets bigger and bigger every year. If the company survives—so it can make those contributions to your pension every year—by the time you're sixty-five, with the contract you have, you'll be a millionaire. Okay? Okay. Super. No problem.

"But, if it doesn't ... If the company goes down the toilet, as in: *insolvency*; as in: *paying off* if anything happens to that manuscript ...Well, you may wish you'd have re-upped when you had the chance and stayed in the army. That's one thing about the army, it can never go bankrupt. Congress just raises taxes and prints more money."

Scotty looked defeated. "Well, shit. Thanks for making my day."

Gorman finished his cigarette and lit another. "Hey, I just wanted you to know where you stand. You have as big a stake in this thing as I do."

Scotty frowned. "Bigger. You probably got a shitload salted away. If we do go down the tubes, you just fall back five yards and live off your interest."

Gorman's laugh was part cough. "Don't I wish. Everything I have has been sunk back into this little venture we both know and love as Jefferson National. The more I made, the bigger percentage I bought. It was in my contract; I could bite off as much as I wanted to chew." He laughed again, lower this time, in a "funny weird" not "funny ha ha" kind of laugh. "I sold all the stock I owned, took out a second mortgage on my house, cashed in all my chips so to speak, and put it right here. My goal: Own it all. Huh? Smart, right? Own the whole damned thing. Well, old Greedy Gorman may have finally outsmarted himself." He drew deeply on his cigarette, then bit a thumb nail. "Don't misunderstand, everything's fine, if we stay frosty. If. The big if ..."

Scotty ripped the wrapper off a stick of Juicy Fruit, folded it over twice and tossed it into his mouth. Chewing gum took his mind off his problems and helped him concentrate on the issues at hand. It worked, too. It brought him back from Viet Nam alive. Of course, that was only war, simple life and death kind of stuff. Juicy Fruit may not work on something as big as this.

Scotty pushed his six-foot-three-inch, two hundred and twenty pound frame up out of the chair. He ran a meaty hand through long brown hair. "I think maybe I'll shoot on up to New Brighten tomorrow and check out that system one more time."

Parker Gorman nodded. "I think that would be wise."

Chapter 3
Monday Evening

"Busy day?"

Marcella closed the door and flipped the lock. Then she reached up to the top of the door and turned on the security switch. She turned and started walking toward Michael, metal heels clicking on the tile floor. Her navy-blue cardigan sweater was buttoned all the way to the top.

"You're telling me," she said. "Ever since good old Mark Twain sauntered in here, we've been mobbed."

Michael Parks stood over the glass display case that held the prize manuscript. Michael was the curator of the Winslow Addison Museum and Gallery in New Brighten, Connecticut. Marcella was his assistant. His pale face and shiny scalp reflected off the glass as he peered down into it. Male pattern baldness had begun to creep into Michael's life at an early age, right out of high school as a matter of fact. After four years at Georgetown the pattern had spread, mowing a deep swath down the center of his scalp all the way from the top of his forehead to the back of his neck. If it was any consolation (which it wasn't, not to Michael anyway), ten years later the twin patches of hair shading each ear were still completely brown, with nary a trace of gray. Of course, Michael Parks was only thirty two years old, so why would he be gray? On the other hand, one could also ask: Why was a thirty-two-year-old man practically bald? It was a good question. Unfortunately, Michael didn't have a good answer. His father was sixty-four and still had a full head of hair. Michael had to be content knowing that although he didn't have a lot of hair, what hair he had *looked* young. And he had a young-looking face. Thank God for little favors.

"That's really something, isn't it?" Marcella said, joining Michael at the display case. She stuffed her hands into the pockets of her sweater. "I still can't believe it. Not really. A manuscript actually written by the hand of Mark Twain himself. Doesn't it just give you goose bumps?" She sighed, looking down into the glass case in awe, then turned toward Michael. "I'm a big fan of Twain, you know."

"Really?" Michael smiled. "You have all his albums?" Michael's eyes twinkled.

Marcella made a face. "Very funny. Seriously, I've admired the man all my life."

Michael didn't push it. "I didn't know that."

"It's true. Ever since the fifth grade," Marcella confirmed. "Twain was an extremely remarkable writer, you know. Exceptional. One of a kind, actually."

Michael shrugged his shoulders. Marcella didn't care for that response. "I'm serious. He was probably the first, and last, really great American writer. Hemingway and Faulkner both said so."

"Oh, yeah?" Michael raised his eyebrows.

Marcella noted Michael's suspicious look. "They did. Honest. They both said he was the greatest. He possessed utter clarity of style. That was one of the things that made him so great. He made other writers seem archaic, fusty, redundant."

"Fusty?"

"Right. It means stale, stuffy. Not up-to-date. Old-fashioned."

"Right."

Marcella didn't stop to breathe; she was on a roll. "Twain had supreme command of vernacular American English. Before Twain there was only dialect; after Twain there was an American language—an *all new* American language." Marcella paused, proud of her little speech, almost as proud as if it had been said about her. Then, "And he was damned funny, too." So there.

Michael didn't comment; he was waiting for the lecture to end before he jumped in. He wondered just how he'd opened this can of worms to begin with.

"I'll bet I've read *Huckleberry Finn* twenty times, at least," Marcella said.

Silence. Staring. Michael's cue. "No kidding?" Brilliant, Michael thought to himself. The man of a thousand phrases. At least it kept the conversation going.

"That's right," Marcella said. "I'm on my third copy. First two I beat into the ground. Bindings shot, pages worn from use."

"Dog-eared." Michael nodded, knowingly.

Marcella looked startled. "Dog-eared? Good God, no. I'd never dog-ear a page. A true reader, a connoisseur of fine literature," she peered at him over the top of her granny glasses, "a lover of books, would never dog-ear a page. You've got to be kidding. I'd die first. Why that's ... that's blasphemy."

Michael smiled and pushed bifocals that were always sliding down back up to the brim of his nose. "Sorry. I'm a Stephen King fan, myself. I've never been all that big on Twain."

Marcella looked like she'd bitten into a rotten apple. "Stephen King? Surely you jest? Yuck!" She looked down at the manuscript. "We're talking about real literature here, Michael. A classic. A masterpiece. Stephen King? Outside of making all the bestseller lists, what has he ever done? Name one thing that he's produced that will survive time. What has he ever written that will go down in history as a classic?" Her face was filled with disgust, and disappointment. "Stephen King. Good God, Michael! Honestly."

"Hey, *Cujo* was pretty good. And *The Stand*. And *Pet Sematary*, what about that? Did you ever read *Pet Sematary*? I'm serious. It was great. The way he developed that old man, saying he could easily have been his father. I thought that was pretty neat. He may never get credit for it, but I think it was a fine piece of work. Literature even."

"Literature?"

"Yeah, literature."

Marcella looked suspicious. "Right."

"Have you read it?"

"No. And I don't intend to. I have better things to do with my time."

Michael shrugged his shoulders. "Well, then, you're no judge. You can't judge what you haven't experienced."

"Not true. I don't need a case of scarlet fever to know it's bad news."

"That's not the same."

"Sure it is."

"It is not."

"Is too."

"Is not."

"Is too."

"Child."

"*Adult.*"

"Baby."

"Old goat."

"Adolescent."

"Octogenarian."

"Dim-witted simpleton."

"Obtuse buffoon."

"Stupid—"

Marcella didn't give him a chance to finish. She attacked. The best defense was a killer offense as far as she was concerned. "Mental dwarf, ignorant pond scum, prehistoric clown, semi-humanoid, dolt, dunce, blockhead, dip—"

"Okay, okay." Michael held up his hand in a STOP motion. He laughed. "I give up. You win."

They smiled at each other. Two children at play.

Employer and employee had argued this way many times in the past, even before their working relationship had begun. Years of experience had made them expert at it. Michael and Marcella had been friends for the past nine years. Platonic friends.

Michael was only three years Marcella's senior, but most times acted more like a parent than a peer. It was an act that royally ticked Marcella off. She'd been on her own for a long time now; she could take care of herself, thank you very much.

The other thing about Michael that always set Marcella spinning was the fact that Michael never seemed to notice that Marcella was female. In their entire nine year relationship Michael had never once asked her for a date. Never "How about dinner?" never "How about a movie?" never *How about a lousy cup of coffee?* for crying out loud! Marcella would not have been the least bit surprised to learn that Michael had never once fantasized about sleeping with her. He seemed dense to the fact that she was the opposite sex. To Michael Parks, Marcella Givens was just a younger friend, another human being. She was neuter.

That, however, was not the case with Marcella. Frolicking in the pleasures of the boudoir with Michael Parks had tested her imagination on several occasions. She decided now, however, those romps of illusion may have been somewhat premature, an error in judgment on her part. She could never again fantasize about going to bed with a man she now knew was a fan of—she almost couldn't bring herself to even think the words—*Stephen King*. Good God!

Smiling at each other, the two of them turned in unison and walked down the hall together. Time to close up shop for another day. Once again metal heels clicked on the tile floor, with the added sound of rubber soles squeaking. If two hearts beat in rhythm no one heard.

Michael continued his argument, "All I'm saying is you shouldn't judge something until you've tried it. You may find you're missing a whole big world out there."

"Sure."

They walked on, switching off lights as they went. After a few minutes, Michael said, "You turned on the alarm, right?"

Marcella gave him a irritated look. "Of course I turned on the alarm, Michael. I always turn on the alarm."

Michael always asked her that. It was another thing about Michael that ticked her off. The fact that he'd even think for a minute she'd forget to turn on the alarm irked her to no end. Why must he always treat her like an infant? Couldn't she even be trusted to turn on the stupid alarm? It wasn't that difficult a thing to remember.

Marcella fumed. She wouldn't forget to turn on the alarm anymore than she'd dog-ear a page, for crying out loud.

Henry switched off the snowblower and stared at his driveway. He was discouraged; the driveway was turning white again. Ten minutes before the job was finished it had started to snow, *again*. So what else was new? When hadn't it been snowing? All the time it seemed. Fourteen inches since Thanksgiving. It was downright depressing.

Henry took a deep breath, then watched his exhaled puff of lung-warmed air turn to fog in the thirty-degree weather. So far the winter had been a real bitch. For the third time since Thanksgiving—and it was only December fourth—Henry had been forced to crank up the old snowblower (which was a job in and of itself—the damn thing started great in August, but seemed to prefer hibernation to animation once the temperature fell below forty degrees) and clear the driveway. December fourth—what the hell was it going to be like when winter got really serious?

"What's it gonna to be like by January?"

Henry turned. It was his neighbor, Bill Freely. Henry had been so immersed in his own snow-clearing efforts that he hadn't noticed his neighbor was duplicating that activity not more than ten feet away in his own driveway. Talk about devoted to your job.

"God, I don't want to think about that," Henry groaned. "This winter's gonna kill me yet."

"Do you believe it?" Freely said. "I don't think I've ever seen a winter this bad, this early."

The two driveways were exactly ten feet apart, minimum distance according to the zoning laws. Neighbors for eleven years, the two men had talked across that distance many times, but this was definitely the largest amount of snow their voices ever had to carry over. In that ten feet there was a mountain of snow, piled high first by the hand of God, and then added to by Henry Nash's snowblower and William Freely's mighty shovel.

Henry talked to Freely over the top of the snow bank. "It's been a bitch, hasn't it?" Henry looked down at his snowblower. "If it wasn't for this little baby here I'd probably have died of a heart attack weeks ago."

Freely raised his shovel to shoulder height. "Ah, what happened to your pioneer spirit? Our forefathers didn't have snowblowers. This old shovel is good enough for me. Lot better exercise than pushin' that dumb thing around."

Henry shook his head. "Sure it is. If you want to kill yourself."

Freely laughed. "Bull."

Henry countered. "Hey, that's the truth. Don't you know that shoveling snow is one of the most dangerous things you can do? Everybody says so. Doctors say so."

"That's a crock of medical meadow muffins."

"No way," Henry argued. "Check the stats. More people die every year from heart attacks from shoveling snow than from any other cause." Henry wasn't positive about his facts, but he knew one thing for sure: Freely didn't have any data to prove him wrong. Throw out a bunch of numbers, and if people don't know any better, they assume you know what you were talking about. Works every time.

Freely leaned on his shovel. "Henry, you don't really believe all that propaganda hogwash, do you? I'm serious. They're brainwashing you. All it is is the damned snowblower lobby in Washington just trying to scare people, so they'll all get shook up and go out and buy a great big, over-priced, you-only-have-to-use-the-damn-thing-once-or-twice-a-year-at-the-most snowblower," Freely rolled his eyes, "like somebody I know." Freely waved his shovel, smiling.

Once more Henry's nose started to run. He sniffed, then put his sleeve to use again. "Don't worry. If things get that bad I'll resort to: *God put it here, He can take it away*. Besides, winter's probably all over with anyway. I bet we got the worst part behind us."

Freely looked up at the black sky, then at Henry. "Sure, you go right on believing that. *Almanac* says you're wrong. Says the worst is yet to come. Now the cold part is on the way, my friend. Frigid, that's what the book says."

Henry looked at his driveway, then at the sky, then at his neighbor and said, "Screw this. Wanna come in for a beer?"

Bill Freely stopped shoveling. "Thought you'd never ask." He stuck his shovel into a snow drift, pulled back the sleeve of his coat and looked at his watch. "I got thirty minutes, at least, before supper. Marge isn't home yet. I'll hit this again later, if it stops snowing."

With the snow piled high between the two houses, Freely had to take the long way around by walking down his driveway to the street, then coming back up Henry's driveway. Henry put away his snowblower while Freely made the trek, then the two men walked to the back of Henry's garage, to a door that led directly to Henry's finished basement.

Henry's finished basement was eight-hundred square feet of pride and joy. It had a fireplace, a pool table and a wet bar. All his life Henry had wanted a wet bar, and he'd finally gotten his wish last Christmas. A gift from the family. They came up with the down payment and the bank was happy to come up with the rest. First Federal Bank and Trust owned more of it than Henry did, but Henry spent a lot more time there. Bill plopped down on the sofa in front of the fireplace and Henry took up his position behind the bar, got two cans of beer out of the small refrigerator tucked underneath the bar and then joined Bill on the sofa. He handed one of the cans to his neighbor and popped the top on the other. "Cheers," he said, raising his can.

Bill raised his. "Power to the people."

After a couple swallows Freely leaned back, looked around and said, "This is one great room you got here, Henry."

"Thanks," Henry said. Henry smiled inside; it *was* a great room. "And reasonably priced, too, only one arm and one leg."

Freely nodded his understanding. "Don't I know it. We priced doing something like this to our basement ... made my head hurt." He took a drink of beer. "Bet you spend all your time down here. Am I right?"

"As much as I can get away with. Let's just say that Gladys knows where to look if she needs me. If it would ever quit snowing I could spend less time in that damn driveway and more time down here," Henry winked, "where I belong."

Freely had a solution for that. "Why don't you hire Billy to shovel your driveway for you?" The Billy Bill Freely was referring to was William Freely Junior, his sixteen-year-old son. "He's always looking for ways to earn gas money now that he's got his driver's license."

Henry took a long pull on his beer. "Sure, and why don't I fly down to Rio for a couple of weeks? I mean, I got plenty of money, right? Hell, I'm in the UAW, I got money coming out my ears. We all know those UAW guys make at least twenty-five bucks an hour. For doin' nothing. For just screwing off all day. Those lazy bums, screwing up the whole country because they gotta get paid big bucks and don't do anything to earn it, don't produce nothing for it. That's why the damn Japs are kicking our butts all over the map. It's all the UAW's fault, the spoiled little babies who'd rather go on strike than listen to reason. The little brats who sit around and whine and pout if they don't get their way."

Freely gave Henry a strange look. "What the hell are you talking about?" Freely said. Then it dawned on him. "Oh, hey, that's right. I forgot all about that. Your contract's up. So, what's the scoop? You going out?"

Henry lowered his voice, as if somebody might hear, as if there might be a reporter hiding in his chimney. As if anybody really gave a damn besides him. "Looks like it. Don't say anything though; I haven't told Gladys yet." He shook his head. "Anyway, if we do, I'm gonna have plenty of time to clear my own driveway, thank you. Shit, I may even take up the business of clearing driveways myself. Compete against your kid. I may need the gas money more that he does."

"Come on, who're you tryin' to shit? You got it dicked. Out on strike, walking the picket line, what, once a week? The rest of the time it's down here in the old rec room suckin' up beers and watching the Soaps. Wish I could go on strike. Wish I had it as easy as you."

"Yeah, right. Ever hear of 'no tickey, no washey?' As in: 'No work, no pay?' I don't get paid to sit on my duff and read magazines like you guys. Talk about having it dicked. If anybody has it made it's you firefighters. How do you get to be a firefighter anyway? What do they do—make you all sit around a big table and then hire the first guy who falls asleep?"

Freely had to laugh. "Very funny. Your house ever catches on fire, don't call me."

"Hey, I wouldn't want to wake you up."

Freely sipped his beer. "Wouldn't do you any good if you did. Damned truck probably wouldn't start anyway; it's a Chevy, you know."

Henry forced a laugh, but, in truth, he didn't think it was all that funny. Sure, he made fun of GM himself, but when it got right down to it, he'd be dead without The General. He changed the subject. "So tell me, how's Billy doing, now that he's driving? Bet it keeps the old man awake at night worrying about what the hell's going on out there—all those drunk drivers and all. I got a feeling that when my little monsters start driving it's gonna cost me a lot of sleepless nights."

"You got that right," Freely verified. "He's doing okay, but I got a hunch he drives a lot faster than he should. From what I hear, neighbors and all. They say things. Never nasty things, just things, like: 'Boy, he sure doesn't waste time going around corners, does he?' and, 'Brakes are going to last forever on that car since he never uses 'em.' That kind of stuff. But I never see it. He's too smart to hotdog around the old man. King Kong would stomp his young butt if he did. *And* take his keys."

Henry was curious. "Tell me, does the insurance really go up as much as they say it does when you add a teenage driver?"

Freely choked on his beer. He couldn't wait to answer that one. "You bet your bunnies it goes up. And if you have *one* accident, just one, it doubles." Freely's look said *how's that grab you?* He took another drink before he continued. "Two, and it doubles again." Freely raised his eyebrows in question. "What do you think of them apples?"

"What happens if you have three?"

Freely said "*Ha*" then, "First, they cancel your policy. Then they send a guy named Vito after you, your wife, your kids and all your relatives."

Henry laughed out loud, then raised his beer in salute. "Hey, better you than me."

Freely looked at his friend knowingly. "Your time'll come."

Henry killed his beer and offered Freely another, which Freely accepted, saying it would have to be a quick one, Marge was probably home from the doctor by now and in the process of setting the supper table at that very minute.

"Doctor? Anything wrong?"

"Naw, just feeling kind of punk. You know. Probably coming down with the flu or something." Bill took a drink of beer. "She's been real tired lately. It's not like her. Might be her iron; she has to watch her iron."

Henry nodded.

Then Bill asked, "Did you happen to see the winning number in the Lottery yesterday?"

Henry shook his head no.

"I was only off by one," Freely said. "Can you believe it?" He held up his hand, showing Henry that his thumb and forefinger were a fraction of an inch apart. "That close to five million."

"That's nothin'. Peanuts. Did you read about that broad in Connecticut who bought an old trunk for thirty bucks and found a manuscript written by Mark Twain in it? A manuscript that had never been published. A manuscript that nobody even knew about. Paper says it could be worth billions and billions." Henry gave him a "so there" wink.

"You're kidding."

Henry shook his head. "Nope, it was in the paper."

Scotty poured himself another drink.

It wasn't the fact that Parker Gorman had lied to him—he hadn't—it was more a matter of just not telling him everything there was to tell.

Scotty set the bottle of Chivas Regal back down on the bar, picked up the third scotch he'd poured himself in the past forty minutes, walked around the corner of the bar and headed back into the living room.

He thought Parker was his friend, someone he could trust.

Scotty normally drank beer; hard liquor dulled his senses too much. But tonight beer wasn't strong enough. Scotty sat down on the couch and leaned back. He took a drink. The scotch didn't seem strong enough either. This was his third drink and he didn't feel a thing. Getting drunk must be more mental than physical, Scotty thought to himself. Otherwise, why would his head start spinning sometimes after just one drink, and other times, like now, he could practically pour it down and not feel a thing? Mood, that had to be the most important factor. Mood and mental state. When you were in the mood to feel it, you felt it. Scotty wasn't in the mood.

He took another drink, then looked around the room. Well, if good old Jefferson National went down the tubes he could say good-bye to all this.

Scotty had moved into his new apartment exactly two weeks ago today. Well, *moved* wasn't exactly the right word. *Occupied* was more like it. *Moved* implied that he'd moved something, when in fact the only thing he'd moved was his person, and a few personal belongings: clothes, a few books, a set of dishes his parents had sent him from Syracuse (factory seconds, but still top quality), a couple of souvenirs from his days in the army, and his Olympia exercise machine that he'd set up in the spare bedroom. No furniture. He'd left his furniture behind. All of it. It was no loss; it was junk. Even if he hadn't moved into a new apartment Scotty would have had to buy new furniture soon anyway. The stuff in his old apartment had started out used; he'd bought it from an old army buddy who decided he liked it a lot better in Germany than in the good old U. S. of A., and, "It just isn't worth the expense to ship it all the way to Frankfort, Scotty. You can have it cheap; a thousand bucks buys it all," the guy said.

Hell of a deal.

But, as Scotty found out, you get what you pay for. It was cheap in more ways than one. It didn't last long. But that was okay; it had served its purpose. It had gotten him to this point and now it was time to move on. He had a new job, a new apartment, a new beginning. He should buy new furniture; he was starting a new life.

And he sure as hell didn't want to load up this baby with junk. This was a class place; one of a kind. The real estate agent said something like this didn't open up very often.

Scotty had to agree; it was something all right. Twenty-five hundred square feet of wool carpet and easy living, with a view of the Atlantic Ocean out one window and the New York skyline out the other, on a clear day. Scenery like that didn't come cheap. Scotty would never have been able to afford anything like this if he'd stayed at Prudential.

Actually, Scotty wasn't certain he could afford it even at Jefferson. The way he calculated it, he worked the first four months of the year for Uncle Sam, the next four months to pay for the apartment, and the last four for himself, for necessities: food, clothing, Kendo lessons. If he lost his job he wondered if Uncle Sam would be willing to give up his portion first.

Scotty sipped his scotch and listened to music that came from the stereo by the fireplace.

The five-thousand dollar stereo. For a guy with a tin ear. Not too bright. Granted, it looked neat. And sounded great. But he probably wouldn't have been able to tell the difference between this high-tech model and the five hundred dollar job at Service Merchandise. He wondered if it was too late to return it.

And the sofa he was sitting on: $3,295.00. Sure, it was gorgeous, and he had to have someplace to sit. But a half-circle of genuine leather that could seat ten was just a little extravagant, considering his lifestyle, and the fact that he didn't know ten people he could invite over.

Actually, it was more than a little extravagant when you combined it with the new bedroom outfit, the dining room table, the eight chairs, the hutch, the serving unit, three lamps, two end tables, one coffee table, the matching floor-to-ceiling bookcases and the Persian rug that graced the foyer. Total hit: $24,611.11. Really kicked the shit out of the twenty-five grand bonus that Parker had seduced him with. Talk about a drunken sailor.

Okay, he hadn't had to buy it all at once. He could have waited, until things were a little more definite.

But Scotty *had* been waiting—all his life. When you come from a poor background you get tired of waiting. After a while you just want things at any cost. Damn the torpedoes.

Wanting things had gotten Scotty in trouble before. Like the time he bought that used Corvette. He just had to have a Corvette. Couldn't afford a new one, so a used one would have to do.

Tell it to the mechanic who smiled and said the engine, transmission, and rear end were all shot. Three, four grand should cover it.

Scotty took another drink. It tasted like water.

Damn, he should never have left Prudential. He would never have gotten rich at Pru, but he wouldn't have ended up in the poor house either. Prudential was safe. Prudential was solid. Prudential was guaranteed.

Like he thought Jefferson was. Like he thought his contract was. He should never have let Parker talk him into leaving. He had security there. Seniority. A future.

Short-term thinking was, without a doubt, Scotty's biggest flaw.

Oh, he never over-extended himself; he never spent money he didn't have. That wasn't his problem. Debt was not Scotty Hunter's albatross. Scotty's problem wasn't that he spent more than he had, his problem was that he just spent *everything* he had.

He should never have left Pru. But how could he walk away from the kind of money Parker had offered him? Christ, not only had he gotten a bonus, but he'd tripled his salary. Tripled! A guy would have to be a complete idiot to turn something like that down. Well, he certainly qualified on that count.

Scotty looked at the gold clock on the mantle. Eleven-ten, he should get to bed. He had a long day in front of him. The drive to Connecticut wasn't long in terms of miles, but fighting New York City traffic for the first half going up and the last half coming back made it long in terms of time. He needed his rest. A tired mind always screws up before a rested one. A tired mind makes mistakes. Scotty couldn't afford any mistakes. Not this time.

He took another drink. Hey, no problem. Scotty Hunter didn't make mistakes, right? Scotty Hunter was the best there was. Ask anyone. Ask the people at Pru. Ask Parker—he knew. That's why Parker had come after him in the first place. All Scotty had to do was make sure nothing happened to the manuscript and everything would be fine.

And why should that be so difficult? Hey, that was his job, wasn't it? That's what he was getting paid the big bucks for. That's why he could afford to live in this luxury. Hell, if he couldn't do that he deserved to go down the tubes; he'd have nobody to blame but himself. Everything depended on him. *He* depended on him. He'd never let himself down before, so all he had to do was make sure he didn't let himself down this time.

No problem.

And that's the way he liked it, too. He liked counting on himself, liked being in control. It was when he had to depend on someone else that things got all screwed up. You just couldn't count on other people. If you wanted it done right you had to do it yourself.

Scotty liked that. He was a pro. Pros liked being in control. He knew what to do. All he had to do was do it. He was good. He was damned good. No problem.

He finished his drink.

Chapter 4
Tuesday

"Okay, we're down."

Henry looked up from the pit. It was Luther Mills.

Luther shook his bald black head. "Goodyear's late again." Luther was looking at Henry. His expression said *I know you've heard this before, but.* "We'll be down for a half hour at least. Maybe an hour. Load's just coming in now. Clean up your area or take a break, I really don't give a shit." Luther walked away, shaking his head in disgust.

Luther Mills was shift foreman over Henry's section of the assembly line: tires, hoods, rear decks, rocker panels and fenders. This was the third time in the past two months that Goodyear was late with a shipment. And when Goodyear was late, GM was down.

The shut-downs were not a surprise; Luther had expected them, and had warned his people in advance. It was right after the last plant-wide meeting. Luther called his crew together and informed them that management had decided it was a good idea (and a necessary one, if they were to compete with the Japanese) to keep only a thirty-minute supply of tires on hand (Luther rolled his eyes when he said that)—something about the fact that they (supposedly) had too much inventory in the plant and had to reduce it at all cost. *Kanban* was the word they used. It was Japanese for "no inventory." If they were to compete with the Japanese they would have to use Japanese techniques. Which meant: No inventory. Which meant: When Goodyear sneezed, GM caught a cold. Talk about your major pain in the butt.

The "no inventory" concept may have worked if everything else was half-way normal, but everything else was not half-way normal: Goodyear was on strike. And that meant that management people were working around the clock to keep things going as best they could. Which wasn't very well. Four hundred people could not take the place of four thousand. Assembly line shut-downs had been a serious problem since the model-year changeover last summer. Luther's section had been spending a lot of time on break lately, as had the entire assembly line. There was a saying in an assembly plant: You can drive a tired man but you can't drive an un-tired car.

The big problem was that Henry and his buddies might be spending even more time on break in the near future. Permanent break. If their own contract talks didn't start going a hell of a lot better than they had up to now, The Chevrolet Assembly Plant, of The Chevrolet Motor Division, of The General Motors Corporation, in Fort Lee, New Jersey, would also be on strike, just like their brothers at Goodyear. The last word was that the UAW and GM were not even close. If a strike came, they wouldn't be needing any tires at all.

If a strike came, Henry Nash would be in deep shit.

Henry couldn't live on strike pay. Henry had a hard time making ends meet at full pay. Cut that in half and life turned real sour real fast. Henry had too many bills, that's all there was to it. They'd struck at GM six years ago so he knew what it was like. He was still trying to catch up.

"Call it." Roger flipped the quarter into the air.

Henry said, "Heads."

Roger caught the quarter in his right hand, slapped it over onto the back of his left, took his hand away and smiled: tails. "You buy," he said.

Henry grunted. "What else is new?"

Roger grinned. "Hey, you know what they say across the street at the Clorox plant: 'Life's a bleach and then you dye'."

Roger laughed out loud. Henry didn't even smile.

Henry reached into his pocket, dug out a quarter, then reluctantly slipped it into the slot of the coffee machine as Roger dropped his quarter back into his pocket. Roger pushed the button under BLACK. "Thanks, chief," he said.

As Roger's cup filled, Henry dug for a second quarter.

"Don't mention it," Henry said, his heart not in it.

Roger retrieved his coffee and Henry reloaded the machine. He hit CREAM, then EXTRA SUGAR, then stood there, frozen in disbelief, as his cup got caught halfway down the chute. Before he could react, most of his coffee squirted down the drain. "Son of a bitch," he cursed, fumbling for the cup, trying to salvage as much as he could.

He salvaged a third of a cup.

"Story of my life," he said.

Roger led the way to an empty table.

The plant cafeteria was a cornucopia of vending machines and picnic tables. The vending machines had every culinary delight the mind could imagine; the picnic tables had Formica tops and bench seats. It was a lot different than the good old days. The Glory Days. The days when the plant had a complete full-service cafeteria, with a hot food line. The days of fruit juice and salad and the best damn French Fries in the whole damn world. Better than McDonalds, even. But that disappeared when the Japanese came over and started kicking the US automakers' butts, and the US automakers started cutting costs. One of the first things to go was the full-service cafeteria, then hot food, and finally the fries.

The two men slid into their seats. Roger started the conversation. "Willie said the chances of a strike are lookin' pretty good."

Henry nodded, taking a small sip of his coffee, rationing it. "Willie should know; he's steward. Stewards should know that kind of thing. That's what they get paid for." Henry put his coffee cup on the table, carefully, not taking any chances. He didn't want to risk spilling any. "They sure as hell don't get paid to work."

Roger agreed. "I'll be honest with you, Henry. I'm not all that excited about going out, if you know what I mean."

Henry agreed. "Yeah, me neither."

"Willie says it could be a long one."

"Wonderful."

"Willie says the company doesn't want to give us a thing. Says the word is they're even asking for give-backs. You know, give back gains we've already got. Stuff we fought for over the years. Doesn't look good." Roger took a swallow of his coffee.

"Hey, can you blame them?" Henry said. "Look around. The Gooks are kicking our butts, Rog. There's Jap cars everywhere. There may not be any in this parking lot, but I'll bet my pension there's one or two in some driveways around town, and they don't all belong to bankers either. Some of 'em belong to the wives of good old GM employees who work right here, our *brothers*. And they're good cars, too. Top quality. They're sending in a better car," Henry held out his thumb, "with a smaller ticket," then his first finger, counting his points as he made them, "and a bigger warranty. Tell me the truth, Rog, would you buy a Chevy if you didn't work here?"

Roger was silent, but the guilty look on his face answered Henry's question.

Henry followed up. "Company's got to do something."

"Hey, who's side are you on?"

Henry looked at Roger over the edge of his cardboard coffee cup. "I'm on my side. The company, the union, you don't think either one of them really gives a shit about us, do you? The company fat cats sure as hell don't give a damn about you and me. Not for a second. They're out to protect their own fat jobs and their fat pay checks and their fat wives' fat asses, so they can go to their fat country clubs and gulp down fat martinis and eat fat prime rib.

"And the union's no better, Rog. Bunch of guys trying to protect their cushy jobs so they don't have to go to work for a living. 'Brother,' my ass! There ain't no such thing as brotherhood. It's every man for himself."

Roger stared at his friend. "Boy, you really get pissed when you have to buy coffee, don't you? You're downright ornery. Or maybe you just got out on the wrong side of the bed this morning. Is that it? You're a real bitter soldier today, Henry Nash."

"Hey, just call me Mr. Sunshine. Goddammit!"

Roger laughed.

Henry finished off what was left of his coffee. Roger still had two-thirds of a cup. They both looked down at the Formica-topped table and didn't say a word.

Three hours wasted.

Well, maybe not wasted, not completely anyway.

Driving back from New Brighten, Scotty had to admit that he did feel a little more comfortable now, even though he hadn't discovered anything he didn't already know. He'd put his mind to rest, at least. He'd confirmed, re-confirmed, that The Winslow Addison Museum had an excellent security system. State-of-the-art, as a matter of fact. And a state-of-the-art system for a small operation like that was very unusual.

Scotty snickered. Yeah, it was unusual all right, a dead bolt and a good old Yale or two was what he usually had to deal with. *Cross your fingers and pray* was more the norm. For some reason people thought that a padlock was the answer to any and all their security needs, the safest thing this side of Fort Knox. Maybe because padlocks were heavy and made out of steel, and looked imposing, maybe that's why they gave people a secure feeling.

Big mistake. A whole lot of property had disappeared over the years because of that feeling.

But not this time. Winslow Addison was into laser beams and sound-detection equipment. Even heat-sensitive devices. Any movement in the temperature, up or down, and bingo. Frosty the Snowman dressed in thermal long-johns could not walk into the place and keep from changing the temperature enough to trigger the alarm. The system was tied into the thermostat, which allowed the temperature to fluctuate within set limits without causing any problems. However, any variation and "Hello, Mr. Burglar, we're from the police. You have the right to remain silent. You have the right to ..." and so on and so on and so on.

Scotty cracked open the driver's side window a notch and let in some fresh air. The temperature outside was frigid, but the day was sunny, and even with the heater turned down the passive solar energy beating through his windows was turning the inside of his car into a sauna. He loosened his tie.

The traffic was a bitch, but it didn't require all of Scotty's concentration; he could still think about some of his other problems, the main one being his pension. And the fact that he didn't like the shit he'd found out one damn bit. The more he thought about it, the more it pissed him off.

And the fact that Parker hadn't told him pissed him off even more.

Sure, The Rock *could* go under, but what were the chances of that happening? Damn slim, if you asked him. Prudential was too big to go down the tubes. Shit, the government would step in before they'd let that happen. They'd have to. It was just like that Savings and Loan thing that happened a few years back. The government couldn't afford to let something as big as Prudential take a fall. It would screw up the whole economy, the whole country.

But little Jefferson National—we're talking peanuts here. Nobody'd even notice if Jefferson went belly-up. Nobody but the two hundred employees whose livelihood depended on it. Nobody but Scotty Hunter and his whole damn future. Nobody.

Scotty burned. Parker had no right to bury Jefferson that deep. He had no right to risk the whole company on one policy for chrissake! This wasn't a crapshoot we were talking about here. These were people's lives he was screwing with. People's futures. Scotty Hunter's future! You didn't put your life on "double-zero," and then hope like hell that the wheel stopped just in time to pull your hot burning ass out of the fire. It was stupid.

Stupid, stupid, stupid.

Watching reruns of *I Love Lucy* brought back a lot of fond memories.

Ralph thought Lucille Ball was one the funniest comics he'd ever seen, man or woman. She was so alive, so full of energy. Certainly filled with more life than the woman sitting at the far end of the sofa not saying a word, not even smiling.

Ralph didn't like it when Lilith was quiet. Granted, it wasn't all that pleasant when she was noisy, but at least then Ralph knew what she was up to. When she was quiet she was planning. That concerned Ralph.

"They don't make 'em like they used to, do they dear?"

Ralph tried to start a conversation, but Lilith would have none of it. She just turned toward him then turned away without saying a word.

"Lucille Ball, Jack Benny, Jackie Gleason ... Remember how we watched them every week, like clockwork? And Uncle Miltie. Texaco, remember? 'We - are - the - men - of - Tex-a-co, we - work - from - Maine - to - Mex-i-co, we'—how did that song go?"

Ralph got another dirty look from his partner.

"Every Tuesday night, right? Can you believe it, here we are, what, thirty, thirty-five years later, and Lucy's on Tuesday nights again?"

No response.

Ralph turned back to the TV. "'Course, everything was black and white in those days. But there was something about black and white, you know? Made it all kind of mysterious, magical, don't you think? Allowed the imagination to work a little. Color takes that away, tells it like it is. Can't hide anything with color."

Lilith rubbed her chin absentmindedly.

"Black and white, that's the way dogs see things, isn't that right? They say dogs are color blind, see everything in black and white. Wonder how they know that."

Lilith looked disgusted.

A commercial came on. Ralph stood up. "Want anything from the fridge, dear?"

Lilith didn't respond. She was sitting on the end of the sofa with her elbow on the arm, her hands resting in her lap and her ankles crossed. She had been like that for the past forty minutes. She was staring at the TV, but she wasn't seeing it.

Ralph walked out of the living room and into the kitchen and opened the refrigerator door. What looked good? Not a lot. The pickin's were bleak. The refrigerator had seen better days. Ralph leaned over, reached in and moved a couple of jars around to see if anything was hiding in the back, found nothing, gave up and closed the door. Then he checked the freezer; maybe an ice cream sandwich had escaped Lilith's eagle eye. Not a chance. The freezer offered no more than the fridge. There were two packages of frozen green beans in the freezer but what the hell kind of a snack were green beans?

Ralph shut the door and moved over to the pantry. Maybe a cookie. He opened the door and looked for the Nabisco Wafers. They always kept Nabisco Wafers on hand. Almost always. The cupboard was bare. A cracker? Ralph's eyes scanned for the box of saltines. He saw none. He called to Lilith in the living room, "We got any crackers?"

Silence.

Ralph took that for a no.

To himself, "Ah, I don't need anything anyway. Wouldn't hurt if I dropped a few pounds."

Ralph closed the panty door and made it back to the sofa just as the second half of *I Love Lucy* was starting.

"Did I miss anything?" Ralph asked, as though anyone was going to respond.

This time Lilith surprised him. "Yeah, you missed the crackers." She pointed at the coffee table in front of them with her nose.

There, sitting on the coffee table in plain sight was the box of saltines and the jar of peanut butter that Lilith had brought in—at Ralph's request—while they were watching the local news.

"Hmmm, knew I saw crackers somewhere," Ralph said sheepishly.

He bent over and picked up the crackers, placed them on the sofa at his left hip, picked up the peanut butter, put that between his legs, put his feet on the coffee table, twisted the cap off, grabbed a cracker, dunked it in the Skippy Chunky Style, being careful not to break it, and then proceeded to lose himself in Lucy while Lilith went back to her planning.

Gladys Nash was in the bathroom brushing her teeth, getting ready for bed.

Henry was already in bed, but on another planet, in spirit at least. If not on another planet, certainly in another world.

Lying in bed with his head propped up on a doubled-over pillow, granny glasses balanced on the tip of his nose (bringing into focus print that seemed to be getting smaller and smaller each day), lips moving slowly and silently to themselves, hands and book resting on bare chest, there was no doubt as to where Henry's mind was. It was in another world all right. And not just any old world. It was in Henry's favorite world: the world of the Wild Wild West.

The reading lamp clipped to the headboard squeezed out every last watt of the fifty it had to offer, lighting Henry's way as he thumbed eagerly and religiously through each delicious page. It was food and Henry was famished; he was a prisoner of that hunger. He bit into each phrase like a starving man dining on his first meal in weeks. He chewed on every word, savored each morsel of literary nourishment as if it were the only food his system could digest. Food for the soul.

The Great Twain Robbery 47

Montana Territory— The Dalton Gang, hard at work, was Henry's latest obsession. This time cattle rustling was the name of the game. Henry's wife didn't exist; his family didn't exist.

Henry Nash didn't exist.

Damn, he thought to himself, damn, those were the days.

Gladys finished brushing her teeth, turned off the light and walked out of the bathroom.

"I didn't get a chance to tell you earlier," she said as she took off her bathrobe and laid it across the cedar chest at the foot of the bed, "because I didn't want to say anything in front of the children, but," pause, "we got a notice from the bank today."

Bank?

The word hit Henry like a baseball bat right between the eyes. Chapter Ten: The Dalton Gang had just decided that maybe cattle rustling was not such a hot way to make a living after all. It was hard, dirty work. *Too* hard and *too* dirty, that was the problem. The hours were long and the rewards were small, and even after you rustled the cattle all you had to show for your efforts was a bunch of damned cows. You still had to find a buyer—a buyer who always refused to pay what the cattle were actually worth, never any more than thirty cents on the dollar, because he couldn't *afford to pay more and be picky about the brand, too, now could he?*

Maybe Jesse James had the right idea: robbing nice clean banks looked to be a lot easier than dealing with dumb dirty cows. And it was not only cleaner, it smelled a whole lot better. "You don't end up with cow shit all over your boots," Cole Younger said, laughing. "And when you're done, you're done, money's already money, it don't have to be turned into money like beef. And you don't get cheated out of half of it neither." Cole Younger was all for the idea; he thought it was about time that Jesse James wasn't the only one living the easy life. Clay, his younger brother, argued against it—too much risk, everybody and his brother gets on your trail when you rob a bank. The Youngers had teamed-up with the Daltons three chapters back, and now the meanest bunch of hombres west of the Pecos was raising a ruckus all over Texas.

Henry loved it.

The story was quicksand and he was in up to his bald spot. The world could stop spinning and Henry would never notice. Nothing grabbed Henry's attention, piqued his imagination, *turned him on* more than sagas of The Old West. Especially tales about the Bad Guys—the guys in the black hats and the dirty boots with beards like cactus and skin like leather. Jesse James and the

Dalton Gang and Billy the Kid. You could have your Wyatt Earps and Bill Hickcocks and Bat Mastersons. You could take that tin star and throw it in the dust. Henry didn't want any part of the Good Guys.

It wasn't that Henry Nash actually rooted for the outlaws. Or, for that matter, that he believed in breaking the law; Henry was a very law-abiding citizen. Henry didn't see them as outlaws; he saw them as Robin Hoods. He saw them as men who had to fight to survive, in a time when fighting was the only way you could survive; it was a time that was not as clear cut as it was today. A time not sketched in black or white; a time painted in shades of gray. It wasn't a question of right or wrong, good or evil; it was much simpler than that. To Henry Nash it was the ability—and, yes, the necessity, too—to live free, to do what had to be done, and in so doing, the freedom to do it on your own, without interference. It was the Every Man for Himself rule that Henry found so electrifying. The ability to run wild, free as a breeze, responsible to no one.

It was a time when the law was not as fully-defined as it was today (if there was any law to begin with, that is), so you had a little more freedom to do things. You were forced to make it up as you went, that's what Henry liked. Rules? There weren't any. Right and wrong? No question. "Right" was the five pounds of steel strapped to your hip that went by the name of Colt .45. Back then you didn't need an attorney to figure things out for you. Your "mouthpiece" was a .45 that spoke loud, clear, and final. Back then they didn't have one attorney for every two people like they do nowadays, so you *had* to figure it out for yourself. A man had to fend for himself and make up his own law.

The only law that mattered was the law of survival. And the law of the six-shooter.

You could do it back then. You could take care of yourself, you could take care of your family, because every man was the same, every man was equal. There weren't any hot shots with MBAs and law degrees and personal computers to screw everything up. Nobody was any bigger than anyone else. Every man was the same size: six feet tall—his Colt .45 said so.

Henry argued that that wasn't really breaking the law—how could you break something that didn't exist? It was more like defining it for yourself, deciding what was right and what had to be done, and then doing it. Every man had to protect what was his: his property, his family, his rights. He had to do whatever was necessary in order to survive. Some said that was breaking the law; Henry called it survival. A man had to survive, didn't he? Hell yes!

Henry looked up from his paperback as Gladys pulled back the quilt, kicked off her slippers and climbed into bed.

"What was that you said?" he asked. "Something about the bank?"

Gladys looked worried. Usually a bubbly woman, the spring was missing from her demeanor tonight. Even though she'd tried to hide it at dinner, even though she'd tried to keep the conversation peppy, Henry could tell something was wrong. Gladys Nash was not a good actress.

This was not the first time it had happened. Gladys had not been herself for the past six months. Henry was concerned. He knew she was worried about her father. Her father was not handling Gladys' mother's death last April very well at all. Neither was Gladys, for that matter. It was affecting her a lot more than she let on. Gladys and her mother had been very close. Henry was afraid that sooner or later her health might suffer. It had already affected her blood pressure; she hadn't had high blood pressure problems before her mother died.

But she did now. The doctor said it was nothing to worry about, not as long as she took care of it. But still.

It bothered Henry. It would any man. He didn't like it when his wife seemed so *down*. Gladys was a good woman. She deserved to be happy. If there was anything wonderful about Henry, it was his wife. The one time in his life he'd picked a winner. She was fantastic. She was always there for him, always supporting him, always trying to make him feel good, make him feel as if he was really worth something.

Although he didn't buy it. Not today. Not next week. Henry remembered reading somewhere that the chemicals in the human body were worth about seven bucks, total, and he figured, in his case, that was just about right.

Henry was in a real woe-is-me mood. And he recognized it. He'd been feeling sorry for himself lately, jealous because the other guy always seemed to be doing better. And he didn't know why; it wasn't like him. But he did know one thing: His world was not built on bedrock. Henry Nash was not on solid financial ground. His empire could crumble around him at any minute. If there was a strike, if the company got fed up and moved out of town, if he lost his job ... If ... Henry had one foot in quicksand and the other in shit and he could sink just like that. How much would he be worth then? Gladys deserved more. If anything ever happened to her ...

Gladys pulled the quilt up to her neck. She stared at the ceiling for a second, then turned to look at her husband. "Our second mortgage—the one on the rec room?—just went up. Well, actually, it *will* go up. Next month. Another eighty-seven dollars and sixty-four cents a month."

"What?" Henry closed his book. "You can't be serious. I thought— It hasn't been a year already, has it?"

"Well, it will be. In February."

Henry let out a sigh. It had been a year. It was just last Christmas they'd finished the basement. Where on earth did the time go?

Gladys frowned. "Henry, I don't understand something. If it won't be a year until February, then why are they raising the rate in January? I thought we had a whole year before they could do that."

A puzzled look washed over Henry's face. He studied the question, even though he knew deep down inside that he wasn't going to come up with an answer. He cursed his lack of a formal education.

"Hell, I don't know," he finally said. "I thought it was supposed to be a year, too. All I can say is that they probably understand those papers we signed a lot better than we do. It's their job; they do it every day. I didn't think it was supposed to change until February, but what do I know? I'm not a banker." Banker hell, Henry thought, you gotta be a Philadelphia attorney to understand that stuff. "I gotta figure the bank knows what it's doing. They're not going to cheat us, not intentionally anyway." He shook his head in defeat. "I'll call them if you want me to, but I don't think it'll do any good."

Gladys aimed her eyes back at the ceiling. "No, I'm sure you're right. It's just, well, I don't know where we're going to get the money, that's all."

It was a question disguised as a statement.

"We'll manage somehow," Henry offered. "We always have." He didn't want his wife to worry.

Gladys wasn't finished. "Oh, it's not just the mortgage, it's just that everything seems to be coming at once, you know what I mean? The mortgage, Christmas. The car's acting up again; that could cost some money. I have to pay the second half of our property taxes by the middle of this month. Our VISA's at its limit. We're almost paying more in interest than we're paying on the principle. And the mortgage on the rec room is just the first blow, because, since it went up, I'm sure the mortgage on the house will go up too, in March."

"Hey, we'll make it. Don't worry."

"And we don't have a thing put away for college."

"College? Good God, Gladys, that's—"

"I know it's a few years away, but it'll get here before we know it. Elementary school certainly disappeared over night. And one day Sandy will be getting married, and we'll have to pay for that, too."

Gladys handled the finances in the Nash household—writing checks, balancing the check book, budgeting expenses—which meant that when there was a money problem she was the first to feel the heat because she was the closest to it. Which meant that she was the one who knew when it was time to start worrying.

Jesus, she's more upset than I realized, Henry thought. She's thinking about problems five years away. He tried to be positive. "Hey, maybe we'll win the Lotto this week, and all our problems will be solved."

Gladys was not in the mood to be light. "And then there's Brian's teeth. I was looking at them at dinner. Did you ever look at your son's teeth? I mean really *look?* They're getting worse, Henry. Do you realize it's been six months since the dentist told us that Brian would need braces, too? I hoped that we could put it off until we got Sandy out of hers, but now, I don't know."

Brian was a late bloomer. His teeth hadn't started to grow crooked until after his younger sister's. Gladys and Henry thought they were going to get away with only having to pay for one set of braces. They were wrong.

However, Henry had an easy answer for the problem.

"Well, if we can't afford braces for Brian, he'll just have to wait until we can. He'll just have to live with less than perfect teeth for a little while longer. Besides, it's different for a guy anyway. Perfect teeth are more important to girls; guys could care less. I never had braces when I was a kid and I lived through it." He winked. "And I got you, didn't I?"

Gladys smiled, but it didn't last. "What about the bank?" she said. "Do you think they'll wait?"

She was not intentionally being sarcastic; she actually hoped Henry might have an answer.

Henry had a question instead. "What about the money you inherited from your mother? Can't we use that?"

Gladys gave him a strange look. "Use it? We've already used it."

Henry didn't understand. "What do you mean?"

"It's gone."

Stunned. "It's gone?"

"That's right."

"I— What do you mean 'it's gone?' All of it?"

Gladys frowned, looking just slightly perturbed. "Henry, it wasn't that much. Ten thousand dollars doesn't go very far these days. Not when you have two kids growing like weeds. And two mortgages. And bills to pay."

"You mean we went through the whole ten thousand that fast? I can't believe it. Where'd it all go?"

Gladys built on her perturbed look. "It *went* to pay bills, dear," she said, drawing out the *dear*, not even bothering to try to hide her irritation. "Henry, we've been living off it for the past five months. Frankly, it wasn't until August that I managed to pay off most of our bills from last Christmas. We knew at the time we might have gone a little overboard—we keep saying we're going to cut back, but we never do. We talked about it, remember? We were counting on the interest rates going down, not up. Right?"

Gladys didn't mention the rec room in so many words but they both knew what she was talking about. It was the killer. If they only had one mortgage they might be able to handle it.

"I've been pinching pennies trying to make ends meet." She rolled her eyes. "I'm pinched out."

Henry said out loud what they were both thinking. "I guess we should never have put in that rec room."

Gladys turned back toward the ceiling. "You bring home a very nice paycheck, sweetheart. You always have. You're a good provider." Then back toward Henry. "But—admit it—we've been living above our means ever since mother died and left me that money. We both knew it would run out sooner or later."

Jesus, Henry thought to himself. Is this where we are? Is this all there is? Surely there's more to life, Henry petitioned.

There used to be. He remembered. There were times.

He recalled those times, times when he was full of life. Times when he could babble on and on about absolutely nothing. Exciting times, invigorating times. Back when *everything* was important. Where had all the flowers gone?

And just like that, Henry Nash felt completely alone. Abandoned, marooned. The only man in the Milky Way.

What the hell was wrong with him? Were the potential problems at the plant getting to him? Was the strike on his mind? The thought of a strike had never seemed to bother him before. He'd walked the line a number of times in the past and never thought a thing about it. Why was he so screwed up all of a sudden?

Was he going through some kind of mid-life crisis? Was he getting old? Was he going through male menopause? Jesus, talk about a cold slap in the face. Henry let out a sigh. Maybe that was it. Maybe he was over the hill. Forty-six didn't sound all that old, but life seemed out of balance all of a sudden; nothing seemed to fit. It was as though Henry had just awakened from a long dream and life had somehow passed him by. Life was depressing as all hell.

He turned toward Gladys. She was waiting for an answer. This time all Henry had to offer was silence. And more bad news. After a few minutes he said, "Now's not a good time to bring this up, but I guess I'd better tell you. There's a good chance there's going to be a strike at the plant."

Shit, Henry wished he hadn't said that. Gladys didn't need anything else to worry about.

Gladys stopped breathing. "You're kidding."

Well, it was too late now. Henry guessed it was better that she find out from him rather than hear it from someone else. He shook his head, discouraged. "'Fraid not. That's the word."

"How good a chance?"

"Better than fifty-fifty."

For the fourth time in as many minutes the ceiling was on the receiving end of a Gladys Nash stare. "Damn."

"I'm going to New York. That's it. I've made up my mind."

Ralph Bright turned toward his wife. "What?"

Lilith Bright didn't like to repeat herself—which she wouldn't have to do if her husband paid more attention to her when she spoke. He said he did, but Lilith knew better. It really ticked her off. And the fact that he refused to admit it ticked her off even more.

She gave Ralph one of her patented dirty looks, stood up, walked over to the doorway that led from the living room into the kitchen, stopped, turned, then began tapping her foot up and down. "I said, 'I'm going to New York.'"

In addition to the look, the tone was also patented. It was Lilith's famous You-got-a-problem-with-that? tone.

Ralph should have known; Lilith's silence was the tipoff.

But, since she hadn't said anything in the past two days about the manuscript, Ralph thought that maybe, just maybe, the whole thing had blown over; maybe his dear wife had decided to let the silly thing drop.

Wishful thinking. Lilith never let anything drop.

Playing dumb probably wouldn't work, but Ralph decided to give it a shot anyway. "New York? Lilith, why on earth would you—"

"Ralph. Try to follow me on this. I'll go slow. I'm - going - to - New York. Nothing you can say will stop me. That manuscript belongs to me, and you know it. And I intend to get it."

It had been worth a try. Ralph let out a sigh and gave her a sorry look. "I was hoping you'd forgotten all about that."

Lilith's look was sinister. "Yeah, right. Well, you hope in one hand and crap in the other, and see which one fills up first. Hope—I've been hoping for years that one day I'd get what was coming to me—my rightful inheritance—but all I ever got for all that hope was a handful of you-know-what. I'm done hoping, Ralph. It's *acting* time. I'm going to New York. Period. You can come along if you want, or stay here and whine. I could care less."

Here we go again, Ralph thought. "Now, Lilith, you know—"

"Don't 'Now, Lilith,' me, Ralph Bright. I know what you're going to say and I don't want to hear it. I've heard it before, and I'm not going to listen to it anymore. I've wasted enough time. Mark Twain was a relative of mine and they owe me. And I don't intend to give up on this thing just because you have. Lilith Bright does not knuckle-under to anyone. If you want to be a wimp and let those high-powered New York attorneys shove you around, if you want to crawl into a corner like a sniveling dog, then just you go right ahead. But I'm not. By God, I'm not!"

"But, honey ..." Ralph's voice was soft and low this time, soothing, as if he were talking to a wounded bear, which, in a sense, he supposed he was. "You know we've gone through this whole thing before, over and over, again and again. This won't be the first time you've tangled with those people. You have been *acting*, dear, and it's gotten you nothing but heartache. Please, give it up. They just have too much muscle for us. They have all the money and all the resources and all the time. They can out-spend us, and out-wait us. It may be a noble effort, Lilith, but it's just no use."

Ralph knew it had nothing to do with *noble; greed* was the motivator here. But *noble* was a butter-her-up word, a calm-her-down word, a make-her-think-reasonable word.

It didn't work.

"Balls," Lilith said.

Ralph fidgeted in his seat. He waited for the inevitable. He knew what was coming.

"That's all it takes," Lilith challenged, her words a hopeful dare. She'd sent out this same invitation before. "Balls," she repeated.

Ralph said nothing.

When Lilith saw that once again she was not going to get any response, she closed the issue the same way she always closed the issue, with a sigh and, "I guess we both know who has the only pair in this family." Lilith stared down at her husband, almost begging him to disagree.

Ralph knew better than to argue; living with Lilith was tough enough under half-way compatible circumstances. He did not want to make waves. He did not want to aggravate things; it was easier.

Ralph put his hand on the arm of the sofa and pushed himself up. He bent down and picked the jar of peanut butter up off the coffee table, put the crackers back into the box, cradled the box in the crook of his elbow, then reached over and switched off the floor lamp. After doing that he walked over and flipped off the TV, then turned toward Lilith. "When are we leaving?" he asked, sticking out his chest and smiling proudly, expecting at least a smile return. Your knight in shining armor has arisen m'lady.

Lilith grunted and walked out of the room.

Sometimes Ralph expected too much.

Chapter 5
Wednesday

3:20 AM

It was a sand storm. The wind whipped across the plains like a tornado, kicking up clouds of dust that made it impossible to see where he was going. But he had to keep going. They were right behind him. He couldn't stop now. If he ran headfirst into the side of a mountain, or went sailing out over a cliff, it was still better than what they had in mind for him. Anything was better than the rope.

They'd been after him for nine straight days. Picked up his trail outside Indian Fork. They were relentless. Texas Rangers were like that: hound dogs that wouldn't quit.

The dust burned his eyes, like salt in a wound. He tried to brush it away with the back of his glove, but it was no use. He could cover his nose and mouth with his bandanna, but he couldn't do a thing about his eyes. He just had to let them burn.

Hooves pounded like thunder against the sun-bleached plain. Beneath him, his ever-faithful Diablo. The horse under him was a machine whose legs were driven by a heart as big as the sky. He would never quit, never surrender. Diablo would die for him, and Jesse knew it. But then Diablo stepped into a prairie dog hole and Jesse heard his leg snap. It was like a rifle shot, CRACK! and Jesse knew it was over. He was a goner. His mighty steed started to fall and Jesse started to fly.

He seemed to sail through the air forever. Time stopped and he was in a world all his own. Everything became quiet and he was a bird, flying free, flying home.

Then the ground came up to meet him in a sudden rush, and he wasn't flying anymore. It was hard ground, unforgiving. The dry, cracked earth felt like solid rock that struck his chest like a battering ram and took his breath away.

"Ahhhhh," he screamed, as the air was forced out of his lungs.

Thud. He hit, then bounced, then hit again. Then rolled. Then came to a stop. His chest exploded. Pain shot through his entire body.

Jesus, he was on fire; his flesh felt as if it had been ripped from his body. His chest screamed. Bands of flame squeezed at his ribs like a vise. Then everything exploded, and his body was white-hot. The sun that had been above him was in him now.

Jesse had never felt such pain. His chest, it must be crushed. He couldn't breath.

"I ... I can't breath."

It felt as though a great weight was pressing down on him. *Better than a rope* flashed through his mind.

"It hurts sooooo ..." The pain was agonizing.

"Henry?"

What?

"Henry? Henry, it really hurts. I ..."

Henry?

His eyes popped open. It was Gladys.

Henry flipped on the light. She was sitting up in bed, holding her chest. Gasping for air. Trying to catch her breath.

Jesus, he thought he was dreaming.

Wait, he *was* dreaming. No, *had been* dreaming. But not now. This was no dream. He sat up. "Gladys, what's wrong?"

"It's my chest. It's ... It hurts so ..."

"Jesus." Henry put his hand on her back. "Try to relax. Breath slowly, take deep breaths. You'll be all right. You'll be okay. Just relax. Take it slow."

Henry was scared to death. Chest pains—one thing flashed through his mind: heart attack.

Gladys was sitting up, but bent over, making faces, faces that indicated to Henry that she was in a great deal of pain. She had her hands pressed to her chest, massaging.

Henry didn't know what to do. He tried to reassure her, tried to calm her down. "Everything's going to be okay. You'll be fine. It's okay. Just take it slow and easy. Slow and easy."

He felt so helpless. There was nothing he could do. His incompetence infuriated him. Being absolutely helpless when someone needed you was the worst kind of incompetence imaginable.

After a few more minutes—painful minutes for Gladys, frightening, agonizing minutes for Henry—the pain seemed to begin to recede. Gradually Gladys began to relax. She let out a sigh.

"Oh, my God, I don't know what happened to me." She took a deep breath, then let it out. "All of a sudden I just couldn't breath, and then my chest started to throb and I thought I was dreaming. And then—God, it—The pain woke me up."

"Are you all right?"

She didn't answer right away. Then, "Yes. I— I think I'm going to be okay now."

"Are you sure? Maybe I should call a doctor."

"No, no, I'll be fine. Really. Just give me a minute. I feel a lot better. I don't know what it was, but whatever it was, I seem to be over it."

Henry stared at his wife.

She let out another sigh. "Wow." She looked at Henry and smiled.

"*Wow* is right," Henry said. "You had me scared to death. Good God, Gladys."

She looked embarrassed. "I'm sorry. I— I'm sorry I woke you up."

"Hey, I'm not talking about that. It's you. Jesus; are you sure you're all right?"

She continued to breathe deeply. "Yes. I'm sure. Whatever it was seems to have passed."

But she continued to rub her chest.

"Glad-ys?"

"No, I mean it. My chest still hurts a little, but it's probably just the aftershock. It hurt pretty bad there for a while. But most of it's gone. I feel a lot better than I did. I'm sure I'll be okay."

Henry looked suspicious. "Well, I still think you'd better give Doc Williamson a call in the morning and have him check you over, just to make sure."

Another sigh. "Ah, I don't think that's necessary. I'm sure it was just a bad case of heartburn, something I ate that didn't agree with me. I don't need to bother Doctor Williamson for something like that."

"Baloney. Doctors love to be bothered. At the rate of thirty dollars a visit I'd love to be bothered too."

Gladys laid back down. "Well, we'll see. I know one thing for sure, if it was something I ate, I don't ever want to eat it again. I certainly don't need to go through something like this again, not for a long, long time."

Henry turned out the light. You and me both, he thought to himself. You and me both.

Over the intercom: "Mr. Romaine, there's a Mr. Samuelson here to see you."

Samuelson? The name didn't ring a bell.

Victor checked his calendar: Wednesday, December 6th. No Samuelson.

Nothing scheduled all day. He got up from his desk and walked over to his office door. When he opened it, a giant greeted him.

A man, easily six-foot-four or -five, weighing well over two hundred and fifty pounds, and standing by Victor's secretary's desk, smiled. He was dressed in a tan topcoat. Sitting on the desk in front of him was a box roughly a foot tall, and approximately a half a foot wide and a half a foot deep.

Victor scanned the man as he approached. On top, long, wavy, sand-colored hair; a square head; eyes dark and darting; face rugged, eagle-like; skin lined and leathery; neck thick, almost non-existent; shoulders that went on forever. A physical man. An outdoorsman. He was wearing a white shirt and a red tie that showed beneath his coat on top. Sticking out from the bottom was a very expensive-looking pair of alligator cowboy boots. In his hands he held a cowboy hat, which he shifted to his left hand when he proffered his right to Victor.

Victor took it. "Mr. Samuelson, Victor Romaine." The grip was firm, a vise, and the hands were callused. "How may I help you?" Victor asked.

"Sir," the man said with a half bow, "Nice to meet you." The voice had a Texas drawl, deep and melancholy, almost sad. "It's about this here piece I got here." With that he moved his hand to the box that was sitting on Mrs. Copperman's desk. "I was wondering if you might be interested in selling it for me."

Victor nodded noncommittally. "Well, that's why we're here. Why don't you bring it into my office and we'll take a look at it, and see what we can arrange."

Victor turned and held out his hand, gesturing for Samuelson to lead the way into his office. When Samuelson hesitated, Victor gave him a curious look.

Samuelson said, "Well, you see. I'm kinda in a hurry. So, if you think you'd be interested, there's the problem of time. I'd really like to have it sold as soon as possible." He gave Victor a shy look. "By this weekend, to be exact."

Victor lowered his hand. "Oh, I see. Well, I'm sorry, Mr. Samuelson, but I'm afraid that would be impossible. We already have an auction scheduled for this weekend. Even if we didn't, we couldn't possibly do it that fast. Auctions take a minimum of three months to organize. Many take longer. Some as much as a year. You understand, these things take time. The first thing we have to do is notify prospective buyers, people who would be interested in this type of merchandise. Just what kind of merchandise do you have?"

Samuelson didn't answer right away. He was thinking. Then, "Oh, ah, it's a vase. Chinese. Ming. I bought it in London three years ago. One-point-two mil—but I'm sure it's gone up since then."

Victor nodded knowingly to Samuelson, and then thought to himself: You bet your life it's gone up since then. How's five-fold sound? Ming had been the hottest property on the market in the last two years. It wouldn't bring as much as the Twain manuscript, but it certainly wouldn't go for a song either. "Well, I'd be happy to take a look at it and give you my opinion as to what it's worth."

Samuelson drifted away again. When he came back he had a proposal. "I thought maybe, well, would you be interested in buying it, and then auctioning it off for yourself? You ever do that sorta thing?"

Victor smiled and shook his head. "No, I'm sorry. The investment to do that would be much too prohibitive. With the interest and all, it just wouldn't pay us to get involved to that degree. No, we're simply an outlet, I'm afraid, not an investor."

Samuelson nodded, disappointed. "I see."

Silence. Waiting. Thought. Alternatives.

Finally, Samuelson held out his hand. "Well, Mr. Romaine, thank you for taking the time to see me. I think we would have made a great team. Maybe some other time. This time I can't wait; I really have to sell right away. I got some finanacial matters that just kinda came up all of a sudden, you understand." He looked at Victor and winked shyly. "I think I'll check with some of the other houses. Maybe they can fit me in quicker. If not, I guess I'll head for the airport and see if I can grab a flight to London. Heck, I bought it there, I oughta be able to sell it there. Right?"

Victor smiled and once again shook the bear paw. "Well, I wish you luck. If things don't work out, give us a call. Like I said, we'd be happy to assist you in any way we can, but we need a little more time."

Samuelson returned the smile. "I appreciate that, but time is the one thing I don't have."

With that he put on his Stetson, picked up his package, nodded to Mrs. Copperman, turned and walked out.

Mrs. Copperman said, "Gee, that's too bad. I would really have liked to see that vase."

Victor shrugged his shoulders. He didn't care, there were bigger fish in his sea.

Chapter 6
Thursday Evening

HENRY PICKED UP THE TELEPHONE ON THE SECOND RING. It was Roger Muldowney.
"Did you get the word?"
Henry said, "No."
"We walk."
"Shit."
"Yeah, I agree," Roger said. "A strike is the last thing I want, too."
"Are you sure?"
"Positive."
"How'd you find out?"
"Just talked to Ernie Paul. Shively called him. Said they just broke off talks. It's definite. Grab your sign; time to hit the bricks."
"That's a bunch of horseshit, Rog."
Silence.
"So," Henry said, "what are you gonna do?"
Roger was stunned. "What am I gonna do? What do you mean 'What am I gonna do?' You mean like I got a choice? I'm gonna take the big hike, man, like everyone else. Round and round we go, when we stop, nobody knows."
"Hey, I don't know, Rog. I just don't know."
"What do you mean, you don't know?"
"I mean, I don't know."
"Hey, I know what 'I don't know' means. I just want to know what *you* mean when you say 'I don't know.'"
"I mean, I don't know. Jesus Christ, Rog! I don't know! I don't know! All right?"

Henry fumed, then paused. In union terms a pause was referred to as a cooling off period. And Henry needed cooling off; Roger was really pissing him off. Finally, as calmly as he could put it, Henry said, "It means, I just don't know what the hell I'm gonna do, Roger. It's the exact opposite of knowing what I'm going to do. Do you understand? Can I make it any clearer?

I'm not prepared for a strike. I have to think. Okay? I don't know. It's as simple as that. I don't know."

Roger thought for a minute. Then, "Jesus, Henry, you're not thinking what I think you're thinking, are you?"

Silence.

"Henry, talk to me. You're not thinking about crossing the line, are you? Don't tell me you're thinking about crossing the line."

Henry didn't answer right away. There was much to think about. Then, almost a whisper, "I don't know, Rog."

More silence.

Then Roger said, "Jesus, Henry, I know, I know this whole thing really stinks, but crossing the line ... A guy's really got to think about that. I mean, Jesus Christ, man. Jesus Christ."

"Hey, I'm not stupid, Rog. I know what you're saying. It's just that I don't really think the membership supports this strike, you know? Not the majority, anyway. It's mostly that loud mouth Vacossi, and his cronies."

Jesse James wouldn't put up with this kind of shit, Henry thought. Other people robbing you of your rights, stealing your right to make a living. Taking away your right to support your family. And there was Gladys to think about. She didn't need this kind of shit. Not now.

"Maybe so, Henry, but he's the president of the union. What he says goes, whether he's a loud mouth or not."

"It's horseshit, Rog."

"Horseshit or not, if the boss says we walk, we walk."

"Hey, you talk to the other guys—the ones our age who have gone through this kind of thing before—and they'll tell you they don't want this strike any more than we do. Not really. They got families, kids, bills to pay. The company's talking about moving the whole damned thing down south, you know that, don't you? If that happens, then what do we have? A piece of the pie's better than none at all."

"Come on, Henry. They'll never move. There's eighty-five hundred people workin' here. And all that equipment. Do you know how much that would cost? Plenty. Hell, they can't afford to move."

"Hey, I'm just saying if, if they do, then I'm shit outta luck, pal. I got nothin' else, Rog. Nothin' to fall back on."

Roger had to agree that he, too, would be shit outta luck if the company moved the plant. But that didn't really make any difference. "Okay, Henry, so tell me our options. Like we got any. What can we do?"

Henry looked down at Thursday's folded newspaper lying on the coffee table, and the paperback western next to it. The newspaper ... Sunday ...

The Mark Twain manuscript.
Jesse James.
Light bulbs flashed.
Henry reached into the side pocket on his easy chair; the Twain article from Sunday's paper was still there where he'd left it. He took it out and stared at it.
Yippee yi-oh ki-ay.
"Why don't I meet you at Broadway Joe's in, say, half an hour, and maybe we can figure something out over a brewski or two. You know beer has a way of clearing out the old cobwebs."
"You got any ideas?"
Henry smiled down at the newspaper. "Maybe."

Since Lilith hadn't said anything about the New York trip since Tuesday night, Ralph assumed the whole thing had blown over. Wednesday came and went. By the time he got home from work on Thursday it was out of his mind completely.
Big mistake. It came up at dinner.
"Ralph, right after we finish I want you to call the airport," Lilith commanded. It caught Ralph just as he was shoveling in a forkful of pork chop. "I want to leave Dallas-Fort Worth around one or so. We'll leave here between ten and eleven, grab a bite at the airport—no, wait, we'll eat here, that rip-off airport charges an arm and a leg for a lousy cup of coffee. We'll eat, then leave for the airport precisely at eleven; that should give us plenty of time to find a place to park, get our luggage checked in, and then get to the gate without having to rush around like a couple of chicken farmers. We need to get into New York sometime late Friday afternoon, fourish. We'll check into a hotel, and then I think we should go to the auction house first thing Saturday morning. Then—"
Ralph swallowed his pork chop. "—Leave tomorrow? Tomorrow's a work day, dear. I—"
"Call in sick. Jesus, do I have to think of everything, Ralph?"
"Well, I was just thinking that—"
Lilith stopped him, the way she usually stopped him, by interrupting. "Don't think, Ralph. Thinking always gets you in trouble. Just do what I say and you'll be fine."

Broadway Joe's had two customers: Henry Nash and Roger Muldowney. The forecast of a coming blizzard had apparently scared most of the people away. Even the regulars, the normally tenacious barflies, were nowhere to be seen.

Chet Ramsey, the bartender and owner of Broadway Joe's (he bought it off a guy named Joe Filabresse and never changed the name because he thought Broadway Chet's sounded stupid) busied himself behind the bar wishing he had two *less* customers so he could close the place and get the hell out before he got snowed in.

Henry and Roger sat in a booth in the back.

"Did you see the weather forecast, Henry?" Roger asked. "That shit scares the hell out of me."

Henry studied the comment, then tossed it away with a wave of his hand. "Hey, what's a little snow?"

"Ten inches? That's 'a little' snow? And *wind*. The guy on the radio said thirty-mile-an-hour shit. That means drifting. We got a bitch coming our way, Henry. A real bitch."

Roger nervously played with his drink.

The howling wind outside didn't seem to bother Henry. He calmly sipped his draft. "Rog, quit acting like a big wimp. It's just snow, for chrissake. White powder. Fluffy rain, that's all. It's not the end of the damn world."

Roger looked around the bar; he wasn't so sure of that. It sounded like the end of the world to him. The racket going on outside sounded like the end of everything. The wind howled and whistled. Roger was scared to death and didn't try to hide it. The fact that he didn't want to be there was an understatement.

"This is dumb, Henry. Really dumb. I should be at the grocery store right now, stocking up on food just in case we get snowed in, instead of sitting in some stupid bar," he looked down at his drink, "drinking a stupid beer," he looked at his friend, "talkin' to a crazy man."

Henry frowned. "Christ, Rog, you're worse than a little old lady. Those weather people always make it sound worse than it really is. You know that. Forget it." Henry drained his glass. "Have another beer."

Roger drummed the table with his fingers. Eyes darted here and there. "Yeah, well, I don't know." He spun his glass, studied it, then raised it to his mouth and emptied it in one swallow.

Henry raised his hand in the air. Chet saw it. Henry twirled it in circles: another round.

Chet grunted to himself.

The two men sat in silence, Roger on the edge, Henry thinking. After a minute Chet delivered the drinks.

"You guys hear the weather forecast?" he asked. "Way they talked, a fellow might want to think about gettin' out while the gettin' was good."

Hint.

It didn't work.

"Propaganda," Henry said. "Cops just want to keep everyone off the streets so they can all go home early."

Chet walked away grumbling to himself.

Henry said, "I've decided, Rog. This strike is bad news all the way around." He bit his lip and shook his head. "I can't handle it right now and that's all there is to it. It's as simple as that."

Roger gulped. "What the hell's that supposed to mean?"

Roger was afraid he already knew the answer to that but hoped he was wrong.

"It means 'forget it.' It means 'no way.' It means 'thanks but no thanks, I think I'll pass.'"

Even though Roger knew what was coming he asked anyway, just in case. "You mean you're gonna cross the line?"

Henry didn't respond. Roger gulped again.

"Henry, are you out of your damned mind? That's suicide. You can't do that."

"Who says?"

Roger's eyes got big. *Who says?* Henry, Jesus, you know better than that. You can't buck the system, even if the system's wrong. It's too big, too powerful. You're more than a day old; you weren't born yesterday."

"Rog, I don't have any choice. I can't take that kind of financial hit right now." Henry was a man defeated. His eyes had an emptiness to them, his face shallow and barren. "My mortgage just went up. Can you believe it? With Christmas coming and all—my mortgage just went up. How's that for an early Christmas present? That rec room I put in the basement last winter? Remember? Well, it came back to haunt me. Gladys and I knew it might. The bank warned us. They said if interest rates went up we could expect to see an increase. Well, interest rates went up, and they were right. Ever hear the saying: 'I have seen the increase and it is mine'?"

Henry tried his best to snicker at his sorry attempt at humor but realized there was nothing at all funny about the mess he was in. He paused to collect his thoughts, then said, "And if that wasn't bad enough, I got one kid in braces, and another one all primed and ready to get braces, stompin' at the bit, if you know what I mean? Rog, do you know what braces cost?"

Roger looked confused. "Braces? I thought our insurance covered that."

"Yeah, right. It does—up to eight hundred bucks. Eight hundred bucks, *per* kid. At last count I had two kids. Two kids who couldn't have their mother's perfect set of pearly whites. Oh, hell no, they had to inherit their old man's come-in-at-any-angle-it's-okay-who-gives-a-damn teeth. The orthodontist said Sandy's will probably cost twenty-five hundred by the time we're all done, and Brian's should come in around three thousand."

This time Roger really gulped. "Three thousand? Dollars? Jesus, you're kidding. Braces cost that much?"

Henry frowned and nodded.

Roger thought for a minute, then offered a solution. "Well, shit, Henry, listen. I got an idea. I got some extra cash I'm not going to need for a while. It'd be no problem for me to—"

"Forget it, Rog," Henry interrupted. "Thanks, I really appreciate it, but that's not the point. That's a short term fix and I got a long term problem, like they say on *Wall Street Week*. A problem I gotta do something about. And I gotta do it now."

Roger searched for an answer. "Henry, listen to me. I know things look bad, but don't be crazy and do something now that you'll regret later. We don't know how long this strike's gonna last. Hell, it could be over in a day or two."

"Rog, that's horseshit and you know it. This son of a bitch is gonna last forever, at least into the new year. Probably *way* into the new year. Both sides are mean and both sides are pissed and both sides are hungry. Vacossi's up for re-election next year; do you really believe he's gonna cave in? And what do you think the company's gonna do, back off now? Shit. Forget it. It's too late. Both sides have been making their By God We're Tough speeches for the last two months. They'll squeeze us dry before this thing is all over." Henry shook his head. "Nope, this son of a bitch is showing all the signs of being one long and bloody bastard. You know it and I know it. Let's not try to shit each other. Okay?"

Roger's thoughts were no longer on the weather. "So, you're gonna cross the picket line, is that it? *That's* your solution? No matter what I say, no matter how dangerous it is. You've made up your mind and that's that. You're gonna do it."

Henry looked at his friend and smiled, then slid the newspaper he'd brought with him across the table. "I'm going to do something even more dangerous than that, Roger Ramjet," he said. "Cross a picket line? Dangerous? Hell, you ain't seen nothing yet."

Chapter 7
Thursday Night

Stanley Kowalski never missed *The Tonight Show*. First Steve Allen, then Jack Paar. Then Johnny. And now, Jay Leno. Stanley wasn't fully into Leno yet; "Big John" was still his favorite. But he watched every night because he had nothing else to do. Stanley had tried David Letterman, but, frankly, Stanley didn't understand Dave. He couldn't quite figure him out. So Stanley watched Jay, and all the time wished Johnny'd come back.

Stanley could stay up and watch *The Tonight Show* because Stanley didn't have to get up early. Stanley could sleep as late as he pleased. As a result of that freedom, Stanley never flipped off the TV much before 3:00 AM. Stanley's job allowed him to sleep in because most of Stanley's work came in the afternoon or evening, or night, but never before noon. That was the best part about Stanley's job—he got to pick his own hours. If he didn't want to go to work until 7:00 PM, then he didn't go to work until 7:00 PM. Stanley could do that because Stanley was self-employed. Stanley was a hit man. Stanley Kowalski killed people for a living.

Lying flat on his back in the center of an unmade bed, in underwear he'd worn for the third day in a row, Stanley stared at Jay Leno over naked hammer toes. The volume on the nineteen-inch RCA color television on the dresser at the foot of Stanley's bed was turned up just loud enough to hear. Loud enough for your normal person to hear, that is. Stanley Kowalski, however, was not your normal person. It was almost too loud for Stanley. Stanley Kowalski had an extremely keen sense of hearing. Ears like sonar. Hearing like a dog, Stanley used to brag.

Good, right? Wrong. Extra-sensitive hearing was a curse, as well as a blessing. It helped in Stanley's line of work to be able to hear better than the next guy—especially if the next guy just happened to be your target, and the lights were out, and the only sound in the room was the heavy breathing of a man about to die.

But it also hurt. *Hurt*, as in *pain*. Hurt, as in normal daily sounds were extremely painful to very sensitive ears. Horns and whistles and *illegal mufflers!* They were the worst.

Rotten snot-nosed, pimply-faced little bastards that drove those cars—why didn't the police do something? They punched Stanley's hot button like nothing else, making him so angry he could kill somebody for free. Noise pollution was a real bummer in Stanley's case, maybe explaining why Stanley Kowalski got so many migraine headaches.

Stanley's "spare tire" stretched the sweat-yellowed, tank-top T-shirt he wore beyond the point of no return, beyond the manufacturer's recommendations, voiding any warranty, *implied or otherwise*, that promised it would always *spring back* to its original form.

But Stanley didn't care. Stanley didn't think about T-shirts that had lost their spring, or beer guts that invalidated guarantees. Stanley didn't think about much of anything. Stanley just lay there and let the ugliness that had taken years to perfect hang out over the elastic of his striped boxer shorts in a fat, disgusting roll.

Stanley was a large-boned man, whose body had apparently been assembled by a blind man; a blind man who had an excellent feel for parts, but who had no perception at all when it came to the whole, because everything was completely out of proportion to everything else. Nothing seemed to go together; body parts simply didn't mesh with each other. His basset hound ears were far too large for his diminutive head; and his tiny head was too small for his bull neck; the lipless mouth sliced into the front of his face—little more than a line drawn with a Number 2 pencil—had settled too far south of an eagle beak. The two-day growth of beard that decorated his double chin gave him an especially surly look, matching his surly mood. His W.C. Fields nose stuck in the lower half of a expressionless, pear-shaped face, dwarfed eyes that looked like, according to his buddy Lou Monetti, "two pissholes in a snowdrift." Doughy-white flesh draped loosely over a bulky form (even though Stanley was overweight his flesh hung on him) as if he'd bought the wrong size coat of skin at a garage sale simply because it was a hellava buy. From the neck down it didn't get any better. His arms were gangly and his hands were stubby and his knees were knobby.

But beer guts and dirty T-shirts and unshaven chins and "two pissholes in a snowdrift" didn't bother Stanley Kowalski; he was a man who had neither the ability nor the inclination to improve his appearance. Stanley simply didn't give a damn.

Jay's guests tonight were Burt Reynolds, Carl Reiner and some woman named Louise Ann Bridges.

Who the hell is Louise Ann Bridges? Stanley wondered.

Jay told him. Louise Ann Bridges was the woman who'd found the Mark Twain manuscript at the bottom of an old trunk.

Fuck, Stanley thought, as he fired-up a Pall Mall. Who gives a rat's ass about some dinggy broad and a dipshit book?

He sucked in a lungful of smoke and then spit a small piece of tobacco off his lower lip as he exhaled. Stanley didn't smoke those filtered jobs. Filtered jobs were for pussies. He liked his cigarettes straight. A bean-bag ashtray, balanced precariously on Stanley's large belly, jiggled every time he adjusted his position against the two pillows he'd stuffed between his back and the bedroom wall that served as the headboard. Stanley took another drag on his Pall Mall and then tapped the ash into the ashtray with the fat index finger of his right hand. In his left hand was a Seagram's Seven-and-Seven, Stanley's favorite drink dating back to his Reform School days. The glass hadn't been washed in weeks but that didn't bother Stanley. The fingernails at the ends of his stubby fingers were dirty and needed trimming, but that didn't bother him either. Stanley noticed their condition and thought that he might take care of that one of these days.

Stanley reached over and grabbed the bottle of Seagram's Seven off the night stand and poured three gurgles into his half-empty glass. He put the whiskey back on the table and picked up the can of Seven-Up. One gurgle of Seven-Up was plenty—too much Seven-Up made him burp. He put the can back and then proceeded to enjoy life, drinking with one hand and smoking with the other. A two-fisted drinker and two-fisted smoker was our man, Stanley Kowalski.

Commercials flashed across the screen after Jay's monologue.

Stanley took a sip of his drink, then burped. Damn Seven-Up.

Life between jobs was one boring son of a bitch as far as Stanley Kowalski was concerned. The thrill of the hunt—the thrill of the kill!—that's what Stanley lived for. Without that the nights were long and the days just piled up against each other one after another, row upon row of check marks on a blank calendar, nothing to look forward to, only back on. Things had definitely been too quiet for too long. Stanley needed a contract real bad. And not for the money, either. Stanley didn't need money; he needed something to do. Something to live for. *Anything.* Why the hell hadn't Carmine called? Business couldn't be that slow. Surely somebody needed dusted, or leaned on at least. Stanley's trigger finger was itchy.

"You're gonna what?"

Roger couldn't believe it.

Henry pointed to the newspaper and repeated himself. "I'm gonna steal the Mark Twain manuscript." He found it a lot easier to say the second time.

Roger blinked, twice, with difficulty; his coordination seemed to have deserted him. Then, not knowing what else to do, he ordered two more beers.

Henry said, "I told you about it, Rog. Remember, that woman in Connecticut bought an old trunk and—"

"I know you told me about it, Henry. What the hell does that have to do with anything? Telling me about it is not the same as telling me you're going to steal the damn thing. That is what you said, isn't it? You're going to steal it."

Henry nodded.

After the bartender delivered the order and walked away, Roger said, "You're pulling my leg. Right? This whole thing is some kind of joke."

No comment.

"Henry?"

Roger could not believe what he was hearing, or, more accurately, what he was not hearing. Denial is what he wanted to hear. "You're out of your mind. You know that don't you?"

Henry smiled.

Roger shook his head. "You've flipped, Henry. I knew sooner or later it would happen. It was just a matter of time. Sooner or later the guys in the white jackets—the room with the padded walls—" He stared across the table at his friend. There was a note of pleading in his voice. "Henry, tell me this is a joke. Tell me you're making a funny."

Henry was silent.

"Henry, talk to me. This is bullshit, right?"

"I'm sayin' it like it is, Rog."

"You can't be serious."

"Rog, would I lie to you?"

Roger Muldowney was at a loss. Henry Nash had come up with some pretty dumb ideas before, but this had to be the dumbest of all time. This might just be a new world record for dumb.

"Henry, you've come up with some pretty weird shit in the past, I mean real left-field kinda stuff, but this is the weirdest. I've known you for a long time, and every time I thought you'd finally topped yourself, you always managed to dig just a little deeper and pull something new out of the hat, but this time, Jesus, Henry." Then he stopped. He thought for a minute, looked off into space, and then, suddenly, just like that, started laughing. He looked back at Henry, "Henry, you asshole," and laughed some more. "You really had me going for a minute."

Henry stopped smiling. "You think I'm pulling your leg?"

Roger increased his laughter. "You bet your ass I do. Nobody in his right mind would try a stunt like that. You gotta be pulling my leg."

Henry's voice was deadly serious. "Not this time, *Kemo Sabe*."

Roger was silent. Even the wind outside seemed to stop blowing. Finally, "Henry, I can't believe it. Where in the hell did you come up with this shit?"

Henry shrugged. "Outta the blue, kinda. Not a bad idea though. What do you think?"

"What do I think? I think it sucks—that's what I think. I think it sucks royally."

Henry shook his head back and forth slowly. "Roger, Roger, Roger. That's just because it's new to you. New ideas always take awhile. Give it a minute. Let it sink in."

"Give it a minute, my ass! A minute or a year, it still sucks. I'll spell it out for you: S-U-C-K-S. Sucks. Repeat after me, Henry: This idea *sucks*. And for crissakes, it's *robbery*. Grand larceny."

Henry tilted his head to the side. "I don't look at it as robbery. I look at it as," Henry thought for a second, tossing various choices around in his mind, then said, "borrowing."

Time again for Roger to recheck his hearing. "Borrowing?"

"Yeah, borrowing. I'm just gonna borrow it for a little while."

"Right. And then you're gonna to give it back after a while?"

Henry's expression said that he agreed with that statement. "Yeah, more or less. That's about it."

"Right. First, you're gonna steal—borrow, excuse me—it for a little while, and then you're gonna give it back?"

Henry nodded his head.

"Oh, yeah? Well, ask me something, old buddy, how do you think the police are gonna look at that? Do you think the police are into 'borrowing?'"

Henry laughed. "They probably won't think it's such a neat idea. They might even think it sucks."

"Jesus, Henry," Roger said, "do you really think so? No damn sense of humor, right? Police are funny that way. Not big on borrowing, are they? You want my advice? Do you? I'll tell you: *cross the line*. Yeah, that's right. If you're serious about this robbery bullshit, then cross the picket line. I mean it. I'll back you all the way. That's your best bet. The picket line—hey, you're only talkin' broken windshields, maybe a scratched fender or two, nothing real serious." He raised his eyebrows and shook his head from side to side. "None of this 'fifteen-to-twenty' bullshit, maybe with time off for good behavior. Know what I mean?" He shook his head up and down. "Not nearly as painful, Henry."

"Not nearly as profitable, either," Henry countered.

"Henry, you ... you, you dumb shit! Henry, you don't know anything about robbery. Have you thought about that? You couldn't steal a pencil from a blind man. How the hell do you figure you can handle something like this?"

"I got a plan."

Roger took a deep breath. What? "A plan?"

"Right."

"Henry, you mean to tell me that you've actually worked up a plan? You've gone that far? Jesus, tell me you're not serious."

Henry smiled again.

"Henry, you're a crazy man. A plan? Wonderful. That's just great. Everything's fine. Everything's okay. You got a plan, you got all you need." Roger shook his head in disgust. "Jesus H. Christ, Henry."

Henry let Roger talk. Roger didn't find that a problem at all. "Okay, I'll bite," Roger said. "I'm curious. I gotta hear this. It's bound to be good. Tell me about this plan of yours. How're you gonna do it?"

Henry shrugged, and said matter-of-factly. "I'm just gonna do it."

Roger gulped. "You're just 'gonna do it?' *That's* your plan?"

"Right."

"Henry, that's no plan. That's dumb, that's what that is. That's stupid. That's horseshit. Henry, I'll go slow, read my lips: Your brain has turned to shit, pal. The old pipes are clogged and the plumbing's backed up and the shit has started to flow uphill."

"Roger, trust me."

"Trust you? Henry, listen to me. *You* trust *me*. We're not talking about stealing a pack of cigarettes from a damn drug store here. We're not talking about a little shoplifting at your local K-Mart for chrissake. We're talking bigtime, skinny-dipping, for-real robbery kind of shit. Felony kind of stuff. Serious crime.

"And I'll tell you something else: They don't put a thing like this manuscript, something this valuable, in some asshole's shoe box and tuck it under the bed. We're talking real, high-class, no-nonsense security here, not just a couple of dome mirrors hanging in the stupid corners for crying out loud. Jesus, Henry. They got alarms, and guards, electronic shit. What, tell me, do you all of a sudden know about that stuff? Shit, Henry, who the hell do you think you are, Jesse James?"

Henry smiled. The thought had occurred to him.

"Henry, you dipshit. They'll send you to jail."

"They gotta catch me first."

"Yeah, right. 'They gotta catch me first.' That's what they all say, Henry. Every guy in the Big House right now has said those very same words. But, Henry, they all got caught, didn't they? That's how they got put in the little gray room in the first place. That's why they're in the slammer to begin with."

"Roger, hear me out. Just listen. That's all I ask. My plan is foolproof. I mean it, it really is. I've been thinking about it ever since we hung up."

Roger choked on his beer. "Ever since we hung up? Jesus, that's, what, an hour ago? Hey, no problem. That's plenty of time, right? Hell, if you can't put a major robbery together in an hour, you better get into another line of work."

Henry smiled. "I'm serious. It's not that complicated. The whole thing just seemed to come to me. Believe me, I know what I'm doing. It sounds crazy, but for some reason it's like it was meant to be, like I was born to do this. If you'll just listen for a second, I know you'll agree. Rog, seriously, we can pull this thing off."

Roger froze. *"We?"*

Chapter 8
Late Thursday Night

Burt Reynolds sucked, and Carl Reiner didn't have shit to say—talked about his dip-shit kid, Meathead, the whole damn time. If the pros weren't any good, you could bet your ass the broad was gonna be a waste.

Stanley would have switched channels but he was too comfortable lying there in bed. If he only had a remote.

More commercials: "*Toyota, what you do for me*," "*Oat Bran fights cholesterol*," "*Tastes great, less filling.*" Stanley drank and smoked.

And flicked the ash of his cigarette at the ashtray. And missed. There, that proved it, he thought. He needed work. He was getting rusty, couldn't even hit a dumb ashtray less than a foot away for chrissake. The ash landed on his T-shirt. He brushed it away. The gray smudge that remained blended in and disappeared.

Louise Ann Bridges was introduced. An ugly, fat broad, Stanley thought. Jay told Stanley and the world about how Mrs. Bridges had found a manuscript written by Mark Twain in an old trunk. Then his eyes twinkled. "So, what do you think you're going to get for that little sucker?" Jay asked. "Twenty million?"

Twenty million!

Stanley's lazy eyes popped open. Jesus! For a lousy fuckin' book?

Louise Ann Bridges had a high voice that grated on Stanley's sensitive ears. "Oh, I don't know," she laughed. "We haven't really thought about that. Everything has been moving so fast. We just can't believe this is all happening to us."

Jay smiled. "So, tell everyone, how'd all this come about? You found it in a trunk, is that right?"

Stanley listened in disbelief as Louise Ann Bridges told her story.

"Yes, that's right. We went to this estate sale, you see, in Carmel Cliffs—that's on Route Twenty-Two about fifteen miles south of where we live in New Brighten—and I spotted this trunk. I told Raymond—Raymond's my husband—that I just had to have it. It was just the thing I'd been looking for

for the sun room, you see. It would make a perfect coffee table. So Raymond says if it didn't go for too high a price then I could bid on it," Mrs. Bridges said.

Louise played with a button on the front of her dress.

"So, anyway, as it turned out, there was only one other person interested in it, besides me. So I bid on it, and then he bid on it. And then I bid on it, and he bid on it. After a few minutes of that he said twenty-nine dollars, and I said ah, what the heck, thirty. It was my last bid. If I didn't get it for thirty dollars, I was going to quit.

"Well, he must have had the same idea, because he quit first—twenty-nine was his limit. The auctioneer said thirty once, thirty twice, sold for thirty dollars to the lady in the blue dress, which was me." She smiled proudly. "And that was it. Then Raymond says, 'I hope we can get it in the car.'"

She stopped and shook her head at Jay. "Which was a fine time to think of that, don't you think?"

Jay raised his eyebrows and said right.

"Well, anyway, we managed to get it into the trunk of our Ford and—" Louise stopped talking and quickly slapped her hand to her mouth. "Oh, my gosh. I, I shouldn't have said that, should I? I mean, mention a car, like that, by name."

Jay pretended he was embarrassed. "Ah, that's okay. Normally I'm the only one allowed to use four-letter words on the show, but I guess we can excuse you this time. Just don't let it happen again."

The audience laughed. Louise laughed. Jay smiled.

Stanley said ah shit.

Louise continued, "So, anyway, we got it home and opened it up—after we broke the lock—and guess what? It was filled with all these files stuffed full of papers, and we didn't know what it was. We just assumed it was a bunch of junk we were going to have to throw away. I had no idea it would turn out like this when I bought it. I just bought it for the trunk, not what was in it. Like I said, I was going to use it for a coffee table."

There was a pause. Jay prompted. "And then ..."

"Oh, right. Well, don't you know, I was about to throw away all them papers when Raymond said, 'My gosh, look at this, Louise,' and there, as big as you please, was Mark Twain's signature at the bottom of one of the pages. At first we got real excited. But then we looked some more and saw that some of the other pages had the name Sergeant Fathom at the bottom, so we figured, heck, somebody was probably just fooling around, you know, writing Mark Twain's name on stuff to be cute. Playing games, that kind of thing."

"Sergeant Fathom?" Jay asked.

"Yes. Well, as it turns out—from what the people at the museum told us later—apparently Samuel Clemens used a bunch of different names for his writing, before he finally decided on Mark Twain. Sergeant Fathom was one of them?" She stated it like a question, then paused, waiting for Jay to nod his understanding, which he did, and then she continued. "He used other names, too, of course. Thomas Jefferson Snodgrass. Wilber Bubble. And, are you ready for this? W. Epaminandos Adrastus Blab? Can you believe that?"

Jay repeated the name and said you're kidding.

Louise shook her head no. "So, what I think is: If anyone else knew about the papers being in there, they probably never realized that they were written by Mark Twain. I mean, it was only that one page that had his name on it—the name Mark Twain, that is. So, if you didn't happen to see that one, and if you didn't know that Samuel Clemens used other names, well, heck, you'd never have thought anything about it."

Jay said you know, you're probably right.

Louise went on, "Well, I'll tell you, when we found out it really was written by Mark Twain—*the* Mark Twain—I just about spit out my teeth." The audience burst out in laughter. As did Jay. "Why, it still makes me shake all over when I think about just how close I'd come to throwing it all away. I already had half of it stuffed into a Hefty bag getting it ready for the garbage man, don't you know. That was on a Tuesday night. I remember, because we have garbage pickup on Wednesday morning—if they come on time, that is, which they never do. It's usually Wednesday afternoon before they get there—but you're still supposed to have it out first thing in the morning all the same, so it can sit there all day lookin' ugly and all.

"Well, anyway, my heart skipped a beat, I'll tell you that for sure. I said to Raymond, 'Do you suppose we should keep it, just in case, and ask someone if it means anything? We can always throw it out later.' Raymond said, 'Heck, you got magazines in the attic that you ain't looked at in twenty years, can't do any harm to hold onto this stuff for a little while.'" Louise gave Jay a sheepish look. "Raymond was right, you know—I do have stuff from years back. I just hate to throw things out that I might want to look at one day, you know what I mean? Just be my luck as soon as I pitched it, I'd need it." She rolled her eyes. "So, I said to Raymond, 'My, gosh, Raymond, you don't suppose—I mean, do you think all this stuff really could be worth something?' And Raymond says, 'Who knows?'"

Louise smiled and looked out at the audience. "And here I am, on *The Jay Leno Show*, don't you know."

$$$

Roger sipped his beer as Henry talked. The faster Henry talked, the faster Roger sipped.

"First," Henry said, "you're right. No way could we break into a place like that. I'm sure they have security out their ears. Alarms, TV cameras. I don't know anything about that kind of stuff and neither do you. So a B and E is out."

"B and E?"

"Breaking and Entering."

Roger coughed, then cleared his throat. "Oh, B and E. Right. I thought you said 'Bring me some tea.' I misunderstood. The old B and E trick. Of course." He curled his upper lip. "Jesus, I'm dealing with a freaking pro here. Even knows the language. I feel a lot better now, Henry." Roger was being as sarcastic as he could possibly be. "I'm impressed. I really am. And here I didn't think you knew a thing about robbery."

Sarcasm didn't bother Henry at all. "Hey, I told you, I've got this thing all figured out. Bear with me, okay? So, what do we do, if we don't break into the place?" Henry whispered. He raised his eyebrows. "It's obvious—we steal it while it's in transit." Henry nodded his head up and down, accenting each word with motion. "*On the way* to the auction house." That said, he winked.

Roger blinked. "Huh?"

"Yeah. They're moving it from that museum in Connecticut to the auction house in New York, right?" Henry pointed to the newspaper on the table. "It says so, okay? So, that's when we grab it. *Between* security systems. We shoot on up to Hartford, real early, pick them up right when they start out. They'll come down Ninety-One to New Haven, then grab Ninety-Five. We'll follow them and hit them just before they swing west, where Ninety-Five crosses Six-Seventy-Eight, somewhere around Baychester, or the Bronx Pelham Parkway." Henry raised his eyebrows up and down twice. "The Plan. That's where we put in The Plan. Remember like that little guy used to say on—what was the name of that TV show? Something *Island*. 'Dee plen, Boss, dee plen.'" Henry laughed at his joke. "We grab the manuscript, hang a right on Ninety-Five, sail over the George Washington Bridge, and we're back in The Fort before anybody knows what's what." Henry smiled and nodded. "And that's the name of that tune. That's why I need you, Rog; it's a two-man job."

Roger couldn't believe it. "Jesus, you do think you're Jesse James."

Henry winked again.

"Henry," Roger said, "what the hell kind of a plan is that? What are you gonna do—jump on Old Paint and chase them across the plains? That'll never work. You think they're gonna send that thing down here unprotected? There'll be guards. Police. You think the museum has a badass security system, you ain't seen nothin' yet. You ever heard of a thing called an escort? You can bet your ass somebody will be riding shotgun, like the cavalry, for instance."

"Hey, Rog, we're talking about a book here. We're not talking a strongbox full of gold bouncing around in the foothold of a stagecoach for crying out loud. We're not talking Wyatt Earp or Marshall Dillon. Jesus, Rog, gimme a break. They're just gonna put it in the back seat of some bozo's car and drive it down."

"And how the hell do you know that?"

Henry shrugged his shoulders. "Makes sense to me."

"Makes sense to you?"

"Yeah. That's how I'd do it."

"Oh yeah? What you'd do doesn't mean ding dong. And what if you're wrong? Then what? What if they do have a whole posse of bad asses riding shotgun?"

Henry held out his hands, palms up. "Then we back off."

"That's all they have, dear. The woman says—"

"Give me that damn phone, Ralph. There's no way in hell that I'm going to take a damn midnight flight to New York City. Who the hell do they think they're dealing with?"

Lilith grabbed the phone out of Ralph's hand. "Hello! Who the hell am I speaking to?"

Outside, the wind continued to whistle and the snow continued to blow. Drifts began to take control of the city. For the first time that evening the storm didn't bother Roger Muldowney at all. Not any more. Snow was the last thing on his mind.

"Okay, let's suppose you're right and you can pull this thing off—which I ain't saying for a minute that you can, you understand? I'm just saying suppose. I haven't heard the details, so we'll just say for argument's sake, okay?" Henry said okay. "Okay, what the hell do you plan to do with the thing once you get it?"

Henry tilted his head. "What do you mean?"

"Henry, the only fence I know is the chain-link job I got in my back yard.

You have to dispose of the stupid thing, you know? Do you know any fences, Henry?"

Henry smiled a knowing smile. "Nope, don't know any, as a matter of fact."

"Well?"

"Rog, my man, that's the beautiful part. My favorite part. It's the part that gets my tit out of the financial ringer, and the part that gets our asses out of the legal sling. We steal it; we collect the bounty; we walk away as free as birds. Stinking rich."

Roger waited. Henry didn't say anything. Roger quit waiting. "Okay, you win. I give up. Tell me, how do we do all that?"

Henry spoke like a man who was proud of what he had to say. "Simple-a-mondo. We sell it to the insurance company, that's how."

Short and sweet. Enough said.

It was not enough for Roger. "What?"

"That's right. We sell that little dude to the insurance company. Is that great or what? That's what I meant when I said I was only going to borrow it."

Roger shook his head. "I don't get it."

Henry was happy—no, *eager*—to explain. "Don't you see? We steal the manuscript, then we sell it right back to the insurance company that's got it insured. We get our money, and, as part of the deal, if they want the thing back, they have to let us go free. We make them agree to that up front. No coming after us; no trying to track us down. No trying to find out who we are. We walk away, and they walk away. Nobody turns around and everybody lives happily ever after. End of story."

Roger gave him a distrusting look.

"Hey, it'll work, Rog. Trust me. I mean, we don't hit 'em for twenty million or anything like that, not enough to really piss 'em off. Nothing even close to what it's insured for; that's the secret. They'd never let us alone for that kind of money. And they'd have no reason to pay us instead of the owner if we tried to get them for that. We just ask for enough to solve a money problem or two and that's it. Just enough to soothe our pain. Say a hundred grand, maybe two. We get healthy, and at the same time the insurance company saves millions. Get it? Everybody's happy. Everybody wins. A win-win situation."

"Henry, why on earth would an insurance company agree to that?"

"Rog, they do it all the time. It's a hell of a lot cheaper to make a deal than to pay off on the policy. Right? I mean, is two-hundred thousand dollars less than twenty mil, or is two-hundred thousand dollars less than twenty mil?"

Roger looked suspicious. "You're trying to tell me an insurance company would submit to blackmail?"

"They would if it made sense from a business standpoint."

Not yet convinced, Roger said, "Okay, say you're right. What happens if they agree, and then after we get the money and they get the manuscript, they call the cops?"

Henry shook his head. "No way. They wouldn't do that. You know why? Because, if they did, they'd never be able to make another deal again. And they know it. The next time they'd be out the whole ball of wax. Not smart, Rog. Very expensive shit." Henry held up two fingers to the bartender then turned back to Roger. "Rog, remember one thing: these guys are businessmen. The only thing they can see is the profit line. They're just like the guys we work for. They don't give a shit about anything else. It's purely mathematical—two hundred thousand is less than twenty million, so it makes sense."

Once again the bartender came and went. He no longer seemed irritated. Apparently he had resigned himself to the fact that he was going to be stranded here until spring. His only hope was that his two new friends had a VISA card with a hell of a limit.

After a few seconds of thought, Roger said, "Henry, I still don't like it. But, just for the sake of argument, just for the sake of knowing, just so I can say I gave your your shot—and I know I'm going to be sorry I said this—detail the plan for me."

Chapter 9
Friday Evening

Roger had told Henry he'd think about it and get back to him.

Henry said he wouldn't be in the plant on Frday; he was taking the day off. A sick day.

Roger said he'd call him at home.

Henry'd said fine.

After they'd left the bar Roger did think about it—for ten minutes—then made up his mind. *No way in hell.* It was the dumbest thing he'd ever heard, absolutely out of the question. He was out of his mind to give it even ten minutes.

Then, for the rest of the night, he tried to talk himself into it.

It wasn't that it was a bad plan; the plan was actually pretty damned ingenious. It could work. It was obvious that Henry had given it a great deal of thought.

That surprised Roger a little—he wouldn't have guessed it of Henry in a million years. He'd known Henry a long time and had never pegged him as the criminal type. A little crazy, maybe, but not criminal. Desperate people do desperate things was the only explanation he could think of.

So, if the plan wasn't the problem, what was?

It was against the law, that was the problem. It was against the damn law for chrissake! No matter how many times he rolled the dice they always came up the same: Don't be a schmuck, it's against the law. It's go-to-jail kinda shit. It's lose your job, lose your life, lose everything kinda shit. It's GO DIRECTLY TO JAIL; it's DO NOT PASS GO; it's DO NOT COLLECT $200. Going to jail was not on Roger's letter to Santa Claus ... not this year.

And he sure as hell didn't need the money. So, he asked himself: Why should I pull a dumb stunt like that? Friendship, that's why. He'd do it because his friend needed him. Bullshit, that didn't wash either. A true friend would try to talk a friend out of doing something stupid like that. Guts then: Maybe Roger Muldowney just didn't have the guts to go along with it? Wrong! It wasn't a question of guts; brains were the issue here. Doing something stupid versus doing something smart. Roger concluded that he had too many brains to do something like that. He was simply too smart to do something dumb.

It didn't make him feel a whole lot better.

Finally, after hours of arguing with himself, he gave up. It was no use. No matter how much he wanted to help his friend the answer always came up *no*.

There's a fine line between chicken and genius, he told Henry over the phone. It was a saying he made up, paraphrased from one he'd heard somewhere. It didn't make a hell of a lot of sense to anyone but Roger.

Henry tried to talk Roger into it.

Roger tried to talk Henry out of it.

Neither succeeded.

After a while the silences between arguments grew longer, and each man knew that for all practical purposes the telephone conversation had just about reached its conclusion. Neither man had any more to say.

Roger took one final shot. "Henry, let me lend you the money, for chrissake. It's no big deal. I have money just sitting in the bank doing nothing. We might as well put it to some good use. If it'll make you feel better I'll charge you interest. Isn't that a hell of a lot better than pulling a dumb stunt like robbery?"

"No way, Rog. I already told you that was out."

"Henry, quit being a jerk. Are you saying that you're too proud to borrow from a friend, but you're not too proud to steal? Is that what you're saying?"

Silence.

"Don't be dumb, Henry."

"It's a good plan, Rog."

"It's against the law, Henry. It's stealing. You'll be a criminal, Henry. A thief. A crook."

Henry sighed. "It's a good plan, but I can't do it alone."

"Henry, it doesn't matter how good of a plan it is, it's still illegal. That's the main thing—that's the only thing. Say that to yourself, Henry. Say it over and over. It's not borrowing, it's stealing. It's against the law. You think about that."

"I will."

"Will you? Promise me."

Pause. Click.

"Yeah?"

Stanley Kowalski was a man of few words. *Yeah*, said it all. The phone rang; he picked it up. "Yeah?" What more was there?

"Stanley, my man." It was Lou "The Weasel" Monetti.

"Lou," Stanley said.

"You got time to deliver a package for us?"

"Package" meant *contract*; "us" meant *Carmine Rico*.

"Sure. When?"

"As soon as possible."

"No problem. This a rush job? Special D?" Special D meant kill.

"Naw. We want it to go out soon, but you can take whatever time you think. It ain't a big deal; maybe ain't even necessary, but what the hell. Can't hurt, right? Regular mail will be fine."

Regular Mail meant just rough him up a little, bend a bone or two, make sure he understands the seriousness of this whole mish-mash. Make sure he gets the message but don't kill him. Dead men don't pay their bills.

"Whatever you say."

"Hey, that's great, Stanley. We appreciate it. We'll get it to you right away."

"Right."

The line went dead.

An hour later an envelope slid under Stanley's door. It contained ten one-hundred-dollar bills and a wallet-sized photograph with a name and address written on the back. Stanley studied the photo, turned it over and memorized the name and address on the back, and then ate it.

Henry was in some real pretty shit now—his best friend had just let him down. And Roger Muldowney, unfortunately, had been a major player in Henry's little scheme.

Roger had been an integral part of Henry's plan right from the beginning. He was not just somebody Henry could simply scratch off his list and then move on to the next name. Henry had been counting on Roger. It was a two man job, and Roger was the number two man. One guy couldn't pull the thing off by himself.

But Roger said no thanks, I'll pass. And now Henry was right back where he started: Outta money, outta time and outta luck. And maybe outta friend.

Henry felt lousy. The best friend he had hadn't come through for him when he really needed him. The man he thought he could turn to in a pinch, the man he thought he could count on, the one constant in Henry's universe had just turned his back and walked away.

Henry thought about it; hell, could he blame him? It wasn't really Roger's fault, it was Henry's—that is, if Henry wanted to be completely honest with himself. Face it, Henry Nash was the one asking *his* friend to break the law for crying out loud. He was the one asking his best friend to become a criminal. What did he expect? *Henry* was the one who had turned his back on a friend. Henry was the one who had forsaken the friendship, not Roger. Henry felt sick about it. Roger had tried to talk him out of it. Roger had tried to talk him out of becoming a criminal. Roger had tried to do what any true friend would do. Henry smiled. Of course, Roger had done exactly what any real friend would have done: He tried to save Henry from himself. He'd tried to talk some sense into the crazy fool.

Roger was right; it was good plan, but it was stupid. And it was wrong. Breaking the law wouldn't solve Henry's problems, it would just add to them. Roger Muldowney—Henry Nash's best friend—was absolutely right. He should scrap the whole stupid idea. It was just plain dumb.

And it *was* a two man job. There wasn't any way one man could do it, and there was no one else Henry could ask to help him.

The solution was simple: forget it. Henry would call Roger later, apologize, swallow his pride, and tell him that he might just take him up on that offer of a loan after all. Roger was right: If he was not too proud to steal, then why should he be too proud to borrow? Yes, Roger was his friend. A *true* friend. A friend he *could* count on. Roger was right, if—

Henry's doorbell rang.

When he answered it he found his neighbor, Bill Freely, standing there on his front step, as white as a ghost.

By the time Tommy Kosuri got through to Tokyo it was almost 10:00 PM in New York, which made it 11:00 AM tomorrow, in Japan.

But the hour was of little consequence; Tommy would have stayed up all night trying to get through if he had to. Tanaka-san, himself, had called. What an honor! To have the Chairman of the Board call. To have the Chairman of the Board want to speak to a lowly salesman, why, it was unheard of!

Tommy had been with SENSEI OF JAPAN for eleven years, and in that time had never even met anyone who had had the honor of speaking personally to Nobuko Tanaka. Many had worked their entire lives for SENSEI OF JAPAN and had never been granted that most rare privilege.

And he called *me* personally. Tommy's hands were sweating.

Tommy couldn't imagine what it was about. He was very excited, but at the same time somewhat concerned. Maybe even a little frightened. It couldn't be his performance; he was ahead of his quota. This was his best year ever. But, what could it be? A man of Tanaka-san's stature wanting to talk to a lowly salesman like himself. What a mystery!

The operator answered the telephone. "*Mosimosi. Nihon-Sensei de gozaimasu.*" [Hello. This is SENSEI OF JAPAN.]

Tommy said, "*Tanaka-san. Onegai-simasu.*" [Mr. Tanaka, please.]

"*Sotira dotirasama de rassyaimasu ka.*" [Who is calling, please?]

"Tommy Kosuri *desu ga.*"

"*Ee, Nyuuyooku? Beekoku?*" [New York? America?]

"*Haa, sayoo de gozaimasu ga.*" [Yes, that's right.]

"*Tyotto matte kudasai.*" [Just a moment.]

Tommy waited. Then, "Tommy. *Ogenki desu ka.*" [How are you?]

Tommy? It was Tanaka. He called him Tommy?

Tommy cleared his throat, then spoke. "*Okagesama de anata wa?*" [I'm fine, thank you. And you?]

"Fine. Fine. Thank you for returning my call so promptly."

It did not register in Tommy's mind that Tanaka-san was speaking English. Tommy's mind was somewhere else. "*Doo itasimasite.*" [You're welcome.]

"Tommy, let's speak English, shall we? I need to practice."

Tommy quickly agreed. "Ah, yes. Of course."

"I get so little practice. You forget, you spend all your time in America. You get to practice your English every day."

"Yes, sir. That's fine. Very good." Pause. "Sir, I'm sorry it took me so long to get through, the lines are a problem and—"

"Nonsense," Tanaka interrupted. "You did excellent. I understand. Things are difficult sometimes—the distance, the time."

Tommy breathed a sigh of relief. He couldn't believe that Tanaka sounded so *common*. He seemed so *ordinary*, so *normal*. Not at all like the god Tommy had expected. Tommy was astounded. It was amazing to Tommy how a man of Tanaka's importance could humble himself so as to make a lowly salesman like Tommy Kosuri feel completely comfortable. Tanaka-san was indeed a great man. Without thinking, Tommy bowed and said, "*Doo mo arigatoo gozaimasu,*" [Thank you very much.] Then felt silly because he'd bowed over the telephone.

"So, young man, how are things in America?"

"Very good, sir. Business is strong."

"Yes, the board just met today. Sales appear to be doing very well in America. Very good."

"*Hai.*" [Yes.]

"They are up in Europe, also."

"*Aa, soo desu ka.*" [Oh, is that so?] "That is good news." Mr. Tanaka sounded pleased. "SENSEI OF JAPAN is very strong all over the world. Thanks to men such as yourself."

"Thank you, sir."

"No, it is true. It is to you—the loyal, the devoted—that we owe our success."

Tommy felt humbled.

"Tommy, the reason I wanted to speak with you," (*Tommy*, there it was again. He insisted upon calling him *Tommy*.) "I would like you to do something for me, ah, for the company. It is a very, ah, *delicate* matter, and must be handled with utmost *discretion*."

Tommy held his breath. A delicate matter? "Yes, sir. I understand. Whatever I can do. I'll do my best."

"Yes. Yes. Of course you will." Tanaka paused. There was silence. Tommy knew Tanaka was searching for the right words. Tanaka's English was very good—no, excellent—for a man who spent so little time using it, but he had to think before he could speak. Tommy wished he knew what Tanaka wanted so he could help him with the words. Finally, "It involves a purchase we would like you to make for us. A rather large purchase."

An acquisition? Tommy didn't know anything about acquisitions! My God! He wasn't qualified for that. He was a lowly salesman. His hands started to shake, the palms that had begun to dry out began to sweat again. He reached into his hip pocket and pulled out his handkerchief. He wiped his brow.

Tanaka continued, "Ohuiri Shubioshi, our treasurer, has already contacted our bank in New York and has arranged for the transfer of funds as soon as you have successfully completed the transaction."

As soon as you have successfully completed the transaction.

The choice of words did not sail by unnoticed. Tommy had gained control of himself and the inference had not escaped him. Tanaka did not say *if* you complete the transaction; he said *when*. It *must* be done, therefore, it was assumed that it *would* be done. And that Tommy Kosuri would do it.

"You are authorized to bid as high as twenty-five million American dollars."

Tommy thought he was going to pass out.

Bill Freely left at eleven. The conversation had lasted an hour.

Henry told Bill not to worry and closed the door behind him, then joined

Gladys in the kitchen. Gladys said, "Isn't that just terrible. Poor Marge. I feel so sorry for her."

"Yeah, me too. God, I can't believe it."

"Henry, what would we do if that kind of thing happened to us? I mean, could it? Could it happen to us? Does our insurance cover us for a problem like that?"

Henry reassured her. "Yeah, we're okay. Don't worry. I remember. A flyer went around the plant last year some time. Same thing happened to a guy in the Cleveland stamping plant. Everything's okay. We're covered, but let's hope nothing like that ever does happen to us."

Gladys filled Henry's cup with coffee, put the coffee pot back on the stove and then sat down with him at the kitchen table. "What on earth are they going to do?" She looked and sounded so worried that Henry felt almost as sorry for her as he did for the Freelys.

He shook his head. "I don't know. I don't know."

Henry lied. Henry knew exactly what Bill Freely was going to do. He and Bill had talked about it while Gladys was in the kitchen making coffee. Henry made Freely an offer he couldn't refuse. Everything was going to be all right. For the Freelys *and* the Nashes.

But he couldn't tell Gladys, even though he wanted to. Even though it was the solution to all their problems. Even though she wouldn't have to worry about money anymore. It was not the kind of thing Gladys would be able to handle. Not the kind of thing he wanted her involved in anyway. It was his job and he would do it.

It was too bad though, Gladys looked like she could use some cheering up. She looked so worried sitting there. She looked like a little girl. Henry's heart ached. He wanted to squeeze her to pieces.

Twenty-five million dollars! *American!* For a book!

Tommy still couldn't believe it. It had been two hours since he'd hung up from talking to Tanaka-san and the telephone conversation continued to pound at his brain, haunting him into a state of insomnia. He tossed and turned. He couldn't get comfortable. His mind would not stop churning. Every fiber of his being was on fire. He closed his eyes; they popped back open. The conversation kept replaying in his mind over and over and over. For the hundredth time Tommy heard the words that Tanaka-san had so carefully chosen ...

"It must be handled in a most delicate manner," Tanaka explained. "The Americans are becoming more and more upset with the Japanese every day. There are many who do not like the fact that Japanese companies are buying so much American property. We see it in the newspapers, hear about it from our representatives in Washington. They say we do not understand, but it is they who do not understand. The Americans seem to favor capitalism only when it is to their benefit. It is too bad they do not listen to one of their own sayings: What is good for the goose is good for the gander. I believe that is how the expression goes."

Tommy let out a mild chuckle, but not out of disrespect. To hear a man like Tanaka say it simply sounded funny. Words of a mortal spoken by a god.

"So," Tanaka continued, "I am sure that you can see, it would not be in the best interests of SENSEI OF JAPAN if the Americans were to find out that a Japanese company was bidding on such an American treasure. A manuscript by the famous writer, Mark Twain, I am sure is deemed to be a very valuable artifact that the Americans will not part with in—how do they say?—a congenial manner? That is why it is imperative that you understand our position."

There was a momentary silence and then Tanaka added, "I know of your loyalty to Japan, Tommy. My colleagues have told me that you have demonstrated that loyalty time and time again. They tell me that you can be trusted and I believe them. And I believe in you. I will be completely honest with you, Tommy; we realize this is a great burden to place on one so young and so inexperienced, and, I know, it is probably unfair of us to ask you to do this. But please believe me when I say that we have no other choice. You are our only hope.

"You no doubt wonder: Why is that so? Why you? I will explain. The main reason we are asking you to assume this great responsibility is because, and please forgive me, I do not mean this to be disrespectful in any way, but, it is true, Tommy, you do not look Japanese."

It was at that point Tommy swallowed so hard he almost hurt himself. How on earth did Tanaka-san know that? How did he know what Tommy looked like? There was only one answer: He must have looked at Tommy's personnel file. How else would he know? He had never seen Tommy in person. At least as far as Tommy knew.

And if he looked at his personnel file, then someone must have told him about Tommy, otherwise, why would he have known to look at Tommy's file in the first place? SENSEI OF JAPAN had fifty-four thousand employees around the world; he certainly wouldn't stumble across Tommy's by accident.

And how did he know of Tommy's loyalty? How? The mystery was growing.

But one thing was not a mystery. It was as plain as the nose on Tommy's face. His American face. And his American nose. Tommy Kosuri did not look Japanese. Tommy knew that better than anyone.

But it was not his fault. An American mother with very dominant American traits, and a Japanese father who was half American to begin with, had produced a son destined to wear a Caucasian mask over an oriental soul. A mask Tommy hated. If there was one thing in his life that Tommy would change if he had the power it would be his looks. His Japanese spirit was being held prisoner in an American body. At times he felt almost like a traitor.

As soon as the significance of Tanaka's statement sunk in, Tommy felt sick. Tanaka-san, the Chairman of the Board, a man he worshipped, the founder of SENSEI OF JAPAN—a man who had taken American technology, redefined it, redirected it, and then transformed it into an entirely new line of products the Americans never dreamed of, products that were made better and marketed better than the so-called American state-of-the-art versions, products that in effect had beaten America at its own game—knew Tommy Kosuri looked like an American. His one major disgrace in life had not gone unnoticed after all. Tommy never really believed that it had, but he had hoped. And now even hope was gone. Even the Chairman knew. His idol *knew!* Tommy Kosuri had been chosen for this assignment not because he was qualified, not because he was the best man for the job, but because he *looked* like an American. It was as simple as that.

And the fact that he happened to be in the right place at the right time.

Tanaka had also said there just was not enough time to get anyone else there: the auction was Sunday afternoon at 2:00 PM. "I am so sorry I have to impose on you like this," Tanaka had said, "but I am afraid we have no other choice."

Impose? The word had hit Tommy like a bullet. My God, Tanaka had humbled himself. Tommy hadn't wanted that; Tanaka-san had to humble himself to no man, least of all Tommy Kosuri. My, God, this was not an imposition, this was an honor. Tanaka-san must understand, he must be told. It was an honor to be chosen at all, no matter what the circumstances.

The more Tommy thought about it the more he realized that *honor* was the right choice of words—the reasons didn't matter. *Why* was not important. All that really counted was the fact that he had, indeed, been the one chosen. He was the one they were all depending upon. He was the one Tanaka-san was depending upon. Finally his American looks would serve him, instead of shame him. Finally his deformity could be used to enhance the glory of his country, his *true* county.

"You will not be able to get into the auction without credentials," Tanaka had said. "We have arranged with our attorneys—right there in New York—Marshall, Hughes and Stone, to provide you with identification and Power of Attorney. Please understand, they have no knowledge of any of this; they are, after all, Americans, too. We simply requested that they provide you with a letter of introduction in order that you may call upon a new client. The Power of Attorney authorizes you to withdraw funds from our account as necessary, but it does not specify the purpose." There was a long silence, then, "I hope you realize the great trust we are placing in you, Tommy. This is not a minor task. It is very important. Not just the purchase of the manuscript, but the entire image that we of SENSEI OF JAPAN project in all America could be blackened if anyone were to find out. Our reputation rests in your hands. As I said, it is most, most delicate."

"Yes, sir."

"The parcel will be delivered to your hotel first thing in the morning. *Wakarimasu ka?*" [Do you understand?] Tanaka had asked, sounding a little concerned that Tommy did not fully understand the gravity of the situation.

Tommy had assured Tanaka that he needn't worry. "*Ee wakarimasu,*" Tommy replied. [Yes, I understand.]

He understood all right. He understood it all too well. He understood it was his ass on the line, that's what he understood.

"Good," Tanaka said. "We are counting on you. I know you will succeed."

"Yes, sir."

"*Oyasiumi-nasai.*" [Good night.]

"*Sayonara.*"

And Tommy's eyes had been wide open ever since.

"I still don't understand why the hell you can't smoke on airplanes anymore. That's a bunch of crap." Lilith Bright, once again, was pissed.

And it was not the first time she'd raised the issue. Thirty minutes at thirty thousand had not numbed her anger the slightest.

"Look back there, Ralph," she said, leaning out into the aisle and looking toward the rear of the plane. "I'll bet half the people in this plane are smokers. I know. I can tell. I can recognize a smoker a mile away."

Ralph turned, stretched his neck, and looked over the back of his seat toward the rear of the plane, as directed. They just looked like plain ordinary people to him. His response at what he saw was a simple *ah-hmm*.

"It really ticks me off, Ralph." Lilith raved on. "Who the hell came up with all this No Smoking junk anyway? Probably some wimp in Washington, some goody two-shoes. You can bet your butt it wasn't a smoker."

Ralph Bright didn't smoke; however, he, too, was sorry you weren't allowed to smoke on domestic flights anymore; it would have given Lilith something else to do with her mouth. Ralph decided that would be an observation best kept to himself.

Unfortunately, the fact that Lilith couldn't smoke had not been the first thing to ruin her day, or, last night, actually. She was on the phone over an hour, and no matter how loud she screamed they didn't budge; they simply could not get her on a flight that departed at an earlier time of the day. Everything going East late morning or early afternoon was booked solid. If she wanted to book a ticket standby she could—*Hell, no, she didn't want to book a ticket standby! Were they crazy? She could sit in the stupid airport forever waiting for some dope to find her a seat.* Then, the only other choice, if she wanted to get to New York before Saturday night, was the flight that left Friday at midnight. That would get her into New York at 4:38 AM.

That was all Lilith needed to hear to set her off. *Of course she wanted to get to New York before Saturday night you jackass. Why on earth did they think she'd called in the first place? Were they complete idiots or what?* The fact that she didn't call (didn't have Ralph call) for reservations until the day before she wanted to leave was not an issue, not as far as Lilith was concerned. Hell, short notice was no reason not to have something available. Flying people was their job, wasn't it? What kind of damn airline were they running for chrissake?

4:38 AM! A gawdawful time to get into anywhere.

Look at the bright side, Ralph had said. There shouldn't be a lot of traffic going into the city at that hour. But Lilith was not the kind to look at the bright side.

Then the weather reared its ugly head. Winter storms were moving into Chicago; O'Hare was shut down. Which didn't make any sense to Lilith whatsoever; she wasn't going anywhere near Chicago.

"Yes, ma'am," the flight attendant for TWA had explained, "but when O'Hare closes down it pushes all the flights scheduled to go into O'Hare off on to other airports, and that creates back-ups and delays all over the place. That's why this flight's been delayed. When O'Hare has problems, the whole country has problems. I'm sorry, but there's nothing we can do about the weather."

Can't do anything about waiting for that other damn plane, either, Lilith had tossed at her. Get to the airport at ten, sit there for two damn hours waiting for a flight that's supposed to leave at midnight, only to have to wait another two hours because of the stupid weather, and then, when the weather says okay, they have to wait another hour for some other plane to get in. They just *had* to wait so they could pick up a couple more lousy passengers—and a few more lousy bucks—no matter how it inconvenienced the passengers already on board. The hell with them; they already got their money.

I'm sorry ma'am, but there's nothing I can do, the flight attendant said for the hundredth time if she'd said it once.

Sorry, shit! Everybody was sorry but nobody did a damn thing about it. Three hours without a cigarette. Jerks!

And it wasn't like that was bad enough—the fact that they wouldn't let her smoke during the flight—but the dummies who worked for the stupid airline had made them sit in the plane, on the ground! and wait for the entire three-hour delay, waiting on that other stupid plane for crying out loud! With the NO SMOKING light glowing the whole damn time. Can you believe it? Would they let them get off the stupid airplane and go into the terminal and have one lousy cigarette? Hell no! That would make sense. Why on earth would they do anything that made sense?

A three hour delay, a three and half hour flight—that's six and a half hours without a cigarette! SIX AND A HALF HOURS!

And thanks to the delay, and those selfish people who just *had* to get onto their plane, the chances of getting into Manhattan before the heavy traffic started to converge on the island were getting slimmer and slimmer.

If they got in at all. If Lilith could survive that long without a cigarette.

"I can't believe it, Ralph. Thirty-five—no, forty percent of all people smoke, okay?—I read that in a magazine. So tell me: Why the hell do forty percent of us have to suffer just because some Surgeon General says No Smoking On Airplanes?" Lilith answered her own question. "Because it's Screw Lilith Day, that's why. It's always Screw Lilith Day." Lilith shook her head. "They're pulling the same kind of crap in restaurants, too."

Ralph leafed through his *Newsweek*. To his recollection Lilith's forty percent didn't sound completely accurate. He'd read the article she was referring to and it seemed to him that she may have switched a couple numbers around, stacked the deck a little in her favor. Lilith was inclined to do that on occasion. Ralph chose not to contest the point. "I don't know, dear. You'd think they'd be able to figure out a way to make both sides happy, wouldn't you?"

"It really ticks me off, Ralph."

Ralph nodded, staring down at the magazine. "It's probably that anti-smoking lobby in Washington. They got a lot of clout, you know."

"Hey, I pay taxes, too. What about my clout? I got half a notion to call one of those stewardesses back here right now and give her a piece of my mind."

"Flight Attendant."

Lilith gave Ralph a sour look. "What?"

"Flight Attendants. That's what they call them nowadays."

"Oh, excuse me, Mr. World Traveler."

"That's right. They're not stewardesses anymore. Too many men getting into that line of work, I guess. Probably didn't like being called stewardesses so they changed the name. Can't say as I blame them."

Lilith grunted. "Call them what you will, they're still stewardesses to me. Even the men."

Just then a male flight attendant walked by. Lilith watched him carefully, a suspicious smirk turned up the corners of her mouth. She leaned over to Ralph and whispered, "Especially that one, if you know what I mean." Then she laughed.

Saturday

December 10

The Act

Chapter 10

THERE WAS A KNOCK AT THE DOOR AT 7:00 AM.

Tommy moved to answer it—showered, shaved, dressed and ready. The early hour had not caught him off guard; he'd struggled with sleep until five, then finally surrendered to the excitement of the task at hand and realized he would not sleep again until all this was behind him. He opened the door.

It was the messenger, who handed him the envelope. Tommy signed for it, said thank you and closed the door.

No sooner had he turned and started to walk back into the room than there was another knock. "Room service," came the voice from the hallway.

Tommy opened the door a second time and stepped back out of the way, allowing the waiter to push the serving cart into the room. Normally Tommy would have checked under the covered plates to make sure they hadn't screwed up his order (Americans were notorious at that—screwing up meal orders, screwing up everything. Their lack of concern for quality was why their country was in such a mess right now, Tommy observed. And why it deserved to be, he concluded), but these were not normal times. Tommy was in a hurry to get started. He had bigger things on his mind than scrambled eggs and bacon.

"Would you like me to pour your coffee, sir?" the waiter asked.

Tommy reached into his pocket and pulled out what little cash he had—two tens and two fives. No surprise there; Tommy survived on plastic, like everyone else. Tommy never really needed much cash. Until now.

He made a mental note: He'd better get some serious cash just in case. You never know, this little venture he was about to start might call for the greasing of a palm or two. And you can't get a lot of grease out of a ten dollar bill. Better to be safe than sorry. Tommy certainly didn't want the lack of ready cash to hamper in any way what he might have to do. He peeled off a five dollar bill and handed it to the waiter. "No thank you. I can do it."

The waiter handed him the check and a pen. "Thank you, sir. If you'd sign this, please."

Tommy signed. The waiter thanked him again and disappeared, closing the door behind him.

Tommy picked up the coffee pot and poured himself a cup of the steamy black liquid, then sat down on the end of the bed and opened the envelope. He sipped at the coffee as he read.

Tommy was very impressed. There it was, in black and white, just as Mr. Tanaka had promised: the letter of introduction, and the Power of Attorney. *To whom it may concern.* Tommy read every word.

He sipped his coffee and read it a second time. Tommy liked what he saw. Especially the parts where his name appeared: *Thomas J. Kosuri*. This was such an honor. Such an honor, indeed.

Tommy got up from the bed and walked over to the serving cart, proud of himself, eager to get started. Such an important assignment. This would surely put him in great favor with his superiors. His chest swelled as he took the lid off the largest plate.

Damn! He knew it. He knew it. He should have checked.

Every time Tommy didn't check he paid the price and this time was no exception: two eggs, poached, and link sausage stared up at him from the plate. You'd think he'd learn. You'd think after all the times he'd been screwed he'd know better. How many times did this have to happen to him before it sunk in? *Jesus, Tommy, what's the matter with you?* He was so angry at himself. Damn! Every time he didn't double-check them, they screwed up. Stupid, stupid Americans.

Well, you can bet I won't leave the rest of this thing up to chance, Tommy vowed. Right after breakfast—his wonderful breakfast of poached eggs and sausage—he'd go to the bank, pick up some serious cash and then check out the Carneby-Glenn Auction House, just to get a feel for the place. Do a little reconnaissance, so to speak. Size up the situation.

Tommy looked out the window. It was snowing. And blowing. The weather looked terrible. It didn't matter. This was too important to let a little bad weather slow him down. Tommy had to plan his attack. The Carneby-Glenn Auction House was about to become *Tommy Kosuri's* Pearl Harbor.

"Hartford! Shit!"

The announcement of the rerouting of TWA Flight #453 from New York's Kennedy Airport to Bradley International in Windsor Locks, Connecticut, north of Hartford on I-91, had just come over the PA system. The pilot was very apologetic, but that didn't buy him squat as far as Lilith Bright was concerned. Apology was just another name for incompetence. The fact that

Kennedy was under blizzard conditions was not her problem; it was the airport's Administration Department's problem. If the airport officials got the deadass maintenance crew off their deadasses they'd be able to keep the damn runways clear. *That* was the problem.

And then Lilith Bright wouldn't have to drive all the way from Hartford to New York in a damn blizzard, for chrissake!

"Can you believe that?" Lilith exclaimed. "What a bunch of horse crap. First, no damn flights are available—we have to leave in the middle of the damn night, for chrissake. Then they stick us with a two hour weather delay. And we have to sit for another hour in one stupid airplane, waiting on another stupid airplane, waiting for the stupid weather to clear, and the whole damn time I can't even have a damn cigarette. And now *this*! Rerouted to Hartford, Connecticut, for chrissake. I'll tell you, Ralph, this is really beginning to burn me."

Ralph nodded. "I just hope we make it to Hartford," he said cautiously.

Lilith gave him a dirty look. "What do you mean by that?"

Ralph turned his face toward Lilith but he didn't look her in the eye. "The pilot said the weather all over the east coast was iffy. We could get to Hartford and what happens if it's socked in, too?"

"So?"

"So, what if we can't land?"

The light bulb finally went on in Lilith's brain. And it made her mad—madder. "Oh, great, Ralph. Cheer me up. That's all I need."

Ralph turned back to his magazine. He tilted his head to the right and made a face. "It's a possibility."

"Ralph, listen to me. Sooner or later something's got to start going our way. All right? I mean it. Now quit being so damn negative."

Ralph let Lilith's comments slide off his back. "I'm just crossing my fingers, that's all. Hartford may not be as good as Kennedy, but it's a dang sight better than turning around and going all the way back to Dallas."

"Dallas? Dammit, Ralph, bite your tongue. We're not going back to Dallas. Understand? If that dipshit pilot comes back on that dipshit PA system and announces that we're turning around and going back to Dallas, then you better start looking for a couple of parachutes, because I have absolutely no intention of turning around and going all the way back to where we started. You can bet your boots on that."

That said, Lilith dug into her purse. Ralph watched out of the corner of his eye as she pulled out a pack of cigarettes.

$$$

"Are you sure it's secure?"

If Michael asked her that question one more time Marcella was going to scream. She looked at him over the top of her granny glasses. "Michael, if you ask me that one more time I'm going to scream."

"I just want to make sure."

"Would you like to unwrap it and redo it yourself?"

"No, of course not."

Marcella seemed satisfied. Not pleased, but satisfied. At least he trusted her enough not to go through the whole process all over again. Then Michael added, "That would take too much time."

Marcella exploded. "Take too much time! Oh, so you mean if you had the time you *would* open it, just to make sure I didn't screw it up?"

Michael teetered on the brink of the hole he'd just dug for himself. "Well, I, er, ah, what I meant was—"

"What you meant was you just don't trust me. That's what you meant."

"No. That's not it at all. Don't be silly."

"Silly? Am I being silly? As in silly little girl? As in silly female?"

Michael thought he might jump into that hole after all. Voluntarily. It just might be the safest place for him right now.

Marcella didn't quit. "Michael, face it, you're always checking up on me. Double-checking everything I do. For example: You always ask if I've turned on the security system. Every night. I've been working here for three years— you've known me for nine—and you still find it necessary to ask me that same question every night. Even though I've never forgotten. Even though I'm batting a thousand, you still ask. And now this, the manuscript. *Is it packaged properly? Are you sure?* Michael, don't you trust me to do anything? If you don't trust me, why'd you hire me in the first place?"

Michael held his breath, looking for an answer. When he finally exhaled, one came rushing out. It had a name. It was called Plead Guilty and Throw Yourself on the Mercy of the Court. "You're right, Marcella. I'm sorry. Forgive me. You've done an excellent job since you've been here. I couldn't ask for more. I'd be the first to admit that. If I've been treating you like a child, well, I'm sorry. From now on, I'll trust you completely. I promise."

Michael seemed proud of his little speech. He hoped it would save him.

Marcella was speechless. Obviously she should have taken Michael to task ages ago. "Well, that's better." She gave him a suspicious look. "If you really mean it."

"I do. Honest."

Marcella bent over and picked the manuscript up off her desk. It was packaged in a cardboard carton about the size of a small suitcase—twenty-by-fifteen-by-ten—and weighed roughly twenty pounds, give or take a thousand words or so. It was sealed shut with masking tape and tied with heavy twine, then wrapped in white wrapping paper. A big red bow decorated the center. The bow was Marcella's idea of cute. Michael thought it was silly but there was no way in hell he was going to point that out. He'd take it off once he got it into his car.

"It looks good, doesn't it? Real Christmassy," she said. "Something anyone would be proud to have under a tree." She winked. "You don't think I'm being silly, do you, Michael? Wrapping it up like a Christmas present?" She smiled at the look on Michael's face. "So sue me." She handed him the box. "It's all yours. Take good care of it. I'm off to Aspen."

Michael grunted under the weight of the carton. It was heavier than he'd expected.

"If you have any problems," Marcella said, taking off her granny glasses and giving him a sly look, "don't call me; I'll call you." She put on her ski jacket, hung her purse over her shoulder, wedged her hands into black leather gloves and added, "Not that you'd be able to reach me anyway; I'll be on the slopes every second."

Michael puffed, still holding the manuscript. "If I run into a disaster I'll send out a St. Bernard."

Michael's words bounced off Marcella's back since she had already left her office and started down the hall. Back over her shoulder she said, "Just make sure he has plenty of rum."

Michael smiled, then hollered after her. "Don't break any legs or anything." Funny, he thought to himself as he watched her walk away, he missed her already. And then, "Wait, I don't have your number. Where can I reach you if—?"

Marcella raised a hand in a wave without turning or speaking. Michael wondered if she really had forgiven him.

Marcella went directly to her car. The snow was six inches deep in the parking lot and three inches deep on her windshield.

She unlocked the door, leaned in and started the engine, slid the lever to DEFROST, flipped the fan to HIGH, and then took her ice scraper out of the back seat and began to clean off her windows. It took five minutes.

That done, she got into her car and carefully backed out of her parking space, noting that her windows were already beginning to cover over with snow. The storm the weather man had projected was turning out to be for real. She hoped there would be no trouble with her flight.

Marcella turned right coming out of the parking lot onto Lake Avenue and drove straight to I-91. The traffic was slow. The streets had not been cleared. The clock on her dash said 7:15 AM. She wasn't worried; she had allowed plenty of time to get to the airport.

She crossed her fingers as she eased her way onto the ramp that lead to the expressway. Below her she could see the expressway traffic creeping along at a snail's pace. It was not a good omen. If any road was clear it would be the expressway. I hope they're doing a better job at keeping the runways clear than they are the expressways, she thought to herself. She had planned on everything except this. The weather could really screw her up. She was ready; the question was: Was the Highway Department? Her bags were packed and in the trunk of her car. Her skis were clamped to the roof. She was ready for a vacation. She had everything she needed. The one thing she didn't need was a weather-related flight problem.

The snow pelted her car; her windshield wipers hummed. If they had as much snow in Colorado as they were getting in good old Connecticut, she was in for a grand time, assuming she could get there.

She entered the expressway at the New Kensington Exchange and headed north.

Chapter 11

THE PLANE TOUCHED DOWN AT PRECISELY FOUR MINUTES AFTER EIGHT, five hours after it took off.

Ten minutes later an angry Lilith Bright climbed out of her seat grumbling. "Not bad. Only three hours late. Three hours, no cigarette, *and* the wrong airport. Other than that, everything was perfect."

"I'm just glad to be here," Ralph said. "Look on the bright side."

Lilith harumphed. "*You* look on the bright side."

Eager to get moving, Lilith fumed as she was forced to stand in the isle stuffed between a sweaty fat man with bad breath and a young mother carrying twins. Waiting for everyone to open the overhead storage compartments and drag out all their carry-on luggage grated on Lilith's nerves. She turned to Ralph, who stood hunched over, head pressing against the NO SMOKING light, waiting for someone to move so he could at least inch forward enough to stand upright, and said, "I'll bet you a hundred bucks the stupid cargo hold isn't even half full. From the looks of this crap, I'll bet we were the only ones dumb enough to check our luggage on this whole stupid airplane. You know, they should have outlawed carry-on bags instead of smoking, then it wouldn't take people a damn year to get off a damn plane."

Lilith watched a woman three rows in front of her struggling to disengage one of the four full-sized suitcases she'd crammed in over her seat. They appeared to be wedged so tight Lilith doubted that they'd have come loose in a crash. She leaned over to Ralph and squeezed the words out of the side of a partially-closed mouth. "Look at that, Ralph. Do you see that? That jerk has more luggage than we do and the dumb broad had the gall to carry it on. Why the hell do airlines let people get away with that kind of crap? Answer me that."

Ralph tried. "I suppose if they had a better record of not losing people's luggage, people would be more inclined to check their bags. Don't you think?"

Lilith didn't respond. She wasn't listening.

The traffic jam in the center isle started to clear. The cattle were being herded out. They'd move a lot faster if I had a bullwhip, Lilith thought to herself.

CANCELED

The word made Marcella's heart race, then rise up in her throat.

She gulped and swallowed it back down. No, this could not be happening. Not now.

People began to scurry everywhere. The sounds of idle chatter turned to frantic buzzing. Soon the lines behind the ticket counters would be flooded with stranded travelers looking for help. Marcella rushed to the first open spot she found.

"Yes ma'am," the female ticket agent behind the counter said, "that flight has been canceled. For that matter, all flights are about to be canceled. We just received word that the airport is officially closed. Nothing will land and nothing will take off." She turned and motioned with her head toward the gate where a TWA plane had just parked. "That's the last one to get in. Just made it under the wire. I'm sorry, but we're shut down until this storm lets up." She raised her eyebrows. "If it ever does."

Marcella stared in disbelief at the TV monitor. The word CANCELED now appeared behind every flight number, departures *and* arrivals. She was sick. And stuck. There was nothing she could do, nowhere she could go. She was trapped. She—like all the airplanes—was grounded. This couldn't be happening to her. Not now for God's sake!

As reality set in, the energy drained from Marcella's legs. Her breathing came in spurts. Perspiration dotted her forehead. She wanted to run but she couldn't move; she wanted to scream but her throat was dry; she wanted to die but even death rebuked her. She felt like she was going to collapse—which, when she thought about it, was probably the only thing Marcella knew she *could* do for sure: she could sit down right there in the middle of the floor, in front of God and everyone, and cry her eyes out. *That* she could do.

Instead, she somehow managed to regain control of her faculties. She had to. She didn't have a choice. She took a deep breath, bent over and picked up her suitcase, tossed her carry-on flight bag over her left shoulder, reached down and grabbed her final package by the make-shift masking tape handle she'd made, and then turned and reluctantly walked away from the ticket counter feeling as low as she'd ever felt in her entire life. What on earth was she going to do? This couldn't be. It just couldn't. All the planning, all the time. The arrangements. Everything was down the drain.

Marcella had to think. She had to figure a way out of this. There had to be something she could do. There had to be an answer.

The airport lounge looked like a safe haven for the time being. She could think there, gather herself.

With all the canceled flights the bar was quickly filling to over-flowing, but Marcella lucked out and got to a table just as an older couple decided it was time to leave. First, she had to clear off the mess they made, then she put her suitcase down beside the table that overlooked the snow-covered runway, leaned her skis against the wall and sat down. The passengers on the TWA flight that had just landed were disembarking. Lucky fools, she thought to herself, you got to where you wanted to go.

Ten minutes passed. Then twenty. Thirty. Marcella dug deep, but there were no solutions to be found. She was getting desperate. She chewed on a fingernail.

It continued to snow.

Gladys answered the phone.

"Hi, Gladys. Roger here."

"Oh, hi, Roger. How are you?"

"Okay, I guess. All things considered."

"Yes, I know. You mean the strike."

Roger hesitated, then, "So, Henry told you?"

"Yes. He did. It's just terrible, isn't it?"

"Yeah. It sure is. Not the kind of thing I'm looking forward to, that's for sure."

"Neither am I. I remember the last one—when was it, six years ago? God, it seems like yesterday. I can't believe six years has passed that fast."

"Yeah, time flies when you're having fun."

Gladys laughed.

Roger said, "Is Henry home? I need to talk to him for a sec." What I need to do is see if he still has that dumb idea in his head, Roger thought. I need to see if he's wised up since I talked to him last.

"No, as a matter of fact, he's not. He and Bill Freely—that's our next door neighbor, the fireman—took off real early this morning. Said they wanted to get into the city, do some Christmas shopping before everything got really crowded. Can you believe it? Henry? Christmas shopping? With another man? Why, I practically have to drag him kicking and screaming to get him to go the store with me when it's to buy something *he* needs. He hates shopping. I don't know what's come over him. Bill was over here last night and for some reason I guess they decided to get together and do it. Will wonders never cease? Maybe after all these years the Christmas spirit has finally sunk in."

Roger was stunned. Christmas shopping? Henry Nash? The Henry Nash he knew?

Gladys added, "He said that they might be gone all day. Personally, I bet they spend most of their time in some bar watching a dumb football game."

"Yeah," Roger said, thinking. "I bet you're right."

"Well, I suppose that's the kind of thing Bill needs right now, poor man."

Roger didn't understand. "Why? What do you mean?"

"Well, I don't suppose I should say anything, it's not really my place. But when Bill was over here last night," Gladys paused, "he told us, well, Bill's wife has to have a liver transplant."

"You're kidding."

"No, they just found out."

"That's serious stuff."

"It's going to cost a hundred and fifty thousand dollars."

"Good God."

"And the bad part is—where is a guy like Bill Freely going to get that kind of money?"

"You mean his insurance doesn't cover it?"

"Apparently not."

"What's he going to do?"

"Gosh, I don't know. What could any of us do if we had a problem like that? Henry tells me that our insurance covers that kind of thing."

"Yeah, it does. I guess we can be thankful for that."

"We sure can, even if we do have to go on strike every six years, right?"

"Right."

"So, do you want me to have Henry call you when he gets home? If he gets home; the weather looks absolutely terrible. I can't believe they went out on a day like this."

Roger thought some more. Jesus, was Henry really going to go through with it? Had he found a new partner? Fumbling for an response he said, "Uh, no, that's okay. I'll catch him another time. It was no big deal."

"Well, I'll tell him you called. I just hope he has enough sense to get off the roads before this thing gets any worse. Even if he has to stay in the city overnight, I would feel a lot better knowing he wasn't on the highway in this stuff. Weather like this scares me to death."

"Oh, don't worry, Gladys. Henry'll be fine. He has a way of coming out of things. Don't worry."

Gladys said she wouldn't and hung up.

Roger hung up to, but he didn't follow his own advice. He *was* worried. Damned worried. And not about the weather. Henry Nash may have had shopping on his mind, but it wasn't for a bunch of Christmas presents.

Roger poured himself a cup of coffee and sat down at the kitchen table. Now what the hell was he going to do?

"What the hell do you mean, it's lost?"

The TWA service representative turned white. "Well, ma'am, it's not exactly lost. It's just been *rerouted* to someplace else."

"Someplace else!" Lilith Bright screamed. "Someplace *else*! That's all you can say? It's been *rerouted* to someplace *else*?" Lilith huffed and puffed. "Let me tell you something, young man." She looked at his name tag. It said his name was DOUG. "*Doug*," she accented it like it was a dirty word, "that just isn't good enough. This airline has been screwing me from the very first second I scheduled this stupid flight and this is the last straw. Losing my luggage! Jesus, I can't believe it."

Doug didn't say anything. More than likely, even if he had, he would not have been heard over the roar of the raging fire burning in Lilith's soul.

Finally, "Ma'am, I'm very sorry. All I can say is that as soon as we locate your luggage we'll have it shipped here. Chances are, it's probably on its way here right now." He stopped and thought for a second. "Well, actually," he said, "if it was misrouted, then it's probably on its way to Kennedy, since that's where it was checked to originally."

Lilith looked suspicious. "Oh, is that right? On it's way to New York, is it? Tell me, just how in the hell is it going to get to New York, if Kennedy's closed?" Her face was twisted in sarcasm. "You couldn't get *us* there—how do you expect to get our luggage there?"

Good question.

It was Doug's first day in Customer Service and he'd picked a real beauty. The worst snow storm in a decade; flights were canceled and rerouted all over the place, and those idiot baggage handlers had to lose the one piece of luggage that belonged to a direct descendant of King Kong. He drew on the experience he'd gotten in his last job as a Service Rep for AT&T. Talk fast. Don't give them time to think; don't give them time to respond. Say anything. It doesn't matter *what* you say, just say a lot. "They'll be open in no time, I'm sure. Closing Kennedy causes big problems all over the country. They can't afford to allow it to stay closed for long. If you'll just tell me where you'll be staying in New York, I'll let our people know so that you won't be inconvenienced any more than you all ready have been. We'll contact you the minute it shows up."

It worked. But only because Lilith didn't have any choice. She could beat the shit out of the little twerp behind the counter, but that wouldn't accomplish anything except make her feel better. She grumbled as Doug wrote down the hotel, the baggage claim check number, and then got out one of their "handy-dandy-pick-out-the-bag-that-closest-resembles-yours" laminated eight-and-a-half-by-eleven sheet of cardboard.

Lilith was still fuming as they walked toward the Hertz counter. She was about to say something when she stopped abruptly and listened.

"What is it?" Ralph asked.

Lilith held up her hand. "Shhhh." After a second, "Ralph, did you hear that?"

"Hear what, dear?"

She looked down at him, wearing one of her disgusted faces. "Jesus, Ralph, don't you ever pay attention? It just came over the PA system."

"What did, dear?"

"A page. Someone is paging Louise Ann Bridges. She's here. Louise Ann Bridges is here, Ralph. In this airport."

Ralph looked confused.

Lilith put an even uglier disgusted look on top of the first one. "Louise Ann Bridges, Ralph. You know, the woman who stole my property. The woman who has my uncle's manuscript."

Uncle?

"Come on, we've got to find her."

Lilith grabbed Ralph by the arm and led him away, coat tails flying.

The wind was the hand of a cold heartless witch. Filled with thumb tacks it slapped his face, and then seemed to laugh with glee as it whistled its way through Manhattan's forest of plate glass and I-beams and reinforced concrete. Gusting to thirty miles an hour it brought with it a wind-chill of twenty below. Flakes of snow transformed by the frigid temperature into tiny bits of stone greedily pricked at any flesh left exposed and unprotected.

Tommy turned up the collar of his tan mohair topcoat and leaned into the storm. The footing was fragile, the traction non-existent. The snow gave way under his feet as he struggled forward. It was almost impossible to stand, much less walk. It was not a fit day for man nor beast, but Tommy Kosuri had a mission, and, he had no choice. And he sought none.

He turned north and headed up Park Avenue. Traffic was sparse. It was the only time that Tommy Kosuri had ever seen the normally busy thoroughfare when it didn't look like a parking lot. Today it was little more than a barren wasteland of blowing snow; a frozen tundra; a raging river of billowing powder that if viewed by a waking Rip Van Winkle might easily have been mistaken for the South Pole—a place where he had somehow been magically transported while swooning away in the joys of nocturnal bliss. Or maybe he was still sleeping and it was all a dream. Or a nightmare in white.

The buildings offered no protection. The slicing wind hurled by the invisible hand of centrifugal force actually seemed to gain momentum as it darted around the sharp corners of the skyscrapers. Faster and faster it came. The BB-like grains of frozen snow could not have been more penetrating, Tommy concluded, if they had been launched by the sling of David. Existence was the war; weather was the enemy.

Tommy had finished his business at the bank; his wallet was now full of *serious* cash. Twenties, fifties and one-hundred dollar bills, just in case. Just in case he had to grease a greedy palm. The bank had not opened until nine, and apparently all of the tellers had not made it in because of the weather; he'd had to wait for nearly twenty minutes in the only line open. Making an eager man wait was cruel and unusual punishment. Tommy did not want to wait; he wanted to get the action moving. But then, Carneby-Glenn didn't open until ten anyway, so waiting at the bank was no worse than waiting in his room.

Tommy crossed Fifty-Sixth Street and turned east, then worked his way across Lexington Avenue. His heart raced when he raised his eyes and saw Bloomingdales shooting up into the cold winter sky before him. Carneby-Glenn should be no more than a block or two south. He knew now how his ancestors must have felt at that first moment when Pearl Harbor climbed over the horizon. Did they, too, Tommy wondered, feel the excruciating need to urinate?

The huge projection TV in the corner of the airport lounge showed the same picture that Marcella could see just by looking out the floor-to-ceiling plate glass windows in front of her: snow, wall-to-wall, floor-to-ceiling, ground to sky. The whole world was hospital-white. Damn! of all the luck.

Marcella thought the man with the gray hair and gray suit reporting the weather on the TV looked a little like her father. Like he used to look. She really missed her father. He had died at such a young age. Motherless since birth, the rest of Marcella's family had died when he died. No brothers, no sisters, no aunts, no uncles, nephews or cousins; Marcella was left truly and absolutely alone. She had always hoped that someday she and Michael ... No, that was ridiculous; they were complete opposites. She looked out at the snow and shivered inside. It made her feel even more alone. Alone and trapped, with nowhere to go, and no way to get there. Her life suddenly seemed like the blizzard, random and erratic, purposeless, going nowhere, until one day it would just blow itself out. Her mind drifted. Although she was staring at the TV, she did not see it, or hear it; she was far away, in another world, looking for the one thing she could grab hold of and hold on to, that one thing that would give her a feeling of belonging. Every day was winter on a planet of strangers.

Then she got mad at herself—self-pity would get her nowhere. She had to do something. She had to rethink her options.

Chapter 12

MICHAEL'S MIND WAS LIKE A MOUSE IN A MAZE, darting first to the right, then to the left, trying to figure out which way to go, which way to turn. Disbelief was the first intersection he came to—the corner of Disbelief and Confusion.

And it had taken him a full thirty minutes to get there.

Michael still couldn't believe that he'd been driving around for nearly a half an hour before he even realized the manuscript was missing. He'd looked down at the dashboard to check his gas supply, noticed out of the corner of his eye that the seat next to him was empty, and then felt something click in his brain: *empty ... something's not right here.*

It took a second to register. It was the manuscript. The manuscript was missing!

Maybe he'd put it in the back. He knew he hadn't, but he was desperate. Michael jerked his head around and looked into the back seat. It wasn't there. The floor. Maybe it slid off the seat when he slid off the highway. Maybe it was lying on the floor. Of course it wasn't there either. It was nowhere. It was gone. Michael's heart sank to his feet. Where? He felt light-headed, then his head started to whirl. How? It—

That's when it hit him: My God, he'd been robbed. The accident—that's when it happened. The accident was no accident; the accident was on purpose!

But when? How? He—

Of course, that was it. He'd gone back to look at the other car, to check for damage—to see if everyone was all right—and one of the guys from the other car came forward to look at his car. And when he was back there they had *robbed* him!

Then it dawned on him. The whole thing must had been *planned.*

Jesus, he felt sick when he thought about it. He'd been robbed. He, Michael Parks, had been the target of "robbers." And more than that, they must have been watching him. The whole time. Waiting for him. *Stalking* him. The thought alone was frightening.

But they didn't seem like thieves. They seemed like friendly, normal, ordinary people. Your average Joe. The driver looked like a *kid*, for crying out loud.

And all the time he'd thought the storm was going to be his biggest problem—navigating I-91, then I-95, in the middle of the worst blizzard of the twentieth century. All the time bragging to himself *about* himself. Good job, Michael. Way to go, Michael. Keep up the good work, Michael. How proud he was of Michael Parks driving all the way from Hartford in a blinding snow storm. By himself. Hardly able to see. Sliding all over the road. Risking life and limb.

Delivering the mail, so to speak.

"'Through sleet and wind and hail'—however that saying goes," Michael had said aloud to himself as he looked out at the snow and took a deep breath, filling his lungs with pride, smiling. He was doing one heck of a job. He was doing good. Mile after dangerous mile.

Michael had made the trip from Hartford to New York many times—I-91 got him as far as New Haven, then he switched to I-95—but he'd never driven it in the middle of a blizzard before. That made it more than a little scary. But he kept telling himself that he could handle it. And he could, too. Why, even with the snow slowing him down, the towns seemed to fly by: West Haven, Milford, Bridgeport, Fairfield, Westport, Norwalk, Stamford. NYC was right around the corner. He'd done a great job. He had it made.

Wrong. Robbery was the only thing right around the corner for Michael Parks. Robbery, and the bursting of an overactive, over-inflated ego.

After all Michael had gone through, robbery never entered his mind. Driving took all his concentration. Besides, who on earth would pull a robbery in this kind of weather? Who *could*? Impossible. It couldn't be done. You could barely drive in this stuff.

After I-91 Michael figured that I-95 would be a piece of cake—they always kept I-95 plowed. Why, the traffic alone would probably keep it clear.

Not even close. I-95 was a jungle. A white jungle. A jungle where the beasts of prey were Fords and Chryslers and four-wheel-drive vans that wished they'd waited for another day to test their driving prowess. Michael, himself, barely missed becoming party to accidents on three different occasions in the first ten miles, escaping only at the last second thanks to some very deft driving on his part. That's why he didn't see anything especially unusual about the accident that finally got him. To be truthful, he was expecting it. He figured he was lucky to have lasted as long as he had.

Sweat spotted his brow when he thought about it. Yeah, he was lucky all right. Michael Parks, Mr. Lucky.

Jesus, a thing like this could ruin him. Who would trust him after this? How on earth could he face his friends? He was such a jerk. He'd lost the manuscript. Ten million dollars. One of a kind. In Mark Twain's own hand. He'd lose his job—that was the least that would happen.

And what would Marcella think, after the way he'd acted about *her* security measures?

He had to get off the expressway, that was the first thing he had to do. There certainly wasn't any help here. What was he going to do? Flag down the first cop who just happened to be cruising by? Or maybe grab another motorist and ask him for help? That was a joke. New Yorkers were so famous for their benevolent spirit, after all. No, all the expressway had to offer was other drivers lost in their own problems, fighting for their own survival. Nobody had the time or the inclination to care about Michael Parks' problem. His only hope was to get to a phone and call the police.

The first exit he came to was Columbia Avenue, which meant nothing to Michael. It could have been an exclusive area, loaded to the gills with "old money," people who knew the Chief-of-Police personally; or it could have been the heart of the slums, a place where his wheels would get ripped off his car while he waited at a traffic light.

Although he'd been to the city many times, Michael did not spend any more time in New York than he had to. It was *too* big. It frightened him. It seemed almost like a living thing.

Which meant that Michael was anything but an expert when it came to finding his way around The Big Apple. Although he'd made the trip before, the Triborough Bridge and the Queensboro Bridge were the only two landmarks he was familiar with, and that was on a clear day, when you didn't have to worry about sliding into other cars. Or having other cars slide into you. He could find his way into Manhattan and back out again, as long as he limited himself to one street in and one street out, no driving around, no sightseeing, just aim at the Empire State Building and pray you didn't run into any detours.

Michael looked out his windshield; he had no idea where the Empire State Building was. New York City had no skyline today. It wasn't even there.

The exit ramp was jammed. The weather had traffic backed up all the way down the ramp and onto the expressway itself.

Michael eased his way over to the side of the road and tapped the brakes. His heart stopped as he started to slide. He tapped the brakes again. He kept sliding. He turned the steering wheel to the right, nothing. To the left, nothing. He tried the brakes once more, hoping. Hoping didn't work either. Jesus. He held his breath. The rear bumper on the white Mercedes that was stopped twenty feet ahead loomed before him. It came closer. He kept sliding, and tapping. It grew in his eyes. Closer. Perfect, just what he needed, to run into a Mercedes. Probably an attorney behind the wheel. Whiplash and a lawsuit for twenty million, not to mention the delay. Lose ten million in a robbery and another twenty million in court, and get stuck here for hours. Jesus.

Michael stopped two inches shy of a rear-end collision. He started to breathe again.

Premature. The driver in the car behind him wasn't as lucky; his car didn't stop. The collision sent Michael sailing into the back of the Mercedes with a bang.

One word came to mind: Help! He wanted to scream it at the top of his lungs. Help! He wanted to shout it to the world. HELP! What word better expressed how he felt? What word could be more clear? A word worth a thousand pictures. It was the only thing he could think of doing.

The three drivers got out of their respective vehicles and headed for the car in the middle—Michael's. The driver of the Mercedes was a woman.

"I'm sorry," said Michael. "I—"

"It was all my fault," the man behind Michael said as he came running up. "I couldn't get stopped." The man was short with a big nose. "Is there any damage? Is anyone hurt?" Fear was written all over his face.

Michael checked his front bumper first, and then the Mercedes. They both looked fine. He didn't have time for this.

"I don't see any damage up here," he said, hoping the lady would agree with him.

She did. "No, mine looks okay. There's a little scratch, but for all I know that might have been there already. There's nothing major anyway, that's the important thing. Which is good, because I don't plan on standing around in this kind of weather waiting for the police. I don't need that."

With that she turned and got back into her car.

Police? Michael thought. That's the one thing I *do* need.

Michael and the short man with the big nose walked around to the back of his car. There was a dent in Michael's bumper big enough to see but not big enough to worry about as far as Michael was concerned, under the circumstances. The short man with the big nose agreed.

"No big deal," Michael said. "I say we forget it."

The last thing Michael wanted to spend time dealing with was whose insurance company was going to pay for whose bumper. He wanted to talk to the police all right, but it had nothing to do with a Mickey Mouse fender-bender. The short man with the big nose agreed again.

Michael got back into his car and then sat there in silence waiting for the line to start moving. Lines, actually. The exit ramp had two lanes, one for people who wanted to turn left onto Columbia Avenue, and one for people who wanted to turn right. They need three, Michael thought, one for people who don't know which way to turn.

Michael glanced to his left and looked at the woman sitting in the blue Dodge van next to him; she looked scared to death. He could see her staring straight ahead, eyes wide open, hands gripping the steering wheel, holding on for dear life, chewing on her lower lip. Lose ten million dollars and I bet you'd bite that little sucker off, Michael thought.

The Mercedes in front was completely covered with snow, including the scratch on the rear bumper that thirty seconds ago had been clearly visible. Michael's rear window was covered as well, so he couldn't see the car behind him, or the short man with big nose who had run into him. But he would bet money the man was anxious to get moving before the fool he'd hit changed his mind and decided that maybe the dent was worth reporting after all, and that just maybe he had a little case of whiplash to go along with it.

"Forget it friend, I have bigger problems than whiplash."

Michael noticed the eyes in the rear view mirror that stared back at him. He spoke to them. "You got major stuff to worry about, don't you pal?" The image in the mirror said nothing.

The traffic light thirty yards away shined red through the white.

"Come on, light, change."

Michael was losing valuable time. The longer it took him to get to a phone the farther away the thieves were getting.

Come on, dammit. I have to get moving.

Michael was not alone in his desire to get out of there. Everyone around him looked eager to find cover. Everyone was looking for a place to hide.

Hide. That was not an option for Michael Parks. The last thing he could do was hide. On the contrary, Michael Parks was going to be in the spotlight, the limelight, under a magnifying glass, like it or not. He was about to become a celebrity. Once the story got out, his face would probably be plastered all over the newspapers, the TV screen. Michael Parks, The Man Who Lost The Mark Twain Manuscript.

The Storm of the Century and the Robbery of the Century, all in the same day. Michael looked at the snow and shivered. If the Bible didn't say the second ending of the world would come by fire, Michael would have bet that this was it: End of the World by Blizzard. It may not last for forty days and forty nights, but this mess was going to stay a mess for awhile.

Well, at least he could be thankful for one thing: he was getting off the expressway, getting away from the crazy traffic and the crazy people. I-95 had been more like a war zone than a super highway. Brightly colored chunks of steel rocketing toward each other out of control. Projectiles flying through space. It was a battlefield loaded with vehicles whose rear ends decided to race their front ends to the next exit ramp; vehicles loaded with people who didn't know how to drive in this kind of weather—accidents waiting to happen. Brakes were useless; steering wheels were just decoration. One-eighties turned into three-sixties with the flick of a wrist. Round and round we go. Fender-benders extrapolated into serious accidents. Stopped, stalled and damaged vehicles were everywhere, weeds in a garden. Wreckage.

Every cloud has a silver lining, popped into his mind. He looked for the bright side, but found only darkness. Then his mind offered an alternative. "Things could be worse. You could be dead." What? "That next accident, you know, the one around the next corner, the killer, maybe it had your name on it." What? "Maybe the robbery saved your life."

Yeah, right. A thought, but not one that brought rejoicing. Michael found no solace in what might have been, or what he might have been spared; he had to deal with the reality of what was. And, frankly, death did not seem like all that bad of an alternative at the moment.

Ahead, Michael could see that the traffic on Columbia Avenue was moving very slowly. All the thoroughfares were bound to be clogged on a day like this. On a day like this no one in New York City was going anywhere fast. That had to be almost as catastrophic as the storm, Michael thought. New Yorkers without their hustle and bustle—that could be terminal.

The string of headlights that came toward him in the southbound lane of 95 looked like a giant centipede—a centipede with a hundred yellow eyes as well as a hundred squiggly feet. The world was a cold and eerie place. The light changed and Michael started to move.

Ten feet. Columbia Avenue, like the expressway, was overloaded with traffic going nowhere. Nobody could get off until the people in the intersection moved, which they did at about the same time that Michael's light turned red again. Two cars made it through.

Waiting at the light gave Michael time to think, and time to be angry at himself. Damn, how could he have been so stupid? A work of art, a priceless manuscript, for chrissake, sitting in the front seat of his car and for all practical purposes he acted as if it wasn't even there. Ten million dollars sitting beside him and as far as he was concerned it was just so much paper. How dumb could one man be?

Michael had to wait through four green lights before he made it to the front of the line. He would make it through the next time the light changed, that is, if someone didn't pull into the intersection and block traffic. Michael used the time to see if he could spot a phone booth. He couldn't. Nothing right or left. Damn.

But at least Columbia Avenue looked promising. It was a wide street, with shops that lined both sides. An affluent area. He should be safe here. He could go into one of the shops if he couldn't find a phone booth.

The light turned green. Michael was in the right lane so he had to turn right.

He found himself behind an orange dump truck, a municipal vehicle, creeping along at an even slower pace than the rest of the traffic. The truck had a blade in front, and was shooting out salt, or sand, or something, from the back. The yellow flashing lights on top of the cab spun. There was something warm and comforting about flashing yellow lights in the middle of a snow storm. Michael was in a hurry, but gladly accepted the speed; for the first time in hours he felt as though there was some friction under his tires. The snowplow would clear his path. Cross off one concern: he didn't have to worry about the snow any more. One problem down, one to go.

Two, if you counted finding a phone. But that was solved in two blocks. He found one next to a McDonalds. He thanked God for small favors. There was a place to park in front.

Michael pulled over to the side of the road. He got out of his car, turned up the collar of his coat and leaned into the wind as he worked his way toward the booth. The air was frigid; it whipped at his face. Even in his despair he felt the bitter cold.

Inside the booth he closed the doors with one hand and dug for a quarter with the other. He thanked God again; he had one. He deposited it in the slot and dialed 911.

The police arrived in twenty minutes. Considering the weather, Michael couldn't complain. They sat in his car while he told them his story, which one of the officers wrote down in a small black notebook. It took ten minutes. Then the one who wrote it all down went back to the police cruiser and radioed it into headquarters. The other police officer sat in Michael's car and stared out at the snow, saying nothing. Michael felt like a fool.

And now, as he inched his way through the blinding snow, he felt like an even bigger fool, for it suddenly dawned on Michael that he had another problem: he was lost. By getting off the expressway to find a telephone he'd dumped himself in a part of New York City that he was not familiar with. Maybe he should just stay lost, he told himself, for the rest of his life. Lost in New York might be a less painful fate than explaining things to Parker Gorman.

Chapter 13

"I'M SORRY, BUT WE HAVE TO CLOSE NOW."

Victor Romaine was beside himself with panic. The telephone call he'd just received had knocked the stuffing right out of him. His mind searched for answers, tried to make some sense out of the whole thing. But nothing seemed to compute. If Phyllis was right—and why the hell wouldn't she be? Why the hell would the newscast be wrong?—then any minute now all his sins were about to form a Conga line right before his eyes.

"I— I don't understand," Tommy Kosuri said.

Tommy stood in the lobby of the Carneby-Glenn Auction House dripping melting snow all over the blue Italian-tile floor. Now that he was inside Tommy realized just how cold it had been outside. He had apparently been numbed by it. As he began to warm up he felt the cold for the first time.

But his feeling of warmth quickly passed. The frigid weather he thought he'd left behind when he stepped into the building was resurfacing again. Tommy quickly discovered it was equally as cold inside—the greeting he'd just received was even icier than the ordeal he'd just gone through. That didn't make sense. Something was wrong. One thing was for sure, Tommy hadn't braved the great outdoors on a day like this to have some fool walk up to him and say "I'm sorry, we have to close now." Certainly not today. The Yellow Pages had said OPEN 10:00 AM to 4:00 PM. Tommy looked at his watch. It was 10:10. Just what the hell was going on anyway?

Victor searched for a reason—why was he closing? He found one no more than a few feet away. "The storm!" he blurted out. "That's it! I have to close because of this terrible storm." There, that sounded good. That made sense.

Tommy stood his ground. "But I—"

"Please," Victor interrupted, grabbing Tommy by the arm and trying to lead him to the door. "You understand—the storm and all. I don't know about you, but I certainly don't want to get stuck in this city overnight if I can help it. They want an arm and a leg for a room in this town." As an afterthought, he tossed out, "That is, if there are any left." He motioned to Tommy to look out the front door. "This kind of weather, they're probably filled up."

Tommy jerked his arm free of Victor's grip. He would not be ushered away. "Sir," he said smartly, "my name is Tommy—*Thomas* Kosuri. I have some papers here that will introduce me."

Tommy reached into his coat pocket and pulled out the envelope that had been delivered to him just that morning, the envelope that had been messengered to him *personally* at the direction of Tanaka-san, himself. When the insolent fool saw his papers, Tommy knew he would be more than welcome.

Tommy's eyes opened wide when Victor pushed away the envelope he so proudly offered.

"I'm sorry," Victor said, "but I don't have time for that now. I have no choice; I have to close. I'd be more than happy to review your documents another time, preferably when we're not under such a terrible winter storm alert." He gently eased Tommy toward the door. "Forgive me, but I really must insist."

Stupid Yankee dog, Tommy thought. Then he blurted out, "But it's about the Mark Twain manuscript!"

As crisp as a soldier, Victor came to a halt. "What?"

That's better, Tommy thought. Show a little respect.

"Yes. That's why I'm here. For the auction." Again he tried pushing the envelope back into Victor's hand. "I plan to buy it. I'm authorized to spend—" then Tommy stopped. No, don't tell them what you're authorized to spend, you fool. That will only give your hand away and cause the price to go up. The cheaper you can get the manuscript the better, for Tanaka-san, and SENSEI OF JAPAN. *And for Tommy Kosuri.*

When Tommy said the Twain manuscript, Victor, at first, thought (hoped) he might have more information about the message he'd just received from Phyllis—a retraction maybe, it had all been a mistake—but when he'd said "buy," Victor quickly realized the man was nothing more than just another potential bidder, someone trying to get inside leverage before the auction. He'd waste no more time dispensing of this nuisance. Time was the one thing he didn't have. Victor Romaine was a man in a hurry. "There's not going to be an auction," Victor said curtly.

Tommy's jaw dropped. "What?" His head spun.

This time Victor was able to escort the dazed man to the door with ease. The surprise had stolen Tommy's will to resist. "That's right. There's not going to be an auction," Victor confirmed.

"But—What on earth do you mean?" Tommy wanted an explanation. He demanded one.

Victor opened the door and steered Tommy through it.

"Haven't you heard?" he said. "The manuscript's been stolen."

It was no use; there were no options.

In the last two hours Marcella had gone over everything she could think of, and now, finally, she had to face facts; there was nothing she could do. There was no way she was going to get out of here—not today, that was a given. All forms of transportation were either at a standstill, or too slow. There were no trains she could take; she'd checked Amtrak before she'd scheduled the flight. Even if she had been able to get a ticket, they were probably shut down too. And the buses—if they were running—were too slow. As was a car. No, there was only *one* way to get far away, in a hurry, and that was by plane.

Unless all the planes were grounded, of course.

Marcella chewed on her lower lip and tapped her finger on the table. She was running out of time.

Marcella stared at the TV. The commercial was over and the news anchorwoman came back on: a news flash, just off the wire service. It caught Marcella's ear. Even knee-deep in her own problems something rang a bell. Her mind twitched as her eyes brought the woman into focus. Her hearing snapped to attention.

What! What was she saying? Marcella couldn't believe her ears.

" ... the manuscript, considered by many to be priceless, was scheduled to be sold at auction Sunday afternoon.

"Once again, our lead story: The Mark Twain manuscript has been stolen."

Marcella grabbed her luggage and skis and ran from the bar.

Stolen?

Tommy stood in the entry way to the Carneby-Glenn Auction House hypnotized by the shock of what he'd just heard. Stolen? He ignored the wind and blowing snow that whistled by. Stolen? The word echoed over and over in his brain. How could that be? Especially now, of all times. How could some thief, some robber, some lunatic, steal Tommy Kosuri's shot at stardom? *Stolen.*

Tommy began to shake all over, and not from the biting wind. His legs rejected his brains' request for support. His stomach grumbled; his head floated. His heart pounded inside his chest. My God, what would Tanaka-san think? His first assignment and he'd failed, even before he'd started. He would be branded a failure, a disgrace. How could he ever again look into the mirror?

Tommy didn't move. Snow fell. Time drifted by.

"Hello. Hunter here."

The last thing Scotty Hunter needed in this traffic and this weather was a call on his car phone.

"Scott, Parker." Parker Gorman sounded out of breath. "We got a problem."

A million things raced through Scotty Hunter's mind but only one made it to the finish line. "Tell me it doesn't have anything to do with the Twain manuscript," he said, hoping.

"Give the man a cigar."

"Shit! You're kidding."

"I just got the call, from Michael Parks, the guy from the museum."

"What happened?"

"Some son of a bitch stole it on its way down here from Connecticut. Sometime around nine, give or take ten minutes either way."

"In transit? You're joking."

"I wish I were."

"In a blizzard."

"You got it."

"Who took it, a couple of polar bears?"

"That's hilarious, Scotty."

It wasn't meant to be funny. Scotty was too mad to be funny. Scotty was on fire. He wanted to scream and holler, and call Parker Gorman the biggest lying, misleading bastard he'd ever met, but he didn't. Scotty was a pro.

"What happened to the escort?" Scotty asked.

"Did a half-gainer into the median strip. Out of the ball game just like that."

Scotty shook his head. "Okay, tell me about it. Are the police on it?"

"As much as they can be. It's not real easy finding someone when you can't see more than twenty feet in front of you. The weather's terrible. It's a bitch out there."

Scotty fought to see through the snow piling up on his windshield. "Yeah, I heard." The heavy snow combined with the freezing temperature proved to be too much for his wipers.

"Scotty, I don't have to tell you what this means."

Scotty Hunter squeezed the steering wheel with all his might. No, you sure as hell don't, he thought. You already explained that to me. You explained it real good you son of a bitch. "Are there any leads? Anything to go on?"

"Nothing. The guy from the museum said they just drove him off the road. Said he thought they'd lost control of their car in the snow, while they were passing him. Never occurred to him that there was any problem—other than a traffic accident, that is. He said he got out of his car and two guys got out of the other one. The second driver stayed in the car."

"There were three of them? In total?"

"Yeah. Right. Three. So, Parks says the one guy walked up to him—he assumed to check on the accident—while the other went around the side of his car—he assumed to check it for damage. The first guy asked if he was all right, and he said sure, no problem. Then guy number one proceeds to engage him in conversation. He said he was so busy looking at the cars and worrying about the accident and the weather that he never paid any attention to the second man. After a few minutes of that, man number one led him back to his car to see if there was any damage, while the second guy walked around our guy's car, supposedly looking for the same thing.

"Now, get this, guy number one points out a dent in one of his rear doors, okay? So, he opens the door—to see if it still functioned properly, right? Everything seemed okay so he slams the door shut. Pretty hard, as our guy remembers. Well, this is where we assume guy number two was doing the same thing to our car with the manuscript—simultaneously slamming the door so the two sounds blended together. The guy from the museum said it was snowing like crazy and there were cars sliding all over the place. The only thing on his mind was the weather and the accident, and the fact that he could get hit by a car just standing there. It never dawned on him he was being robbed. Said the guys just seemed like your normal run-of-the-mill people. Never would have guessed in a million years they were crooks. Like the bad guys always wear black hats or something so we can spot them."

"What kind of car were they driving?"

"Didn't notice. Just said it was white or tan, something light."

"What'd they look like? Can he ID them if he sees them again?"

"I doubt it. He said they were average. They were both wearing jackets with the hoods turned up so he never got a real good look."

"Average? Wonderful."

Parker didn't say anything.

Scotty asked, "White or black?"

"White."

"Well, I guess that's something."

"Right. How many average white guys can there be in the New York area?"

"What about the driver? Was he wearing a hood?"

"No, as a matter of fact, he wasn't. Parks said he was young. Just a kid. If fact, he said that was the only thing that seemed a little strange."

"What's that?"

"Said the kid didn't seem shook up about it at all. Calm as a cucumber. He said you would have thought an accident like that would have really messed up the mind of a young driver."

"An accident probably would have," Scotty said. "But this was no accident."

A man approached.

He entered the alcove, ignored Tommy and tried the door.

When he found it locked he mumbled something to himself that Tommy couldn't make out. What on earth is he doing here? Tommy asked himself. The man did not look like the kind of person who would have any business at an establishment like Carneby-Glenn. The man was *vulgar*-looking.

More than vulgar, crude. Almost primitive. An insult to the eye.

Tommy did not have to dig beneath the skin to know that this was a man with no class at all. He was big, but disproportioned. Bulky, cumbersome, a hulk. He was completely out of place at Carneby-Glenn, that's all there was to it. Where style and flair and elegance ruled, he contributed only size. And he was not only big, but he had big parts as well. Nose, ears, hands. Parts that didn't ... *match*. The flesh on his face hung down over his jaws—*jowls*—in layered folds, flaccid skin over a bone structure that defied description. *Bumpy*, was the word that came to Tommy's mind. The strange man turned to Tommy with questioning eyes.

Tommy wanted to ignore him, but there was no retreat.

"He just locked up," Tommy said, in response to the silent question, hoping it would send the man away. "Closed because of the weather," Tommy offered, almost as an apology, although he wasn't exactly certain why he felt obligated to apologize to this riffraff.

The man grunted. "Just now, you say?"

"Yes," Tommy said. "Just ..." Tommy looked down at his watch and couldn't believe what he saw: he'd been standing there for a full twenty minutes. He was stunned. He corrected himself. "Ah, about twenty minutes ago, I'd say."

The man's reaction surprised Tommy. He seemed upset, perturbed by the fact that Tommy had changed his story. Actually, he seemed downright angry.

Stanley Kowalski was like that. Stanley Kowalski could fly off the handle for very little provocation. Stanley was upset because if Tommy had been right the first time, and the guy had just closed the place, Stanley might have been able to catch him going out the back door. But now it was too late. The little son of a bitch had gotten Stanley all excited, for nothing. Sometimes people really pissed Stanley off.

Stanley grumbled to himself as he stepped back out into the storm.

Tommy watched him walk away.

Pig, he thought.

Victor Romaine walked head-first into a blinding blast of winter hell. Wind and snow whipped at his face as he stepped into the parking recess behind Carneby-Glenn.

It didn't faze him at all.

Nor did the snow that managed to find its way around the turned-up collar and down the back of his neck; it was ignored as well. Victor Romaine had other, more pressing matters to worry about.

Six inches of the freshly fallen fluffy stuff guarded the path to Victor's car—a joy or a nuisance, depending on your point of view. A joy if you appreciated virgin beauty; a nuisance if your name was Victor Romaine. Mother Nature had created a winter wonderland that was breathtaking, majestic, a masterpiece—a panorama in cotton-white on a canvas called New York. Everything in sight was covered by a generous helping of powdered sugar. It made the city look fresh and pure and clean. Almost edible. It was genuinely magnificent.

If you had the time.

Victor Romaine didn't. It was, in fact, less than a nuisance; it had no meaning at all.

Sinking in over his ankles Victor kicked up waves of snow as he plowed his way toward his car, ignorant of the fact that his hands were freezing; it had not entered his occupied mind to put on the fur-lined gloves that were still buried in the right pocket of his Chesterfield.

He got to his car. Numb fingers dug for keys. He found them in his coat pocket, buried beneath the gloves. Fumbling with the lock, he scratched the car door with a bouncing key that refused to hold still. The sailing is never smooth for a desperate man in a hurry.

Victor cursed to himself, then finally managed to unlock the car door and crawl inside. He slammed the door behind him. As his hot breath filled the interior of the car, a thin coat of steam quickly hushed over the windows. It didn't matter; Victor had to get to the airport before Arthur Samuelson's plane took off—that was his only concern now. The ability to see would come as soon as the car warmed up. Victor Romaine would just have to struggle with the inconvenience of being partially blind until then. It was no big deal; it would be short-lived. Not at all like a broken leg. The remnants of a broken leg were with you forever.

Carmine Rico employed people who broke legs for a living.

Victor trembled at the thought. Then he tossed it aside; he couldn't think about that now; he had to get to the airport. Arthur Samuelson's vase was all that mattered. Ms. Copperman had called Samuelson's hotel—Samuelson had not left town on Thursday as he had planned. She talked to the reservations clerk who had booked his flight. It left for London at four-seventeen. Victor could make it, no problem. But he didn't want to waste any time, not in this weather. He had to—Victor stopped. No, he had to take a moment, he was still in shock. His hands were shaking and his chest was pounding. Before he could do anything he had to get a grip on himself.

Victor dropped his forehead down onto the steering wheel and closed his eyes. He took deep breaths. He tried to relax. He tried to concentrate.

He failed. Phyllis' words ricocheted through his mind—her call had come directly from the Jaguar dealer. Her voice was choppy, in a state of panic: *The manuscript has been stolen; what does that mean, Victor? Should I still order my car?*

He raised his head and pounded once on the steering wheel with the heel of his hand. All she could think about was that stupid car, like a goddam car was the most important thing in the world!

Irritated as he was, Victor had tried to calm her down. Everything will be fine. Don't worry.

But the news had sent him into a tailspin of his own, and he wasn't doing all that well himself. He had things to do, plans to make. Contingency plans. *Emergency* plans. He had to THINK! The last thing he needed to deal with now was an hysterical wife whose only concern was to make certain the color of the interior of her car complimented the color of the exterior. If anyone needed calming down it was Victor Romaine.

His hands squeezed the wheel. He needed to pull himself together. Okay, he had a problem, but he had a solution, too. All he had to do was get to the airport before Samuelson's plane took off and everything would be fine. He would sell Samuelson's vase—surely one of his Twain bidders would be interested in buying a Ming vase once they found out that the manuscript would not be available. It was better than nothing. Better than nothing for them, and better than nothing for him. It would not generate the same kind of commission that the manuscript would have generated, but it would be better than *nothing.* It might take a little while to set up, but he could do it. He could do it; he *had* to.

Carmine Rico would understand. He'd wait. He was tough, sure, but he was also a businessman. As long as he got his money, that's all he cared about.

Victor jammed the key into the ignition with frozen fingers. The engine turned over once, then started. Victor breathed a sigh of relief. He flipped on the windshield wipers. Heavy-duty wiper blades installed in early November easily pushed the snow off the windshield. Victor moved the heater lever to DEFROST and flipped the fan switch all the way up to full power. The fog on the windshield started to disappear. He shifted into REVERSE and began to move backwards.

The rear view mirror was filled with gray; snow covered the back window. Victor lowered the driver's side window and stuck his head out. That's when the gravity of the storm finally dawned on him. The wind was coming in gusts, calm one minute, a blistering, raging monster the next. Gray sky, followed immediately by thick clouds. Blowing snow pelted his face. He squinted, tried to see. Good God, the weather was a nightmare. Panic flooded back. Would he be able to get to Samuelson in time after all? In this weather? Traffic jams flashed through his brain ... bumper-to-bumper, fender-benders, delays. He said a silent prayer.

He'd only gone a few feet when his car hit something and the rear wheels started spinning. Oh, shit! He gunned the engine, which only generated faster spinning. Victor rammed the shift lever back into PARK, opened the car door and charged to the back of the vehicle to find out just what the hell was going on.

He discovered the problem immediately. Apparently a snowplow had just gone down the alley behind Carneby-Glenn, and, in doing so, had pushed a ridge of snow roughly a foot high all along the exit from the parking alcove. As a matter of fact, Victor could see the plow was still there, moving along slowly at the far end of the alleyway. Victor's mind worked. He quickly estimated that if he pulled forward and then hit the ridge hard enough he could blast his way through.

Or, he could get stuck right in the middle, and spend the rest of his afternoon straddling a snow bank.

It was a chance he'd have to take. It was the only chance he had.

Victor got back into his car, eased the nose of his Mercury forward until it just touched the rear of the building, shifted into REVERSE, and then slowly, allowing the car to pick up speed as it moved, pushed the accelerator all the way to the floor.

The car raced backwards, snow flew from spinning radials. The big Mercury hit the ridge of snow with a thud, stopped momentarily, then bounced through. Victor said a silent thank you.

He looked down the alley. Damn! He couldn't get out that way. Based on its current speed—which appeared to be zero—the snowplow looked as though it had visions of killing the entire afternoon in this one alley. He'd have to go all the way around to the front of the building and circle back.

Victor gingerly guided the Mercury along the slippery surface, eased his way cautiously out onto 57th Street, turned south at the intersection of 57th and Lexington, and then proceeded to drive slowly by the entrance to Carneby-Glenn.

The snow was coming down like chunks of giant confetti, but the traffic was light. The gods are with me, Victor thought. If there weren't too many assholes on the roads, he could make it.

But being able to see would help. His windshield was clear, but there was still a fog on the side windows. He moved the heater lever to VENT.

Even if visibility had not been problem, Victor had too much on his mind to notice the two men standing in the doorway to his building. He'd met one of them. The other, he didn't want to meet.

Blowing snow or not, the larger of the two men certainly noticed Victor. Stanley Kowalski recognized him from the picture Lou Monetti had included with the ten bills. Stanley's eyesight was almost as good as his hearing.

Chapter 14

LILITH SPOTTED HER QUARRY BY THE BANK OF WHITE COURTESY PHONES.

Louise Ann Bridges looked exactly like her picture in *Time* magazine. A stout woman with a puffy face that, as far as Lilith was concerned, was about as exciting as a bag of flour. *Dense* was the word that popped in Lilith's mind.

As Lilith got closer she swore the woman was wearing the same stupid flower-print dress she was wearing the day the photographer from *Time* snapped her smiling kisser. The winter coat she wore looked dowdy, as did the man standing beside her—no doubt her dipshit husband, Lilith concluded. The only thing that looked any different at all about the woman was the shocked expression engraved on her face. *Dense as granite,* Lilith reiterated. Lilith, with Ralph in tow, got to her just as she hung up the phone.

"Mrs. Bridges, my name is Lilith Bright." A declaration more than an introduction.

Lilith extended her hand. An order more than an offer.

Louise Bridges took it absentmindedly. It was apparent to anyone with even negligible observation skills that Louise Ann Bridges' mind was still on her telephone conversation. Lilith, however, had more important concerns to deal with than one dizzy broad's inability to focus on the issues at hand. Lilith revised her original appraisal: *Denser* than granite. She bulldozed ahead. "I read the article about you in *Time* magazine."

Louise Ann Bridges blinked. Her eyes momentarily flashed a hint of recognition then quickly retreated behind a curtain of fog. "Ah—Yes. Ah, I see."

Lilith's eyes were crystal clear and hard as ice. "You and I have something in common," she said, with a half-smile, half-sneer.

Louise Bridges was at a loss; her mind was still sorting through the data she'd just received, data she couldn't believe. Terrible news. A tragedy. She turned to her husband, Raymond, for help. Raymond turned to Lilith to speak but never got the chance.

"That's right," Lilith continued. "You have something that used to be in my family. Well, actually, I don't mean 'used to be,' in the strictest sense. I mean it *was* in my family, until just recently. And still is, I guess, if you want to be technical about it. Legally, I mean. It's just not in our possession at the moment, is what I'm trying to say." Louise Bridges' eyes were still glazed over. Lilith liked that; strike when the enemy's confused. "The manuscript you found was written by a relative of mine. You see, my dear, Mark Twain was my great-grandfather."

Ralph Bright choked.

Lilith greeted the reaction with eyes of steel. Ralph looked sheepish. He hadn't realized his gulping had been so loud. He was sorry, but Lilith had caught him off guard; just minutes ago Twain was her uncle, and now he was her great-grandfather. Ralph understood: "grandfather" had a much stronger ring to it, a bigger title. Ralph was angry at himself; this had happened before; he should have been ready for it. Lilith was always promoting Twain from in-law to blood relative and then, for no apparent reason, demoting him back again. This, however, was the first time Ralph had been caught in the middle of a swallow.

Lilith turned back to Louise. "So, you can see, I'm as interested in the manuscript as you are." She cocked her head; her jaw locked. Time for the real zinger. Lilith braced herself, ready to do battle. "Which brings us to the question at hand: ownership." It wasn't a question; it was a dare. "I realize, of course, that you discovered the manuscript, and, as a result, are certainly entitled to a reward. There's no question about that. I agree completely. You deserve it. You should be compensated—and compensated quite handsomely—for your part in recovering this, ah, property of mine ..." She let the words hang in mid-air, waiting to see if anyone snapped at them. When nobody did, she went on. "I'm sure that you will agree—Mark Twain being my grandfather and all ..." She looked at Ralph out of the corner of her eye, waiting for the gulp that never came. Ralph knew better this time. He was ready. He wasn't the least bit surprised that Twain was now only two generations away, "that there's no question about who really *owns* it."

Before Louise Bridges could respond, Lilith grabbed her by the arm like a Boy Scout about to help a little old lady across the street. "But don't you worry, my dear. We'll get everything straightened out and you'll get a nice big reward. I'll see to that." She turned to Ralph. "Well, Ralph, don't just stand there. Help them with their bags." She turned back to Louise. "We don't have any bags." An ugly grin crawled across her face. "The wonderful airline we came in on lost all of our luggage. Can you believe it?"

Lilith started to lead her away. Louise allowed herself to be led. She was in too much shock to resist.

"So, my dear," Lilith said. "The first thing we'll do when we get to New York is to go directly to that auction house, what's the name—Carney and Green? I want to talk to that auctioneer personally. I don't trust those guys, you know? As far as I'm concerned, all they're interested in is a quick sale so they don't have to work too hard. Well, by God, they won't get away with that this time. I know what that manuscript is worth and I expect to get every penny. And I don't want any crap." She squeezed Louise's arm with encouragement and smiled. Two buddies. Arm in arm. "The more I get, the more you get, right?" Lilith's smile was wicked. "So, if this jerk wants his commission, then he damn well better earn it. Right? For instance: Just what has he done up to now? Like—who has he contacted? What arrangements has he made to make sure the big-money people will be here? People who can afford to spend more than a hundred bucks for chrissake. He better not have just been sitting around on his dead duff waiting to collect his commission or he'll be a dog's breakfast by the time I'm through with him. Which, by the way, reminds me: Just how much does this turkey expect to rip us off for anyway? It better not be more that ten percent—which I think is too high to begin with, all they do for chrissake is pound a damned gavel and say going, going, gone—or he's going to have some explaining to do."

For the first time since she'd met Louise Ann Bridges, Lilith Bright waited for an answer. The one she got she didn't expect. It knocked her socks off.

"It's, it's been stolen," Louise said from her trance.

Lilith stopped dead in her tracks. Ralph, carrying the bags directly behind her, slammed on his brakes just in time to keep from climbing up her back. Lilith glared at Louise. Her eyes seemed to glow now, neon-like, inhuman. "What?"

"It's been stolen. The manuscript's been stolen. I can't believe it, but ... That's what they said. I— I just talked to them on the phone and they said—"

Lilith didn't wait for the rest of the explanation. The woman was obviously a blathering idiot. She didn't have time to stand around and wait for some excess piece of cargo to gather her senses; she had to react. And she had to react now. Times-a-wastin'. Lilith Bright had work to do. She turned to Ralph. "Ralph, don't just stand there. Get us a damn car for chrissake."

Stanley couldn't believe his luck. When he thought he'd have to go to all the trouble of finding out where this Romaine character lived, the pigeon jumped up and flew right out in front of him. Stanley charged into the street like an excited bull looking for a cab.

Tommy Kosuri watched curiously from the alcove. He, too, had noticed the man from the auction house drive by but it had meant nothing to him. What did he care? His world had just come to an end, shattered beyond repair. He would be forever a failure. Even though it wasn't his fault—fault had nothing to do with it. You either succeed or you fail. Tanaka-san had said *when* you do it. He did not say *if.* If was not an option, not an alternative. If was not acceptable. What on earth would he do? Where could he hide? Such disgrace. If only ...

Stanley, waving his arms frantically in the driving snow, caught the attention of a cab half-way down the block. Actually, two cabs at the same time noticed the wild man running down the street and pulled over. Stanley could have his pick. He grabbed the first one he got to.

Why on earth is that crazy fool ... Tommy jumped to attention. *Maybe he knows something I don't,* Tommy thought. *Maybe he—*

As Stanley moved down the street in the first cab, Tommy made his way to the second and climbed in. What do I have to lose, he thought.

Stanley gave the cab driver instructions to follow the black Mercury turning right at the intersection just ahead. Tommy issued similar instructions to his driver, who turned and gave him a suspicious look. "Follow that cab?" the cabby said. "Jesus. That went out with high button shoes, pal. You been watchin' too many old movies."

Tommy handed the driver a hundred-dollar bill.

The driver flipped on the meter, eased the accelerator toward the floor and said, "You want me to head 'em off at the pass for you too, *pard-ner,* just say so."

Panic, the word blinked on and off in her brain. A strobe light as hot as it was bright.

Marcella's heart had not stopped pounding since she'd heard the news. She tried to calm herself down, tried to tell herself to relax. But the words kept coming back to haunt her: *"The Mark Twain manuscript has been stolen."*

Marcella told herself there had to be some kind of mistake. The newscaster had to be wrong. The woman must have gotten the facts wrong, or read them wrong. Something. Surely.

But if it wasn't wrong. If it—

Marcella knew she could not afford to wait around and find out. She had to do something. She had to find out what was going on, and she had to find out now.

Marcella raced to her car and practically flew out of the airport parking lot. She had to get to New York. She didn't know what she'd do once she got there, but she had go. This whole thing was so *absolutely unbelievable!*

It wasn't until Marcella got to I-91 that she realized that the blizzard was still going on. In her haste to get moving she had forgotten all about it. But it had not forgotten about her.

She had to be careful. She had to think about her driving. She had to pay attention. She had to get her mind off the manuscript and think about what she was doing. Driving came first, the manuscript came second. Marcella had to forget that her chest hurt; she had to forget that her heart was pounding; she had to forget that her world may just have come to an end. She had to forget about everything and drive.

She could feel the dampness under her arms, the drops of perspiration running down the small of her back. I never sweat, she thought to herself.

The manuscript had been stolen.

Picking up the television newscast like that, at the end, the only information Marcella had was what the headline had told her. No details. No specifics. She tried the radio in her car, but it seemed that the world was against her; each station she tuned in offered one of three choices: Hard Rock, Easy Listening, or Golden Oldies. In between: static. The weather must be playing havoc with the airways as much as it is my driving, she thought. She quit turning the dial. It was unlikely that she'd get any more news now until the beginning of the hour. She looked at her watch; that was forty-two minutes away. Damn, she'd never be able to wait that long. She had to find out what had happened to the manuscript. She couldn't— She— The manuscript— It—

My God, what about Michael? Was Michael all right? Marcella took the exit ramp that led to I-91 South. Jesus, she hadn't even thought about Michael.

As Marcella drove down the ramp and approached the expressway, a feeling of dread came over her at what she saw. The scene before her was as wicked a sight as she'd ever seen. It looked like a desert. A desert of white blowing hell.

I-91 was a God-forsaken island of snow and cold that looked like a scene out of a science fiction movie. It was somewhere on a foreign planet and the earth seemed to be almost *alive.* It was *pulsating,* constantly changing its configuration, redefined by the wind every other second. What was a mountain one minute was a valley the next. Flatland to rolling hill and back again.

What was a passable highway then, was quicksand now.

But, unlike a desert, it was anything but deserted. The twin yellow headlights of the traffic roamed the highway like lost souls. They moved toward her in slow motion—the eyes of iron turtles that crept along one agonizing step at a time. Either they were like Marcella, here because they had to be here, or they were trapped, caught in the middle of the storm with their only goal to get away. Oh, God, I hate this, Marcella thought. I hate driving in snow.

As much as she loved skiing, as much as she loved winter, when it came to driving in it, Marcella hated snow more than anything else. Skiing was one thing, driving was another. She could handle herself on a pair of skis. She knew what she was doing on a pair of skis. She didn't have to worry about another car running into her on the slopes.

As she pulled onto the expressway her car started to slide, and Marcella's heart skipped; she stopped breathing. Don't lose control. Please. It's okay. Steer into the skid. Don't panic. Don't jerk the wheel; don't slam on the brakes. Pump the brakes.

Marcella rediscovered her breathing skills once the car found its traction and righted itself.

But her heart kept pounding.

Wow, that was close. I almost lost it there. I hope that doesn't happen again. Stay calm. Just stay calm.

If she only knew more about it. If she only knew what was going on. What she knew was bad, but what she didn't know was worse—the fear of the unknown. A phone—she should look for a phone and call Michael and find out what was going on. That sounded right. That's what she should do. She needed to find an exit; she needed to get off the expressway; she needed to call Michael. She'd just gotten on, but she needed to get off. Get off, that was the thing to do. If she could just get hold of Michael, well, then she'd feel better. No, that was no good. She couldn't get off. What good would that do? Even if she found a phone, where would she call? Where would Michael be?

If he was anywhere. Maybe he was ...

No, he was not dead. She would not think that. He had not been killed. The newscaster said the manuscript was stolen. She did not say anyone was injured. If anyone had been injured—or killed—the anchorwoman would have said so. Murder was a bigger story than robbery. Of course, the woman would have said robbery *and murder*.

No, Michael was probably with the police right now. He was somewhere safe. Yes, that's right. That was undoubtedly how the TV station got the story to begin with; otherwise, how else would they know? Michael got to the police and reported the robbery. Of course he was all right.

It was just a question of where *was* he. A question of *where* she should look.

Marcella was confused. She didn't know what to do. She had never been involved in anything like this before.

She drove on, headfirst into the storm. There was only one thing to do. She had to keep going; she had to find out. She had to know for sure. She had to know what happened to Michael. She would search him out. She would find him. She had to, for her own sake even more than his. She had to get to New York.

"Well, hell, I don't give a damn what kind of car you get, Ralph. Just get one, for chrissake."

Ralph had been standing in line at the Avis counter for twenty minutes listening to Lilith grumble about how slow the clerks behind the counter were. What the hell were companies hiring nowadays—monkeys? Wasn't there anyone competent anymore?

Pick any car. Ha. Ralph knew better. Ralph had gone through this before. He knew if he didn't let Lilith pick the car he'd never hear the end of it. She'd complain about it all the way to New York. And then some: *"It's too small," "There's not enough trunk space," "You should have gotten a four-door, Ralph," "Why on earth did you let them stick you with bucket seats?" "Where were your brains for chrissake?"* And so on and so on ...

"Well, I don't suppose we have much choice anyway," Ralph offered. "Looks like everybody and his brother wants a car. I just hope they have one left by the time we get to the front of the line."

Lilith gave him one of her looks. "Jesus, Ralph, there you go again. Don't you ever have a positive thought in that head of yours?" She turned to Louise Ann Bridges who was standing at her side. "Is your husband like that, always thinking the worst? Never thinking anything is ever going to work out?"

Louise opened her mouth to respond, but she never got the chance. Not knowing Lilith that well, she didn't realize Lilith was rarely, if ever, interested in a response, even to her own questions. Lilith knew what was what, and she didn't need anyone cluttering up her thinking by dropping in their two cents worth. Before Louise could say anything, Lilith turned back to Ralph and said: "Just don't let them give you any crap about 'all they have left are Cadillacs.' They tried to pull that on us before, remember? That's bullshit. They *always* have more that just Cadillacs. Who's kidding who? They just don't want to give us an inexpensive car, that's all. They'd much rather soak us for all they can get. Money-grubbing bastards." She turned to Louise. "They try to convince you that you can get it for the same price as a regular-sized car, but don't you believe it. I know better. I've been screwed too many times in my life to fall for that line." Back to Ralph. "A Cadillac will cost us an arm and a leg and we can't afford an arm and a leg." Again to Louise. "Can we, dear? I mean, we'll split the costs, of course, fifty-fifty, but we both want to save money, don't we?" To Ralph, "We aren't made of money, Ralph. We aren't interested in Cadillacs or Lincolns or any of those fancy high-priced foreign jobs. So when you get up there don't act like some big-shot big-spender type, just because some cute little blonde bimbo behind the counter smiles at you."

"Yes, dear," Ralph said. "I think a Ford, maybe. A nice Ford—"

"No damn Ford," Lilith interrupted. "I hate Fords. Get GM. Ford hasn't made a decent car since Henry the first died."

"Yes, dear."

"I don't have anything against Ford, personally, you understand," Lilith said to Louise. "It's just that we had a Ford once, and every time it rained it leaked in the window. The passenger side window. My side. Not Ralph's side; he always stayed as dry as a bone while I got soaked." She stopped to give Ralph a look, as though he'd done something—on purpose—to cause the leak. "We took it back to the garage, naturally, and they looked at it and looked at it and looked at it. But they never did fix the damn thing. Leaked the whole time we had it."

"Cars can be a real nuisance sometimes," Louise agreed meekly.

It didn't win her a friend. Lilith gave her a look that said twit, then turned back to Ralph and gave him a shove.

"Step up there, Ralph. People will crowd in front of you if you just stand around with your thumb up your butt."

"There's nowhere to step to, Lilith. The line's moving as fast as it can."

Lilith's lips were pressed together in a tight, straight line. Her back was as stiff as a two-by-four, and the knuckles of both her hands were white from the death-grip she had on her purse. "Ralph, there's," Lilith stopped, raised her finger, stretched her head so she could peer over the line and counted to herself, "five clerks back there, and I'll be damned if I can see any of them doing anything. They just seem to be standing back there with their heads up their you-know-whats, staring at their stupid computers. Tell me, what the hell have they accomplished the entire time that we've been standing here? I ask you. How many cars have they handed out? Has the line moved? Hell no. Jesus, you'd think they could have taken care of a hundred people by now. Am I missing something, Ralph, or is the whole world overloaded with incompetent assholes these days?"

The line inched forward.

Out of the blue, "You have insurance on the thing, don't you?" Lilith said, staring straight ahead.

Silence. Louise gave Lilith a questioning look. Was she talking to her?

After a few seconds Lilith tried again. This time an irritated look accompanied words sharp and crisp, impatient, nasty, as if she were disciplining a child. "On the manuscript. You have it covered, don't you?" *Jesus, did she have to explain everything?*

"Oh, ah, yes, of course it's insured," Louise said. "That was the first thing we did—take out insurance. Raymond said—"

"Good," Lilith interrupted, "at least somebody's thinking besides me. I don't have to do everything for a change." The comment was meant for Ralph, and he knew it, but he didn't say anything. "Maybe that should be the first place we go, before the auction house." Lilith thought about that. "You know, maybe we should hit the insurance company right out of the shoot; find out just what the hell they're doing to recover our property, and then go to the auction house. I don't know about you, but my experience with insurance companies has been all bad. They spend more time trying to figure out ways to keep from paying off on a policy than they do trying to find the stuff that the policy covered to begin with." She looked at Louise. "What's the name of the company?"

"Ah, Jefferson National."

"What?" Lilith looked disgusted, and little angry. "Who the hell is Jefferson National? Never heard of it. Why didn't you insure it with a big company?"

"Well they—"

"Ah," Lilith waved her off, "it probably doesn't make any difference anyway. The big ones are just as bad, and they have more people to think of ways to rip you off. Thousands of bodies whose only job it is is to figure out how many different ways they can screw the customer." She gave Louise an evil eye. "You did check them out though, didn't you? You did make sure they were qualified to handle something this big? Like, for instance, did they have enough money in the cash box to pay off the claim if anything happened to the manuscript? Which it did."

"Well, I don't know. I just thought that ..."

Lilith rolled her eyes in disgust. "Wonderful. Just wonderful."

Louise looked like a child who was being scolded.

"Well, never mind," Lilith said. "It's too late to worry about that now. If they try to pull anything, we'll just get us a good lawyer and sue the everlovin' crap out of 'em. That's the only language they understand anyway. Fight fire with fire, that's my motto. That's the only way to deal with people like that." She grabbed Louise by the elbow and pulled her closer so she could whisper in her ear. "Let me tell you something, Dearie—and you can take this to heart, I've learned it over the years—the only way to deal with people is grab them by the balls and squeeze."

Louise Ann Bridges turned red.

Chapter 15

"WELL, WE DID IT," HENRY SAID.

Bill Freely agreed. "Yep, we sure as heck did. I can't believe it, but we did."

"The Nash-Freely Gang rides to success," Billy Jr. exclaimed.

The three desperadoes congratulated each other with all the gusto they could muster: *Outstanding! Way to go! Everything went perfect! Damn, that was easy! Did we kick butt or what?*

But the celebration lasted only a few minutes and then a hush came over the car, and three minds began to wander. Soul searching. Each tried to define in its own way what it had done, what it had just become. Slowly it began to sink in: They were, in fact, real live criminals. Outlaws. They could go to jail.

To the slammer.

The Big House.

Solitary.

The Chair.

Frightened minds play frightening games.

Henry visualized a shootout at the OK Corral, tracked down by the Earps. Biting the dust in a blaze of gunfire. Dying with his boots on.

Then he thought about Gladys, and the kids, and a bitter chill bit at his neck.

Bill Freely thought about spending the rest of his life in jail, and Marge never getting her operation after all, because the whole plan exploded in their faces.

Billy Freely Jr., on the other hand, was not at all fearful; he was too busy basking in his own glory. This just might be a really nifty way to make a living, Billy thought. Hell, it was fun. And easy. A piece-a-cake. Why not? He was glad he'd kept pushing and pushing, arguing, refusing to quit until his father finally gave in and agreed to bring him along. He replayed the whole thing over again in his mind ...

"We've been following him for over two hours now, Henry. When are we going to make our move?"

Bill Freely was getting anxious. Bill, Henry Nash, and Bill's sixteen-year-old son, Billy, had picked up Michael Parks as soon as he came out of the museum. He was carrying what they all assumed was the object in question: the manuscript. A box the size of a small suitcase was just about the right size for a manuscript, wasn't it? Therefore, it must be the manuscript, right? I mean, if it looks like a duck, and it walks like a duck, and it quacks like a duck, it must be a duck. Right?

However, the big red bow in the center (even parked across the street from the museum in a blinding snow storm, the bow could easily be seen from their car), they all had to admit, seemed just a little strange. But, in the end, they agreed that it had to be the manuscript, because, after all, what else could it be?

Right?

"Do you really think that's it?" Billy Jr. asked.

Henry spoke from the back seat, "That's it all right."

Bill Sr. wasn't so sure. "Are you sure? I don't know. If that's the manuscript, why would there be a red bow on top? That doesn't make sense. It may just be a Christmas gift."

"Bullshit. That's gotta be it." Henry tried to sound confident, yet a sliver of doubt peeked through.

"Maybe Dad's right," Billy said. "Maybe it is just a gift for someone."

"It's a gift all right," Henry said. "For us."

"I don't know, Henry," Bill came back. "What if it is just a Christmas present?"

Henry tried to reassure them both. "Hey, listen, it's got to be the manuscript. This is the day they're going to take it to New York, right?"

Father and son nodded their agreement.

"And that's the guy who runs this place, right?"

Yes, again.

"So it makes sense that he's the one who's going to be delivering it, right?"

No argument.

"But what about that girl who came out earlier?" Bill tossed out.

"What about her?"

"Maybe she had it."

"Ah, she probably just works at the place," Henry said. "She didn't have anything with her that looked like a manuscript, did she?"

Henry interpreted the silence as agreement.

"Okay, so it stands to reason that has got to be it." Henry waited a second to see if anyone had a comment. No one did. "I mean, what else can it be?"

Bill finally thought of a possibility. "Maybe she had it," he said quickly. "Maybe it was already in the trunk of her car. Maybe she put it in the trunk of her car before we got here."

"We've been here since five in the morning for crying out loud, Bill," Henry countered. "She got here at six; he got here at six-ten. She was the first one who came out of the building since we got here. It wouldn't have been in the car already. If it was in her car, then that means they put it in her car last night, which means it's been in her car all night. Now why the hell would they do that? Why the hell would they leave it sit around in her car all night? They have a nice safe, secure building and they're going to leave the thing in the trunk of a car all night? No way. That doesn't make any sense. Besides, she looked more like someone who was going on vacation to me, not like someone delivering a manuscript to an auction. She had skis on the top of her car for crying out loud. You think someone who was delivering a package all the way to New York City would drive there with skis on the top of her stupid car for chrissake?"

Bill Freely wasn't convinced, not a hundred percent anyway, but he didn't have much choice; they only had one car so they could only follow one person. If they'd picked the wrong one, it was too late now. He prayed they'd picked right, because if they hadn't, they were in some real deep weeds.

"Well, I hope you're right, Henry. Because if you're not, we're really S-O-L. It's bad enough that we're committing a crime, but to break the law and not get the manuscript—to have nothing to show for it but somebody's set of pots and pans, or a new VCR—that would really be bad news. That'd be the pits. I don't think they'd look the other way just because we made a mistake and took the wrong thing."

"Bill, don't sweat it. That won't happen. Listen, everything is going to be fine. Trust me. We'll know if we're right as soon as he hits I-ninety-one. If he turns south, he's our man. If he doesn't, then we back off. But I know he's the one. I just feel it."

Henry sounded sure of himself. He was the only one in the car who knew the way he sounded was not necessarily the way he felt.

As it turned out, waiting wasn't necessary. Five minutes later a state trooper showed up and they knew he was their man.

But now they were approaching the outskirts of New York City and they had done nothing but follow the man with the big white box with the big red bow. In another thirty minutes they'd be in downtown Manhattan. Billy Jr. was driving; Bill Sr. was riding shotgun and running out of patience.

"Henry, we'd better do something, and soon. We don't have much more time left. We just passed Baychester; if we want to do it and still be able to swing west on ninety-five we have to make our move. Besides, I don't know if I can wait much longer. Every second we delay I lose a little more of my courage, you know what I mean?"

Henry was in the same boat—waiting had given him time for second thoughts also. He, too, wanted to get the whole thing over with. Like his neighbor, the longer he waited the more frightening it all became. Hours ago it had seemed like it was no big deal. Nothing to it. Just do it. He'd even started to give the order a couple of times to kick the plan in gear, but every time he did it was like jumping out of an airplane; each time he thought he was ready, each time he'd gotten to the point that he was convinced it was just a matter of taking a deep breath, closing your eyes, jumping, and then pulling that cord, he stopped himself. Every time, at the last second, his mind screamed: *You're jumping out of a goddam airplane you jackass! You're committing robbery you jackass!*

Henry wondered if he was getting cold feet, too. Was the realization of what they were about to do finally sinking in? Roger Muldowney's words kept haunting him: *Don't do it, Henry. It's dumb. It's stupid. It won't solve your problems; it'll only add to them.* Henry was struggling within himself—

"Henry?" Bill Freely prompted.

Henry shook his head. "Bill, it's this damn weather. We can hardly see the road. I don't know if we can pull it off under these conditions. I didn't figure on this. Hell, you know the plan; you tell me, can we do it in a blizzard? And what about the state trooper—how do we handle him?"

Freely didn't know. It was a good plan, but only under the right conditions. No one had plotted-in the worst snow storm in the last ten years as a factor. "Shit, Henry, I don't know. All I know is—we can't wait forever."

"Well, what do you suggest? I'm open for ideas."

"Hell, maybe we should call the whole thing off," Bill said. "You're right, under these conditions. I just don't know. We could screw everything up and then we'd be in a hell of a jam."

Henry's mind raced. Jesus, this whole thing was crazy. Who was he trying to kid? He wasn't Jesse James; he was an auto worker for chrissake! He put cars together. What the hell was wrong with him? Roger was right; he was acting like a jerk.

But he had a plan. A plan that would ... Plan—that was a joke. Even *he* was beginning to have doubts about his glorious plan. His plan was taking on water right before his eyes. Funny how it didn't look nearly as foolproof in the cold light of day as it did the night before. It could sink, and drag them all down with it.

And the snowstorm—that was a brand new factor, a new piece to the puzzle. An unknown. Henry wasn't a trained thief; he didn't have any experience at this. He couldn't adjust to changing circumstances. He had to follow the script, the blueprint. He couldn't *innovate* for chrissake! Even without the storm everything would have had to have gone like clockwork. Everything would have had to have been absolutely perfect. The timing, the action, everything by the numbers. Jesus. Jesus Christ. He was not prepared for this.

He looked at Billy. Billy was staring straight ahead, eyes on the road, hands strangling the steering wheel.

And to top it all off, there was Billy.

Henry still couldn't believe it; Bill had actually brought his kid along. What the hell was he thinking? Was he out of his goddam mind? A sixteen-year-old kid driving the getaway car, for chrissake! That was the first thing that had changed, the first new ingredient added to Henry's pie. Henry had not factored-in a sixteen-year-old kid.

So Billy had discovered what they were going to do—so what? Bill should have taken care of that. He should have told him that coming along was out of the question, ridiculous. *No way!* He should have put his foot down. This was no place for a sixteen-year-old. Of course Bill was overwrought. Of course he was worried sick about Marge. Of course he had a lot on his mind. But that was no excuse. He should never have admitted to Billy what they were doing, and he should not have allowed him to come along.

Okay, so the kid was a good driver, and an extra man (boy), someone to drive while Henry and Bill worked Henry's magic plan, made sense. But a sixteen-year-old? A juvenile?

If only they hadn't needed Billy's car, that was the problem. That had screwed up everything. He never would have found out what was going on if they hadn't asked to borrow his car.

But, as fate would have it, they didn't have any choice. The first factor that Henry had not factored-in was waking up the morning of the Big Heist to find a three-year-old station wagon that wouldn't start. Talk about an auspicious way to begin the Crime of the Century. (In truth, using a station wagon had always bothered Henry a little right from the beginning. People would probably remember a station wagon more than they would a regular car. Not that Billy's car was regular, the loud Hollywood muffler was anything but regular.) Henry shook his head in disbelief. Can you believe it? he thought, the dumb car wouldn't start. Not that he shouldn't have expected it. Gladys had warned him that the car had been acting funny.

Thank God it chose to die *before* the robbery. Imagine stealing the manuscript, then trying to make your getaway and the stupid car stalls out and won't start again. If it wasn't so sad it would have been funny. That's all Henry would have needed: a car that quit running in the middle of a robbery for chrissake. Henry wondered if Jesse James ever jumped on his horse and found out it was dead.

They couldn't use Bill's car because Marge had to use the Freely car to go to the doctor's. And they sure as hell couldn't postpone it, the manuscript was only going to be in transit for a short period of time, and then it was back to vaults and alarms and 2000 volts of wired floor that would turn a person to toast as soon as he stepped on it.

So they'd had to get down on their knees and ask a sixteen-year-old kid if they could use his car.

Talk about a couple of pros.

But to bring him along—that was the ultimate stupidity. Bill had to be out of his mind.

And Henry had to be out of his mind to have allowed it. Contributing to the delinquency of a minor *and* highway robbery. Henry could see the headlines now: Arrested: Henry Nash, Bill Freely and Billy——

Jesus, Billy *the Kid*. Henry sighed. They'd throw away the goddam key.

Call it off, that was the only reasonable thing to do. Get out while the gettin' was good, as Jesse would say. Too much had changed, too many new variables: a blizzard, a teenager, an escort. How the hell could they make their getaway in a damn blizzard with a damn teenager?

But what about Gladys? Henry couldn't turn his back on Gladys. She needed him. They needed the money. That was why they'd started this whole thing to begin with. That's why they were here. He had to do something. He couldn't just say the hell with it and walk away. Say the hell with it and walk away and they'd be right back where they started. He'd never let her down before and he couldn't let her down now. What the hell should he do?

And then God and His weather came to their rescue. The trooper lost control of his vehicle, did an "exit stage right" into the median strip, and Henry was down to one problem: God and His weather. And how the hell was he going to work his plan in these conditions. His answer came from a most unlikely source.

"I got an idea, Mr. Nash," Billy Jr. said. "Why don't we just pretend that

I lose control of the car, see—say, as I'm passing him, for instance? I start around him just like I was going to pass, okay? And then, as I get up beside him, I pretend I lose it. I swerve, and run him off the road. He won't know what happened; he'll think it was just an accident. Then you and my dad get out of the car, and while Dad keeps him busy—pretending to be looking for damage, you know, that kind of thing—you grab the book. In this weather everybody will be so busy trying to keep from sliding off the road themselves, they won't pay any attention to us. They'll just be thankful it's us sitting along the side of the road and not them."

Out of the mouths of babes. And it worked like a charm ...

Billy Freely Jr. smiled to himself. And it had been *his* idea. They didn't even want to bring him along. If he hadn't smelled a rat the way his father was acting last night (his father never was very good at hiding things), and then kept badgering him the next morning about why he wanted to borrow his car (and why couldn't he go along?), until he found out the whole story—until he found out about his mother's illness and the robbery and why shouldn't he help? After all, it was his mother, wasn't it? They would never have pulled this thing off.

His idea. His driving skills. His plan.

Hell, he was the key to the entire operation. And, Billy mused, not only had he pulled it off, he may have also just found a career path for himself as well. He was a natural for this kind of work. He felt proud. Confident. Grown-up.

"Billy, will you please slow down!" Henry was not lost in Billy's glow. "We *have* the manuscript now. There's no reason to drive so fast. Especially in weather like this."

Billy ignored him. Billy liked driving fast. He knew what he was doing. That's why he was along, wasn't it, to drive? He was the best damn driver of the bunch, that was for sure. He had a talent for it; it was a skill that came naturally. Until he'd stumbled onto this new line of work, he thought that he might be a race car driver one day.

Don't worry, Mr. Nash, I can handle the weather. Any weather. Slippery roads don't bother me. I didn't have any trouble sailing by those two taxi cabs that were creeping along like little old ladies, did I?

Hell no. Billy the Kid Freely was a damned good driver. The other drivers were just a bunch of wimps afraid of the weather. (If you can't drive it, get out and lead it, that was Billy's motto.) Billy still couldn't believe that the last cab driver he passed had the gall to blow his horn at him, like he was some kind of nut or something for driving over ten miles an hour. Billy just smiled and gave him the finger.

"Actually, in weather like this, Mr. Nash, driving too slow is even more dangerous than driving fast," Billy said.

But that was not what Billy wanted to say. He wanted to tell Henry Nash: *Drop dead, I know what I'm doing; I got you this far, didn't I?* But he knew his father would not let him get away with that. Respect your elders and all that kind of crap. Billy just had to be content in knowing that he was in charge, whether the two old farts in the car knew it or not. It had been his plan—all his—and it had worked. Without Billy Freely they'd still be French-kissing that bald-headed dummy's exhaust and not have a damned thing in their car but a couple old coots trying to figure out what to do next.

But they'd listened, and now they had a million bucks in their car.

And Billy Freely was the *man* behind the wheel, driving them all off to safety. They should be damned grateful he was along. This was a job for the young. Young muscles can handle this kind of thing better than old muscles because young muscles have quick reflexes. If it wasn't for his young muscles his father and Mr. Nash would be standing around with their old wrinkled thumbs up their old wrinkled butts. Say thank you for saving our asses, Billy coached in his mind. Billy Freely, Man in Charge.

And then it happened. Without warning, the car started to fishtail. Billy's eyes opened as he turned the steering wheel to correct the problem and nothing happened. He pressed on the brakes. Again nothing happened. His blood turned ice-cold as the realization came to him that he had absolutely no control over the vehicle he once dominated.

Billy tried the steering wheel again. It spun uselessly in his hands—a free-wheeling circle of metal that didn't feel as if it was connected to anything. Shit! He spun it clockwise, then counter-clockwise. Billy's heart rose up in his throat. He tried the brakes again: nothing. No matter what he did the car kept charging down the highway out of control. The Nash-Freely Gang was little more than a lifeless projectile—a three thousand pound bullet flying aimlessly through space.

The car's rear end slid forward and passed the front end on its journey to the rear. They'd done a one-hundred-and-eighty degree turn and were now sailing down the expressway backwards. Instead of looking where they were going, they were looking where they had been; the past, not the future, lay before their eyes.

Then Billy looked up and was staring into the saucer-like eyes of a cab driver—the same cab driver who just seconds before had been the ungrateful recipient of Billy's middle finger. When the cab driver tried to slow down to avoid hitting Billy, he, too, lost control and started to spin. The second cab driver behind him saw what was happening and tapped on his brakes but it was too late. He, like his brothers before him, began to make loops in the falling snow.

It was a circus. Each car was under the big top, taking its turn in the center ring, spinning circles while flying down the highway. Billy's car completed a three-sixty and started a second rotation when it bumped into the car in front of it, which, in turn, sent it spinning. (Victor Romaine didn't know what hit him but he knew, just like that, he was out of control.) Now there were four cars in the circus train. The only thing missing was the calliope music.

The snow was thick and heavy, and continued to pelt the earth. *Turn into the spin* ran through Billy's mind. That's what it said in the manual. Billy turned into the spin.

Nothing happened. Panic knocked. His heart began to pound, sweat glands filled to overflowing, his head spun, his stomach felt nauseous. The manual didn't tell you what to do when you turned into the spin and nothing happened, *when your steering wheel was a useless as tits on a bull. Jesus. Jesus. What do I do?* An old joke flashed through Billy's mind: Put your head between your knees and kiss your ass goodbye.

On Billy's third spin, to his utter disbelief, he saw one of the taxicabs actually pass him. It flew by in a yellow flash and disappeared behind a white curtain of snow, heading, at last sighting, toward the median strip. Concern for the cab never entered Billy's mind; he had problems of his own. His car was facing forward again, but neither his forward motion nor his spinning seemed to have slowed down. As a matter of fact, it felt as though they were gaining speed.

Out of the corner of his eye Billy saw Victor Romaine's Mercury off to his right dart to the right, spin to the left, hit the guard rail, and then bounce across the highway directly into Billy's path. The man behind the wheel saw it coming at the same time as Henry.

"We're going to hit him," Henry screamed.

Henry was right. Billy's car smashed into the left rear fender of Victor Romaine's car and then careened to the right.

Which turned out to be just the beginning. Crunching sheet-metal screamed for mercy as Billy bounced off Victor Romaine's car and into a second car that had come out of nowhere. Bumpers banged together, locked. Then, in tandem, the two vehicles began their waltz down the snow-covered expressway as one.

But they didn't get far. Seconds later they started to spin, once, twice, and then BANG! a red Ford Explorer entered the fray and made it a threesome. The sounds of twisting and tearing metal sang in the air. But the trio split up after just one chorus. The Explorer had four-wheel drive and while that did little for its own traction, it did manage to knock Billy loose from his dance partner so he was free to pirouette one more time before ricocheting off a fourth and final vehicle, a vehicle that sent him soaring into the median strip backwards.

To the inhabitants of Billy's car, it felt as though they'd flown for hours before they finally came to a stop. When they did, steam hissed out from under the hood. The red temperature light flashed three times, the car backfired once, and then the engine died. To the eye the world was a peaceful white, but to the ear there was a war going on; the sounds of other cars crashing together could be heard exploding through the blinding snowstorm.

Seconds later Henry crawled up off the floor in the back seat and tried to gather his senses. "Is everyone all right?" he asked. "Is anyone hurt?"

Bill Freely snapped open his seat belt. "I'm okay." He looked across the seat at Billy. There was as ugly blue-red bump over Billy's right eye. It wasn't bleeding, but Bill watched it swell to tennis-ball size before his eyes.

"I think I banged my head against the steering wheel," Billy said, touching the bump on his forehead, then pulling his hand away as if he'd touched a hot skillet. "But I'm okay."

The three robbers tried to right themselves. The car had not flipped over onto its top; it was still sitting upright on four wheels. That was the good news. The bad news was—it might as well have flipped over on its top, because they were trapped all the same. Not trapped in the car, but trapped in the middle of an auto accident, in the middle of a snow storm, in the middle of a robbery. Other than that, everything was perfect.

The once proud members of the one-and-only Nash-Freely Gang were no longer as cocky as they had been. There were no high-fives and boy-we-really-kicked-butts this time. Getting away with this wasn't going to be easy after all. Reality had opened its doors and said welcome, suckers. From hero to has-been with the twist of the steering wheel.

Henry looked around. They had a big problem. A couple of big problems. The storm, as bad as it had been, seemed to be getting worse, if that was possible. It was blowing more now, whipping across the highway in tornado-like gusts. And the most important part of any robbery—the escape, the get-away, that's why they called it that, dummy, you have to *get away*—did not appear to be possible under the circumstances. There was no escape route here; everywhere Henry looked he saw nothing but snow and other cars sitting—and lying—at very weird angles. Wonderful, snow on the outside, stolen property on the inside, a car stuck somewhere in the median strip, and a major traffic accident to top it all off.

And, a traffic accident meant police. Probably ambulances. *Questions*.

"Billy, try the engine," Henry said. "See if it'll start. We have to get out of here."

Henry crossed his fingers. Billy sat up in his seat. His head spun. He felt dizzy, but he fought through it and managed to reach up and turn the ignition.

Click. He tried again. This time not even a click. The ignition was as useless as the steering wheel had been. Billy looked at Henry. Henry looked back. Seconds passed, turned to minutes. Three minds worked. The Outlaws Three searched for answers. The snow kept coming.

Then red lights flashed through the raging storm.

Billy leaned forward, trying to see. A police car or an ambulance? Frantically he looked around. There had to be a way out of this. Jesus, there had to be something they could do.

He looked at his father: Confusion. He turned to Henry: Panic. Billy tried to think. Even with his head pounding he tried to come up with something. He'd come up with something before, surely he could come up with something now. There must be a way to—

He stopped. Outside, through the windshield, through the snow, something appeared to be moving toward them. He strained to see. What was it? He couldn't make it out. He shook his head, but his head hurt and the cobwebs wouldn't go away. Something was out there all right, a dark shadow outlined in the blowing white and flashing red. It was large and dark and ... *menacing*. For some reason, *menacing* was the word that came to mind. It was coming toward them. He squinted. His head began to clear. It came closer. What the hell?

Then he saw. It was *a man*. A large man. A giant-like man walking toward them through the snow. Billy winced. The man was really weird-looking. Billy had never seen anything like this before. The man had hands that dangled from arms that dangled from shoulders that stooped. The arms hung down at his sides, ape-like.

Ugly dude, Billy thought. He looked closer. There was something in his hand. It moved through the snow. It looked like ... Naw, it couldn't be. Billy gasped. It was. Jesus, it was. In the man's hand was a *gun*. My God, the man approaching their car was carrying a gun.

Why on earth would ..?

Billy could see his face now. His eyes. He looked angry. Very angry.

If there was one thing Stanley Kowalski could do it was look angry. Stanley was very good at looking angry. Stanley was one of the best. He moved toward the car. Stanley Kowalski didn't like smart-ass kids, smart-ass kids who gave him the finger, smart-ass kids who caused accidents and kept him from doing what he was supposed to be doing, smart-ass kids who drove cars with mufflers that almost burst your goddam eardrums even in a goddam blizzard. It made Stanley mad. Damn mad. Mad enough to kill.

Chapter 16

JESUS CHRIST! WHAT THE HELL HAPPENED?

Victor Romaine was beside himself, physically as well as emotionally—his body, like his mind, was upside down.

Victor's car was in the median strip of I-95 lying on its right side, and Victor was lying on his head, wedged against the passenger-side door with his feet sticking straight up in the air. The last thing he remembered was driving down the highway, trying to see, trying to keep from sliding into other cars, trying to navigate his way back to Highway 678. Trying to get to Arthur Samuelson before his plane took off.

Driving, hell—*crawling*, that's what he'd been doing. Victor wasn't driving, he was creeping. Plodding along at five miles an hour. A snail. He could get out and walk faster. Damned weather. Victor turned off Third Avenue onto 59th Street; the Queensboro Bridge was only a couple blocks away.

Victor toyed with the idea of speeding up. Just a little bit. Just ease the accelerator down a fraction. Should he risk it? Should he rev it up a notch of two? He had room; traffic was surprisingly nonexistent. Only fools are out driving in weather like this, Victor thought.

No, don't take the chance. Samuelson's flight did not leave until four something; it was just after eleven now. He had plenty of time, even in this weather.

Victor looked to his left, then to his right. Jesus, he'd never seen weather like this before. Every other second or so he was, in fact, driving blind. Everywhere he looked there was nothing but blowing snow. Swirling, spinning, *a white whirlpool from hell*, he thought to himself. Then it would clear up, just like that, just long enough so you could see how bad it was out there, and then the visibility went back to six inches again.

Better not take the chance, Victor concluded, not in these conditions. It would be foolish to try to go any faster. Okay, he was moving slow, but at least he was moving. He was going as fast as he dared given the fact that the road was slippery and visibility shifted from clear to impossible just like that. Only a couple more blocks and then he'd be over the bridge and on Highway 25. He'd take 25 to 25A, 25A to 278, 278 to the Grand Central Parkway, and then: "Hello, La Guardia." And "Hello, Samuelson."

And "Goodbye, Rico."

Victor's heart pounded. It was bad enough that the road was slick, bad enough that he could lose control at any second, but those gusts of wind, the blowing snow, not being able to see, that was the scary part. The roads looked fairly barren, but for all he knew there was a taxicab somewhere out there, stalled, just on the other side of the next wall of snow, waiting for him to plow into it. He had to get to Samuelson, but because of the damned weather, he couldn't go any faster. He couldn't take the chance. Going faster would be stupid.

There it was, the Queensboro Bridge. He had plenty of time. He'd make it.

As Victor approached the bridge the traffic got heavier, but it was moving better than he expected. Okay, okay, everything was fine. He felt good. Keep moving. Just keep moving.

And he did. Unfortunately, not in the direction he wanted to go. The flashing yellow arrow at the entrance to the bridge directed him north, away from the bridge. Jesus, the goddam bridge was CLOSED FOR REPAIRS! Shit!

Okay, okay, stay calm. No problem. He'd just have to go up to the Triborough Bridge, come back down south on 278 and shoot on into La Guardia that way. No big deal. He had plenty of time.

At 11:43 Victor turned onto the Triborough Bridge. Thank God the city wasn't working on this bridge too, Victor thought. But it was a wonder; it seemed as though it was the mayor's plan to shut down the whole damn city every chance he got.

But now everything was fine. Everything was okay. Just keep moving. Just keep—

Damn! Flashing red lights through the snow, up ahead. At the far side of the bridge. No, not now. Don't tell me. Dear God, don't let there be an accident. Don't make me sit here for hours.

It turned out worse. Victor's prayer was answered; he would not have to sit there for hours. But when the snow cleared Victor could see his next obstacle; red lights everywhere. The accident he had worried about had happened, at his exit, the south exit ramp—he couldn't get off. Policemen were everywhere, waving people to the northbound ramp. Victor followed the traffic. He couldn't go south. Jesus! Now what the hell was he going to do?

Victor fought with his emotions. The first thing he had to do was to stay calm. Okay, okay, he'd just have to go all the way around. That's all there was to it. He'd go north on 278, hit 95, grab 678 south, and then circle back down to 278 from the other side and come into La Guardia from the east. It was one hell of a long way, but he didn't have one hell of a lot of choices. He looked at the clock on the dash: 12:02. Okay, he still had plenty of time.

Except the ramp onto 678 South was closed as well. Another damn accident. Jesus Christ, Victor swore to himself. Am I ever going to get a break? Will this shit ever end?

His only choice now was to continue going north on 95, take the first ramp off, get back on going south, and then pick up 678 from 95. Talk about your damn jigsaw puzzle. If Victor pulled this off he'd be a genius.

Or, maybe he should get off the expressways all together. Take city streets. The shortest distance between two points is a straight line. The shortest distance between Victor Romaine and La Guardia were city streets. But how passable would they be? If the expressways were bad, Victor could only imagine how bad the city streets—the *secondary* city streets—must be. Victor thought about it, then rejected it. No way. Getting from point A to point B (and staying out of Rico's gun sights, at point blank range) in the quickest time was the issue, not which route was the shortest. He'd better stick to the expressways.

Wrong choice. Just after Victor exited 95, then got back on again going south, he'd gone no more than a quarter of a mile when Billy Freely issued his invitation, "Greetings Mr. Romaine, Want to go for a spin?"

And suddenly Victor Romaine didn't have all the time in the world any more.

It happened so suddenly, at first it didn't register in Victor's mind what was going on. His brain did not interpret it as something that was happening to him. Concerned as he was about getting to Samuelson, his mind, naturally, was already fully loaded. Over-loaded. His mind was thinking about more important things: Arthur Samuelson, Ming vases, manuscripts, the time, IOUs. Carmine Rico. He didn't have time to think about accidents. The crash—it was just a sound that meant nothing. He'd heard the thud, felt the jolt, but he didn't pay any attention. He was busy. It was happening to someone else. His mind ignored it.

Until he started to spin. The car lurched forward, and then the steering wheel went lax in his hands, and the vehicle started to sail, *float*, out of control, and Jesus! What?

When it finally dawned on him what was happening, his heart began to race even faster; a gong pounded in his head. This couldn't be! Not now! Not a traffic accident! He had enough problems. He didn't have time to be out of control, sliding down the highway. He didn't have time to crash. Physical injury, loss of life, damage to his car—these were thoughts that never entered his mind. Time, the loss of precious time—not getting to Samuelson in time—that was the monster that reared its ugly head in Victor Romaine's nightmare. He was running out of time to spare; he had to get to that vase. He'd spent the last two and a half hours driving all over goddam New York; he didn't have time to worry about death and destruction.

He had a man named Samuelson to worry about.

And a man named Rico.

Things bad had suddenly gotten worse. Even before the accident Victor was a man dangling from a string, nervous, jittery, upset with all the forces that seemed to be against him, the weather most of all.

But it was more than the weather, it was what the weather meant. His lack of skill at handling this kind of situation was Victor's major weakness, and he knew it. He was not a man of speed, not a man who could think on his feet and adjust to changing circumstances; he did not do well when it came to improvising. Victor was a planner, a contemplator, he had to have a program in front of him in order to function. When he had a plan he was great, the best in the business. Planning, that was his forte. Everyone said so. Victor was proud of his abilities to put things in a logical order, to develop a plan of attack, to program every move, a chess player who anticipated every possibility under normal circumstances.

Under normal circumstances, that was the problem. These were not normal circumstances. *Under normal circumstances* there was time to plan.

Victor remembered Arthur Samuelson's words; they echoed in his brain: *Time is the one thing I don't have.* Victor knew the feeling.

What irked him the most was the fact that he had not anticipated that something like this might happen. He had not *planned* for all the contingencies just-in-case. He knew better than that. He couldn't believe that he could be so unthinking. The Great Planner had not developed a Plan B, just in case something happened to Plan A. What was it the Chairman of the Board had said at the last board meeting? "Victor is a man who plans everything, a man who charters each step, organizes every detail down to the nth degree, carries each calculation out to the fourth decimal place. He is a man who leaves nothing to chance."

Except this time. The one time in his life when a back-up strategy was necessary—no, absolutely vital—he'd skipped right over it. The one time in his life when just maybe his life depended on it, it never entered his mind. And if he was honest with himself, it was the greed more than the snow that was responsible for his blindness. As soon as he had signed the contract to sell the Twain manuscript a new philosophy had taken over: Damn the torpedoes, full speed ahead.

The most important time in his life and Victor had no plan to fall back on. He had only one choice: He had to charge headfirst into the fray. And, as luck would have it, this time the fray was a thirty-mile-an-hour gale. Filled with snow.

Then it hit him. Wasn't it Mark Twain who'd said: "Everybody talks about the weather but nobody does anything about it?" Talk about irony. The Mark Twain manuscript and a Mark Twain line. It was almost as if fate had planned on having the two of them collide.

Fate and automobiles. It was the last car that hit him that had caused most of the damage. The first car started it all, but it was the last one that really screwed things up.

Victor couldn't remember everything that had happened—it happened too fast—but he did remember the last car that hit him, the last of many. It had been like a cannon—a rocket that launched him into orbit. It banged into his left side and sent him skidding out of control and into the median strip. He might have been able to work his way out of the first hit, or even the second, but it was that last one that was the real killer. Victor remembered that no matter what he did he couldn't stop his flight, his free-fall. The steering wheel, the brakes, useless. As his brain began to clear he also remembered that once he sailed off the highway even the snow got out of focus; he was just a twisting, turning, rolling cage of steel with flashes of light and dark, the only images that registered on his brain. And then he banged into something—something that grabbed at his left front tire—which sent the car rolling head over heels, ass over tin cups, as his late grandfather used to say. It turned over three times before coming to a stop on its right side. Useless. Dead.

And quiet. That's what Victor noticed first—his car was not running any more. Which meant he was not moving, even at a snail's pace. Victor Romaine was going nowhere. Which meant Arthur Samuelson was getting farther and farther away. And Carmine Rico was getting closer and closer.

Victor had to get up. He had to get moving. He tried to turn over. *Ouch,* a sharp pain jabbed at his back. "Jesus," Victor gasped. Damn, that hurt. Then the pain was the least of his worries. Jesus, what if he was injured? Seriously?

What if his back was *broken?* Then he'd never get to Samuelson. Then he'd never—

No, that was ridiculous. If his back was broken he couldn't move at all. And there would be no pain—he wouldn't be able to feel anything.

He moved his feet. He felt his feet. He had feeling. He had pain. Thank God, he had pain. Victor took a deep breath, put the palms of his hands against the car door and pushed himself into an upright position. He did it slowly, cautiously, moving each muscle meticulously, an inch at a time, waiting to see if his back was going to respond by stabbing at him with the stiletto of pain as it had before. It didn't. So far so good. He worked his way to his knees.

Don't move the victim of an accident; it can cause more harm than good popped into his mind.

How many times had he heard that warning? It applied to self-inflicted movement as well as externally assisted, Victor was sure of that. If he was injured he'd better be careful; he could move and really screw things up. Before going any farther, he decided that he'd better take a second and check his body for damage.

As if he really had anything to lose, he thought. If his back wasn't broken now, it would be, once Rico's men got hold of him.

Victor moved his eyes and his hands slowly over his body, pressing here, probing there. His chest, stomach, legs. He felt around his head. As best he could tell there was no bleeding. He seemed to be in one piece. At least nothing appeared to be leaking out; the only moisture he felt was sweat.

He decided it was safe to proceed to Step Two: Stand up and see if anything was broken, see if anything fell off when he shook it.

Stupid thought, Victor thought. He was getting giddy. Fear was making him giddy. Jesus, Victor, get hold of yourself.

He reached up and grabbed the steering wheel. Now-or-never time. He pulled.

He was standing.

More or less. Hunched-over was more like it. He was vertical at least. His muscles ached and he could expect a little soreness, a bruise or two, but nothing seemed broken. At least nothing ached like it was broken. Satisfied that he was not knocking at death's door, Victor looked for a way out.

There was only one, and that was through the driver's side door—the passenger side of his car had an entire planet pressed against it. That meant climbing, assuming he could manage to get the door open in the first place. It might be jammed shut as a result of the accident; that side of the car had taken a powerful hit during the barrage. If it was crushed, it might not open. Then what?

He tried the door handle. Click. Thank God. He pushed up. It weighed a ton. It didn't seem that heavy when the car was sitting upright, when he just pulled on the handle and it popped right open. He didn't even think about it then, he just crawled in and drove away.

But now it was the heaviest damned thing he ever had to move in his entire life. He pushed up. Jesus, the door was heavy.

Was it really a gun—or was his mind playing tricks on him?

It could be his mind, Billy thought. He had taken a pretty good whack on his head when he'd banged it against the steering wheel. His head hurt, and he still felt a little dizzy. And either his vision was screwed up, or all of a sudden the world had gotten just a tad bit on the fuzzy side.

He blinked. It didn't help. It still looked like a gun.

"Is that guy carrying a gun?" Billy's father asked.

Billy swallowed hard. Holy shit, his father was seeing it too. That did it. If his father saw it then it wasn't his imagination.

"What?" Henry asked, leaning forward in the back seat.

Bill Freely Sr. repeated himself. "That guy coming toward us—does that look like a gun in his hand to you?"

Henry squinted. It was hard to see. Once the car had stopped running, naturally the windshield wipers had stopped working, and when that happened the snow quickly began to cover the windshield. It did look like a gun though. But that didn't make any sense. Why in the hell would some guy be walking toward them in the middle of I-95 with a gun in his hand?

"It can't be," Henry said. "Why on earth would some guy be out wondering around in the middle of a snowstorm with a gun in his hand?"

Billy gulped again. "It sure looks like a gun to me, Mr. Nash."

Bill Sr. added, "And he's not just wandering around, Henry, it looks like he's headed right for us."

Henry didn't say anything.

"Jesus, Henry, you don't think it has anything to do with the robbery, do you?" Bill said.

How could it have anything to do with the robbery, Henry thought. "What? What the hell are you talking about?"

"Maybe he's after us," Bill said, eyes straight ahead, fixed on the man coming their way. "Maybe he's after the manuscript. Maybe he's after—"

"Bill, are you out of your mind? Why the hell would he be after us? You ever see that guy before? You know him? He has no reason to be after us."

"Jesus, Henry, I don't know."

"Bill, what do you think he is, a private eye? You think the guy from the museum found himself a private eye in the middle of I-Ninety-five, one who just happened to be looking for a case, so he hired him, on the spot, to track us down? Jesus, Bill, get a grip on yourself."

"Maybe he's a cop," Billy said.

Oh shit. Silence. Maybe it was a cop. Nobody wanted to think about that.

"What—what ar—are we gonna do, Henry?" Bill was stuttering.

"Hey, Bill, the guy's not a cop, okay? Why would he be a cop? And even if he is a cop—why would a cop be after us? I mean, it doesn't make any sense. Think about it: Nobody knows about the robbery. Not yet. They can't; it's too soon. Nobody knows we swiped the manuscript, except for the guy we stole it from. And he hasn't had time to tell anyone anything. A cop would have no reason to come after us, okay? A cop would have no reason to suspect us of anything. We're just a couple of people involved in a traffic accident, like everyone else. Relax. Just relax."

But it did look like the man had a gun. And he *was* walking toward them.

The man stopped. Ten feet away. He stood there, staring, a huge black shadow in a field of white. A phantom, with eyes as cold as the snow. His image was crystal clear now. It was no longer a question of *what* he had in his hand; it was a question of *why*.

Why would the man have a gun? Henry asked himself. Why would he have ... The man raised the gun and pointed it at Billy.

Jesus, Henry thought. What the hell!

Billy's mind screamed. *Jesus! He's aiming that thing at me. He's—what the hell do I — Duck! Duck you fool! Drop down in the seat, get behind the dashboard. MOVE!*

But he couldn't move. Billy was frozen in fear as he stared down the cold hollow barrel of the cannon aimed at the center of his forehead.

Billy could see the man's eyes. Death was written there. Jesus.

The man cocked the hammer.

Jesus; I'm gonna die.

Then an ambulance with red lights flashing and sirens blaring slid to a halt in front of their car and two doors flew open and two paramedics jumped out.

People were suddenly everywhere, and the world was filled with noise and chaos. Medics, police officers, other drivers who had stopped to help. A carnival of police cruisers and ambulances and tow trucks and damaged and disabled vehicles surrounded them. They just showed up, out of nowhere. It was as if God had sent the cavalry to help them, as if God had come to their rescue. The Nash-Freely Gang was sitting in the middle of an avalanche of activity and all hell was breaking loose. Snow and wind and sirens and flashing lights, people hollering and running about. Clutter. Disorganization. Bedlam.

The gun vanished inside a coat.

That seems odd, Henry thought. He's hiding the gun. He's acting as if he doesn't want anyone to see that he has a gun. A cop would have no reason to hide his gun, certainly not from other cops. Which meant Henry was right; the man wasn't a cop. But if he wasn't a cop, then what was he? Why had a man, a complete stranger, a man with a gun, walked toward their car in the middle of a snowstorm, in the middle of a major traffic accident, as if he were on a mission, as if it was his intent to shoot someone? Why?

Goofy, Henry thought. Really goofy.

"Here, let me help you with that."

The car door jerked out of Victor's hand.

"You okay, pal?"

It was a paramedic. A huge paramedic. Paul Bunyan in a white coat.

"Yeah, I'm okay," Victor said. "I don't think anything's broken."

Victor hoisted himself up onto the rocker panel of his car.

"Be careful. Don't try to do too much, or move too fast," the paramedic warned. "You could be hurt and not know it. Injury sometimes starts out as numbness—the body's involuntary reaction to protect itself from pain—so, for awhile, you don't feel anything, but then you move and bang! Serious damage."

The paramedic helped Victor crawl down out of his car. Victor's legs were wobbly. The paramedic helped him stand as a second paramedic wheeled a stretcher toward them. He struggled to force it through the snow. He made it. Together they laid Victor onto a stretcher. Paul Bunyan said, "You just lie here. We'll get you to the hospital right away and they can check you over."

When Victor heard that, he tried to get up. "No, wait, I can't go to any hospital. I have to—"

The big, sandy-haired man pushed him back down. "Sir, please lie down. Like I said, you could have internal injuries that haven't shown up yet. It can be very dangerous to move around."

The man's forearm was like a lead weight pushing against Victor's chest. He struggled to free himself, but it did no good. "No, you don't understand," Victor said. "I have to get out of here. I'm in a hurry. I have to—"

"You don't have to go anywhere but to the hospital, sir. We'll take you in; they can check you over; and then, if everything's okay, you can go wherever you please."

"But I don't have time for that. You don't understand. I have to get to the airport. I have to get—"

"Sir, you don't understand. We have to take you to the hospital. That's our job. Once we assist someone in an accident, we have to take them in and have the doctors check them over. Otherwise, if something did turn out to be wrong, and we didn't insist that they go to the hospital, well, take my word for it, we can get in a whole lot of trouble. We could get sued."

Victor couldn't believe it. "That's baloney. I don't have to go to the hospital if I don't want to."

"No, sir, it's not baloney; it's the truth. Happened to a friend of mine. Last summer. Let a woman walk away from an accident—very similar to this one as a matter of fact, six-car pile up over on the Jersey Turnpike. Turned out she was pregnant; then she lost the baby. She sued him. Sued the hospital, too. Sued the policeman who was there and a tow-truck driver. Sued everybody in sight. Jury gave her ten million." He nodded his head up and down. "Hospital says if we help anyone, assist them in any way—assist them by actually touching them, I mean—then we have to bring them in and have a doctor check them over, just to be sure."

Victor pleaded. "But I'm fine. I tell you, I'm fine."

"Woman said the same thing." He shook his head. "Sorry, but, you understand, we can't take any chances. You just relax and this whole thing will be over in no time."

Victor's frustration turned to anger. "Listen young man, if I say I don't want to go to the hospital, that means I don't want to go to the hospital."

The paramedic said yes sir, but he didn't let Victor up.

"Now, will you please let me up? I have to get out of here. I have a very important business appointment to get to. So, if you'll be so kind to get your arm off my chest so I can—"

With that Paul Bunyan pulled a leather strap across Victor's chest, snapped it into a chrome buckle and pulled it tight. Victor's eyes opened wide in horror. "What! What the hell do you think you're doing?"

The medic didn't say a word as he attached a second strap across Victor's legs and pulled it tight. Victor was immobile. A prisoner.

"Damn it, man. Let me out of this thing," Victor screamed. "I'll have your ass for this."

Paul Bunyan never lost his cool. His voice was calm and matter-of-fact. He said, "Maybe I should give you a shot to help you relax. You seem a little paranoid to me, a little too excited. You might struggle and accidentally hurt yourself. Sleep would do you a lot of good. Twenty-four hours of sleep might be just the thing you need."

Victor interpreted that as the threat it was meant to be. He closed his mouth and didn't say a word.

Petals of snow covered his face as the two paramedics wheeled him off toward the flashing red lights of the ambulance.

I'm a dead man, Victor thought to himself.

Chapter 17

"Is anyone hurt?"

Henry turned away from the man with the gun.

The paramedic standing outside Billy's door waited for an answer. He was wearing a white, waist-length coat with a Red Cross patch on the shoulder; the name over the breast pocket said "Walter."

Billy rolled down the window but didn't say anything. He was too busy to speak; he was staring straight ahead, wondering about things, like men with guns, that kind of stuff.

"Walter" looked like a kid. He had a young, smooth-looking face—was he old enough to shave? Henry asked himself—with blonde hair and blue eyes. And a tan. A tan in the middle of December? A surfer, washed in on a big wave from California, was the first thing that entered Henry's mind. Christ, that's all we need. A teenybopper. A punk kid who didn't know diddly about squat, or squat about diddly. He looked even younger than Henry's own son—and nobody looked younger than Brian. Were paramedics getting younger these days, or did he just look young because Henry was getting old? Then Henry thought about the man with the gun and quickly turned back to the windshield.

He was gone.

Henry's eyes searched through the snow. Right, then left. Behind them. To the front again. The man had disappeared. Henry did not understand.

Neither did Walter. He did not understand why everyone in the car was just sitting there staring out the windshield. Were they injured or weren't they? Were they in shock? He decided not to wait any longer. He opened the door, then noticed the bump on Billy's head. "I'd better take a look at that," he said. "Come with me."

Billy hesitated. He didn't see the man with the gun either, but that didn't mean he wasn't out there. He could be hiding somewhere in the snow, waiting. Billy could be in his sights at that very minute. What if he stepped out of the car and the crazy bastard blew his head off? Jesus, he'd never been in such deep shit —deep shit he didn't understand. He couldn't go, and he couldn't stay. He couldn't move. He didn't know what to do. He looked at Walter. And he couldn't ask for help. What was he going to do—ask the paramedic to get the police? Great idea. Hey, Walt, old pal, wanna call a cop? There's a crazy guy out there with a gun. I think he's trying to kill me. Why? Who the hell knows? What's that in the back seat, you say? Oh, nothing, just twenty million or so in stolen property. Don't pay any attention to that.

Why—that's the part that ripped at Billy the most. Why in the hell would a complete stranger pop up out of the snow and aim a gun at him?

Billy turned toward his father, his eyes questioning what to do.

After a second of thought Bill said, "He's right, son. We need to have that taken care of."

"But ..?"

Bill understood. "I know, but first things first. A bump like that can't be ignored."

He looked back at Henry. Henry nodded his agreement. Bill was right; they had to take care of Billy first. They could worry about the man with the gun later. Besides, it was not as if they had a hell of a lot of options; they weren't going anywhere.

"Your dad's right, Billy," Henry said. "We'll come with you." He looked at the paramedic. "Okay?"

"No problem," Walter said.

As the paramedic helped a dazed and confused Billy Freely out of the car, Bill Sr. opened the door on his side and got out too. The first thing he did was look for the man with the gun. All he saw was snow. His concern for Billy made him forget about the man, and he ran around the front of the car and joined his son as Henry climbed out of the back. Henry was about to shut the door when he looked back into the car and realized that the manuscript was still lying there on the seat. Damn, the storm, the accident, the man with the gun; he'd completely forgotten about his buddy, Mark.

As he stared at the box, Henry wished for the first time that he'd never heard of the Mark Twain manuscript. He wished it would disappear for real as easily as it had vanished from his mind. Jesus, talk about your hot potato. Now what? What the hell was he going to do about the manuscript now? It was not the kind of thing he wanted to carry around with him, but, on the other hand, it was not the kind of thing he could just leave lying around either. An hour ago it was the one thing Henry wanted most in life; now it was an albatross. What should he do?

Henry leaned back into the car and picked it up; he didn't have any choice; he had to take it with them. He didn't want it, not now, not as they were all about to shuffle off in an ambulance to who-knows-where, but it looked like he was stuck with it. One thing he knew for sure: He couldn't leave it in the car. He didn't know where he was going to end up much less the car—but he knew that leaving it in the car was the same as signing a confession. He tucked the manuscript under his arm and closed the door. When he looked up he saw Bill staring at him. He shook his head and shrugged. His expression said, "We can't leave it here." Bill looked at Henry, then at the paramedic. Then back to Henry. Bill did not look comfortable.

Together they followed Walter as he took Billy by the arm and led him toward the ambulance. Every few steps Henry would turn around and look behind him, expecting to see the man with the gun turn up again at any second.

He never did.

Did Jesse James feel the same way just before "that dirty little coward" shot him in the back? Henry wondered to himself. Did he feel the bullet coming?

When they got to the ambulance, Walter helped Billy climb into the back. "Watch your step," he said. "These aren't the easiest things to get into."

Henry and Bill waited outside, nervously looking around, wishing Billy would hurry and get in; they were eager to claim the protection of the steel-sided vehicle.

When it finally came Henry's turn to climb in, he realized that Billy was not the ambulance's first customer. A man was already inside lying on a stretcher watching them. Henry looked at him and wondered why he was strapped down like that. He didn't look injured; he looked angry.

The paramedic took Billy up to the front of the ambulance while Henry looked for a place to sit. A canvas, fold-down bench strapped to the wall solved the problem. Henry unhooked it and sat down. He put the white box in his lap. Resting his elbows on the manuscript he locked his fingers together and dropped his chin on his hands. This was not good, this was not good at all. What the hell was he going to do now? He had to think. He had to figure something out. Analyze the situation, go over it in his mind. They were in an ambulance, in a snow storm, probably headed for the nearest hospital. One of them may be injured, and may need medical attention. (Jesus, God, don't let Billy's injury be serious, give us a break, the one thing we don't need is to get stuck in a hospital.) The other two were fine—at least physically. And outside, somewhere, was a man with a gun, who, for some reason, seemed to be extremely interested in the Nash-Freely Gang. Henry looked down. He had a box full of stolen property sitting in his lap. Property worth millions.

Henry looked up and noticed that the man on the stretcher was staring at the manuscript. His eyes were glued to the big red bow on top. Shit. Of course he was staring. Why wouldn't he stare? Henry thought. Why wouldn't anyone stare? It wasn't like the damned red bow was a beacon or anything. A real eye-catcher. Sticks out like a damn sore thumb, Henry thought. Just what I need. Why don't I just wear a damn neon sign over my damn head for chrissake? Get rid of the bow, Henry. It's too much.

Bill Sr. was staring at the bow too. He had gone forward with Billy, and was standing by him as the paramedic went through his examination, but he was looking at Henry, and at the package. He watched without saying a word, waiting to see what Henry was going to do.

Henry, too, was waiting to see what Henry was going to do. Easier to wait than act. Finally he decided: He would continue to do exactly what he was doing, he would sit there and do nothing. Nothing but sweat. When in doubt, sweat. Maybe something would come to him. Wait and sweat. And maybe panic a little.

And feel sorry for yourself. Feel like a trapped rat on a sinking ship. Here we are, Henry's mind said, the James Gang, trapped in a stupid ambulance. Trapped by the storm, trapped by circumstances, trapped by money problems. Trapped by fear and incompetence. Frank and Jesse and Billy the Kid, three trapped rats. The sheriff was probably out rounding up a posse at that very minute. *"Come on men, when we catch 'em we'll string 'em up."*

Talk about major shit.

And what about the man with the gun—who was he? Who was the big man with the big gun? A bounty hunter?

Jesus, Henry wished he were somewhere else. Things had gotten real complicated real fast. This was not the way it was supposed to turn out. So far everything had gone about as wrong as it could go. The weather, the accident—the only thing that went right was the actual robbery, and that had been Billy's idea.

Henry felt like a complete fool. Henry Nash, Master Thief. Jesus, how about Master Jerk? Jesse James would have been so proud. The only part of this whole mess that had turned out halfway right was the robbery, and they had a sixteen-year-old kid to thank for that.

Of course, if it hadn't been for the sixteen-year-old kid, then they probably wouldn't be up to their ass in alligators at this point either. Highway robbery, traffic accidents, on their way to the hospital with a stolen manuscript in his goddam lap. With a sheriff's posse after them, no doubt. And a bounty hunter. Maybe even the cavalry. If it wasn't for the sixteen-year-old kid, they'd all be home right now thinking how great a plan it had been, and it probably would have worked if it hadn't been for the damned weather.

Okay, they wouldn't have the manuscript, but they wouldn't be in deep shit either. They'd be right back were they started, and all of a sudden being right back where they started—outta work but outta jail—looked pretty good to Henry.

Henry jumped when the driver of the ambulance slammed the doors shut. Is that what the doors of the slammer sound like when they lock you up for the night? Henry wondered. Is that what it sounds like in the hoosegow?

The paramedic finished his exam and stood up. He looked down at Billy and said, "I think you're going to be all right. You seem to be focusing okay." To Bill Sr., "It's a nasty bump, but I have a hunch that it looks worse than it is." Back to Billy, "We'll get you to the hospital right away, and they can give you a thorough exam just to make sure. It's my bet that you probably have nothing more serious than a minor concussion." He looked at Billy's father again. "It's nothing to worry about. If it looks like he's getting sleepy, talk to him. Don't let him fall asleep, okay?"

Bill nodded and sat down beside Billy.

Walter then asked Bill if he was all right. Bill thought for a minute, then said his shoulder hurt a little—punctuating it by moving his right shoulder and grimacing—but he was sure it was nothing serious, he'd be fine. Walter nodded knowingly and said they'd take a look at that, too, as soon as they got to the hospital. Then he turned to Henry and asked him the same question. Henry didn't hesitate. He said he was fine. He didn't bother to tell Walter that his wrist had just started to throb. He didn't want anyone knowing about his wrist. He'd have to put the package down to have someone look at his wrist, and no way was he going to do that. Walter ended by making the mistake of asking Victor Romaine if there was anything he could do for him.

Victor had a list. "Yeah," he blurted out. "The first thing you can do is let me out of here. I told your friend up there that I was fine, but he wouldn't listen. Okay? I'm fine, honest. I feel great. No problem. And I'm in a hurry. I don't have time for this. I'm not hurt, and I don't need to go to the damn hospital. So, if you'd be so kind, would you please take off these stupid straps, let me out of this stupid ambulance, and let me get back to my business?"

The paramedic leaned down and put his hand on Victor's shoulder. He was young, but he'd dealt with hysterical people before. "We'll be at the hospital in no time, sir. Just take it easy. I'm sure you're right, but it's better to be safe than sorry." He gave Victor's shoulder a pat and then turned and climbed into the front of the ambulance to join the driver.

"Hey," Victor said. "Get back here."

Walter ignored him. He mumbled something to the driver that Henry couldn't hear and the driver smiled and nodded. Victor said shit as the ambulance turned on its siren and started to drive off.

Shit is right, Henry agreed. "Double shit" was more like it. He looked down at Victor. Hey, I don't want to be here any more than you do, pal. You think you got it bad, you should have my problems. How'd you like to be sitting here with the police hot on your trail, a bounty hunter after your hide, and a stolen Mark Twain manuscript sitting in your lap?

Scotty saw the flashing red lights of ambulances and police cars in the south-bound lane as he turned left on Riverside Drive and crossed over the expressway. It never entered his mind that they were headed in a direction that he should be headed. Just going to—or coming from—an accident, he thought. Not surprising, in this weather there was bound to be a pile-up or two.

As long as he wasn't part of it, that was the important thing, Scotty thought. He had work to do; he didn't have time to be part of a traffic accident.

He turned west on Westchester Avenue and headed back toward Manhattan.

Scotty had work to do all right. He had to recover some property that belonged to him. Not the Twain manuscript—that belonged to Louise Ann Bridges. He didn't give two shits about that. He was after something a lot more valuable. At least to him. He had to recover his life. He had to recover his future. He had to get his pension back.

I could strangle that damn Gorman. If Parker Gorman were here right now I'd put my forearm on his Adam's apple and squeeze until his eyes popped out of his head. One twist of the wrist and Gorman would not have to concern himself anymore with owning The Jefferson National Insurance Company. One twist of the wrist and Gorman would be off to that great big insurance company in the sky, peddling policies for the Holy Ghost. Vengeance is mine, sayeth Scotty Hunter.

But vengeance would have to wait. The NYPD's 16th Precinct was Scotty's current objective. He had a friend in the Robbery Division that might be able to give him a handle on what the hell was going on. If anybody knew anything it would be Inspector Cliff Wiseman.

Apparently nobody knew anything. Wiseman told Scotty he didn't know shit about the robbery.

Not what Scotty wanted to hear. "What do you mean you don't know shit?" Scotty asked. "You're in Robbery, aren't you? Was this a robbery or wasn't it?"

Wiseman gave Scotty a sneer and shook his head as he stuck a cigarette into the left corner of his mouth—a move that looked as though it took all the strength he had. Normally a vital man, the inspector was anything but spit-and-polish today. As a matter of fact, he looked as though he hadn't slept in weeks. His hair hadn't seen a comb for at least the same length of time that his face hadn't seen a razor, and his eyes looked like the eyes of a sixty-year-old.

Scotty knew for a fact, however, that according to the number recorded in the Birth Date box on Wiseman's PQI Form (Personal Questionnaire Indicator), Clifford Wiseman was a long way from sixty—twenty years to be exact. He had moved into a new decade just this past September, but it was the big Four-O, not Mr. Sixty.

Wiseman's bloodshot eyes looked sad and lonely, and the deep lines etched in his forehead would not disappear after a good night's rest. His usually clear features seemed hazy today. Scotty could see he was out of sorts, out of patience, and out of focus. His tie was loose around his neck and his shirt was as wrinkled as his brow. He sat down in his chair, leaned back, put his feet up on his desk and lit his cigarette.

"It's a state problem, comrade," he said, blowing smoke at the ceiling. "Happened on I-Niner-Five. Outta my ball park. It belongs to the governor's boy scouts, and, just between us girls, they're welcome to it. I got plenty to keep me busy just chasin' my own tail."

"State police? You're kidding."

Wiseman smiled. He would never be hired to do a toothpaste commercial.

"Can't you tell me anything?" Scotty asked.

Wiseman shrugged. "Stay off the highways. Weather's a bitch out there."

Scotty frowned. "Cute. Come on, Cliff, quit jerking me around. What do you know?"

The inspector shook his head slowly from left to right. "Don't know squat, and I intend to keep right on not knowing squat. A little knowledge is a dangerous thing. Fat, dumb and happy, that's me."

Wiseman was six feet tall and as skinny as a rail.

"Bullshit," Scotty said.

And he was as smart as they came. "Hey, would I lie to you?" Street smart.

Scotty gave him a suspicious look, then got out a stick of gum and popped it into his mouth. He dropped the wrapper into the wastebasket beside

Wiseman's desk and helped himself to the chair directly across from the inspector. He chewed on his gum and the police detective smoked his cigarette. Time passed.

When Scotty saw that Wiseman was not going to volunteer anything he said, "How 'bout a description of the vehicle the bad guys were driving? You can give that much, can't you? Model? Make? Color? What did they look like? Height, weight, color of hair? What direction they were heading when last seen? You gotta know that."

"Scars, tattoos, distinguishing marks? Like they say on TV? That kind of stuff?"

Scotty could tell Wiseman needed sleep, his demeanor was as rumpled as his appearance. Underpaid and overworked, he'd heard that one before: The Blue Knights' Twin Towers. He felt sorry for Wiseman, but he had a job to do too.

"You know what I mean," Scotty said. "Something that came in over your computers, say, in the last hour or so. Something new. Even if you're not looking for them, you gotta know as much as there is to know, just in case they decide to hide out in your city. Right? So, quit playing games and tell me what you know."

"Ain't my city, man. Belongs to the taxpayers."

Scotty waited.

Wiseman puffed on his cigarette. Then he talked as he exhaled the smoke, "You got the coverage on this, is that what you're telling me?"

Scotty gave him an impatient look. "No, I just love driving around in a snowstorm."

Wiseman raised his eyebrows. His desk was stacked high with files. "Hey, I can live with that. Man's gotta get his kicks any way he can."

Wiseman took another puff and blew a smoke ring straight up in the air. After it faded he lowered his eyes back to Scotty. "How big a ticket we talkin' here? Ten million? Fifteen? Twenty?"

Scotty ran his finger across his throat in the classic cutting-one's-throat-with-a-knife gesture.

Wiseman grinned. "That much, huh?"

"Enough to make us gag if we have to ante up."

Wiseman shook his head. "Must be a bitch havin' to come up with that kind of money. Glad it's you and not me. All I have to worry about is a couple dozen robberies every week, city councilmen trying to cut my budget, newspapers that keep printing about how the good old N-Y-C is turning into a jungle more and more every day—*Good God, it's not safe to walk the streets anymore; where the hell are all the police anyway?* And to top it all off," Wiseman stopped talking and looked over at the corner office, the office of Lester P. Bookman, Captain, NYPD, then turned back to Scotty; when he spoke, his voice was a whisper," I've got a Captain who has aspirations of being Chief some day, so pity the poor bastard that fucks up and screws him out of that next promotion." Pause. Then, in full voice, "And, oh yeah, two kids who want to go to college in a couple of years, and college only costs fifteen grand a year now, what the hell will it cost when they're ready?"

Scotty tried to be cute. "Hey, no problem. I just happen to have the perfect solution for that. For a very nominal amount, I'm sure Jefferson National will be more than happy to set you up with an annuity that will handle all your college problems at one time. Put it away now, and it'll be there for the future when you need it. Want me to have one of our salesmen give you a call?" Scotty smiled. "I'd be glad to do it. Wouldn't be any trouble at all. Honest. I just give him your name and he'll take care of the rest. And you don't have to worry, once he has your name he won't be a pain in the ass about calling you. Whoever heard of an insurance salesman being a pain in the ass? Right?" Scotty's smile was more like a smirk. "What do you say *amigo?*"

Wiseman didn't smile. "What do you say I shoot you six times and then throw you in jail for littering?"

Stanley barely managed to get his gun put away before the ambulance slid to a stop at his side and a paramedic jumped out.

He cursed to himself: So close. Damn. Another second and he'd have taught that kid a lesson he'd never forget. He'd have taught him not to drive cars with loud mufflers. He'd have taught him to show some respect for his elders. And he'd have taught him not to give people the finger. Especially strangers. You never know about strangers. You never know when a stranger just might turn out to be a real bad ass. You never know when a stranger might just turn out to be a killer.

Not that Stanley was actually going to kill the little punk son of a bitch. Hell no, he was too smart for that. Stanley didn't kill people without a plan. That was stupid. It was that spur-of-the-moment kind of stuff that always got your ass in a jam. Just scare him, that was the plan. Point the gun at him and watch his eyes pop out. Make him load his pants. Or better yet "wing him," as the cowboys used to say. Stick a round in a muscle—a lot of pain but no serious damage.

But Stanley knew he couldn't do that either. A gunshot wound would bring a lot of questions, police up the ass. He wanted to. He wanted to real bad. But he had not thought it out; he was reacting to emotion, to anger. He had no plan of attack, no plan of escape. He couldn't shoot some dumb ass kid just because he wanted to—even though the little bastard deserved it—without an escape plan. Where the hell was the way out? Where the hell could he go in a snowstorm? No, he had to be content just to scare him. Show him the gun, let him think about it, let him think about the bullet screaming through his body tearing out a big chunk of flesh on the way in and an even bigger chunk on the way out. Let him think about the pain. Let him think about dying.

Let him think what might have happened, and then walk away. No evidence. Mental pain, but no evidence. Just the imagination of some jerkass kid who didn't know what the hell he was talking about.

Stanley cursed to himself as he looked around for Victor Romaine's car. That's what pissed him off more than anything. He'd had the target in his sight—had been following him all over the goddam city for the last two hours—before that dipshit kid had to act like a wiseass and screw everything up.

The snow was coming down in buckets; Stanley wiped it out of his eyes. He couldn't see twenty feet in front of him. He decided his best bet would be to head back to his cab and start over. He had Victor's home address; he'd just pay him a little visit at home.

He never made it. A paramedic caught up to him before he'd gone ten feet. His eyes went directly to the blood on Stanley's face.

"Better let me take a look at that, sir," the paramedic said.

Stanley's initial reaction was to brush him away. He didn't have time to screw with a pimply-faced kid—a *second* pimply-faced kid. He'd bled before. It was just a little cut. Didn't even hurt. Stick on a Band-Aid and it would be fine. But then the wind stopped blowing, and when Stanley looked around he saw Victor Romaine being wheeled into one of the other ambulances. His prey had not disappeared after all. Just like that, Stanley had a new plan. He decided that the shortest distance between two points might just be an ambulance ride. What better place to put the guy in the hospital than in the hospital? Eliminate the middleman, so to speak.

"Yeah, ah, okay," Stanley said. "Go ahead."

The medic took Stanley by the arm and started to lead him over to the ambulance. "Let's get you out of this weather first," the medic said.

When they got to the ambulance the young man opened the door, stepped to one side, then holding on to Stanley's elbow helped him climb into the vehicle. Inside, another medic was administering to Stanley's cab driver. Seated off to one side was a second cab driver and Tommy Kosuri.

Tommy's right arm was killing him. He'd banged it against the door handle when the cab he was riding in crashed into the cab in front of them. Damn, of all the luck. I bet it's broken, Tommy thought.

Stanley looked at Tommy; recognition flashed. Stanley never forgot a face. Where the hell did *he* come from? Stanley gave him a dirty look, then sat there staring out the back door at Victor Romaine's ambulance as the medic put a bandage on his forehead.

"We goin' to the hospital?" Stanley asked, watching Victor Romaine's ambulance with the eyes of an eagle.

"I think that would be the smart thing to do," the paramedic said. "They can check you over more thoroughly there, make sure nothing's missed."

"We goin' to the same place as that ambulance?"

"Yes, sir. Saint Mary's. We'll be there before you know it."

Stanley smiled.

Tommy looked at Stanley and rubbed his arm. It did nothing for the pain; it was bone pain, not muscle pain. He grit his teeth. Broken arm or not, I'm not letting you out of my sight, he thought to himself.

After a few minutes Tommy leaned his head back against the side of the ambulance and closed his eyes. Never in his wildest imagination would he have ever dreamt that what had happened to him in the last twenty-four hours was going to happen. His whole world had been turned upside down. First the call from Tanaka, the assignment—the *obligation*. Then the storm. The fool at the auction house. The robbery. And then the pursuit, following the pig sitting across from him. And now this, stuck in the middle of a snowstorm, not knowing what to do, not knowing what he was going to tell Tanaka, not—the pain in his arm jabbed at him. *Damn.* And to top it all off, there was a good chance Tommy Kosuri had a broken arm. Tommy had gone from pauper to prince and back to pauper again. A nothing one minute, a hero the next.

Now a nothing again. A nothing with a broken arm. Well, this isn't over yet, Tommy vowed. There are still a few rounds to go. I will succeed. I will. Or go down trying.

"Hey, pal, do me a favor. Unbuckle these straps, will you?"

Henry looked at Victor Romaine. "What?"

Victor motioned at the nylon straps with his eyes. "These things. Take them off, please."

Henry opened his mouth but didn't know what to say. Then, "Jeez, I don't know. I—"

Victor talked fast. "Hey, listen, you gotta help me. I have to get out of here. It's really important. Understand? It's a matter of life and death. I need your help. Okay? Please? Those idiots up front won't listen to me. I have to get out of here and I don't have much time."

Henry looked at Bill. Bill looked at Henry, thought for a minute, then said to Victor, "I, ah, really don't think that would be a very good idea, mister. I mean, I'm sure they know what they're doing. They wouldn't strap you down if there wasn't a good reason."

"That's bullshit," Victor said. "I'm fine. Honest. I told them I was fine. I told them twenty times I was fine. But they're either too stupid or too stubborn to listen. You've got to help me. I've got to get out of here."

Henry was about to say something when he noticed that Billy had closed his eyes. "Bill," Henry said, motioning toward Billy.

"Billy!" Bill Sr. said with a lurch, shaking Billy. Billy's eyes popped open. "Don't close your eyes, son. You have to stay awake. If you have a concussion, you can't fall asleep."

"Uh, why's that, Dad?" Billy asked.

Before Bill Sr. could respond, Victor piped in. "Because if you have a concussion and you fall asleep you could go into a coma." There was no patience in his voice.

Billy swallowed hard, then looked at his father for an explanation.

Bill was looking at Victor. "He could go into a coma?" he repeated slowly, obviously shaken.

Victor Romaine didn't have time for this. "Hey, it's no big deal," Victor said. "Just don't let him go to sleep until they get a chance to check him over. I've had concussions before, a couple of them, and there's nothing to worry about."

Bill Sr. didn't looked convinced.

Victor didn't care. He had a bigger problem than a simple little concussion to worry about. "So, what about it?" Victor asked. "Are you going to let me out? If I don't get out of here now, I won't be fine in a day or two."

Henry wanted more information. "But— Why'd they strap you down if there's nothing wrong with you?"

Victor looked irritated. He didn't have time to play Twenty Questions. "How the hell should I know? They're just a couple of kids. Standard operating procedure, I guess," he said. "They said that's what they're 'supposed' to do, according to the book." Victor turned away, then back again. "Hey, they're just a couple of wet-behind-the-ears punks. They don't know what to do. They do what they're told. They don't have enough common sense to know any better."

Henry could sympathize with that. He didn't know what to do either. And youth had nothing to do with it. Age didn't help when it came to handling a catastrophe. You either had it, or you didn't. Henry said he was sorry, but, "I think we'd better just leave you the way you are. I'm sorry, but if they strapped you down it must have been for a reason. Maybe they know something we don't. They're probably just being cautious. Maybe they're afraid if you move you could hurt yourself."

"Jesus, will you listen to me? Read my lips: I told you, I'm fine. There's not a thing wrong with me. The kid over there has bigger problems than I do, and he doesn't have a thing to worry about." Victor struggled against the straps. "I've got to get out of here and I've got to get out of here now." His face turned red with anger and frustration. "Will you please unfasten these things?"

Henry looked out the back of the ambulance. It was still snowing. He turned to Victor. "Mister, even if we believed you, and I'm not saying that we don't, I mean, why would you lie? Right? But the fact of the matter is, even if we did unhook those straps, where would you go? Look out there; there's no place to go. There's nothing out there but a whole lot of bad weather. So you might as well just relax. Like it or not, we're all trapped here. We're all going to the hospital, so you might as well just lie back and enjoy the ride."

He looked down at the manuscript, then at Bill and Billy, then back at Victor. Then said, "Believe me, friend, nobody wants to be here less than we do."

Chapter 18

I-95 EASTBOUND WAS BUMPER TO BUMPER.

Not that slow traffic was his major problem. Roger Muldowney had a much bigger dilemma than that. Like, for instance, now that he had decided to go after Henry himself, just where the hell was he going to look, for starters? The fact that he didn't have the foggiest idea what he was doing, or where he should be doing it, was the first hurdle Roger Muldowney had to vault. He was after Henry, but where was Henry?

And had Henry been dumb enough to actually pull off the robbery? And was Roger just as dumb to be out here in the middle of a blizzard looking for a man who may or may not need to be looked for? Roger's windshield wipers flapped across the windshield, working overtime, set on HIGH, batting at nothing. He turned them down to NORMAL; the storm seemed to be easing. The snow had regressed to flurries—little white butterflies that skipped across his path—and the wind was no longer the constant force that it had been. But it was still there, coming in random gusts now, buffeting his car, reminding him it was alive and well, still a force that had to be reckoned with. And there was plenty of ice under his Goodyear radials, too, so, although the storm had backed off a little, driving was not a piece-a-cake even with four-wheel drive. On days like this Roger was glad he had his Chevy Blazer. He reached down and flicked on the radio; maybe there would be something on the radio about the robbery.

If there was a robbery.

There was a positive thought, Roger realized. Maybe the robbery never took place after all. Maybe it never happened. Maybe Henry had wised up at the last minute and instead of being a wanted criminal, a highway robber, he was actually home now, sitting in his rec room doing some serious drinking, watching the tube, while Roger was out risking life and limb driving around on a highway filled with frightened drivers and dangerous pavement. Maybe Henry had called the Robbery of the Century off. Maybe this whole thing was just one big waste of time.

Maybe. The world was full of maybes.

Nothing on the radio but noise—music, according to the DJ. But the DJ sounded like a jerk, so what did he know?

As Roger approached I-95 North, he could see flashing red lights just below him and off to his left. Ambulances and police cars were coming off the I-95 ramp heading for 278. That didn't surprise him; it was a perfect day for ambulances and police cars. Their sirens were on, and with red lights flashing the traffic moved out of the way. More or less. As much as you could expect traffic to move out of the way in New York. "Yield" was not a biggie when it came to New York drivers. "Get that piece of shit out of the way!" was more like it.

Roger stared at the ambulances as they approached. Can't be too serious, he thought to himself. They seemed to be taking their good old time about getting to the hospital—out for a Saturday afternoon drive. Okay, the weather forced caution, but if it was a matter of life and death they would have ignored the weather. Those guys were reckless when it came to emergencies, Roger knew that. Back a few years—that Saturday afternoon when he'd cut his finger on the lawn mower, he was hurrying, trying to get done so he could get to the stupid golf course—they didn't stop for anything. Got him to the hospital before the blood even soaked through the towel—sirens blaring, lights flashing, charging through intersections, running red lights. Kind of exciting, actually. Roger did have to admit, however, he was a little embarrassed that they were doing all that for him. He didn't think it was that big a deal—just a cut finger. Okay, he felt a little faint, but that was about it. He had to hand it to those guys—they'd done a hell of a job.

But not today. He didn't want any part of ambulances today. Don't want to end up in one of those, Roger told himself. Don't do anything stupid. Don't hurry. He'd never get to Henry if he was involved in an accident.

Roger reached down and switched off the radio.

"Okay, let's figure this thing out," he said aloud to himself. "According to Henry's plan he was going to swipe the thing on the way to the auction house; 'in transit,' those were his exact words. Didn't have the know-how to sneak in in the dead of night like a cat burglar and lift it like a pro, right Henry? Had to grab it on the run." Roger thought for a minute. "Henry said the heist would go down somewhere between Hartford and New York City." He stopped, unbelieving. "'Heist?' 'Go down?' Jesus, I can't believe it, even I'm beginning to talk like a crook. Henry, you'd be proud of me."

The traffic in front of Roger began to slow down. Then it stopped completely. Roger stopped. What, another accident up ahead?

Roger sat there and watched as two ambulances came down the ramp and moved slowly under his lane. Probably on their way to Saint Mary's, he concluded, then continued the conversation he was having with himself: "Okay, so, between here and Hartford, what's the best place to pull a 'heist'?"

Thought. Then, "I'd say just north of here. Ninety-Five south somewhere around south of New Haven, close to—hey, that's it! That's what Henry said!" Henry's words came back to him. "Now I remember. Henry said he'd hit 'em near Baychester exit, or the Bronx Pelham Parkway. Those were his exact words: Baychester, or the Bronx Pelham Parkway. That way it was just a hop, skip and a jump, navigate the George Washington Bridge, and he was home free." Roger looked out his window. The snow had started to pick up again. "That is, if the weather hasn't screwed everything up. Or if it turned out that the manuscript had an escort after all, and thirty cops in riot gear were too much for you to handle, old pal."

Or if you haven't gotten shot. Or if ... The world had as many "or ifs" as it did "maybes."

Roger's eyes drifted back to the ambulances—speaking of "shot." An ambulance, what about that? Maybe that's where his best friend was right now. Maybe he wasn't at home in front of the tube after all. Maybe at that very moment Henry Nash was lying flat on his back in an ambulance with a bullet in his chest, fighting for his life, trying to breathe. A "sucking chest wound," that's what they called it in the army, because you could actually see it sucking for air. Maybe Henry "Jesse James" Nash had caught a round in the middle of his big dumb gut and at that very moment was on the way to the hospital, sucking for air, one breath away from The Big D.

Dead.

Dead?

No way. Roger didn't want to think about that. He shook his head. "Tell me you weren't really stupid enough to try to pull this thing off, Henry. Tell me I'm just out on a wild goose chase, and you're at home right now wondering what your old buddy Roger is doing out driving around on a day like this."

The ambulances had moved below him and were now coming out on the other side. Roger's lane of traffic started to move again. Roger eased his way forward. He would go north on 95 and hope and pray he would be in time to stop the bad guys. Unless they'd already done it and he'd already missed them and they were already back at the hideout gloating over their loot.

Roger casually glanced down as the second ambulance came out from under the overpass. His eyes drifted to the lead ambulance. Just as he was about to turn away (can't gawk around in this kind of weather) his eyes popped open. The first ambulance, thirty feet or so in front of the second, going up the ramp on to 278, was at eye-level; he had a perfect view into the rear through the door. The light inside was on, the glass windows clear, the visibility perfect. It was like looking at two television screens: One screen was blank; the one with the picture in it made him gulp.

There, sitting in the back, staring off into space, was none other than Jesse James himself.

"Watch out for that truck, Ralph."

Ralph eased the steering wheel to the right, calm as a cucumber. "I saw it Lilith. Don't worry."

"Don't worry? Easy for you to say—you're not sitting in the coffin seat. You sit over here some time, and then maybe we'd see how you like it."

Ralph was driving; Lilith was riding shotgun. Louise and Raymond Bridges were in the back. Lilith had not shut her mouth in the last two hours.

"Your driving has been scaring the hell out of me lately, Ralph. I think you're getting old, you know that?"

"Now Lilith, I'm fine."

"You're turning into an old coot, Ralph."

Unruffled and staring straight ahead, "Sharp as a tack, my dear. Sharp as a tack."

In a disgusted tone, "Yeah, right, a tack. That's a joke. You have a hard time *seeing* a tack." She turned and looked back at Raymond, then at Louise. "Maybe we ought to get ourselves a couple of younger husbands, what do you think, Louise?" She winked.

Louise answered with a friendly but weak smile.

Then Ralph said, "The roads are really bad, that's the big problem. Have been all the way from Hartford. But don't you worry your pretty little head, I can handle it. We're almost there. I think another half hour or so."

Lilith grunted. "Yeah, you can handle it all right. That's what you said that time in Colorado. Remember that? Damn near drove us off the side of that damn mountain and don't say you didn't."

Oh dear God, Ralph thought to himself, would he never quit hearing about that? It had happened over five years ago and Lilith still continued to bring it up. "Now Lilith. That was a long time ago. The road was just narrow, that's all. We weren't as close to the edge as you think. I was—"

"Are you sure those glasses are okay?" Lilith gave him a suspicious look.

"Do they fit okay? Can you see all right? Is everything in focus? When was the last time you had your eyes checked, Ralph? What did Dr. Carter say?"

Ralph shook his head slowly. "Said I was fine."

"When was that?"

"April."

"What year?" There was a smirk on Lilith's face.

Ralph smiled. "This year."

Lilith's lips moved but she didn't say anything. Then, "That was eight months ago."

"Yes, dear."

"A lot can change in eight months, Ralph. Eyes can go overnight, especially at your age."

"I can see fine. Don't worry."

Lilith grunted again and then went silent.

After a few minutes from the back seat came, "Are you sure this is a good idea?" It was Louise. She sounded frightened. "I mean, with the weather being so bad and all, I was thinking maybe we should just find a place to stay for the night—until this thing is over. We can go into the city in the morning. They probably won't know anything about the manuscript until tomorrow anyway. I mean—"

Lilith turned. "Wait 'til morning? Are you out of your mind? After we've come all this way you want to stop now? Get with it, girlie. We can't afford to wait until morning. Hell, those crooks can screw us out of two fortunes by the time the sun comes up tomorrow. Those kind of people stay up nights figuring out ways to rip people off. You have to get with the program, Dearie. The longer we wait the more time it gives the enemy to plan its defense. We have to hit them now, before they're ready for us. We've got to strike while the iron's hot, before those jokers at that insurance company have a chance to make plans."

For the first time Raymond spoke. "Looks pretty bad to me. Maybe we—"

Lilith acted as if he wasn't there. "No way. We aren't stopping. That's final."

Ralph tried to help. "Don't worry, Mrs. Bridges. It looks like the snow is starting to ease a little." He was not only trying to calm down the passengers in the back, but at the same time lend support to his wife. "Maybe the worst is over."

Lilith didn't catch on. She looked out at the storm. "Doesn't look like it's slowing down to me. Looks as bad as it ever did." She turned to her husband. "You sure you aren't going blind?"

Ralph stared straight ahead.

After a few minutes, "Actually, we should have been there by now," Lilith said. "That's what really ticks me off. Waiting around that damned airport forever. Waiting for that other stupid airplane. If we had taken off when we were supposed to take off we could have gotten here before all this happened. Waiting at Dallas on that other stupid plane is what screwed it all up."

Louise leaned forward in her seat. "Dallas—that's where we changed planes. Is that where you're from?"

Lilith was about to respond when something hit her. A light bulb flashed on in her brain. "What do you mean, that's where you changed planes?' You switched planes in Dallas?"

"Yes. That's where we connected with our flight to New York, well, Hartford, actually, as it turned out."

Lilith smelled a rat. "Connected from where?"

"California. We were out there for," she beamed with pride," The Jay Leno Show. We—"

"You! You're the one. It was *your* plane that we had to wait on in Dallas."

The look of pride drained from Louise's face. She didn't know what to say. She'd apparently stepped on a rattlesnake. She leaned back in her seat. "Well, I, er—"

"You're the reason we had to wait around forever," Lilith spit out.

Louise looked sheepish.

"You're the reason we're stuck in the middle of this Godforsaken blizzard."

Louise gulped. "Well, I, I don't think ... I ..."

She let the words trail away. Lilith had turned around and Louise realized it was no use talking; she was staring at the back of Lilith's head.

After they had driven a few more miles Louise leaned over to Raymond and said quietly, "Maybe we should have stayed in Hartford. We could have gone to our house and waited until this storm—"

Not quietly enough. Lilith overheard. "Your house!" she screamed. It just dawned on her. "That's right, you live in Hartford. I forgot."

"Well, actually, we live just outside—"

"Tell me something, Dearie. If you live in Hartford, why in the hell did we rent a car when your car was already at the airport?"

Louise gave her a funny look.

"We could have saved a few bucks, that's what I'm saying. I don't know about you, but Ralph and I aren't made of money. Even splitting fifty-fifty, this little sucker is going to cost a pretty penny."

Ralph knew what Lilith was thinking, but he'd never accuse her of it: *If we had your car, we could have stuck you with paying for it all.*

"But our car wasn't at the airport," Louise offered.

"Ohhhhhhh?"

"No, our car's at Kennedy. We drove to New York when we flew to California, knowing we'd be coming back that way in time for the auction."

Lilith was disappointed; she'd gone for the jugular and missed. She hated it when an apparent advantage disappeared. "Oh."

Another few miles of silence passed. Outside the storm continued. Inside the car, silence, tension. Then, "Ralph! Watch out for that car!" Lilith screamed.

Ralph jerked the steering wheel to the right, more as a knee-jerk reaction to Lilith's scream than to any danger of hitting the car that was passing him on the left.

The car started to slide off the highway. Three people held their breaths. Ralph gathered his calm, turned into the skid, and then, as though he did this kind of thing every day, navigated the vehicle back onto the highway. No problem.

"No problem, dear," Ralph said. "That car wasn't even close. It was just passing. You can relax."

Lilith gave him an evil eye but didn't say a word. As she stared ahead at the car that had just passed them something about it caught her eye. "Ralph, didn't we just pass that car a few miles back?"

"I don't know, Dear."

"Well I do. We sure as hell did. Same damn car. Got those stupid skis on top. Wish to God the jerk driving would figure out whether he wanted to pass or get off the pot."

Marcella didn't notice that the car she was passing panicked and swerved to the right just as she got up beside it. One might have thought that she would have heard Lilith scream, but she didn't; thoughts of the robbery were paramount in her mind and overshadowed all else. Although the condition of the highway was something that concerned her, she was able to ease it aside and concentrate on the matter at hand; somehow she had to get to New York City and find out what happened to the white box with the big red bow.

Sure, other people were looking for it too, but they didn't care about it as much as she did. Not really. Not really *care*. It was just an artifact to them, something to drool over, a commodity, something with a big price tag. A valuable piece of property to be put on the auction block so a bunch of slobbering buffoons could bid on it like starving savages, wolves gathered around a dead carcass. They didn't care about the literary significance, the intrinsic value, the fact that it was penned in the hand of the master, himself. *Dollar* value was all that mattered to them. Commercial potential. As far as Marcella was concerned they were all little more than a bunch of parasites who fed off greed, scavengers whose only interest was to have something that no one else had. They didn't want it; they wanted to *possess* it. They wanted to get it in their hot, grubby little paws only so they could tuck it away somewhere, hide it in a vault where no one else could enjoy it.

Hoard it.

It had made her half-sick every time she thought about the fact that Mark Twain's manuscript, *the* Mark Twain, the *one-and-only* Mark Twain, was ultimately destined to be purchased by some idiot who had more money than brains, some complete fool who could never truly understand or appreciate what he possessed. It was not worth money to Marcella; it was worth more. It was worth everything. It was priceless. It was everything life was meant to be, a once-in-a-lifetime find. History. The kind of thing that made life, existence, worthwhile. Was she the only one who understood that? Was she the only one who cared? Did they not understand that Marcella did not simply *like* Twain? Marcella *adored* Mark Twain. She *revered* Twain, as everyone should.

Michael didn't even *read* Twain. He didn't understand. He would never understand. He *couldn't* understand. He read Stephen *King* for crying out loud.

And, unfortunately, to Marcella's dismay, most people were more like Michael than her. Even the visitors to the museum seemed more or less unruffled by the whole thing. Yeah, it was neat; and, yeah, it was in Twain's hand; but, hey, I remember when I read *Huckleberry Finn*, and it was o-*kay*, but it wasn't *that* great. I mean, it was no *The Day Of The Jackal*, or *The Hunt For Red October*. It wasn't a real exciting adventure story, you know what I mean? Certainly didn't keep me on the edge of my chair. Me, I like exciting stuff. Stuff you can't put down. Danielle Steele; Tom Clancy; Sidney Sheldon. Sure, the critics loved it, but critics never do seem to like what the public likes. Matter of personal tastes, I guess. Still, can't see why they ever made such a fuss about it. But, hey, it's a free country.

Free country? Free to be a complete jerk if you wanted to be, Marcella would concede that point. She would concede it, but she would never understand it. She would never be able to comprehend how people could be such fools. Was life that simple to them? That shallow? They seldom, if ever, even bothered to ask about the book, or about the man. All they ever wanted to know was "How much do you think it's worth?"

Worth? Did Twain's manuscript only have meaning to them in terms of dollars? Was that all there was to their lives: bank accounts, and BMWs, and backyard barbecues?

They didn't deserve the manuscript.

Marcella drove on into the storm.

Why didn't the damn phone ring?

Parker Gorman got up from his desk and started pacing; out of the corner of his eye he watched the telephone. Ring, dammit. His life was on the line here, everything he had. The pressure was suffocating. If this thing exploded in his face it was all over; he was dead, it was body bag time. The pressure in Viet Nam had been peanuts compared to this. He walked over to his window, looked out, then turned and went back to his desk. Why hadn't Scotty called? He must know something by now.

Gorman leaned over his desk and pressed the button on his intercom. "Sheila, you haven't heard from Scotty?"

Sheila Stone was Gorman's secretary. She responded just as she had the first three times Gorman asked her that question. "No, sir. But I'll be sure to let you know the second he calls in."

Gorman reached for a cigarette. He was smoking too much. He knew that. But now was not the time to try to cut back. He had bigger things to worry about. Lung cancer was tomorrow's problem.

His fingers shook as he touched the flame to the cigarette. Who in their right mind would steal a manuscript for chrissake? It wasn't like it was a piece of jewelry, or a painting. It wasn't something you could hang on the wall and admire all day long. It wasn't something you could look at over and over, something you could savor. It wasn't the Mona Lisa, goddammit!

It was just a stupid book. What the hell are you going to do with a stupid book? You read it once and that's it. And you didn't have to steal it to read it; sooner or later the damn thing would be published, and you could buy it and read it then. Or check it out of the stupid library if you were too cheap to buy the damn thing.

Jesus Christ.

He paced back and forth. So why go to all that trouble? Why—

A light flicked on. Hell yes. *Ransom.*

Of course, that was the obvious answer. Auction it off to the highest bidder. Like an insurance company, for instance. Robbery only made sense if the thieves planned on selling it.

If that was, in fact, the plan, then it was something that Gorman had to make sure happened. When that call came he had to do everything in his power to get the police to cooperate. No hero stuff here. No "We'll set a trap for the bad guys," kind of bullshit. He could not afford to take that chance. If a rescue attempt failed, and somehow the manuscript was destroyed, then his whole company was history. So what if they asked for a million bucks? Or even two. Two million was better than twenty. He could handle two million. His company could handle two million. He could live with two million.

He knew the police would disagree. "You can't submit to the demands of criminals," they would argue. "You can't encourage thieves. If you do, they'll just do the same thing over and over again."

Bullshit. Gorman had heard all that crap before. They might be right, but he didn't care about right. He couldn't afford to care about right. He had to take care of today first; he would worry about tomorrow's problem tomorrow.

He stared at the telephone. Maybe the thieves would try to sell it directly to Jefferson National. Maybe they would contact him first, before the police. Keep the police out of it altogether. If they did, that would make things a lot easier. They'd call him, name a price. Naturally, he'd try to talk them down; but he wouldn't be too pushy, he couldn't take a chance and be too pushy. After a while they'd agree. Then he'd give them the money and they'd give him the manuscript and everybody would live happily ever after. Except maybe the police. The police would probably be pissed.

Gorman puffed on his cigarette. Screw the police.

He put out his cigarette.

But how would the thieves know that Jefferson had written the policy?

He lit another cigarette.

Chapter 19

EVERYTHING WAS FUZZY, OUT OF FOCUS. Billy shook his head. That hurt. He rubbed his temples. What was wrong with him? He felt really strange. Then, as his head began to clear and images became less blurred, a new phenomenon took over; suddenly everything seemed to be moving in slow motion. Weird. Billy looked around. What the hell was going on? Where was he? And who was that man strapped in the stretcher?

Then his eyes focused on the big red bow and it started to come back to him. There was Mr. Nash, with the manuscript sitting in his lap. His hands were clenched, fingers locked. He looked nervous. He looked more than nervous, Billy thought; he looked sick. He was looking down at the floor as if trying to pick just the right spot where he might throw up. Billy turned and looked up at his father; his father looked sick, too.

The cobwebs slowly faded and reality settled in. Even though his head hurt, Billy Freely was able to grasp the gravity of their predicament. They were trapped. There had been an accident, and they were in an ambulance on the way to the hospital ... Trapped. No place to go, nowhere to hide, and the stolen property sitting right there in their hot, guilty little paws. Jesus, they had to do something; they couldn't just sit there. He looked at his father; he looked at Mr. Nash; what were they waiting for? They were in deep shit, didn't they know that? His head was spinning and he knew it. Why were they just standing around? They had to react. They had to get out of this mess. They—

A man with a gun. Something about a man with a gun. Something. Billy tried to get a grip on himself. He couldn't panic. He had to calm down. He had to think. He couldn't think. His brain refused to work. A deep breath didn't help. What man? What gun? Slow down. Take your time. Think. Think about what to do.

Okay, okay. Ah, the way he saw it, they had, ah, two choices. Right, two choices. They either had to get the hell out of there, okay, that's right, that's choice number one, get the hell out of there. Or they had to get rid of the evidence. Right. Dump the manuscript. Okay. That was it. Two choices. It was as simple as that.

Wrong! Billy disagreed with himself. That was no good. What the hell was the matter with him? They didn't have two choices; they only had one. Getting rid of the manuscript was not an option. They'd gone too far to pitch it all now. They had the brass ring and *he* was not about to let go. They had it; they'd earned it; they were going to keep it. There was only one solution: They had to think of a way out.

Again he turned to his father, then to Mr. Nash. Forget it. *He* had to think of a way out.

"How are you feeling, son?"

Startled, Billy looked up at his father. "Oh, ah, fine, Dad. I feel better. A lot better. I'm not as sleepy as I was for awhile," Billy lied. He felt terrible.

"You took a pretty nasty bump on the head." Bill Freely leaned over his son and examined the bump. "You got a real goose egg there."

Billy smiled. "I'm okay, Dad. Honest."

"Well, we'll be at the hospital soon. They'll give you a good going over. Don't worry, you'll be all right."

Hospital? They couldn't go to the hospital. What about the manuscript? What about the police? What about— He looked down at the stranger lying there strapped to the stretcher, then he said to his father, "I don't think I have to go to the hospital, Dad. I'll be okay."

His father smiled. "Don't worry. It'll be all right."

Billy thought about that. "Uh, I won't have to stay, will I? I mean, I won't have to stay overnight?"

Bill Sr. understood the significance of the question. Nobody wanted to be detained any longer than he had to be. He wished he had a better answer. "Well, I don't know for sure. It depends on what they find. But I'm sure—"

Victor Romaine piped up. "They usually don't make you stay overnight for a concussion," he said. "Don't worry about it. Concussions are no big deal." He grunted. "I'm sure you'll get out of there a hell of a lot faster than I will." His tone sounded bitter.

Was that true? Billy wondered. Did the guy know what he was talking about? Would they just check him over and let him go? Let them all go?

They couldn't take that chance. They didn't know the stranger from a hole in the ground. What if he was just making the whole thing up? What if he didn't know for sure? What if he was just some asshole who *thought* he knew everything? They had to get out of there, that's what the hell they had to do.

"Of course, you don't have to take my word for it," Victor added. "I mean, what do I know?" Sarcasm. "I think I'm all right, for chrissake."

Who was this guy? "What— What's wrong with you?" Billy asked.

Victor rolled his eyes and twisted his mouth. "I guess I don't speak English—that must be my problem. I can't get those jerks up front to believe there's nothing wrong with me. I tell them I'm fine and they just look at me like they don't understand a word I'm saying." He looked Billy right in the eye. "Let me give you a piece of advice young man: If you're ever in another accident, and you're not injured—you know, nothing serious—whatever you do, don't let those assholes touch you. Once they touch you, once they get their meat hooks into you, they have you. They'll strap you in one of these things and there's nothing you can do to convince them to let you out. You're trapped."

Good advice, Billy thought. The guy wasn't a complete jerk after all. But he didn't need a stranger to tell him that. *Control*, that was the key. Who was in control? As long as they were in the ambulance someone else was in control: the guys up front, the driver. And when they got to the hospital someone else would be in control: doctors, nurses, maybe a cop or two. Not good. They could not allow that to happen. Billy could not allow that to happen. What if they got to the hospital and the doctors decided that they'd better give him a whole bunch of tests, *just in case?* What if they decided that they better keep him overnight, *just to be on the safe side?*

Forget it. As long as they were in someone else's control anything could happen. They could not afford to take a wait-and-see attitude, that would only get them in more trouble. Billy had to act, like he had acted at the robbery. He had taken matters into his own hands. He had to *do* something again.

He looked up at his father and Mr. Nash again. He couldn't count on them, that was for sure. If he waited for them, they might never get out of there. If he had waited on them before, they wouldn't have the manuscript now. No, Billy Freely was the one who had to think of something. His head hurt like hell, but it was up to him. He could do it. He had come through before, and he would come through again. He had to.

How?

Well, ah, first, he had to bide his time, wait for the right moment. Yeah, that's it. The opportunity would come, but he had to wait for it. And while he was waiting he had to think of what to do, think of how to react, so that when opportunity did knock he could charge through that door without thinking. No sitting around on his hands hoping. Billy had to be prepared, ready to jump when the time came. Jump and run.

He stretched his muscles, shook his head, rubbed his eyes. He took deep breaths. Jesus, he felt lousy. Two more deep breaths. He wished someone else would take over, but he knew it was up to him.

The first thing Stanley would do when they got to the hospital would be to make sure he stayed close to that Romaine character. He'd follow him, find out what room they put him in, and then he'd do what he'd been paid to do. If the paramedic tried to lead him off in another direction he would—

"First accident I ever had," Lenny Kravits said.

Stanley glared at him. He didn't like people talking when he was thinking.

"Been driving a hack for eighteen years and never had so much as one fender bender."

Lenny Kravits was talking as much to himself as he was to anyone else. Lenny was Stanley's cab driver. It seemed incomprehensible to him that he was involved in a traffic accident.

"Brother drives a hack. Father drove a hack. Uncle drives a hack. Whole family of hackers." He shook his head. "First one to have an accident. Never gonna be able to live this down."

Stanley agreed. If he didn't shut up he may not live at all.

The second cab driver laughed. "Not me, I've had a shitload in my time. Had one just last week, matter-a-fact. Dumb ass ran a red light. Lucky I'm still alive to tell about it."

You may not stay lucky, Stanley thought.

The two cab drivers had been talking ever since they left the accident. It irritated Stanley. Mouthy bastards.

"'Course I don't mind," the cab driver went on. "Get time off, with pay."

"You don't get a ton of shit for being involved in all those accidents?" Lenny asked.

Tommy's driver gave Lenny a questioning look. "Nah, none of 'em was my fault. Why should I get any shit?"

Lenny shrugged. "'Accident prone,' that's what they call it where I come from."

"'Accident prone?' What the hell's that?"

"That's what they call it when you get into accidents all the time—even if they wasn't your fault. They say you're 'accident prone.' Means if there's an accident around, chances are pretty good that you're gonna be part of it."

"Who's *they*?"

"Insurance companies."

"You're shittin' me."

"No way."

"What the hell do they have to do with anything?"

"They got everything to do with it. Insurance companies refuse to cover people who are accident prone. Call 'em bad risks. And if the insurance guys won't touch you, neither will the company. Friend a mine got fired last month just 'cause he was involved in three accidents in one year. Third one was the one that did it. Third one's the charm. Been with the company eleven years and they just said so long, *adios*, good-bye."

"Well, shit, that don't seem right."

Lenny nodded knowingly. "Tell me about it."

"Wha'd the Union say?"

Lenny shrugged. "Said nice knowin' ya. Better luck in your next life."

Next life, that was Tommy's only hope. He'd certainly screwed up this one, maybe he could do better the next time around.

Tommy rubbed his arm. It was beginning to feel better; maybe it wasn't broken after all. But his feet were cold. It was cold inside the ambulance. He tried wiggling his toes to warm them up.

Every now and then he'd glance at Stanley, think *pig*, then quickly turn his eyes away.

Now he was looking at the two cab drivers as they continued their conversation, but the words sailed by without entering his brain. He had no time for their stories, their ignorance. They were just a couple of stupid Americans who didn't know what they were talking about as far as he was concerned. How this country had ever prospered was beyond him. It could only be attributed to dumb luck; that had to be the answer. And the fact that it never had any real competition.

Until now.

Tommy smiled to himself. America had been successful in the past in spite of itself, but that was all changing. Tommy had been working in the United States for the past three years, and based on what he'd observed America was about to go down the toilet, as they themselves were so fond of saying. It was inevitable. America no longer had anything to offer the world. No superior intellect, no mysterious unique ingenuity. Certainly not ambition—that was for sure. Americans were notorious for their lack of ambition. They're downright lazy, Tommy thought. They were dumb and they were lazy and they were pigs, as evidenced by the swine sitting across from him. The man had no brains at all, no thought processes. Tommy could tell that just by looking at him. It was apparent to Tommy that he operated on instinct alone—

animal instinct. If this was an example of what America had to offer the world, then the walls would soon come tumbling down; the fabric would tear at the seams and America, like the Roman Empire, would exist only in the history books. It was a sight Tommy wanted to behold. He wanted to see America on its knees. But that meant he had to succeed. He had to complete his mission if he wanted to be around for that glorious day.

Tommy stared at Stanley and wondered what the ignorant fool was going to do next.

No way, it couldn't have been Henry.

Roger tried to recall what exactly had he seen? It had happened so fast. Was he just seeing what he wanted to see? Or *was* that really Henry Nash in the back of that ambulance?

Roger thought for a second, then decided that it didn't really make a whole hell of a lot of difference either way; it was the only lead he had. He could either follow the ambulance, or he could drive up I-95 and hope he bumped into Henry.

He decided to follow the ambulance.

In order to do that he had to exit 95 North, swing back on to the southbound lane, and then exit on to 278 just as the ambulances had done. The only question: could he do all that and catch the ambulances?

Probably not, but it didn't matter anyway. If he couldn't catch them, he was pretty sure he knew where they were going. Saint Mary's was the only destination that made any sense; where else would two ambulances be going headed west on 278?

It only took him sixteen minutes to work his way off 95, circle back around, get back on 95 southbound, and then exit on to 278, which meant he was only sixteen minutes behind the ambulances. Which meant he had to make up some of that time by going just a little faster. Which he did. Roger was not totally comfortable increasing his speed, but with four-wheel-drive under him he was able to do some things the other drivers were not.

Roger charged down the Bruckner Expressway, crossed the Triborough Bridge, turned south onto 2nd Avenue, and then zig-zagged his way through the intersections, the traffic, the weather, the construction (New York City was always in the middle of building *something*) and managed to get to 115th Street without crashing, getting a speeding ticket, or drawing the wrath (any significant wrath that is; Roger was sure a swear word or two had been muttered on his behalf) of the other motorists. Saint Mary's Hospital was on

115th and Columbus Avenue, across from St. John's Cathedral, two blocks ahead.

He got to Columbus and turned north—south of 115th Columbus was one-way, but in order for Saint Mary's to be accessible from both directions the city made north of 115th two-way. The sign jutting out from the drugstore on the corner read: TIME 1:38 PM; TEMP 6°. Roger had made up fifteen of the sixteen minutes; the ambulances were just turning into Saint Mary's now.

He stopped for the traffic light. He couldn't complain, it was his first red light.

After a minute the light turned green.

As he approached Saint Mary's, Roger was surprised to find that the ambulances had apparently discharged their passengers and were off again, because one of the ambulances came charging out of the exit lane, bounced off the curb, cut right in front of Roger, almost hitting him, then turned south and sailed down Columbus. That was close, Roger thought.

Columbus was slippery. In his rear view mirror Roger watched the ambulance slide across the north-bound lane, right itself just in time to avoid a collision with a black Dodge van that had to swerve to the right to get out of its way, and then charge back into the south-bound lane where it was quickly absorbed by the traffic flow. Another close call. Roger shook his head.

The driver of the van did not brush the incident aside as casually as Roger. He was mad.

And scared. Pierre Despestre did not want to go up in a ball of flame like his good friend, Francois. They told him the explosive in back was stable, but Pierre was not so sure of that. He didn't believe everything he was told; he'd been lied to too many times by these Gringos. It was new stuff, experimental, and very potent, according to his sources. Even the Army had admitted that it had not been fully tested, and, therefore, they were not one hundred percent certain they knew all of its characteristics. Pierre, and his three friends in the back of the van, had just taken delivery that morning—stolen from Army Ordnance only last night. Pierre yelled something in French, but the driver of the ambulance was already past him, so he didn't hear. Of course, even if he had heard he would not have understood; Billy Freely did not speak French.

Nor did the two men in the gray Ford that Billy also forced off the highway and into a snow bank. They didn't speak French even though they were following the van filled with Bigrements. Many FBI agents spoke a foreign language, but that was not the case with either Lawrence Evans or Carl Ferguson.

$$$

Henry Nash was too stunned to think about black vans or gray Fords. Or near collisions. He was too busy trying to straighten out the mess inside his head. Was he dreaming? Or had Billy Freely just stolen the ambulance that had just delivered them to the hospital? When the two paramedics got out to come around and open the back doors, was that really Billy who jumped into the front seat, rammed the shift lever into DRIVE, pressed the accelerator to the floor and taken off, just like that?

The move caught Henry off guard. He was too shocked to do anything but scream: "Jesus Christ, Billy, what the hell do you think you're doing?"

Bill Sr. was equally shocked. "Billy, what ..?"

Billy ignored them both. He kept the accelerator pressed to the floor. He didn't have time to explain things now, he had to DRIVE! goddammit. He had to concentrate. Didn't they see he'd just missed being involved in two accidents in the past thirty seconds? First, he'd barely gotten by that stupid-shit Chevy Blazer as he charged out of the hospital, and then that dumb ass in that black Dodge van had been halfway in his lane for chrissake. Jesus, didn't anyone know how the hell to drive in this stupid city? It was only because of his superior driving skill, and youth's quick reaction time, that Billy was able to swerve out of the way at the last minute. Jesus, Billy thought to himself, and you want me to explain things *now*?

Then a gray Ford, behind the black van, came out of nowhere. Suddenly it was just *there*, directly in his path. And Billy had to swerve again. Fortunately, as before, his driving skill prevailed; Billy made it.

But the gray Ford didn't. In the rear view mirror Billy saw the four-door sedan plow headfirst into a snow bank. Billy didn't know what happened to the van.

Nor did he care. He had one objective: to get out of there. Not only did he have to protect the manuscript, but there was something else, something in that other ambulance that had pulled in beside them back at the hospital, something he thought was a dream that had suddenly come to life. Something that scared him to death. When the driver opened the door and got out, Billy Freely discovered that the man with the gun was not just an aberration in a spinning brain, he was real after all. Billy *had* seen him. He *had* been there. And then he'd disappeared.

And just a few short seconds ago Billy discovered where he had gone, and that he had not gone far. He was in the ambulance right next to them. And he still looked angry.

Henry: "Billy?"

"I had to do it, Mr. Nash. We had to get out of there." Billy's voice came in pants.

Henry didn't agree. "That's crazy. You stole an ambulance, for chrissake. What's wrong with you? We—"

Henry stopped and looked down at the man in the stretcher. Victor Romaine was lying there with his eyes open wide, a look of shock and horror on his face. His mouth was open and his lips were moving, but nothing was coming out.

Henry climbed into the front seat with Billy. He lowered his voice as much as he could considering the excited state he was in. "Billy, Jesus, what the hell's the matter with you? Do you realize what you've done, what you've just gotten us into? Christ, now they're going to be after us for stealing an ambulance, too. Don't you realize that? Do you have any idea what you've—"

"We already stole the manuscript, Mr. Nash," Billy whispered so the man in back couldn't hear. "What's one more robbery? What's the difference?"

Henry was mad. "Auto theft, Billy. The difference is auto theft."

"Hey, auto theft can't be as big a deal as twenty million worth of Mark Twain. Don't sweat it."

"Don't sweat it? Jesus, Billy, don't you think we have enough problems already?"

"We'll be all right, Mr. Nash. We'll be okay."

"But why? Why the hell did you do it?"

"We had to get out of there."

"But you didn't have to steal a damn ambulance. We could have gotten out of there without doing that. Jesus Christ, Billy, this is just plain stupid. You think we can hide in this thing? Look at it—it's a goddam ambulance. We stick out like a sore thumb. Why didn't you steal a fire truck for chrissake?"

Billy was convinced he was doing the right thing. "I had to do it, Mr. Nash. We had to get out of there. No way could we go into that hospital."

Billy turned east at 110th and was sailing along the northern border of Central Park like a demon possessed, eyes sharp and darting, jaws set, hands clamped to the steering wheel. He was dodging in and out of traffic, swerving to the right, then to the left, avoiding accidents by inches. The red lights on top of the ambulance had not been turned off so they were still flashing, sending out currents of crimson in all directions. Billy would have turned them off but he didn't know how. Besides, he didn't mind, he kind of liked the idea of having people move out of his way.

"Billy, stop this thing right now. We have to get out of here. This is no good."

"Can't stop now, Mr. Nash." He turned south on 5th Avenue. "Gotta lose them."

Henry looked around. Maybe they shouldn't stop after all, not just yet. Fifth Avenue had traffic and people everywhere. If they did ditch the ambulance they'd be on foot and—

On foot? The worst thing that could happen to you according to Jesse James was being *on foot*. Never get caught *on foot*. Had something like this ever happened to Jesse? Henry wondered. Had he ever been up to his eyeballs in deep shit because one of his men screwed up? What would Jesse do? Henry tried to think. It was no use—how could he think at a time like this?

He turned to Billy, "Damn, Billy, if you'd just played it cool for a little while longer we wouldn't be in this mess. We weren't that desperate. We could have gone into that hospital, had you checked over, and then walked out free as birds and no one would have been the wiser. We would have been out of there for chrissake—no problems."

"I don't think so."

"Dammit, Billy, if you'd just have waited, instead of acting like a jerk."

"I couldn't wait. *We* couldn't wait."

"Bullshit! You acted without thinking, Billy. You just took off on your own." Henry leaned closer, turned his head away from the man on the stretcher in back. "They didn't know anything about the robbery. They didn't have any idea who we were. There was no reason for them to even be suspicious. But you sure as hell blew that, didn't you? Now we're in even deeper, for chrissake."

"The, ah, the package. We couldn't take that chance."

Henry was getting madder. "Billy, are you listening to me? Are you paying attention? How big of a chance was it? They didn't know anything. All we had to do was play along and we'd have been home free." He shook his head again, then lowered his voice even more and pointed at the manuscript. "It looks like a Christmas present. That's what people would assume it was. We could have explained the package, Billy. Tell me, how the hell are we going to explain stealing an ambulance? Jesus."

Billy had more. "But that's not all, Mr. Nash. There's more to it than that."

Henry didn't want to hear it. He was busy trying to think of a way out of this new mess. Stupid kid.

"That man with the gun, the one we saw before, back at the accident."

Henry was looking straight ahead, only half listening. "What about him?"

"He was there."

That got his attention. He looked down at Billy, stunned. "What?"

"I saw him. He was there."

Henry turned to Bill. Bill was standing in the back just behind Billy with his body pressed against the back of the seat. He leaned forward. He looked as confused as Henry. Henry turned back to Billy. "What do you mean, 'he was there?'"

"He was there."

"Where?"

"At the hospital."

"What the hell are you talking about?"

"He was at the hospital. I saw him."

Bill said, "You saw him, son? The man with the gun?"

"Sure as hell did."

Henry to Bill: "He's hallucinating."

"Bullshit!" Billy said. "That ambulance that pulled in right beside us—he was in it."

Bill asked Henry if he'd seen him. Henry shook his head no. Henry turned back to Billy and waited.

"He was there, Mr. Nash," Billy said again, eagerly. He looked at his father in the rear view mirror. "Honest, Dad." Back to Henry. "Honest. He was getting out of that other ambulance and he was walking toward us."

"You're sure?" Henry asked.

Billy's voice was firm. "Hey, I'll never forget that guy. He's the ugliest asshole I ever saw. It was him all right."

This made no sense. The man with the gun was back? But—

Henry looked at Bill. Why? What the hell was going on?

Stanley, too, wondered just what the hell was going on. Where the hell were those jerk-ass paramedics going? Why would the fools take off again before they unloaded their cargo?

Then he saw the paramedics standing there and realized something was wrong. *They* hadn't taken off. *They* were still here. But someone had just driven away in that ambulance. Stanley couldn't figure it out. And just as quickly gave up trying. He didn't need an explanation. All he needed to know was the fact that his target was escaping. Victor Romaine was still in that ambulance and he was getting away while Stanley was standing there like a fool. Then Stanley spotted the black van stopped at the entryway to the hospital. He didn't hesitate a second.

Tommy stood by the ambulance and watched, wondering what the crazy man was up to now.

Stanley ran up to the van and tore open the door.

Pierre Despestre was about to say *What the hell do you think you're doing?* when he saw the gun.

"Out," Stanley said.

Pierre didn't argue.

Neither did his three compatriots.

Tommy watched as the four Frenchies (or who he thought were Frenchies, all French people looked the same to him) crawled down out of the van. Stanley's body hid the gun from Tommy's view. What the hell is going on? Tommy wondered.

Stanley climbed up into the van, slammed the door shut and took off in pursuit of the ambulance. Pierre Despestre stood there staring at his friends.

I have to follow him, Tommy thought. But how?

Lawrence Evans and Carl Ferguson managed to get their car pushed out of the snow bank just as the black van zipped by. Assuming that the Bigrements were still in it, they got quickly back into their vehicle, made a U-turn on Columbus and took off after the van.

It was Sonny Grosso's first day on the job; his first day driving a taxicab. He was proud of himself. He just prayed he didn't screw up; it had taken him almost a year to land this job. He'd applied last February. Ten months of waiting for that phone to ring. Ten months of putting Chrissy off. But it finally rang, and now he was all set. He had a good job. Now he and Chrissy could get married.

If he didn't screw up in this weather, that is. If he didn't do something stupid.

Sonny was very nervous. As if driving a taxicab for the first time wasn't bad enough, especially one that sputtered and stalled whenever it felt like it, but add to that the road conditions and Sonny had been on the edge of his seat ever since he'd come on duty at ten. His hands squeezed the wheel. He looked at his watch; almost two, another four hours and he could go home.

Sonny dropped his fare off at the front door of the hospital, thanked the woman for the generous tip, and was about to drive away when he saw a man running toward him waving his arms. He stopped.

Tommy jumped into Sonny's cab. He handed Sonny a hundred dollar bill and issued the same instructions as he had to his previous driver.

Sonny Grosso blinked. Jesus, the first day on the job and it was happening just like it did in the movies. *Follow that car!*

Sonny thought about it for a second—what to do? Then he shrugged. Hey, who was he to argue? The customer was always right as far as he was concerned. Especially customers with hundred dollar bills. Hundred dollar bills would go a long way when it came to furnishing an apartment. If he wants me to follow a black van, then I'll follow a black van, Sonny thought. He said, "You got it," and started down Columbus.

He turned onto 110th, passed three cars, and then pulled in behind the gray Ford that was behind a red station wagon, that was in back of the black van.

Roger Muldowney was glad he was getting off the crazy New York streets for a while. New York drivers were nuts.

As were the pedestrians. Roger couldn't believe that some idiot had just run right out in front of him. Didn't even bother to look where he was going. Trying to hail a taxi is a dumb way to die, Roger thought. Roger swallowed his heart, then gathered his calm. The fool was damned lucky I didn't run over him.

Roger found a place to park directly across from the entrance to the hospital, unhooked his seat belt, got out, locked his car doors, and made it up to the entrance just in time to hear one of the paramedics exclaim:

"Jesus, somebody call the police! They just stole my ambulance!"

Chapter 20

"Pierre, what are we going to do now?"

Jacques Castedo's voice quivered when he spoke. He was Pierre's brother-in-law, and, being six years younger than Pierre, always looked to the older man for answers, even though the older man was only twenty-eight. They all looked to Pierre for answers. Pierre was their leader.

But today Pierre had no answers. Today his mind was spinning. Some crazy man had just come out of nowhere—a man with a gun, a man with insanity in his eyes—and had stolen their van. In addition to the explosive, they were also now missing passports, money, extra clothing (disguises), weapons, and most important, the airline tickets that would take them out of this decadent country. They had nothing but the clothes on their backs and the confusion in their minds. And Pierre, even though he was in charge, was just as confused as everyone else.

The four men stood there on the cold New York street staring at each other; they had nowhere to go and no way to get there. And now, apparently, no hope of accomplishing their mission. Three months of planning, five-hundred-thousand American dollars spent, and it was all about to go down the drain. Jacques asked his question again, "Pierre, what are we going to do?"

Pierre answered his brother-in-law. "How the hell should I know?" he snapped.

Jacques and the others exchanged glances. Then Jacques said, "But Pierre, how can we blow up the United Nations if we have no explosive?"

Pierre's stare was sharp and riveting. How his sister could have married such a man was impossible for Pierre to understand. They were complete opposites; Jacques was shy, meek, mousy; Madeleine was wild, carefree, a free spirit. Impulsive. *Irresponsible*. But to marry a man like Jacques was more than irresponsible, it was insane—the butting together of two contradicting forces was bound to bring rain. And it had. Torrents. In an effort to become what she wanted him to be Jacques had gone too far. He went from simple to complex, not intricate, puzzling; from reserved to rowdy; from almost cowardly to certifiably crazy. *Fearless*—not brave, foolhardy. He took chances. It was almost as if he were trying to get himself killed.

Jacques stood there in his gray sweatshirt, his fatigue jacket, his faded Levi's and his worn army boots waiting for Pierre to respond, waiting for Pierre to tell them all how they were going to get out of this mess. His arms were at his sides, his hands bare. He was shivering. They were all shivering. The temperature was in the single digits. Bigrements, having been born on the small island Isle de la Bigrement in the Caribbean Sea island chain, were not used to this kind of cold. The snow was lighter now, but it continued to fall.

If everything had gone better back in April, none of them would be here now.

You crazy, skinny little runt, Pierre thought to himself. Five-feet-four-inches of skin and bone, with a brain that matched that of a mosquito. How something that small could generate enough energy to move even a frame as modest as Jacques' was a mystery to Pierre. Blow up the UN and yourself with it, is that what you wish Jacques? Is that what it will take to make your wife happy? You would do better to be a farmer than a freedom fighter, grow your corn and feed your chickens and forget about the woman named Madeleine.

Pierre regretted his thoughts. They were an insult to all farmers. His father had been a farmer, had grown corn and fed chickens; he would turn over in his grave if he knew his son felt that way.

But it was true. Jacques had the mentality of a farmer, if not the disposition. He was not stupid, or dense; he was timid. He was a man who presumed nothing—at least not until he met Madeleine. What made him dangerous was the fact that he knew he was withdrawn, an introvert, and made up for it by being reckless. Pierre concluded that was, in a sense, just another form of stupidity. The kind of stupidity that will get you killed, Pierre thought. The kind of stupidity that could get them all killed. Jacques was not cut out for this line of work. His reckless abandon risked not only his own life but the lives of others as well.

Pierre cursed himself for bringing Jacques along. He had already screwed up once—at the exchange this morning. If Pierre had not been able to calm down the men who had delivered the explosive, they might all be dead now. Jacques simply refused to understand that this was not their country. They were visitors here, intruders. Just because the men were willing to sell them arms and the explosive did not mean that they were friends. He should learn to keep his mouth shut. Pierre should not have listened; he should have left Jacques at home.

Not that Jacques' being here was all Pierre's fault, or even Jacques', for that matter. He was here for one reason, and Pierre knew what that reason was. He was here because his wife wanted him to be here. His loving wife—Pierre's adoring sister—had forced him to come. Not with words (hers was a much more subtle pressure than that), but with context. A simple "*un homme* would go" was all it took.

Jacques was here to impress her. He was here to prove that he was a man. He had married a hellcat and he was paying for it with his freedom, his independence, his manhood. And one day, maybe, his life.

Pierre's coal-black eyes bore holes into Jacques. "I do not know how we are going to blow it up, Jacques. We do not have the explosive, so I guess we cannot blow it up. Right, *mon ami*? We also do not have our van, so I do not know how we are going to get to the airport either. And even if we get to the airport, I do not know how we are going to get on the plane because our tickets are in the van, as well as our money, *and* our disguises, *and* our weapons. So, you see, my friend, it is not just the explosive that we have lost, it is everything. We have nothing, Jacques. Do you understand? Nothing."

"But—" Jacques stopped. He saw the look in Pierre's eyes. He thought for a second, then turned toward his two comrades for help.

Marius Petion, the newest member of the group, inducted in May, was the first to volunteer, "But Pierre, we have been planning this for three months. We have got to do something. We cannot just forget it. What about all the money we have spent so far? Are we just going to toss it all away? And what of our imprisoned brothers? They are still rotting in the stinking *Anglais* prisons. Have you forgotten our cause, Pierre? Have you forgotten what we vowed to do? What would Francois think?"

Francois? Francois is dead. The dead don't think.

Marius went on, "Francois Benoit, our glorious founder and leader before you, Pierre, died trying to do what we were going to do today. We must continue what he started. We must send a message to the dirty *Americain* pigs who are always sticking their noses into other people's businesses. We must continue to fight, Pierre. We cannot stop here. We cannot permit our glorious founder to have died in vain."

Make your speeches to someone else, Pierre thought. Our glorious founder would probably still be alive today if the same thing had happened to him that had just happened us. If someone had stolen his explosive it would not have blown up in his face that rainy April morning, and Francois Benoit, my best friend since the sixth grade, would not have been turned into a cloud of pink mist. And I would not have inherited a job I do not want.

Pierre thought back. That's when The Brotherhood of Francois was formed—and when Pierre had become trapped. The name of their little group had been changed from The Isle de la Bigrement Freedom Fighters to The Brotherhood of Francois—a last tribute to their departed leader. However, the new name did not mean that their purpose had changed, it was still the same as it had been the day that Francois Benoit envisioned it: To teach the Americans, and the entire world, that they could not continue to interfere in Latin and South American politics without paying the price, and that the price of that interference was high.

The price had been high for them, too. Six dead, including Francois, and eleven in jail.

"What do you suggest, Marius?" Pierre asked. "Tell me, what should we do?"

"We must find our van. We must finish what we started."

"Where? Where should we look? This is a big city, is it not?"

"We must try. Francois would expect it."

"Francois would not expect more than we can deliver," Pierre said to Marius. "We cannot accomplish the impossible. He would understand. That was part of his greatness. He understood what could be done and what could not."

What bull. Francois was not understanding; he was a lunatic, a fanatic. Pierre knew. Pierre was his closest friend.

And now Pierre was the leader, and he was an even more reluctant leader than he had been a follower. His heart had never truly been in it, his mind never fully convinced, his soul never totally committed. He had followed Francois because he was a friend, and because he had been swept away with the man's magnetism, his power to enflame people, his leadership. His goals were lofty—what more could the son of a poor farmer ask out of life?

That, and the fact that it had been easier to follow than to resist, a creed most followers live by.

But now it was different. Now Francois was gone and Pierre was in charge, and he did not have the strength that Francois had. He did not have the drive or the desire. He was not a born leader. And he did not want to be. He wanted to go home. He wanted this whole stupid thing to end, before they all tasted the same fate as Francois. Sure, they could blow up a building, but would that really change anything? And what if they were killed in the process? Would their deaths change things any more than Francois' death had? Like Francois, they would become martyrs. But martyrs had one thing in common: They were all dead. And death never solved a thing as far as Pierre was concerned.

Pierre thanked God for sending the man who had stolen their van. Maybe now it would stop. Maybe now they could go home. Maybe now his companions would be forced to face reality. They were out of money, out of power, and just about out of time—how much longer could they fool those two stupid FBI agents who had been following them for the past six weeks?

Pierre only had one more problem to overcome. He could handle Jacques, and Marius, but the third member of the group frightened him. Not by what he said, but by the exact opposite, by the fact that he rarely said anything at all. L'Ange was quiet. *Too* quiet. He seemed to be always thinking. What L'*Ange Noir*—the Black Angel—was thinking about was what scared Pierre.

Like now. L'Ange was just standing there staring, waiting, saying nothing, eyes of ink never moving, never blinking.

Thinking?

About what? About taking over control of the group? Pierre wondered. Was that his plan? L'*Ange* Blanchet had not gotten his name from God; it was the devil who'd christened him The Black Angel. And he deserved the name. He was an avenging angel, a killing machine that had no feelings. Pierre feared that what was going on inside L'Ange's head could be even more dangerous than the stolen Army explosive.

Pierre stared back. He would not flinch. He *could* not. There was a rule when dealing with animals: Never show fear. Animals can smell fear.

So Pierre had to fake it. He had to fake it so the others would not know how frightened he really was. He had to fake it so L'Ange would not know.

And he had to stay in charge. Not because he wanted to, but because the consequences of L'Ange taking over were too frightening to think about. As long as he was in charge no one would question his decisions. He was the boss.

At least for the time being.

The group was silent. All eyes were on Pierre. When he decided what they should do he would let them know. That was the boss' job.

Pierre wondered how long he could continue to fool them.

"What's the matter with those crazy bastards?" Special Agent Carl Ferguson said. "They're driving like drunken fools."

Agent Lawrence Evans had both eyes on the black van two vehicles in front of them, and both hands on the steering wheel at his chest. He was leaning forward in the seat of the car, his body tense, strained. He spoke through clenched teeth, "Assholes must be overloaded with red wine. You think they spotted us?"

Carl Ferguson had been watching the van as it zig-zagged its way through traffic for the last twenty minutes. The driving was not at all characteristic of the way that it had been before. It was erratic, unpredictable. Maybe Evans was right; maybe they were all drunk. But that didn't make any sense either; they had always been extra careful about their actions. They had done everything they could to remain inconspicuous. Up to now. Ferguson wondered what the hell was going on. He said, "No. I don't think they made us."

"Maybe they did," Evans said. "Maybe that asshole running us off the road like that tipped our hand."

The van turned east at 86th Street because the ambulance in front of it had turned east at 86th Street. The federal agents were too far back to see the ambulance—the same ambulance that had run them off the road—so they did not make the connection. They only had the van on their minds.

The ambulance got to Lexington Avenue and turned south, as did the van.

"If I ever get my hands on that ambulance driver I'll ring his goddam neck." Lawrence Evans was furious. He turned south on Lexington Avenue.

"Calm down, Larry," his partner said. "I think we're okay."

Evans fumed. "Guy's an asshole."

"No harm done. Forget about it."

Carl Ferguson was the exact opposite of his partner of nine months. Carl never lost his temper. He'd been with the Bureau for twenty four years—he knew it didn't do any good to go ballistic.

Lawrence Evans, on the other hand, didn't agree with that philosophy; he lost his temper every chance he got. "Bullshit!" he said. "What if they spotted us? Couple of gray suits out there trying to push themselves out of a goddam snow bank. You think we look like your typical, run-of-the-mill businessmen? Wall Street tycoons? Two ministers from Omaha, maybe? No way, Carl. No way. Jesus, we stick out like a couple of sore thumbs for chrissake and you know it."

Ferguson tried to calm his partner down. That was part of his job—to train Evans. Teach him the ropes. Teach him how to function in the field. Evans had a lot to learn. Maybe protect was a better word than teach. Shield. Act as a buffer between Evans and the rest of the world.

Evans came to the Bureau from the military and was a little rough around the edges, to say the least. They had assigned him to Ferguson, an experienced agent, so he could learn the proper way—the Bureau way—to do things before he got into too much trouble. It was Ferguson's responsibility to teach him not only the crime-fighting aspects of the job, but the social and political parts as well—like the part about how to deal with the public in general. How to handle the media; how to treat other law enforcement agencies. How to get from Point A to Point B without stubbing his toe or embarrassing the Bureau.

Embarrassing the Bureau was the definitive phrase. No one could do anything to Embarrass the Bureau. Evans had spent twelve years in the military; he was crude. He was not familiar with how things worked on the outside. It was Ferguson's job to show him, to smooth him out as his Bureau Chief had said.

Ferguson had his job cut out for him.

He spoke in a calm, fatherly voice, "Hey, they never made us, Larry. Trust me. Don't worry about it. They came tearing out of that hospital too fast to make anyone. My guess is they didn't even see us."

Evans didn't buy that. "Six weeks on this case—six weeks of following these meatball scumbags through every slimy rathole from Denver to Detroit to DC, just to have the whole thing go down the dumper because some dumbass ambulance driver thinks he has the ride-of-way everywhere he goes. Pisses me off, Carl. Really pisses me off."

Scumbags? Slimy ratholes? Not in the Bureau's official dictionary, Ferguson thought. Not words J. Edgar would have approved of. "Take it easy, Larry. Just relax. You have to learn to relax. We're okay. No harm done. No problem. We're all right."

Carl Ferguson said the words, but even he wasn't certain he believed them. But either way, he didn't see it as that big of a deal. Maybe because he'd been around the agency a lot longer than Evans he was immune to this kind of disappointment. He'd had cases blow up at the last minute many times—it was all part of the job.

"We're screwed," Evans said. "I just know we're screwed. We should have picked them up last week in Detroit when we had the chance. I'd bet my pension they were making a buy. We could have nailed their sorry asses with the goods. We waited too long, Carl. I know it. Now they have us pegged and we'll never catch them with their greasy little mitts in the cookie jar. Screwed, blued and tattooed. Shit!"

Carl was not paying any attention to Larry's rambling; he was lost in thought. Something was wrong. Something didn't fit. He tried to put his finger on it, but whatever it was it managed to stay just out of reach. Finally, he said. "Well, stick with them, Larry. If they did make us, we'll know soon enough."

$$$

Scotty jerked his steering wheel to the right and slammed on the brakes. To his surprise he came to a stop.

Damn, that was close.

Scotty turned and watched the ambulance sail down Lexington Avenue.

"Ambulances all over the place," he said aloud to himself. "Better not fall asleep at the stick today."

Scotty didn't see the black van and the gray Ford go by because by then he was through the intersection and heading west. If he'd looked into his rear view mirror he might have noticed them, but Scotty had too many other things to think about, things that kept his mind churning and his thoughts elsewhere.

Scotty Hunter was not a happy camper. He was thinking about driving back to Jefferson National simply because he didn't know what else to do. However, going home with his tail between his legs was not his idea of a successfully completed mission. But he didn't have a clue as to the whereabouts of the robbers and he didn't know where to go from here. Driving around New York City hoping he'd run into them—if they were even here—seemed like a real big waste of time.

As did wasting his time talking to the state police.

Talking to them was out—Scotty didn't know anyone personally on that force. They had no reason to give him any information at all. He'd tried to enlist their aid once before on another case, and although they were very polite, they'd quickly informed him that it was a state police matter that they could not discuss with a civilian. Lieutenant Wiseman had been Scotty's only hope, and he had been no help at all.

Roger was at a loss. What the hell should he do now? As far as he knew, Henry was still in that ambulance—if the man he thought was Henry was really Henry. And if he was there, he was probably being held captive by whoever stole it.

Or the others in the ambulance were being held captive by Henry.

"Jesus, Henry, what the hell do I do now?" Roger asked of no one in particular.

Roger got back into his car and just sat there, only because he didn't know what else to do, except to wonder if he might just as well give up and go home. Who was he trying to kid? He'd never find Henry. Talk about your needle in a haystack. Hell, he didn't even know what haystack to look in. That ambulance could be anywhere by now. Roger looked out at the city; at least it had stopped snowing.

"What the hell do you mean, 'am I sure I still want to go through with this?' What kind of a dumbass question is that? You think I want to give up now?"

There was no "giving up" to Lilith Bright. Quit was not part of her vocabulary—it never had been; it never would be.

"First Louise, now you, Ralph. We just got here for chrissake," she exclaimed. "You think I want to stop now?"

"I just—"

"Ralph, brain open, mouth shut. Try to stay with me on this. I'll go slow. Your problem is, Ralph, that you're always too ready to quit, too ready to knuckle under. You've got no fight in you. No drive. You gotta be persistent to win in this day and age, Ralph. Can't be a weenie. Read the sign on the front door of the planet, Ralph: NO WIMPS ALLOWED."

"I just thought—"

"Don't think, Ralph," Lilith said shaking her head. "Let me do the thinking. Okay?"

With that she turned and looked into the back seat at Louise. "You know your way around this god-forsaken town by any chance?"

Louise thought for a minute. "Ah, well, not really. I've only been here—"

"That's what I figured," Lilith interrupted. She shot a quick I-told-you-so glance at Ralph, then turned back to Louise with a disgusted look on her face. "You do know where this dipshit insurance company of yours is located though, right? You know, the one you picked to cover the most valuable piece of property in the whole stupid world? The one you picked to insure the biggest discovery of this century? I mean, it does exist, right? It's for real? It's got a building and everything? And you know how to get there, right?" There was as much sarcasm in Lilith's look as there was in her voice.

"Well, it's on Fifth Avenue. I think it's ..."

Lilith rolled her eyes. "Wonderful. Think you can narrow it down any more than that? Like, a street number, maybe? Something that will get us within, say, ten miles of the damn place?"

Louise opened her mouth to speak, then realized she'd better not trust her memory. She opened her purse.

Patience was not a virtue as far as Lilith was concerned. She turned and spoke out of the corner of her mouth so only Ralph could hear. "Jesus, I sure as hell can pick 'em." Ralph didn't respond. Lilith turned back to Louise, who was still fumbling through her purse. "Find anything yet, Dearie?" Louise fumbled faster. "Well, you lemme know when you come up with something, okay? You find that address; I'll do the rest." She turned toward her husband. "Won't we, Ralph?"

Ralph nodded.

As Louise frantically fumbled around in her purse, she prayed she had not left Benjamin Blackwell's business card at home in her file. She had known the Blackwell family for over thirty years—her sister had taught Benjamin, his brother Nathan, and his two cousins, the Landry twins, in the first grade. He had been their insurance agent for the past six years, ever since his father retired from the business because of poor health. When he sold her the policy he said that if she were ever in New York City she should stop by their corporate headquarters and say hello. He was such a nice young man.

As hard as he tried, Michael was unable to stay lost. The one time New York City's size could have been to his advantage it failed him. He was going to have to face Parker Gorman, like it or not—and that scared the living daylights out of him.

He pulled into the parking lot, walked through the foot-deep snow that no one as yet had removed from the sidewalk, announced to the security guard at the front desk who he was and who he wanted to see, and was promptly told to go right up to the sixth floor—Parker Gorman was expecting him.

Ouch. That was not music to Michael's ears. *Parker Gorman was expecting him. Waiting* for him was probably more like it. *Lying in wait.*

The elevator stopped at the sixth floor. Michael made himself get out.

The waiting room to Gorman's office was as silent as a pharaoh's tomb and equally as intimidating—it looked like a shrine. The plush navy-blue carpeting, heavy gray drapes and rich-looking pewter wallpaper quickly absorbed any sound that dared invade this inner sanctum. Michael had been here only once before, and even under more pleasant circumstances he had felt as if he was visiting a funeral home instead of an business office. Everyone spoke in whispers.

Parker Gorman was standing in his doorway waiting for him. He had a frown on his face.

Michael smiled at Gorman's secretary as he walked by. She smiled back. Was that pity he saw in her eyes? A man on the way to the gallows, his last meal a smile from a pretty girl?

Gorman's office was all oak and leather with a smattering of brass. Built-in bookshelves lined two walls. The third housed the bar. The wall behind Gorman's desk was all window; it framed Central Park. On a clear day, and under different circumstances, the view would be breathtaking. Michael didn't notice.

"Please sit down, Michael," Gorman said softly, motioning toward one of the three burgundy-colored, leather-trimmed chairs sitting in front of his massive oak desk.

Was one of the chairs filled with 2000 volts of electricity that turned you to toast when the man behind the desk flicked a switch, Michael wondered, like in those James Bond movies? And then the man pushed a button and the floor opened up and the chair tilted forward and dumped you into the icy river below. Michael knew his imagination was getting away from him, but he couldn't help himself. He sat down, gingerly.

"Can I get you anything?" Gorman asked.

"N-No, thank you," Michael stuttered, then cleared his throat.

"You're sure? A cup of coffee?"

"No, really. I'm fine."

"Nasty day out there. You must be freezing. Are you certain I can't get you a cup of coffee? Hot tea, maybe?"

"No thank you."

"I could have Sheila bring you some tea. Frankly, it would give her something to do. I brought her in here on Saturday just in case."

Why was Gorman being so insistent? And so polite? Fattening up the lamb for the slaughter? Michael shook his head no.

Gorman shrugged.

After a second of contemplation Gorman walked around to his side of the desk, paused, then sat down. The entire time his eyes were fixed on Michael. He didn't say anything for a while, then he leaned back in his chair, put his elbows on the arms, made a church's steeple out of his fingers and put the peak to his lips. He sat like that for a second, then moved the peak to his chin and said:

"So, let's go over it again. One more time."

It didn't take long. There was not much to tell. Michael talked and Gorman listened. It was the same story he'd told him earlier over the phone. When Michael was finished Gorman just sat there staring off into space.

Behind him Michael finally noticed the window and Central Park beyond. It was covered in a blanket of snow, encircling Parker Gorman in a white frame. However, Gorman did not have the look of an angel.

Michael waited. He thought about saying more, but there was no more to say. He thought about apologizing, but that seemed redundant. Besides, none of it would make any difference anyway; nothing would bring the manuscript back. He just had to sit there and take his medicine. Michael shifted uncomfortably in his chair, waiting for Gorman to flick the switch, load the chair with 2000 volts and put him out of his misery.

Just then the intercom snapped on and Gorman's secretary said:

"Mr. Hunter is on Line Two, sir."

Marcella pulled into the parking lot of Jefferson National and in her haste and excitement never realized that she'd parked her car right beside Michael's.

She jumped out and charged forward through the snow, head down. She didn't bother to pull up the hood of her ski jacket.

"Scotty—whaddaya got?" Gorman asked, anxious, hopeful.

The background noise made it difficult to hear, and Scotty's voice had a tinny quality to it. The words sounded like they were bouncing off the inside of a barrel. "Just heard over my police radio that someone stole an ambulance over at Saint Mary's Hospital. The way it sounded the thieves may have been incoming patients."

Gorman was confused. "What the hell does that have to do with anything?"

Scotty responded. "I talked to Wiseman. He said he was glancing over a report that came off the computer a little while ago; the state police reported a major traffic accident—a fifteen-car pile-up—on Ninety-Five just north of Two-Seventy-Eight, not too far from where the manuscript was stolen. He said a couple of the vehicles involved come real close to matching the description of the kind of car that was used by our bad guys."

Gorman looked at Michael. Then into the phone, "So?"

"So, if it was the bad guys, then maybe they're the ones who stole the ambulance."

Gorman frowned. "Come on, Scotty—that sounds a little farfetched, don't you think? What are the chances of that? Besides, how many cars do you figure are floating around this town that come real close to the one involved in the robbery?"

"Half a million or so, probably. But, hey, what have we got to lose? Might as well check it out."

Gorman thought for a second, rubbed his chin, stared at Michael, then: " How far are you from Saint Mary's now?"

"Twenty minutes."
More thought. Finally: " I'll meet you there."
"What?"
"I'm almost as close as you are. I'll meet you there."
"But—why?"
Who was Scotty to question the boss?
"Because I said so," was Gorman's response.

Chapter 21

CARL FERGUSON SMELLED A RAT.

"There's something wrong here, Larry," he said. "Something smells and it doesn't smell good. I don't like it."

Lawrence Evans' eyes were fixed on the black van that was now three cars ahead of him. "What the hell are you talking about?"

"They're not acting like they did before. They're not driving the same way."

The van turned west onto 73rd Street. The two vehicles in front of Evans—which now included the taxicab that had passed him three blocks back (an act that had done nothing but add degrees to his constantly rising temperature), in addition to the red station wagon—followed. Evans had to run a red light to stay with the van, but that was no problem for Evans.

"They're jerks, that's all," Evans said. "How are jerks supposed to act?"

Carl tried to explain. "No, that's not it. You said it yourself: We've been following these guys for almost two months now—right?"

"Right."

"Well, in that time, did you ever see them drive like this before? Drive crazy? Even once?"

Evans worked on that. Then, "As a matter of fact, hell yes, I did. In Chicago, remember? We were coming down Lake Shore Drive and they were—"

Carl stopped him. "No. No. That wasn't the same thing at all. That wasn't like this. Okay, they've driven fast before. *Fast*, yes, but not reckless. Not like lunatics. Think about it, Larry: They've always gone out of their way to obey every traffic law. If you think about Chicago, I think you'll recall that they never actually broke the speed limit that day. Not by much, anyway. They were doing sixty-six, sixty-seven, maybe. But hell, that wasn't bad; everyone was passing them but us. In the six weeks we've been with them, did you ever—in all that time—did you *ever* see them run a red light? Or make a U-turn? Or go the wrong way down a one-way street? I mean, they've never even made a turn without signaling, Larry, or double-parked, for crying out loud. How many people can you name who signal every time they turn?

How many people do you know who can go an entire three months without breaking at least one law?" Carl answered for him. "None. Zero. Zip. And that includes you and me. Up to now they've been nothing but straight-arrow, always the perfect little law-abiding citizens. Squeaky clean." Carl stopped to scratch his bald head. "I can't figure it, Larry. It doesn't make sense. I just can't figure it."

None of that meant anything to Evans. "So, what's your point?"

"My point is, why change now? Why, all of a sudden, are they breaking every law in the book?"

Evans didn't have any problem explaining that one.

"Because they made us, just like I said. Just like I told you. They know we're following them and they're trying to give us the slip. No damn mystery to me, partner. That's why they're driving so nutso. They spotted us in that goddam snow drift back there, and they see us now. They know we're behind them and they're trying to lose us." Lawrence Evans pounded the steering wheel with the heel of his hand. "Shit, I told you. We're screwed."

Carl scratched his bald head again and let out a long exaggerated sigh. "I'm not so sure about that."

"Well, I am. Sure as shit. I tell you they spotted us and they're headin' for the barn, goddammit. We'll never catch 'em with dirt on their hands now. I think we outta grab 'em, Carl—bounce 'em off the wall a couple times and see what cracks. That's the only way to go, before it's too late. We gotta bust 'em and bust 'em hard. Assholes."

Carl didn't say anything as he watched the van slide through the intersection at 5th Avenue, stop, back up, and then turn south onto 5th Avenue. He was lost in thought. He didn't have time to waste trying to convince his partner that something was out of whack. Special Agent Lawrence Evans was all reaction and no feel—he only believed in what he saw, what he could reach out and touch, what he could *bounce off the wall*. Carl Ferguson, on the other hand, had been fooled too many times in the past; he knew that everything was not always the way it seemed. The eyes did not always have it. Over the years he'd learned to trust not what his eyes saw, but what his stomach felt.

And it felt something was wrong.

"Just keep with them for now," Carl said. "You may be right, but let's play it cool for a little while longer. If they did spot us, we should know that for sure soon." He thought to himself: You just keep driving, partner, while I try to figure this thing out.

"Yeah, well, you're the boss. But I'm gonna get closer. These assholes aren't gonna give me the slip."

"Be careful."

"No sweat."

Evans pressed the accelerator to the floor and the gray Ford fish-tailed down the street toward the yellow taxicab two car-lengths ahead. Carl held his breath.

Stanley eased off on the accelerator of the van and tapped the brakes. Who was the idiot driving that ambulance anyway?

They stopped for the traffic light at 71st Street.

Stanley's eagle eyes stayed trained on his prey.

Whoever was driving that thing was a real jerk all right. Whoever taught him to drive ought to have his head examined. Or maybe have a couple of knees busted, Stanley snickered to himself. The crazy fool had almost gotten them both involved in a half-dozen accidents so far. This was the first red light he'd stopped for. Was he color blind? Didn't he know red when he saw it? Stanley had been led on some crazy chases before, but never anything like this. And certainly not in this kind of weather. "The asshole is going to get us all killed," Stanley whispered to himself.

There was a delivery truck, a snow plow and two cars between Stanley and the ambulance. But Stanley had been in these kinds of situations before—he'd had to trail people many times; it was all part of the job, a part he was very good at; he could handle it. He would not let it get out of his sight no matter how crazy he had to drive. It was a challenge now, a dare, and Stanley was the kind of man who could not resist a dare. Everybody better just stay the hell out of his way.

Had Romaine spotted him? That was the question. Was that what this whole thing was about? Was Romaine the one who had stolen the ambulance because he knew that Stanley was after his sorry ass?

The light turned green.

Stanley pressed on the accelerator and smiled to himself. "You can run but you can't hide, my friend."

"Jesus Christ! What the hell do you think you're doing?"

Victor Romaine finally found his voice. Up to now his only sense had been sight, and what he saw scared him to death.

The kid with the concussion had just stolen the ambulance. Victor's head swam. One minute the little twerp was sitting there staring off into space, eyes glassy, head rolling around like one of those stupid little dogs people have in the back windows of their cars, and the next minute he was off like a shot, and before anyone knew it he was behind the wheel and tearing out of the hospital like a race horse with its ass on fire. And for what purpose? Victor was at a loss.

And there was nothing he could do about it. Lying there strapped to the bed while a lunatic teenager drove through New York City like a madman, his only course of action was to ask questions. And protest like hell.

"Hey! Hey! What the hell's going on?" Victor asked. No response. "What do you think you're doing?" Nothing. Victor repeated himself. "I said, 'What the hell do you thing you're doing?" Still no one answered him. "You can't do this," Victor stuttered. "This is crazy." Everyone ignored him. "Hey, you!" Victor screamed at Billy. "Do you hear me? I said you can't do this. You've got to stop this thing right now."

Silence.

Victor struggled against his bindings. It was one thing to get a couple of legs broken by Rico's men, and quite another to die in a ball of flame because some kid with his screws loose ran an ambulance headfirst into FAO Schwarz. "Stop, goddammit! Stop!"

Billy drove on.

Victor could feel himself begin to hyperventilate. Panic attacked. He resisted. It gained a foothold. This was worse than before—before he knew he would be free sooner or later, when he got to the hospital, he'd simply refuse to be examined and leave. He'd just walk out. What could they do, shoot him? But now he didn't know if he'd ever get out of this. And he had to get out; he'd wasted enough time as it was. It was probably already too late, but he had to try. He tried to look at his watch, but the way he was strapped down he couldn't see his wrist. It had to be after two. He fought to remain calm.

"Kid, listen to me. I don't know what you're up to but this is crazy. You don't know what you're doing. You have to stop this thing right now. You're going to kill us all."

Billy Freely acted as if Victor wasn't there.

This was insane. The kid had obviously blown a fuse. The bump on the head must have knocked something loose. Why the hell didn't his father do something? Or that other guy?

Victor stopped struggling and redirected his efforts at Henry. "Please, friend, listen to me. You've got to stop him. He's not right. He's not thinking. That bump on the head—he's dangerous. You've got to do something."

No response. Just staring. Henry was as confused as Victor.

Jesus, I'm in a carriage of lunatics on the way to the nut house, Victor thought.

He tried again. "Look, I don't know what you're up to, and frankly, I really don't care. It's none of my business. Just stop this thing and let me out. Okay? Whatever it is, I'm not part of it. Right? Okay?"

Nobody said a word. The lack of response irritated Victor. He tried to control his emotions but lost to anger. "Pal, read my lips." His tone was harsh, hot, grease splattering on a hot skillet. "I don't know who the hell you think you are, or what the hell you think you're doing, but I want out of here and I want out of here now." Anger didn't work. "What's the matter with you people? Are you all deaf?"

Billy Freely was deaf, at least to Victor's pleading.

Billy Freely wasn't listening because he didn't have time for listening. He had to find a place to dump the ambulance, fast. Mr. Nash had been right; the ambulance did stick out like a sore thumb. It was just a matter of time before someone spotted it.

Victor tried Henry again. "Just stop and let me out of here. Please. We'll each go our own separate ways. Come on, what do you say?"

Still no response. Henry stared at him.

Threats. Maybe threats would work. "Listen, if you know what's good for you you'll stop this thing right now and let me out of here. I mean it. I'm nobody to screw with."

Billy drove. Bill Sr. stared straight ahead. Henry sat in silence.

Threats didn't work. Victor tried a different approach. "Hey, listen, guys, you want an ambulance, fine. Fine with me. Take it; it's all yours. I could care less. I got no problem with that. None. Take it and be happy. Just stop, okay? and let me out. That's all I ask, just let me out of it. You do your thing and I'll do mine. Okay?" More silence.

Then it dawned on him. "Hey, if you're worried about me going to the police, well, you can forget about that." Victor punctuated his words by shaking his head, hoping physical movement would somehow add credence to his pledge. "No way, man. No way. I won't go to the police. Honest. I don't care about the stupid ambulance. Steal every damned ambulance in the city if you want. It's none of my business. It's just that I have to get out of here. Okay?"

Henry finally turned to Billy and said, "Billy, stop the ambulance. We have to let him out. He's right; he's not part of this. We're in enough trouble as it is."

Billy didn't say anything.

Bill Sr. did. He didn't agree with Henry. His voice was low. "But, Henry, he's seen us. He knows what we look like."

Henry gave him a look. "What are you going to do, Bill—kill him so he can't identify us?"

Good point. Add Murder One to robbery, auto theft and kidnapping.

While Bill searched for a response Billy said, "We can't stop now, Mr. Nash. There's no place to stop. And besides, it would take too much time to stop, unstrap him, and then get him out of here. No, we have to keep going until we can find a good place to dump this thing." With that thought Billy reached down and turned off the flashing lights, which he'd just figured out, "And him with it."

Henry wished he had a response for that, but he didn't.

Michael stood up and followed Parker Gorman to the door. "Ah, you're going after them?" he asked, tentatively.

"Hell yes," Gorman said, irrefutably.

Michael wondered what he was supposed to do.

"Don't lose him," Tommy said.

Sonny Grosso spoke into his rear view mirror. "Don't worry, I got him."

"Get closer. You'll lose him staying this far back."

"Hey, don't sweat it, Mister. He's right up there. He won't get away."

"But he *is* getting away. Farther and farther away. Can't you see that? Listen to me, you've got to get closer."

It was cold inside the cab and Tommy was shaking. But not just from the cold; he was frightened. The crazy man in that van two cars ahead was his only hope to save himself; he could not let him get away. At least that's what he assumed. He didn't know for sure the guy could solve his problem, but he did know that he didn't have any other ideas. If this whole thing turned out to be a wild goose chase he was dead.

"Turn on some heat, will you?" Tommy said.

Sonny put on a guilty look. "Ah, it's up as high as it goes. Been having a problem with it all day. Sorry." Sonny didn't tell his fare that he'd been having a problem with the engine stalling-out as well.

"Shit," Tommy half-whispered to himself. He wasn't surprised, however; it was your typical American car. Poor quality, something the Americans were famous for.

The van passed two cars and turned east onto 66th Street.

"There he goes," Tommy shouted. "Stay with him."

"I got him."

Just then a gray Ford swerved in front of Sonny's cab without signaling and Sonny had to jerk his steering wheel sharply to the right to avoid a collision. "Asshole!" he screamed.

Now there were four cars between Sonny and the van, a fact that had not gone unnoticed by his passenger.

"Jesus, what the hell's the matter with you, letting that car cut you off like that? Get up there," Tommy said. "You're too far back. Get closer. If you'd been up there where you were supposed to be in the first place he'd never have been able to cut you off. Come on, what are you waiting for? You stay back here and everyone will get in front of you for chrissake. You're going to lose them. You're going to lose them."

Sonny stayed on the bumper of the Gray Ford. He would not lose them. This was his first time playing Follow That Car and he was not about to blow it. He was not about to blow his first hundred-dollar-bill either. Chrissy was counting on him.

Were all hundred-dollar fares as bossy as this one? Sonny wondered. Sonny prayed with all his might that his engine didn't quit now.

"You just about ran into that cab," Carl said.

Evans didn't say anything.

Carl turned and looked back at the cab. "Crash us into another car and we'll never catch them, Larry."

Evans didn't say anything.

"Relax. We'll be all right. Just stay loose."

Evans didn't say anything.

Carl knew he should be the one driving.

They almost ran her down in their haste.

"Michael!" Marcella exclaimed as the two men came charging out of the elevator.

Michael stopped in his tracks. "Marcella, what—what are you doing here?"

Marcella glanced quickly at Gorman, then turned back to Michael. "I came looking for you. I heard about the robbery and— My God, Michael, are you all right?"

Michael didn't hesitate. "Of course. I'm fine." Then he realized that wasn't quite true. He wasn't all right, not by a long shot. His pride had been stolen right along with the manuscript. He shrugged. "Well, I'm as all right as can be expected I guess, under the circumstances. I'm not physically injured, if that's what you mean."

Marcella repeated the question with her eyes. Michael said, "Really, I'm okay. But— I thought you were skiing in Colorado."

"My flight was canceled. Everything's grounded. When I heard about the robbery on TV, Michael, I couldn't believe it."

Michael rolled his eyes. "Yeah, neither could I."

"What on earth happened?"

Michael stood there staring at Marcella wondering how he was going to explain what happened—even he wasn't sure—when Parker Gorman interrupted: "Michael, I'm sorry, but I have to get going."

Michael looked at Gorman. "Oh, right. Ah, Mr. Gorman, this is my assistant, Marcella Givens."

Gorman smiled. Marcella asked, "Where are you going?"

Michael answered. "There's a chance that the thieves may have been spotted. We don't know for sure, but Mr. Gorman is going to see if—"

She turned to Gorman. "You're going after them?" Marcella couldn't believe it.

Michael couldn't believe it either.

"But isn't this a police matter?" Marcella asked.

Michael agreed with that but didn't say anything.

Then Gorman tossed out, "The police can use all the help they can get. Besides, they don't have the vested interest in this thing that I do."

Marcella turned to Michael. "What are you going to do?"

Michael was silent.

Marcella turned back to Gorman. "We're coming with you," she said.

"We're what?" Michael said, shocked.

But before he could say anything else, Gorman said, "I don't think that would be a good idea young lady. Like Michael said, we don't know for sure it is them. I might just be wasting my time—going on a wild goose chase, that is. It may not be the thieves after all, and, well, if it is, I don't know what to expect. It might be—"

"Dangerous?" Marcella was an expert at anticipating what people were about to say. Michael knew that better than anyone. "I don't care. We're coming."

"But, Marcella, Mr. Gorman is—"

"No way, Michael. If you don't want to come, fine. But he's not leaving me here after I've come all this way. The manuscript means more to me than it does to," she looked at Gorman, "either of you. It won't be any more dangerous for me than it is for you. I'm coming along. And that's that."

Gorman decided he didn't have time to argue.

His black Cadillac was parked in the first stall. He and Michael scraped the snow off the windows while Marcella watched. Then Gorman and Michael climbed into the front seat of the huge black animal and Marcella climbed into the back. Gorman backed out of his parking stall, eased the heavy machine out of the parking lot and started to pull out onto the street.

"Watch out!" Michael screamed.

"Watch out!" Lilith screamed.

Ralph jerked the steering wheel to the right.

"Crazy jerk-ass idiot!" Lilith screamed at the driver of the black Cadillac. "Think you own the damn road?"

Parker Gorman shook his head in disgust and drove away.

Louise Bridges said, "Hey, that looked like the guy from the museum."

Lilith turned. "What?"

"The man from the museum, in Connecticut, where the manuscript was on display. The guy in that car looked just like him." She turned to her husband. "Did you see him, Raymond?"

Raymond spoke. "That was him all right."

Lilith said, "Well, shit!" then turned to her husband. "Well, don't just sit there Ralph. Follow that car!"

Scotty Hunter turned into the hospital just as Roger Muldowney was driving out. He quickly scanned the area around the Emergency Entrance and as far as he could tell Parker Gorman had not yet arrived—if he was here, chances are that's where he would be, Scotty reasoned. Just as he was about to look for a place to park, an announcement come over his police scanner that made him stop. An ambulance, with a very young-looking driver, had been spotted going east on 66th Street, just west of Madison Avenue.

"That's just on the other side of Central Park," Scotty said aloud. He could be there in no time at all, if he didn't have to sit around waiting for Gorman.

Gorman. Should he wait, and take the chance the ambulance might disappear forever? Or should he check it out on his own?

That was easy. Why the hell should he wait for Gorman? He wasn't getting paid to wait for Gorman; he was getting paid to find the manuscript. He had a job to do—thanks to Gorman—and it didn't involve baby-sitting his boss. Gorman would only be excess baggage. Scotty didn't even know why he was coming for chrissake, and he didn't like people looking over his shoulder. Didn't Gorman trust him? Didn't Gorman think he could handle it? *He* wasn't the one who had put Jefferson's neck on the chopping block. Scotty turned his Ford Mustang into one of the parking stalls reserved for emergency vehicles, quickly shifted into REVERSE, backed out, and then drove off as fast as his traction would allow.

Okay, it was a police matter, but the police he knew didn't seem all that interested in making it their matter. Besides, it was just another case to them; it wasn't personal. It wasn't a matter of life and death. It wasn't their future. On the way out of the parking lot he passed Gorman who was on the way in.

"Scotty!" Gorman hollered.
With the wind blowing and the thieves on his mind Scotty didn't hear him.
"Where the hell is he going?" Gorman asked no one in particular.
"Who?" Michael responded.
"Hunter," Gorman said. "That was Scotty Hunter."
Michael turned and looked behind them, then turned back around and looked at Gorman, confused.
"The guy in the Mustang—the one that just about hit us—that was Scotty Hunter, my head of security. Did you see which way he turned?"
Marcella answered from the back seat. "Left. He turned left."
Gorman used the same parking space Scotty had used, turned around and headed after him.
This is crazy, Michael thought to himself. Who did Gorman think he was? John Wayne? Clint Eastwood? Wyatt Earp? Who were they to be chasing a band of thieves?
If they *were* the thieves.

Lilith spotted Gorman. "Well, hell," she said. "The jerk in the Caddy is coming back this way."
As they slowed down Gorman came out of the entrance and flew by them in pursuit of Scotty.
"What the hell is he doing?" Lilith screamed.
They all wondered together in silence.
Then, "Want me to follow him, Lilith?" Ralph asked.
Lilith frowned. "No, Ralph. I want you to stop here and we'll all get out and have a damn barbecue. Hell yes, I want you to follow them." She shook her head. "Jesus."
No one was coming, so Ralph made a U-turn and drove off after the man in the black Cadillac.

Damn, not now, Sonny Grosso thought to himself as he turned the key in the ignition.
"What's wrong? What the matter? What are you waiting for?" Tommy asked, excited, leaning forward in the back seat.

Sonny turned the key again and the engine growled, but wouldn't start. He pumped the accelerator and tried it a third time. "Ah, this thing's been acting up a little lately," Sonny said sheepishly. "Don't worry about it; it'll kick over any second." *I hope,* Sonny thought. The engine had stalled as soon as Sonny stopped for the traffic light.

"What do you mean it's been acting up a little?"

Sonny did not want to answer that question, but he did. "Ah, it just stalls once in a while. No big deal. It'll be okay."

"What do you mean 'once in a while?'"

Sonny turned the key but ignored the question.

"You're telling me this thing's stalled before? Today?"

Tommy waited for an answer, but not for long. He watched the light change to green and the van begin to drive away, followed by the gray Ford. They were only two cars back now; the two cars and the red station wagon had turned north at the last intersection. But two cars could increase to fifty if they didn't get started. "Hey, the van's moving."

Sonny looked up. *Tell me about it.*

Tommy's heart began to pound. "Come on. Come on. Get on it. Let's go."

Sonny turned the key. *Go!*

No go.

"Dammit, man." Tommy was holding on to the wire screen that separated the front seat from the back. His fingers were white with strain. "You've got to get this stupid thing going."

Sonny tried again. No luck—the engine sounded like a dying frog. The people behind them were blowing their horns. "We're okay," Sonny said, trying to stay calm, trying to fake his way through it. "Don't worry. It's just a little touchy, that's all. I think it's the carburetor. But it's just about ready to go. I can feel it. It almost kicked over that time. I think just another shot of juice and ..."

And I'm dead, Sonny thought, when the engine refused once again to start. Bye-bye hundred dollar bills. Bye-bye bigger apartment. Bye-bye Chrissy.

"Goddammit!" Tommy screamed. "He's getting away." Tommy was more than excited now; he was mad, incensed. He shook the wire screen. His face was red. "Come on. Hurry up. Hurry up."

Rrrrrr, rrrrrrr, rrrrrrrrrr ...

Tommy's face was flushed with blood. He let go of the wire screen and leaned back in his seat. "I might have known it. I should have expected this." He grit his teeth, clenched his fists, shook his head in disgust. "It happens every time I assume things are going to be all right. I should know better. I should know better than to expect things to change here. Nothing ever changes. Nothing ever works. First the heater, now the engine. Does anything work in this stupid car? Does anything work in this stupid country? That's the question. Everything is junk. Typical American junk. That's all you people make. American know-how, there's a joke. *Know how* to screw it up is what you mean. Made In America means it may work or it may not."

You people? What the hell did that mean? What's he, Sonny thought, a Martian? Sonny listened to the engine moan.

"And you—you don't know what the hell you're doing. What kind of cab driver are you? I tell you to follow that van and what do you do? You stay five miles behind him. Any idiot could see that you were going to lose him staying that far back. I tried to tell you, but, no, you wouldn't listen. I told you you were going to lose him. Didn't I? Didn't I tell you that? And now this, this, this piece-a-shit cab won't even run. You can't get it started and we're stuck. If you'd been up there—up there where you were supposed to be—at least we'd have some time to spare. Maybe we could have handled a problem like this because we wouldn't be starting out a hundred damned miles behind the goddam thing to begin with."

It was happening again; Tommy swore under his breath. Everything he touched in this stupid country always failed him. America was a disgrace. Americans were such incompetents.

The car started. Sonny gunned the engine, breathed a sigh of relief when it roared. But now the light was red. "See, I told you we'd be all right," Sonny said.

Tommy expected movement but there was none. "What are you waiting for? Get going."

Sonny nodded his head at the traffic light. "Red light."

"What?"

He pointed at the light. "Light's red."

Tommy looked at it. He didn't care. "I don't give a shit. Run it."

"What?"

"Run the damned light."

"I can't do that."

"Bullshit!"

"I—"

"Run it!"

"Look, I could lose my—"

A hundred dollar bill appeared over his right shoulder.

"Run the goddam light."

Sonny ran the light.

$$$

The traffic was thick, and with the snow plowed high against the curbs there was no place along 66th Street for Billy to pull over to the side of the street and dump the ambulance, even if he could get to the side of the street, which he couldn't. There were three lanes of traffic and he was in the center lane. He couldn't stop; he couldn't turn around; and he couldn't go left or right. His only choice was to go straight ahead and pray something good happened.

At 3rd Avenue he hit another red light.

A police car drove slowly through the intersection in front of him. Billy held his breath. The driver turned his head and for an instant their eyes met. Shit, Billy thought. Just before the cruiser disappeared from view Billy saw the police officer lean forward and pick up his microphone. Double shit!

"You're mine, baby," Stanley said to himself. "Ain't no place to go, ain't no place to hide."

Stanley was directly behind the ambulance now—the delivery van had turned down an alley between Lexington and 3rd—no more than six inches separated him from the AMBULANCE, PROCEED WITH CAUTION bold, black lettering.

"You and me," he said, and patted the pistol under his left arm. "And baby makes three."

Stanley grinned.

The light turned green.

"Gonna rip it up, gonna tear it up, gonna smash it up tonight. Ha, ha, ha." Stanley sang aloud. He was a lousy singer but that didn't stop him.

Stanley was about to pull ahead when a car in the right hand lane turned directly in front of him and darted across his path, cutting him off from the ambulance. Stanley took his foot off the accelerator and leaned on his horn. The driver of the other car paid no attention as he slid onto 3rd Avenue, hit his accelerator, and then shot away before Stanley had a chance to curse at him. Stupid ass, Stanley thought to himself anyway. Stanley's hesitation allowed another car to take advantage of the space between Stanley and the ambulance, squeezing in between Stanley and Victor. That pissed Stanley off even more.

"Stay with him, Ralph. We don't want to lose him now."

Lilith's eyes were aflame. She was a born predator.

"Got to be careful, dear. Streets are pretty slick," Ralph responded.

"Bull. The streets look fine; just a little snow. Don't always be such an old woman, Ralph. Don't be afraid to take a chance now and then. Grab a little gusto, man."

The Cadillac turned south onto 5th Avenue. Scotty was a half a block ahead.

Ralph turned south onto 5th Avenue. He was a half block behind.

"If he can drive on these streets, Ralph, so can you. So quit your bitching. Just you stay right up there with him and don't fiddle-faddle." Lilith had her eyes locked on the black Cadillac.

All the stores on 5th Avenue were decorated for Christmas. Strings of brightly colored miniature lights twinkled everywhere, and many of the windows were sprayed with artificial snow. McKesson Robbins, New York City's newest "in" toy store, had a different Christmas scene in each of its six windows that faced the street. Animated characters tirelessly entertained any shopper who was foolish enough to be out in weather like this. Elves in their workshop, reindeer feeding in the stable, angels hovering overhead, a choir of children carolers singing, a family decorating a Christmas tree, and, of course, Santa Claus, all combined to entice the cold and weary potential customer to come in and warm up a bit, maybe browse a little. It was a beautiful sight that no one saw.

"He's got a heavier car than we do, dear. Gives him better traction."

"Phooey. Don't blame it on the damn car. All boils down to the skill of the driver."

Ralph fell farther behind.

"Ralph, you're falling behind. Step on it. Get the lead out of your butt."

"Why don't we just go to the insurance company and wait for them?" Louise tossed out from the back seat. "This chasing people all over the place worries me to death. It's just not safe."

This time Lilith didn't even bother to turn around when she spoke. "Hey, you want to live in the fast lane you can't worry about safe."

"But— Well, I don't really think I'm cut out for the fast lane."

No shit, Lilith thought. "When you deal in millions, Dearie, you don't have any choice. You're in the fast lane whether you like it or not. Millions don't come to people who sit around and wait, people who play it safe. In case you haven't got the point yet, something's going on here; that's why we have to stay on their tail. These people are up to something and you can bet it's not in our best interest." She turned and looked into the back seat. "You feel something slipping through your fingers?" Louise looked confused. Lilith grinned. "It's the money, Honey. The m-o-n-e-y."

It was at that point Billy Freely decided to make a break for it.

Chapter 22

CAPTAIN JOHN WINSTON SHERMAN WAINWRIGHT THE THIRD stood six-feet-four inches tall and weighed two hundred and forty five pounds—without his saber. He liked to be referred to as "Moose." His men complied by calling him Bullwinkle behind his back. Wainwright—a fifth generation Marine—was stationed at the Pentagon, and was assigned to the 121st Quartermaster Group, 35th Marine Division. He had been in the Marine Corps for seventeen years and in those seventeen years had spent a lot of his time swearing under his breath. This was one of those times.

Jesus H. Christ. Talk about your luck running out at the worst possible time.

Captain John Winston Sherman Wainwright, the Third, was a very unhappy captain. For the first time in his illustrious career he had been roped-in to attending—in person, front-and-center—the kick-off ceremonies for the yearly Marine Corps Toys For Tots campaign.

Oh, sure, he'd been part of the drive before; he had to be, it was *expected*. But he was always in the background, never a lead player, never required to actually attend the ceremonies. When called upon he somehow always managed to wiggle his way out of it. In the past he'd report for duty, but once he got there he'd spend all his time sitting around drinking coffee and talking spit-and-polish with the other officers while the grunts did all the work. He took credit for banner years; blamed poor years on lack of effort—sometimes the men just don't get fired up, Sir! But this year his luck finally ran out. This year it was his turn to attend the speeches—standin' tall and lookin' good—and there was no way he could weasel his way out of it. Standing at attention in wind chills that caused the mercury to dip into the double digits on the minus side of the scale, while a bunch of jerks spoke about a bunch of crap they didn't know a damned thing about, was not his idea of a pleasant way to spend a winter evening. Or any evening for that matter.

War—that was the only thing that counted as far as Wainwright was concerned.

Killing slant-eyes, or *Rooskies*—it didn't matter, they were all the same. It was the only game in town he cared about. It was the only game that got you to Major in ten years, then Colonel, then the stars started falling and Hello, General Wainwright. Hell, that's why they invented the term "Gung Ho" wasn't it? I mean, did he join the Marine Corps to stand at attention and listen to dumbasses talk, or did he join the Corps to show the Reds, and the Yellows, and any other damn color for that matter, just what this country was all about? He was not in this thing for parades. Parades and presentations were for wimps. He joined the Marine Corps to kick some butt, Jack!

Instead, he was freezing his butt. Talk about making sacrifices for your country. The Toys For Tots thing was one gigantic nuisance. Shit-duty right from the beginning. He didn't have any kids, so why should he have to collect toys for the snot-nose little bastards? Let the guys with kids do it.

Not having children was no accident—Wainwright didn't have children because he didn't like children. Too noisy, too messy. Bunch of damn whiners, that's all they were. Carolyn, his wife, wanted a family, but so far Big John (another of his favorite names for himself) had been able to talk her out of it. "Hey, you never know when I might be transferred into a combat zone. You know that's no way to raise a child."

And she always bought it.

Wainwright shivered and cursed to himself again. Toys For Tots was a royal pain in the Dress Blues all right, but he couldn't think of a way out of it so here he was.

It's an honor to be chosen.

Bullshit. He'd heard that crap before. That's what they always said when it was bend-over-and-spread-'em time.

But Wainwright did have to admit one thing; it certainly wouldn't hurt his career any. It looked good on his Yellow Sheet. Not as good as combat, but good.

So he'd bite his tongue and play their stupid game: stand tall, chest out, stomach in, chin nailed to his Adam's Apple. As long as he was here he might as well do it right, no time to blow it now, there was too much heavy artillery around, more brass here than you could shake a swagger stick at. Scrambled eggs up the ying yang; four colonels, two generals, even the Commandant of the Corps was here, *in person*. The perfect place to make points. The perfect place to do some serious butt kissing.

Darkness was beginning to settle in; the automatic street lights started to glow.

But why they had to be here more than two hours before the damn thing started made no sense to the Captain. "Hurry up and wait," the Marine Corps invented that one.

Wainwright marched in place, stomping his feet up and down trying to warm up his freezing toes. The rest of his company was huddled in small groups, talking, smoking, waiting for their fearless leader to "command" them. Wainwright stood off to one side by himself. Officers could not mix with enlisted men. Wasn't good for discipline. Gold and tin don't mix. That was not the Marine Corps way; that was the Wainwright way. He didn't have time for grunts; what the hell good could they do his career?

The jeeps that brought them here were parked at the rear. Wainwright noticed there were some people already beginning to congregate around the skating rink; early birds, get here early and stand in front. They kept moving; stay in motion, try to keep warm. Their expressions betrayed their true feelings. Would the wait be worth it? Would sacrificing one's life to death-by-freezing, just to gaze in wonder at the sixty feet of Wisconsin pine as it burst into glorious color when the Commandant pulled the switch, be a fair trade? Wainwright could answer that question for them: Hell no it wouldn't! Were they all nuts? To come out with the temperature in the teens was just plain dumb.

Wainwright didn't understand people; to come out to watch some moron light a stupid Christmas tree was idiotic. He certainly wouldn't be here if he didn't have to be. He shook his head; Jesus, you could stay at home and watch the whole damn thing on the Eleven O'clock News and not freeze your ass off in the process.

The mayor would speak first, then the Commandant.

Wainwright couldn't wait to get out of here. He was cold, and his lips were chapped. But he was able to pucker them all the same. Never know when a general might walk by.

"You want a cup of coffee, Cliff?"

Wiseman looked up from his desk. The voice came from his doorway. The little fat man standing there was waiting for an answer. He got one. "Naw, I think I'll call it a day," Wiseman said. He looked at the clock on the wall: 5:14. He'd been there since seven, ten hours was enough for any man. "I'm all coffeed-out. I'll bet I've gone through a gallon of that stuff today. Thanks anyway, Brownie."

Sergeant Jason Brown had come on duty at four. He was already into his third cup. "Keeps the pipes oiled," he said.

"Keeps the pipes rusty," Wiseman countered.

Brown smiled. "You're just working too hard. Too many hours will do that to a man. Coffee's good for you. Ask your doctor."

Wiseman frowned. "Doctor died last week. Caffeine overdose."

Again Brown showed his pearly whites. Then he motioned with his head to the office next door, the captain's office. "That the case, maybe I should get our fearless leader a cup."

Wiseman grunted. "Make it a barrel."

The two men smiled knowingly at each other.

Wiseman got up from his chair, stretched his aching back, then looked down at the manila folders piled high on his desk. He sighed. Brown punctuated the sigh with a comment. "Still be there tomorrow. And when they disappear new ones'll take their place. No use killin' yourself over a pile of paper that ain't never goin' away."

"Tell me about it," the inspector said.

The two men walked out of Wiseman's office together. As they passed the sergeant's desk, Brown stopped and looked at the paper that was spilling out of his computer. His lips moved as he read. Then aloud he said, "Says here they think they spotted that ambulance that was stolen earlier." Brown looked at Wiseman. Wiseman nodded that he understood what Brownie was talking about. "Out around Third and Sixty-six."

Wiseman turned and said over his shoulder as he walked away, "Good, maybe you guys can solve one tonight while I'm at home watching *A Charlie Brown's Christmas* with my kids."

"Don't want us to save it for you?" Brown hollered after him. "Get you a lot of points with you-know-who."

Wiseman just waved and disappeared out the door.

Lance Corporal Collin McGovern's eyes never moved under the brim of his hat; they were trained on the man in front of him. Bullwinkle Wainwright, his commanding officer.

The guy is such a jerk, McGovern thought. A comic book soldier—King of Parades and Presentations. A "round 'em up, men" kind of guy. He'd never seen combat in his life, but he talked like he'd served with John Wayne at Iwo Jima. The sooner McGovern got out of this chicken-shit outfit the better.

"It's a city matter now. Forget it."

That was not what Officer Howard wanted to hear.

He spoke into his radio microphone. Howard was not afraid to talk back to his commanding officer; he and Mitchell had been classmates at the State Police Academy. "Don't give me that crap, Mitch. The robbery took place in our jurisdiction, on my watch. That means it's our baby. If I hadn't done that three-sixty into the median strip we wouldn't even have this problem. Tell the NYPD to butt the hell out."

Officer Moses Howard of the New York *State* Police Department was not about to let go of this one. He'd been involved in crimes before that had taken him toe-to-toe with the New York City Police Department and he'd always lost, but this time it was going to be different. He was not going to lose this one. He'd started it and he was going to finish it. Beside, losing wears on a person after awhile. Especially when you lose to those guys. Glory Boys, that's what he called them.

Captain Mitchell responded, "The crime *was* ours, but if the perpetrators ended up in the city, the collar's theirs. I don't like it any better than you do, but you can't fight City Hall. I know it and you know it. And it wasn't your fault you lost it, we've got seventy-six cars in the median strip between here and New Rochelle. Forget it, Moses. It was just one of those things. Come on in. It's been a busy day. There's always tomorrow."

Moses mumbled, "Yeah, right," into his mike and turned off the switch. No way in hell was he coming in now. He was too close. The call said an ambulance—a suspicious looking ambulance, maybe the ambulance they were looking for—had been spotted at 3rd Avenue and 66th Street, and he was at Broadway and 63rd. If they turned south, and then came west, and he went south and turned east, they might just run right into each other. Who knows? Crazier things have happened. It was worth a chance.

Moses Howard drove to 59th Street and turned east onto Columbus Circle. He pulled in behind the statue of Christopher Columbus and stopped, shifted into neutral, but did not turn off the engine. He'd wait here and see if the bad guys sauntered by.

It had to be the bad guys; he could smell them. And he was going to bring the bastards in if it was the last thing he did. He was not going to let the Glory Boys break another one off in him. This was going to be his collar and that's all there was to it. He was going to see this baby all the way through to the end. Captain Mitchell could go whistle his tune to someone else. He wasn't coming in until he had those bastards in his cuffs. All they had to do was turn south, swing east and he'd—

Then, in the distance, something white coming his way. Something white, as in ambulance.

It came closer.

Moses saw it. It was an ambulance all right, *his* ambulance, and it was coming straight toward him.

He didn't pay any attention to the black van that followed the ambulance. Or the tan Ford that followed the van.

That's it, he thought. By God, that's it. He shifted his car into low. No siren—no reason to alert the Glory Boys.

The ambulance approached. Moses eased his foot off the brake pedal.

Now that it was almost dark it was harder to see. Lights were everywhere. Car lights. Street lights. Christmas lights. They all looked the same.

But that was the other guy's problem; Stanley had eyes like a hawk. He could spot a pimple on a whore's butt at a thousand paces. Which meant that the sonofabitch in the ambulance could dart in and out of traffic as much as he wanted, he would not lose Stanley.

Carl Ferguson had finally made up his mind. He hated to admit it, but it looked as though his partner was right.

"I think you're right, Larry. I think they did spot us."

"Told you."

With a sigh, "Okay, you win. We've waited long enough. Let's pull them in."

Music to Evans' ears. "Now you're talking," he said, and gunned the engine.

How long were they going to just keep walking? Was this Pierre's plan—walk around New York City forever? They had been walking for hours. And where were they walking to?

"Pierre, where are we going?" Jacques asked.

Pierre did not answer. Pierre did not have an answer.

"I am cold, Pierre," Jacques said.

"I am cold too, *mon ami*," Pierre said.

After a few more steps Jacques repeated his question: " But where are we going?"

Again Pierre did not answer because Pierre did not know.

The southbound lane of 3rd Avenue was closed for snow removal between 60th and 70th Streets; Traffic Department barriers prevented anyone from turning south. Almost anyone. When it came time to make a break Billy The Kid couldn't let a little matter like driving into oncoming traffic bother him.

Not when he was driving an ambulance.

Billy pulled into the intersection, jerked the steering wheel to the right—which meant he was turning south into the northbound lane, the lane of traffic where people were coming *toward* him—flipped the flashing red lights back on and pressed the accelerator to the floor.

Henry's eyes shot wide open. "What the hell are you doing?"

Billy made a quick turn to the right, then brought the ambulance back to the left again, thereby avoiding running head-on into the white Con Ed truck that had been bearing down on him. The driver of the truck swore at him but Billy had no ears for that now.

"We've waited long enough, Mr. Nash. We have to get out of here. We have to dump this thing. I think that cop back there was suspicious."

Billy turned east onto 64th Street.

"Cop?" Bill Sr. said.

"What cop?" Henry said.

"He spotted me at that light back there. Gave me a real funny look. I don't know, but I think I saw him go for his microphone."

"Jesus," Henry said. Then he turned and looked out the back of the ambulance. "I don't see any police behind us. I think we're—"

Henry stopped in mid-sentence. He did not see any police behind them, but he saw a black van that was charging toward them like a wild bull.

Billy approached 2nd Avenue. The light was yellow. As soon as he hit the intersection he turned south, then pushed the accelerator all the way to the floor again. At 59th Street he turned west.

Stanley was gritting his teeth. He forced the words through them. "You ain't gonna get rid of me that easy, pal. You can drive like that, I can drive like that. You want to run red lights, I can run red lights. You go down the wrong lane, I can go down the wrong lane. You think you're screwin' with somebody who ain't played this game before? Ha!"

"Stay with him," Tommy yelled.

Sonny Grosso wasn't so sure this whole thing had been such a good idea after all. "Follow that car" sounded neat, but Sonny had not bargained for this. Running red lights, driving south in the northbound lane ... risking his life had not been part of the deal.

"The guy's driving like a psycho."

"I don't care," Tommy said. "I'm paying you to stay with him. So stay with him."

Sonny shifted into second gear.

"You guys are crazy," Victor said.

The ambulance roared west on 59th Street twisting and turning and sliding its way through traffic, out of control but somehow managing to avoid a collision.

The three men—two men and a boy—ignored Victor.

Victor struggled against his straps, but they refused to give an inch. There was only one way he could get out of here and he knew it. He needed help. And he sensed he would not win that struggle either. These idiots were never going to listen to him. They were crazies and he was a dead man. Hell, it probably didn't make any difference anyway; it was dark out; even if they did let him go, Samuelson had to be halfway to England by now.

Go back to their lovely little island, that was the only thing they could do. Go back and regroup, start over. But how was he going to tell the men? That was Pedro's problem. They would not like it. They were eager for a fight. They were eager to put their lives on the line. How could he tell them it was all over?

How could he tell L'Ange?

"The ambulance was seen heading west on Fifty-ninth Street."

Once again Scotty thanked God for his police scanner—59th was only seven blocks south.

Scotty mentally scanned through his options. He only had one. His best bet was to keep going south. If he got to 59th Street before they crossed 5th Avenue—that is, if they were east of 5th Avenue to begin with—and if they didn't turn off before they got to 5th, then he might just be able to "head 'em off at the pass," as Roy Rogers used to say.

If, however, they decided to turn, or they were already west of him, then once again he was S-O-L, *shit outta luck*—a saying, that in Scotty's case, seemed to be particularly apropos lately.

He checked his side mirror, then eased his car into the inside lane. He did not notice the black Cadillac four cars behind him do the same thing. Why should he? He had other things on his mind. The light at the intersection of 65th Street was green, if he could just get there before it changed.

He was two car-lengths away when it turned yellow. Scotty pushed the accelerator down. He felt the snow beneath his tires give way and his Mustang start to fish-tail. He eased off. He straightened out, but Scotty knew he couldn't stop for the light now even if he wanted to. He was going to make that light regardless, as long as nobody at 65th got antsy and decided to shoot onto 5th before the light changed. Just as he got to the intersection it turned red.

He made it through.

Gorman didn't. "Shit!"

Scotty was not as lucky at the next light. It was yellow as he approached. The car in front of him made it through as the light changed to red. The traffic coming off 63rd Street onto 5th Avenue had already started into the intersection by the time Scotty got there, so he had to stop.

He waited impatiently for the light to change. It did, and he moved forward.

The rest of the lights were green, until he got to 59th. He stopped and looked to his left. He saw no ambulance approaching. Should he turn west, assuming the ambulance had already gone through, or should he try to find a place to wait and hope that it was on its way? The red light gave him time to think.

Time to make the right decision. Because when he turned and looked to his right he saw it, in all its glory, gliding down 59th Street two blocks away.

He was getting close. He smiled.

Chapter 23

Parker Gorman frowned. Scotty was getting farther away.

The traffic had filled-in from the side streets every time Gorman got stuck at a red light, and that made it that much more difficult to keep Scotty in sight. Fortunately, he still had him in view, but just barely. He was up ahead, in the right lane. Gorman could see him waiting at the traffic light at 59th. His right turn signal was on.

"Looks like he's turning west on Fifty-ninth," he said to Michael. "If this damned light would just change." He gave the steering wheel a shot with the heel of his right hand.

By the time the light did change the traffic flow from his left had put another half-dozen or so cars between Gorman and Scotty.

"Damn, I hate New York City traffic," Gorman said. "You'd think in this kind of weather people would have enough sense to stay inside."

"We're didn't," Marcella said.

Gorman didn't respond.

Silence and driving and thinking.

Then, "Uh, what are we going to do if we do catch him?" Michael asked.

Michael asked the question Marcella had been wanting to ask from the beginning.

The answer seemed obvious to Gorman. "We're going to help him— what did you think we were going to do? If it turns out that he's on the trail of the thieves then he'll probably need all the help he can get. That's why we're here."

That's what Michael was afraid of. "But— Uh, don't you think that could be little dangerous?"

Gorman shrugged.

Marcella took a turn. "What can we do to help? We're not exactly a SWAT team, Mr. Gorman."

Good point, Michael thought. His point exactly. He didn't know about Gorman's background, but he could vouch for the fact that neither he nor Marcella were trained in this kind of thing; bounty hunters they were not.

Gorman ignored her question. "I tried to tell you not to come along, Ms. Givens," Gorman said. "We're not here to have a picnic."

Marcella didn't like the connotation of that remark even though the words were more or less accurate. It sounded like just maybe he was suggesting that all the females should have stayed home and tended to the chores: bake a cake, scrub the floor, have babies.

Michael tried to help. "I'm sure that Marcella wasn't just talking about herself. I'm sure she was referring to all of us. Don't you think something like this is best left to the professionals?"

"You're not getting cold feet, are you, Michael?" Gorman asked. "You're free to get out any time you want."

Michael turned to Marcella. His eyes asked the question.

"Not me," Marcella answered. "I'm staying."

Michael turned back around. He had no choice; he was staying too.

Marcella to Gorman: "And besides, whether we were here or not, you'd still be doing this. Am I right?"

"Right as rain."

The light changed and Gorman spun his tires in his eagerness to get moving. "And I'll tell you why." To Michael, "I'll answer that question you asked. No, I don't think something like this is best left to the professionals—not if your definition of professional is spelled p-o-l-i-c-e. Not this time anyway." Gorman had a chance to pull into the right lane so he took it. He wanted to turn right at the next light, and the opportunity to get into the proper lane may not present itself again. New York City drivers didn't like to let an open car length between vehicles go unfilled. "Why? Because nobody cares about that manuscript as much as I do." To Marcella, via the rear view mirror, "Even though you've already indicated that you don't believe that, it just happens to be true. Therefore, that being the case, nobody is as interested in getting it back as I am. The police care about the thieves; I care about the manuscript. Besides, I think we may be vital to this operation because we have something the police don't have. We have the only person in the world who can identify the thieves."

Not even close, Michael thought. "I can identify the thieves just as easily *after* the police catch them. So I'm not too sure I see the advantage of being here now."

Marcella said, "I agree with Michael, and even though I think it's dangerous for amateurs to meddle in professionals' work, and I don't just mean dangerous for us, I mean dangerous for the manuscript as well, I do think we have to go on. What concerns me the most is if the thieves should decide to destroy it, or panic, and just throw it out, so they're not caught with the evidence. From that standpoint I suppose you're right, Mr. Gorman; they may be less inclined to feel threatened by us than by the police. On the other hand, you never know, a caged animal is liable to do anything. If they just tossed it out the window we might never find it again. Then where would we be?"

Michael wished that Marcella was not so committed to this insanity. She seemed to lose all reason when it came to Twain. He understood she was a fan of Mark Twain; she'd made that abundantly clear. But being a fan did not mean that you had to risk your life for a stupid manuscript. Chasing after thieves was police work.

"That's exactly my point," Gorman said, "and the main reason I want to be there. I think they might decide to do exactly that, if the police get to them first. However, if I can get to them before the police do, maybe we can make a deal."

Marcella leaned forward in her seat. This interested her. "Deal? Tell me about this deal."

Gorman kept his eyes on the road. "Well, there's not much to tell. I just believe that the thieves might be willing to sell the manuscript to us, if we keep the police out of it."

"Keep the police out of it?"

"Right. The police can go on with their business and we'll go on with ours."

Marcella was shocked. "Can you do that?"

"I can try."

Michael, who had felt uncomfortable before, but now felt even more so since it was quickly dawning on him that he might not even be able to count on the police for backup, said, "Ah, you'd actually try to keep the police out of this? Altogether? I mean—"

"They have plenty of other things to do." Gorman tossed out nonchalantly.

Marcella laughed. "That's not the point. How busy the police are is not the issue. This is, in fact, a police matter. Robbery is a police matter. You can't just tell them to go away."

"The point I'm trying to make is: I don't have to tell them anything— especially if I can contact the thieves first. Or if they contact me."

"But— Are you sure the thieves will be willing to deal with you?"

"Why wouldn't they be? That's why they stole it, isn't it? You don't think they swiped it just to read it, do you? No way; all they're interested in is money, and ours is just as good as anyone else's."

Marcella was stunned. "But that's blackmail, isn't it? I mean, you'd actually submit to blackmail? You'd really pay a bunch of thieves to get the manuscript back?" *Get the manuscript back*, that was the key, wasn't it? Marcella agreed with the objective, but it was the method that bothered her. Or did it?

"Hell yes I would. In a minute."

Marcella wanted to argue, but she wasn't certain that she believed her own arguments. She and Gorman had, in theory—in theory, hell, in fact— the same objective. But was she willing to do *anything* to accomplish that objective? Marcella was not sure how she'd answer that question. She tried. "Well, of course I want to get the manuscript back, but I don't know that I can condone something like that. I mean, you are, in effect, *paying* them to commit a crime, are you not? Rewarding them. Don't you think that's self-defeating? Don't you think that will only encourage them to pull the same stunt again at another time, another place and another insurance company?"

Even Marcella knew that sounded weak.

"Maybe."

"Maybe? You agree?"

Gorman shrugged again.

"Then why do it?"

"Because, young lady, it's the most expedient thing to do under the circumstances. We don't have a lot of choices. We'll worry about the next time, the next time." He turned toward Michael.

Michael winced. The spear Gorman had just tossed was intended for him. Gorman's way of saying if it hadn't been for Michael there wouldn't be a *this time*.

Gorman continued. "Simply put: Buying it back is one hell of a lot less risky than the other alternatives. And a lot cheaper."

Cheaper, that was the key. Marcella was about to say something when Gorman added, "The only thing important here—the only thing that really matters—is saving the manuscript. I'm sure you'll agree with that." He did not give her a chance to agree or disagree. "Our methods of trying to accomplish that feat would be, I suspect, somewhat different. And our reasons for doing it are probably not the same either. But methods and reasons are not *the* issues; they're side issues. Side issues that are neither here nor there. My method is simple: buy it back if I can. My reason: Saving the manuscript in turn saves the company, *my* company, millions of dollars. Which in turn saves the jobs of the two hundred people who work for Jefferson National. You, no doubt, operate from a much higher plain, a loftier position. I, unfortunately, can't afford to do that. I don't have the ability, or the time, or the right, to deal in truth, goodness and beauty. I have to play in the real world, with real marbles."

Marcella bought part of that, but she didn't buy all of it. And she didn't like being accused of living on Walden Pond. "This has nothing to do with truth, goodness or beauty. And it has nothing to do with the manuscript. It's all about money. You're telling me this whole thing comes down to the almighty dollar. That's basically what you're saying. It has nothing to do with breaking the law. It has nothing to do with right or wrong. It has nothing to do with encouraging thieves. It's solely a matter of dollars. It always has been and always will be. Even before the robbery the only thing people wanted to talk about was how much money, how many *dollars*, the auction would bring."

"Dollars make the world go 'round."

She knew it. "Well, I think that's really sad. You can't define everything in terms of so many dollars. Twain's manuscript is more than dollars."

"Not to me," Gorman countered. "Economics, that's what it's all about, Ms. Givens. Econ One-Oh-One. Money, jobs, people's futures. Jefferson National will be financially ruined if we don't recover that manuscript. You want that to happen? You want to take that chance? You want me to take that chance? If it was up to you, would you be willing to bet the livelihood of two hundred people on the hope that the police care more about recovering the manuscript than they do about apprehending the criminals?" Pause. Then, "Well, I wouldn't. The police have a job to do and I have a job to do. That's why I want to be involved, because I *do* care about the manuscript, because it has the power to affect the lives of two hundred people, two hundred people I'm responsible for. And, I care about myself. And I don't give a damn about the thieves. So, you put it in terms of dollars; I put it in terms of people, and jobs, and families. Will I do whatever I have to do to get it back?" He shook his head with confidence. "Every day of the week."

Marcella took one last shot, just to make sure she understood what was being said here. "What you're really saying then is: You don't care about the manuscript at all, you only care about the effect the lack of the manuscript can have on your company."

Gorman didn't hesitate a second. "Bullseye."

"If you hadn't written the policy on the manuscript you wouldn't care at all."

"Another bullseye."

People sometimes made Marcella ill. "Okay, now that we've settled that, what makes you think the thieves will take you up on your deal?"

Gorman shook his head. "Because I'll make them a deal they can't refuse. Let's face it—and I'm sure you won't want to hear this—but the only value, the only real value the manuscript has is in terms of money. The people who took it couldn't care less about Mark Twain."

That didn't bother Marcella at all; she already understood what people cared about. "Oh, I don't doubt that for a minute. I'm sure your thieves are as big a fools as the majority of the people who came to our museum to view it. I just don't like it when people have to put a price tag on something to define its value."

"People didn't put the price tag on this. You did."

"Me?"

"People like you. You're the ones who shouted to the world how much it was worth. Am I right? Priceless—isn't that the word the newspapers used?"

Marcella did not like the sound of what she was hearing. Priceless was meant to imply that it could not be replaced at any price; it was one of a kind. It did not mean dump it into the greasy hands of the highest bidder, or the sneakiest thief. It belonged to the world. Auctioning it off had ticked Marcella off from the beginning. It made her sick to think that something as wonderful as the Twain manuscript might be crammed away in a safe somewhere. It belonged in a museum. It belonged to the world.

There were only two cars between Gorman and Lilith.

"Stay with him, Ralph. Stay with him." It was not a request, it was an order.

"Oh my," Louise said. "This— This is awfully dangerous."

Raymond didn't say anything.

Lilith harumphed.

Cliff Wiseman was actually looking forward to watching *A Charlie Brown Christmas*. Of course he'd seen it before, a dozen times at least, but that didn't make any difference—it was a story that should be watched every Christmas, along with Rudolph and Frosty and *White Christmas*, with Bing Crosby. *A Charlie Brown Christmas* was as much a part of Christmas as the Christmas tree and the fruit cake.

Fruit cake? There was a sobering thought. If that didn't put a bad taste in your mouth nothing would. Wiseman prayed that this would be the year his dear, sweet, eighty-year-old aunt Bernice in Harrisburg, Pennsylvania, would decide that baking a bunch of fruit cakes was just too much work for her tired old bones, and, she was very sorry, she knew how much everyone enjoyed them, but she was afraid that she would not be able to send her famous homemade Christmas fruit cakes to everyone in the family this year. It was a tradition, but all traditions had to come to an end sooner or later.

This one had gone on too long as it was as far as Cliff was concerned. Getting fruit cakes had been a yearly event ever since he was a child. He thought it was bad then, but then he could dump most of it off on his brothers and sisters. That turned out to be nothing compared to what he had to put up with after he got married. "His" family got a fruit cake of their very own. And "his" wife, and "his" children were not nearly as cooperative as his siblings had been; they refused to eat a bite. Cliff always wrote a polite thank-you letter, but he, too, refused to eat the foul-tasting things. Even the dog refused to eat the foul-tasting things.

But then, what would Christmas be without one of Aunt Bernice's fruit cakes? he asked himself.

More appetizing, he answered himself. Then all he'd have to concern himself with would be the extra workload that Christmas always brought with it: pick-pockets, purse snatchings, crowd control, paying all those bills in January.

And fighting all this traffic. Where the hell did all the people come from and where the hell were they all going? Wiseman asked himself. Now that it had stopped snowing the streets were filling up again, as though nothing at all had happened. Snow six inches deep seemed to deter no one. It's Christmas time, who cares about a little snow? Ho, ho, ho. Wiseman kicked himself for not going over to 1st Avenue the way he'd originally planned, but the traffic report had said the Avenue of the Americas was practically deserted. Granted, that was an hour ago. Wiseman sat patiently at the traffic light at 40th Street and made a mental note to give his pal, Tom Peters in Traffic, a call first thing in the morning and read him the riot act. The light turned green and he just sat there; the traffic across the intersection had not yet begun to move. He wondered if he was going to make it home in time to watch Charlie Brown after all.

"Okay, let's look sharp."

Everyone groaned as Wainwright barked out the words. It was too cold to think about looking sharp, but the company started to fall into formation anyway. Cigarettes were field-stripped, all conversation stopped. Four rows of ten men each began to form.

"Dress it up. Dress it up," Wainwright said as he walked up and down the first column.

My Commander-in-Chief, Collin McGovern whispered to himself. My Hero. Wainwright stopped in front of him. McGovern stared straight ahead.

After he looked him over, up, then down, Wainwright said, "What did you shine you shoes with, Marine? A Hershey bar?"

Without waiting for an answer he turned and walked on to the next man and repeated the same line.

Jerk, McGovern thought. Can't think of anything to say except a line that's older than I am. And I could shave in these shoes, you dipshit, and you know it.

The van had two wheels in the air and two on 59th Street as it passed the final car between it and the ambulance. Needless to say, Stanley Kowalski was not a happy man.

"Crazy son of a bitch," Stanley growled as he managed to straighten out the vehicle and get all four wheels back on solid pavement again. He was fuming. "Dumb bastard. When I catch you you're gonna get a little more than Mr. Rico paid for, pal. I can promise you that. I'm gonna give you a little extra, a little bonus, a little freebie, just for all the trouble you been putting me through."

The van sailed down 59th Street. It bit off the Avenue of the Americas and 7th Avenue in chunks. Evans was getting tired of the merry-go-round.

"These crazy bastards are crazier than we thought. Look at 'em. Look at the way those assholes are driving."

Evans was right. They were driving even more recklessly than they had been before. They were running red lights, cutting people off, and had just about run down two nuns at that last crosswalk. There could be no other explanation. They were definitely trying to get away.

"Stay with him, Larry," Carl said.

Evans groaned. "Don't worry. Those fuzz buckets aren't going to lose me now."

Fuzz buckets? Ferguson was definitely going to have to do something about his partner's language.

That had to be the thieves, Officer Howard thought. No one else would drive like that.

There were no blue-and-white NYPD units anywhere to be seen. Good. It's them, and they're mine. The only question was: Why were all those other idiots behind them driving that way, too? Was the entire city crazy?

"Bill, do you get the feeling that that black van back there is following us?"

Bill Freely turned and looked back at the van, the van that was gaining on them, the van that was gaining on them fast. Bill had to agree that it looked like it was, but he didn't understand. "But— Why would a van be after us?"

Henry shook his head. "I don't know."

Just then a state police cruiser came charging out of Columbus Circle. It pulled in between the van and the ambulance, cutting off the van and almost running into the rear of the ambulance. Henry gulped.

"Shit!" Bill said.

Billy turned his head to the right, but kept his eye on the road. "What? What is it, Dad? What's the matter?"

"State police."

"Whaaaaat?"

"The state police are right behind us. He came out of nowhere, just after you got by Central Park. He was just *there*."

"Jesus."

Bill turned to Henry. "What the hell are we going to do now, Henry?"

"How the hell should I know?" Henry blurted out.

"Do you think they're after us because of the manuscript or the ambulance?"

That was the dumbest question Henry had ever heard. "Jesus, Bill, I don't know. What the hell difference does it make?"

"Doesn't make any difference to me," Billy said. "They aren't going to catch us either way."

With that Billy jerked the steering wheel to the left and floored the accelerator, cutting in front of the traffic coming south on Broadway.

Tires fought for traction, lost. Cars began to slide, spin. Horns screamed. Drivers, trying to avoid the ambulance, saw the inevitable coming and could do nothing about it but curse. Henry was tossed against the door, Bill against the side. And the ambulance, too, started to slide sideways.

State police? What the hell are the *state* police doing here?

Stanley eased off on the accelerator. He was confused, and pissed—a very dangerous and potentially explosive combination in Stanley Kowalski's case. Dynamite in the hands of a child.

Stanley squeezed the steering wheel as this latest predicament bounced around in his brain. This wasn't right; the state police had no business in this. It was not a state police matter; auto theft in the city belonged to the city. If anyone had the right to pull out in front of him it was the mayor's boy scouts, not the assholes out of Albany.

The van began to slow down. A white limo pulled into the growing space between Stanley and the trooper's car. That irritated Stanley even more. He swore to himself: *Asshole.*

Stanley stared at the police car. It was right behind the ambulance. His ambulance. Stanley was frustrated. It wasn't fair. They had no business pulling in front of him; they had no business cutting him off; and they had no business sticking their big fat noses in somebody else's affairs. Why didn't they just go peddle their papers on the expressway like they were supposed to, go play with their radar guns, maybe bust a couple of speeders for chrissake? State fuzz, now what the hell was he going to do?

"What the hell is that state cop doing here?" Lawrence Evans screamed at his partner.

Carl said he didn't know.

"Terrorists are Federal," Evans said. "Don't those assholes know that?" He had his own answer ready. "Hell, yes, they know it. They gotta know it; everybody knows it. They don't have jurisdiction here, Carl."

"They're state. City's part of the state."

"Bullshit. That doesn't make any difference. We've been in ten different states following these meatballs; they're ours. They belong to us. Besides, Federal takes priority. Federal always takes priority."

In his confusion, Agent Evans inadvertently let his foot relax on the accelerator and the gray Ford started to slow down. A Jeep Grand Cherokee with gold lettering took advantage of the opportunity and pulled in front of him. "Shit," Evans said.

The fact that there were now two vehicles between Carl and the van didn't bother him at all, but something else did. Carl watched for a minute then said, "You know, I don't think he's after our guys, Larry."

Still irritated, Evans came out with a quick and confused, "What?"

"Doesn't look to me like he's after the van at all."

As was typical with Evans, without stopping to think or observe he tossed out, "What the hell makes you say that?"

Ferguson had his work cut out for him training this man.

"Because the van seems to be slowing down. Look, the trooper's pulling away. It looks almost as though he's following that ambulance."

Understand it or not, Evans had to agree. "Well, shit. That doesn't make any sense."

Carl raised an eyebrow.

"What the hell is he doing here then?" Evans asked. "And why the hell doesn't he have his siren on?"

Carl Ferguson wondered the same thing.

"Jesus, Ralph. Do you want me to drive?"

Ralph shook his head. "No, dear. I can manage."

Lilith had her doubts. "Then get the lead out of your keister and get the hell up there. Jesus, Ralph. You're going to lose them."

Lilith was visibly irritated. She strained her head forward, making sure the black Cadillac did not escape the grip of her eagle eye. She didn't really want to drive, but she wanted to be in control, and that was the problem. Not being in complete control irritated Lilith more than anything else, even more than her husband's lack of driving prowess. Lilith was not good at being a passenger.

"You're too far back, Ralph. Christ, what are you afraid of? Get up there. Get right on his damn bumper. If he makes a sudden turn you'll never make the light."

"I'll make it, dear. No problem."

I'm married to a damned coot, Lilith thought to herself.

"Will you get closer?"

Tommy was losing what little patience he had left. He just couldn't stand incompetence and that's all there was to it. As far as he was concerned, he'd already had to suffer enough ineptitude in this country; he couldn't take it anymore. He had to act. He had to do something. He'd been more than generous with the idiot driving the cab up to now, but enough was enough. It was time to get aggressive. It was time to take control.

"I thought you learned your lesson the last time," Tommy said. "We almost lost him once; do you want to take that chance again? Listen to me: You have to get closer. You have to stay right behind him. You can't sit way back here and expect to stay with anyone, especially in this traffic, and in this excuse for an automobile. Dammit, man, even I know that and I'm not a professional driver."

But you are a professional pain in the butt.

Tommy was not the only one whose patience was being stretched to the limit; Sonny Grosso felt the jaws of tolerance gnawing at him as well. Hundred-dollar-bills or no hundred-dollar-bills, he didn't know how much longer he could put up with the loud-mouth in the back seat. The guy had been bitching about one thing or another ever since he got into Sonny's cab. Sonny had been in a pretty good mood until then. Not any more.

Okay, Sonny could understand bitching about the cab, it was a piece of junk. He'd bitched about the cab himself. Well, not bitched exactly—"pointed out" was more like it. Sonny was too new on the job to bitch. He "informed" them about the heater and the stalling problem, and, while he was at it, mentioned that there were a number of other things wrong with his yellow chariot. The dispatcher, Connie Filipiack, didn't want to hear about it. But Sonny told him anyway; he felt it was his duty. Connie said that was all they had so he'd just have to make the best of it; if he didn't like it maybe they were hiring over at City Hall. Sonny made the best of it.

Bitching about his driving was understandable, too, Sonny conceded. His driving wasn't the best in the world, he knew that. But, hey, he'd never done this kind of thing before. Following people was new to him. Hell, driving a cab was new to him. *Gimme a break for chrissake.*

But that wasn't the real problem and Sonny knew it. It had nothing to do with the cab or his driving. Sonny could have handled all that. He'd learned real fast that listening to people gripe was as much a part of a cab driver's job as knowing his way around The Big Burg. No, it wasn't the personal assaults that grabbed Sonny the wrong way, it was the constant complaining about America that got under his skin—the this-damned-country's-a-disgrace kind of thing that pricked at his nerve endings and rubbed him raw. Every other word that came out of the man's mouth was a derogatory remark about the United States. *This was wrong, and that was wrong, a loser, no pride, a has-been country, those idiots in Congress, that jerk in the White House. A country of fools run by fools.*

What the hell did this guy know anyway? And who the hell was he to say those things even if he did know? How had he become such an expert on America? Hey, okay, so America wasn't perfect, but it was a heck of a lot better than any other country, that was for damned sure. Sonny thought back; his one and only trip to Mexico, boy was he glad to get back to the good old U S of A after that nightmare. Sonny didn't claim to be a flag-waving patriot, but he was an American, and he was pretty damned fond of this country, and as far as he was concerned talk like that was more than criticism, it was downright disrespectful. And America didn't deserve disrespect. The government, maybe, sometimes, but not America. America had done more good for other countries and other people around the world than anyone would ever be able to repay. If you didn't like something you should do something about it besides bitch, that was Sonny's motto. You don't like it, run for office. Do something constructive. Take action. Talk's cheap, *and* underhanded. As Sonny's mother had taught him: If you don't have anything good to say, shut your mouth and eat your supper. It really ticked Sonny off when people spit on the flag like that.

"And I'll tell you another thing," Tommy said. "Not only is this cab a piece of junk—it is, you know? it really is, I've never seen such a heap of junk metal—and not only are you the worst cab driver I've ever—" A car forced its way in front of them. "—Hey, Jesus, goddammit! There, there, you did it again. You let another car squeeze in front of you. Jesus, will you get the hell up there? Another minute the whole damned city will— Get— Get—You're losing him. Get up there! You're going to lose him. Goddam it, I'm telling you, you're going to lose him!" Tommy grit his teeth. "Dammit, man, move." Sonny eased the accelerator down, but not a lot. Tommy noticed. "Hey, pal, I'm telling you, you better step on it. If you lose that van you've seen the last cent you'll ever see out of me. I'm telling you that right now. I'm telling you you can kiss any more hundreds good-bye real fast."

Sonny made it to the intersection and through just as the light changed.

His success did not slow Tommy down for a second. After Tommy was certain they still had the van in sight, he started again. "You know what bothers me the most? I'll tell you. It's the fact that incompetence here is so typical, you know what I mean? It almost like it's expected. That's what bugs the hell out of me. It's not just you; it's worse than that. It's everyone, every*where*. It's all over the whole stupid country. It's almost like a plague. That's what it is, a plague. A plague that's sweeping the land; that's what I'm saying. A cancer. It's deadly, a real killer. I'm serious. Total incompetence is the name of the disease and you've all caught it and you're all doomed. I've seen it. You can't help but see it; all you have to do is look." Tommy paused, thinking. Then, "You know, I've seen it, and, yet, I still can't believe it. It's— It's impossible to believe, really. It's ... " Tommy stopped and stared, then, "This country—*your* country—is sinking into a whirlpool of shit, friend, and nobody is doing a damned thing about it."

Tommy bowed his head and stared at the floor for an instant. When he looked up he was greeted by the dark eyes of Sonny Grosso watching him in the rear view mirror.

Tommy gave out with a half-smile. "You'd think after a while I'd get used to it, wouldn't you? Is that what you're thinking?" Tommy read Sonny completely wrong. "You'd think after a while I'd accept it, learn to live with it— say, hey, that's the way it is, don't fight it. It's never going to change. It's never going to get any better. Relax. Be cool."

Tommy lost his smile. "But I can't accept it. I can't relax. I can't be cool. I can't ignore it like you people do. I think about it and I get sick. My stomach gets upset. My head starts to hurt and I get mad and I ..." The more Tommy thought about it the hotter the fire burned. "Why, I'll tell you— I'll tell you this and you better listen, friend, you better listen real close, this country is going down the drain because of people like you—incompetents. People who don't give a shit. This country is the worst excuse for a—"

That was it. Sonny Grosso had had enough. A man could put up with only so much. The customer was *not* always right.

Sonny knew what he had to do.

He turned south at Seventh Avenue and headed toward Times Square, ignoring Tommy's screams of protest.

Damn, he'd lost them. They had just disappeared. By the time Scotty Hunter got to the Avenue of the Americas the ambulance he was after had already turned south onto Broadway, and all Scotty found was a sea of traffic; an angry sea that had apparently swallowed his prey.

Cars and lights and people, they all looked the same. Scotty had no alternative but to continue to drive west and hope that somehow, somewhere, they'd turn up. Maybe he'd get lucky again.

He knew better. His head turned and his eyes searched, but his heart was not filled with conviction. The ambulance was gone, probably for good was Scotty's guess. He'd never find it again. It could be anywhere, and he didn't even know where to begin. Scotty didn't know what the hell to do now. He had his chance and he blew it. He'd lost them.

And now *he* was lost.

All was lost. The whole thing was hopeless, and pointless. He would never recover the manuscript. He drove on. The two cars following him had no way of knowing that Scotty Hunter didn't have the slightest idea where he was going.

Chapter 24

NOW WHAT WAS HE GOING TO DO? Times Square was a zoo.

Crowds—no, herds—cluttered the streets. Cattle, Manhattan's own Grade A Prime, grazing in pastures of concrete. Wall to wall, street to street, bumper to bumper. New Year's Eve fivefold.

Given the conditions, it was hard to believe: Christmas shoppers were everywhere. They came in droves. They came committed. They came undaunted. Arms loaded with brightly-wrapped packages ached from the strain, cold feet pounded the snow-caked sidewalks relentlessly, faces turned crimson, mouths exhausting puffs of fog transformed people into angry bulls in search of anything red, anything On Sale. The weather would not stop these hungry beasts; it did not even appear to slow them down. They would not retreat; they would not surrender. Anticipation exhilarated them; the calendar threatened them; there was not much time left. Cold fingers ignoring the temperature stood cocked and ready, willing digits eager to squeeze that last ounce of life out of their favorite piece of plastic, knowing they'd be in financial straits until summer, but not caring. Buying Junkies who couldn't wait to sign their name to one more charge slip: "What the heck, it's Christmas." Christmas was in the air and these frenzied consumers would not be denied.

Tommy, hands crammed into the pockets of his topcoat, kept walking east on 43rd, then north on the Avenue of the Americas. He was not walking any place in particular; he was just walking. The walk of a man with nowhere to go.

Manhattan was a cold and lonely place for a man without a future, a man without a country. The brightly lit stores provided no warmth, the Christmas music no comfort—"Silver Bells" never sounded so sad. The Salvation Army Santa Claus standing on the corner at West 45th Street ringing his bell got a look of disdain in return for his cheery "Merry Christmas." Tommy Kosuri was not in the mood.

Damn that cab driver! Who did he think he was anyway? Who was he to toss Tommy out like that? Stupid American! Tommy had given the man two hundred dollars and the fool had the gall to turn around and throw it right back in his face, and then make him get out of his cab, leaving him stranded in the middle of a bunch of stupid fools whose only ambition was to blow their entire savings on one mad buying spree.

Typical American spender, Tommy thought. Blow it all today, worry about tomorrow when it gets here. No thought of saving. No self-discipline, no self-denial.

No wonder their country was in such sad shape.

Tommy was jostled about by the crowd as he crossed 47th Street. His head was down, shoulders leaning into the wind. He saw and felt little; he was a man inside himself.

The cab driver was an ungrateful pig—and a lousy cab driver as well.

Tommy now knew why Sonny Grosso had turned south, knew why he'd driven him all the way down to Times Square; it was just so he could dump him in the middle of America at its finest. Prove to him everything he'd been saying about America was true. Let him taste it, again. Choke on it.

Tommy cursed to himself, then soothed his wounds by telling himself that he was probably fortunate to be rid of the jackass. He only slowed Tommy down. He was a hindrance, not a help. Tommy was better off on his own. The man was not worth two hundred dollars. He was worth exactly what he got—nothing. He was a fool and an incompetent and—

The light as 48th said DON'T WALK.

Tommy bumped into the man in front of him when the man stopped without warning. Tommy didn't bother to even attempt an apology.

Staring down at the sidewalk he made a vow: This is not over yet. Nobody could treat Tommy Kosuri that way. That stupid cab driver would not get away with it.

They would not get away with it. This *country* would not get away with it!

The more Tommy thought about it the more he realized that was right, it was the country's fault. America was to blame. America was the parent of all its incompetent children, was it not?

America—land of the free and home of the brave. Land of opportunity. Go west young man.

That was a joke. East, that's where the future came from. The sun rises in the east, and with reason; the east brings tomorrow with it. Tommy smiled to himself.

America was a dying flame that was about to burn out. Tommy warmed at the thought—it couldn't happen to a more deserving country. Another ten, fifteen years at the most, that's all he gave it. Then America would only be a memory, a scar left on the face of the planet after the scalpel of reality had sliced it away from the rest of the world. America was the twentieth century Roman Empire.

But there was a problem: Tommy was in America, and America was dragging him down with it. He was trapped in its all-encompassing quicksand because he was here, and he couldn't avoid it. He was sinking, too. Damn, he thought: America was screwing him, again. He had become just another one of America's whores. Guilt by association. *Made In America.*

IT WAS NOT HIS FAULT! IT WAS AMERICA'S FAULT!

Tommy told himself he had failed his mission not because he was a failure, but because of America.

THAT'S RIGHT!

America was the problem, not Tommy Kosuri. This kind of thing would never have happened in Japan.

NEVER!

The theft of the Twain Manuscript, a national treasure, *stolen?* Inconceivable. An impossible occurrence in Japan. Completely incomprehensible. Robbery was more than a crime in Japan, it was a insult, a mockery of human dignity. This would never have happened to Tommy in the Land of the Rising Sun. Japan was civilized.

Tommy raised his head and looked around at the crowd—the *herd.* These were not people; they were animals. They deserved whatever they got. Ignorance—that's what pounded at Tommy the hardest. They were too stupid to even realize that they were bringing about their own destruction. Or maybe they just didn't care. Ignorance *and* apathy. Brothers. Twins.

Hatred swelled. The blood in his veins began to boil. Tommy hated this place. He hated the people; he hated their stupidity; he hated their arrogance. America was a wasteland of blind, diseased fools. It was infected and dying and it was killing him right along with it. He was dying and there was nothing he could—

If only there was something he could do. Some way to make America pay for what it was doing to him. And to Tanaka-san.

WALK

And what of Tanaka?

Yes, what of Tanaka? What would Tommy tell Tanaka?

The crowd pushed Tommy across the street.

Nothing. He would tell him nothing because he would not talk to Tanaka;

he would not face Tanaka. He could not face a man of Tanaka's stature in his disgrace, his dishonor. He was not worthy. He could not admit that he had failed, because to admit his failure would be to disgrace Tanaka as well. Tanaka had trusted him and Tommy had betrayed that trust. He would rather die first. He would—

And then he saw the Marines.

And the Jeeps.

And his anger turned white hot.

Marines. Tommy had read about the Marines, about the war. About Iwo Jima. Gung ho Marines. John Wayne movies; everyone in America thought he was John Wayne. Tommy had studied the war. Read everything there was to read. Become an expert. Pearl Harbor ... Midway ... Hiroshima and Nagasaki ... the slaughter ... the atomic—

Suddenly he had an idea.

This was stupid. They weren't qualified for this. The more Michael thought about it, the more he knew he was right. He turned back to Marcella. "Marcella, I think we should let Mr. Gorman continue this thing on his own. I really do. It's not that I want to desert him. It's not that. It's just that, well, he's probably better off on his own anyway, without us. We've got to be more of a hindrance than a help. I think we should back out and let Mr. Gorman and the police take care of this."

Not on your life, Marcella thought to herself. Now that she'd had the chance to consider all the options, there were things worse that bribing thieves to give back the manuscript. One was not getting it back at all. That was not acceptable. They had to get it back. *She* had to get it back.

Marcella was about to comment when Gorman beat her to it. "That's the smartest thing anyone has said all day. The next chance I get I'll stop and let you out. Take a cab back to my office—I'll pick up the tab—and wait."

Michael recognized the connotation in Gorman's tone. He didn't like it. Okay, he had lost the manuscript, but he was not a quitter. He was not chickening out. That wasn't the issue at all. He was doing what any reasonable person would do. Being logical and recognizing one's limitations was not cowardice. And picking up the cab fare sounded more like charity that generosity. "Well, I just thought—"

"I'm staying." Marcella interrupted.

Not the support Michael was looking for. "Marcella ..."

"I said, I'm staying."

Gorman said, "Ms. Givens, Michael is—"

"If we got out, what would you do?" Marcella asked.

"What?"

"If we got out. You'd continue to go after them, wouldn't you?"

Gorman shrugged. "Of course. I have a job to do."

"Then we'll stick it out, too," Marcella said, as much for Michael as for Gorman. Mostly for herself. "If these are the thieves then I want to be there when we catch up to them."

"But, Marcella, I—"

"Michael, you're free to do as you like. And so am I. And I'm staying."

Michael didn't say anything. He stared at her for a long time. After a while, he accepted it and turned around.

Gorman's smile seemed condescending to Marcella.

The ambulance was out of control.

Henry's eyes were saucers, Bill's the same. Billy was holding his breath. Victor knew he was going to crash and burn and he wasn't certain that he cared one way or another.

Billy turned into the spin and tapped the brakes. There was nothing more he could do but pray. He tried. The van kept sliding. He prayed harder. It worked.

No one asked why God was suddenly listening to Billy Freely now. The only thing that mattered was the fact that the rear wheels somehow found the traction they needed to stop the slide just as they were about to plow into the white Ford Aerostar van that was coming west off 58th Street. As soon as they were straightened out again Billy gunned the engine and they were off like a shot.

After a few minutes, Henry said, "It's got to be because of the manuscript."

Bill gave him a curious look.

"The state police," Henry answered. "They wouldn't be after us because of the ambulance; city cops would be after us for that."

It was the only explanation he could come up with.

Bill didn't buy it. "He could be after us because of the ambulance. A state cop can arrest you for auto theft just as legally as a city cop."

"*Can*, sure, but I don't think that's the case this time. Why would he? Why would a state cop even be in the city in the first place? It's a little out of his way, don't you think?" Henry shook his head. "No, it has to be the manuscript." Then a possibility dawned on him. "Jesus, you don't think it's the escort, do you?"

Bill thought about that. "Oh shit. You don't think it is, do you? And how in the hell would he have found us? Tell me that."

Henry wondered the same thing. "I don't know."

"And how does he know *we* have the manuscript?"

"I don't know that either."

"He can't know, Henry. There's no way he could know."

"Then you tell me, why's he after us?"

Bill considered the possibilities endless. "Speeding. Running red lights. Reckless driving. Hell, I don't know. A hundred different things. All I know is, he's after us. I think we can both agree on that. I don't really think it matters why."

Billy's eyes were on the road in front of him. He had to be careful, not only were the streets dangerous, but New York drivers were crazy, you never knew when one of them might pull right out in front of you, even in poor driving conditions like these. Besides, the state police were not Billy's first concern. He spoke without taking his eyes off the road. "What about the van?" Billy asked. "Is it still back there?"

Henry turned. He let out a sigh. "Sure as hell is. Two cars back."

Just then the van passed the limo that had pulled in front of it. Now it was right behind the state police car matching it move for move.

"Check that," Henry said. "It's one car back."

As Henry watched the police car coming closer, a strange sensation came over him, something tapped at his brain: something was out of place here. Something didn't fit the way it was supposed to fit. He couldn't quite grasp it, but he felt as though something was definitely out of whack.

Then it hit him. "Bill," he said, "tell me something. Why doesn't he have his siren on?"

Bill was caught off guard. "What?"

"Why doesn't he have his siren on?"

"What the hell are you talking about, Henry?"

Billy turned an ear.

"That cop," Henry responded. "Why isn't his siren blaring away? I mean, it's obvious that he's after us, isn't it? So, if he's after us, why isn't his siren blasting, and his lights flashing? And if he isn't after us, if he's after someone else, then why isn't his siren on to warn people, to tell people like us to get out of the way?"

Bill looked back at the police car and realized that Henry had a very good point.

$$$

He should turn on his siren, Trooper Howard knew that.

But he couldn't turn on his siren. If he turned on his siren every city cop within twenty blocks would know where he was. And if they knew where he was, they'd know where the ambulance was. And if there was one thing he didn't want, it was the city boys finding out where *his* ambulance was. Just like he told Mitchell, this was his collar, and, by God, he was going to make it.

Tommy approached the jeeps from the rear.

The Marines were all facing forward, standing at attention and listening to some moose of a man standing in front of them complaining about how sloppy they looked. Tommy could hear his booming voice over all else.

American Marines, Tommy thought. Braggarts. Egomaniacs. The man in front was the typical Marine stereotype—a square head with a gaping mouth, both large and empty. About time they were taught a lesson, Tommy thought. If he could get one of their Jeeps it would not only teach them a lesson, but with his own set of wheels he might be able to track down that ambulance himself.

Okay, the chances were slim-to-none that he'd be able to locate it, but it was the only chance he had. He certainly couldn't do any worse than that idiot cab driver.

"You know," Henry started, then stopped. The lack of sirens was a very good question, but Henry noticed something else that needed his more immediate attention. Bill stared out the back window and waited. When Henry started again, the words came out slow, surrounded with thought. "The guy in that van, he looks an awful lot like ..."

At that moment it hit Bill also. "The guy with the gun! Jesus, Henry, that's the same man we saw at the accident."

This time Billy turned when he spoke; the hell with what lay ahead, he was concerned about his rear. "Wha'd you say? That guy—? That—The guy I saw at the hospital? The guy with the gun? He's— He's back there? He's following us?"

"Guy? Gun? What guy? What gun?" Victor asked.

Henry and Bill stared. The van was at least a full thirty feet away, but there was no doubt—it was him all right. The man with the gun was definitely back.

"It looks like the same man to me, son."

"Are you sure?"

"It's him, Bill," Henry said. "It sure as hell is."

"What the hell are you guys talking about?" Victor wanted to know what was going on.

Bill and Henry ignored Victor and moved back to the front of the ambulance. Bill whispered when he spoke so Victor couldn't hear him. "But—why would he be here? I can understand the hospital, maybe he was involved in an accident. But why would he be here? Do you think he's following us?"

Henry shook his head.

"Why would he be following us?"

Henry added a shrug.

Suddenly Billy's mind was no longer concentrating on driving. "Why the hell is he back there, Dad? I don't get it. I don't get this whole thing. I mean— It— It doesn't make any sense. It— I—Why's he after us? Why's he after *me*?"

Bill shook his head. "I don't know that he is after you, son. If he's after any of us, he's after all of us. But I—"

Billy didn't buy that. "He was aiming at me, Dad."

Bill tried to calm his son down. "I don't know, this whole thing is crazy. None of it makes any sense. It's not just the man with the gun; it's everything. The accident—the guy with the gun, sure—but, then, the state police coming out of nowhere like that. How did he find us anyway? That's what I'd like to know. How the heck did he know where we were? And how did he know about the ambulance? Has he been following us the whole time? Did he hear it on the radio? If he did, then every cop in this state knows about us." He turned to Henry. "Henry?"

Henry didn't have the slightest idea. "Hell, I don't know, Bill. What do you think I am, a goddam fortune teller? Jesus Christ. For all I know, Batman's back there. Everyone else is. Shit, just be thankful the FBI hasn't showed up yet."

"Want me to shoot out a tire?"

Carl almost laughed out loud. Instead he shook his head no. "Ah, no, I don't think that would be wise under the circumstances. It's just a little crowded around here to be letting go with the firepower, don't you think?"

Evans didn't hesitate a second. "Got an Expert in marksmanship at Knox and Quantico both. I bet I could put one right between the grooves in that left blackwall without any trouble at all."

I'll bet you could, Carl thought. The next time they ask you to train someone, Carl Ferguson, tell them you'll retire first.

Tommy bent over and eased his way under the rope that cordoned off the vehicles. All someone had to do was leave one key in one ignition and he'd have a chance.

He looked into the first Jeep. Bingo!

Cocky bastards, Tommy thought. Left the key right there for the whole world to see. Never even entered their conceited minds that someone would have the gall to steal one of their precious vehicles.

Tommy slid into the seat, bent over so no one could see. The only one who could have seen—because he was the only one facing in Tommy's direction—was the big buffoon barking out commands as though he was trying to impress someone with his deep resonant voice. It didn't impress Tommy.

Talk was cheap.

Blow hard talk was free.

Tommy reached forward and turned the key. The jeep roared to life.

With that, heads turned. Shocked expressions filled winter-washed faces. "Hey, what the hell are you doing?" came the cry from the side of beef in front of the group.

X-rated movie theaters, massage parlors, pawn shops. EAST COAST DISTRIBUTORS—50% OFF ON ALL WATCHES. Billy saw none of it, his mind was on something else as he approached Times Square.

Jesus, he'd never even thought about the FBI before. His whole concern had been only with the man with the gun. What if the FBI did show up? The state police were bad enough, but the Feds! Holy shit!

It made sense that they'd be after them, didn't it? After all, they had transported stolen property across state lines. Wasn't that the thing that got the G-men involved? Billy thought back. Yes, it was. He remembered it from Mr. Goulden's class on State and Federal Government.

And the New York City Police were probably hot on their trail, too.

It was the damned ambulance. They had to ditch it and that's all there was to it. It was a beacon that was guiding everyone to them. They might as well have a big red bull's eye painted on their butts.

"We have to dump this thing," Billy said. "It's a goddam neon arrow that's showing everyone where the hell we are for chrissake. We have to get rid of it."

For once, Henry had to agree with Billy. But he didn't like his chances on foot either. How fast could they go on foot? But *on foot maybe they could hide*. Henry looked around. There were people on foot everywhere. The sidewalks were loaded to overflowing. At least they wouldn't stick out on foot like they were sticking out in this ambulance.

"I agree," Henry said. "They're looking for an ambulance, but as Christmas shoppers we can blend right in. They'll never be able to locate us in this crowd. But we have to put some distance between us and them before we do." Henry knew he was going to regret saying it, but he had to say it anyway. He had no choice. "Step on it, Billy. Get us the hell out of here."

Billy didn't have to be told twice.

Tommy shifted the vehicle into REVERSE and gunned the engine. The Jeep was good stock—it snapped the rope barrier like a piece of twine. Must have a Japanese transmission, Tommy thought.

He jerked the steering wheel to the left, spun sideways while still going backwards, shifted into first gear while he was still spinning, and then floored the accelerator. The tires slid sideways in the snow. He eased off the accelerator. The vehicle started to move forward. He could hear the man behind him screaming. He hit the accelerator again and the tires dug in and the Jeep started to pick up speed. As he pulled away Tommy felt happy for the first time since the morning.

"That son of a bitch just stole one of our Jeeps," Wainwright puffed.

No shit, McGovern thought. What gave you the first clue?

Wainwright stood there wondering what to do.

Why don't you call out the Marines, McGovern offered mentally.

Wainwright turned and looked at the podium. The mayor, city brass, Marine brass, dignitaries, politicians. Shit, they wouldn't be any help, they were here to make brownie points; they had no idea what the hell was going on. He looked back at his men; they waited for orders.

Jesus, what the hell do I do?

His eyes locked onto McGovern's. He pointed with a cold finger. "You, come with me." Then he pointed at two other men. "And you, and you. We'll nail that sorry son of a bitch."

McGovern gulped. Ah shit, not me.

"You drive," Wainwright ordered. To Sergeant Potter he said, "You take over here. You're in charge. Ah, just do whatever you, ah ... Ah, hell, just carry on." With that he charged off toward the nearest Jeep. "Come on, men," he shouted at McGovern. "Follow me."

Come on, men? Follow me? McGovern wanted to puke. General Custer. Next line: *What Indians? I don't see any Indians.*

McGovern looked at the other men; they were as sick about the whole thing as he was. He gave them an ah-shit look before he turned and followed his fearless leader.

Billy skidded around 42nd Street and fish-tailed his way for a full half block before he regained control of the vehicle. Henry and Bill watched out the back windows for the police car and the van. Victor strained to see, but his bindings made it impossible to tell what was happening or where they were going. Then, out of the rear window, he saw, just for a second, a red Coca Cola sign and knew they were in Times Square.

"They're both still behind us, Billy," Henry said. "If this thing has any more juice you'd better give it another shot."

The traffic light at The Avenue of the Americas was yellow. Billy put the accelerator to the floor. Billy turned north as the light changed to red.

Fortunately, the traffic was moving and the lights were with him. Billy sailed through one intersection after another: 43rd, -4th, -5th. 46th and -7th. 48th. As he approached 49th Street, he saw a flash out of the corner of his eye. From his right a jeep suddenly appeared. It darted in front of him.

"Look out!" Henry screamed.

Tommy had never felt so cold in his life. Riding in an open cockpit at thirty miles an hour with the wind matching that speed, the chill factor had to be minus a hundred, at least. His gloves were in his pockets. If he could just manage to steer this thing with one hand maybe he could get—

Suddenly he was in an intersection. Something white on his left. Coming at him. He jerked the steering wheel to the right. Jesus, it was a damned ambulance.

It came closer. They were going to crash.

He slammed on the brakes and jerked the wheel.

Big mistake. The Jeep started to spin. A three-sixty. Then another. A spinning top. He was going to crash. He knew it. Tommy knew there was no way he was going to get out of this one. He was a goner. End of mission. The headlights of the big brown UPS truck glared at him as he flew towards it.

Chapter 25

VICTOR WAS GIDDY.

"'Round and 'round we go and where we stop nobody knows."

And why shouldn't he be giddy? His world had already come to an end, hours ago; why the hell should he care that he was going to die?

Die? Of course he was going to die. It was logical—the perfect ending to a perfect day. The manuscript stolen, Samuelson gone, a once-in-a-century blizzard, a zillion-car pile-up on the expressway, kidnapped in an ambulance by three crazed lunatics.

Count your blessings and have a nice day.

And, once more, he was spinning down the highway out of control. What the hell else was new? When weren't they spinning down the highway out of control? Victor had heard someone scream "Look out!" and the next thing he knew the ambulance was off on another one of its exciting journeys.

But this time Victor was determined to enjoy himself. He was a kid again, sixteen, a fresh driver's license in his wallet spinning brodies on the ice just like he used to do in his first set of wheels—a '52 Merc with overdrive. Gun the engine and flip the wheel and have a ball—in the empty parking lot behind the high school, so you didn't run into anyone or anything.

"Can't you get any more speed out of this thing?" Victor screamed at the three madmen in front. "What's the matter? Afraid of a little weather? Come on, gun this sucker."

So he was going to die—big deal. Everybody had to die some day.

Phyllis would be fine without him. She'd survive. She could buy that new Jag with his insurance money. She'd live with her mother. Victor laughed: *A fate worse than death.*

They'll say he was a good man, too young to die. Yellow roses at his funeral; they'd play "How Great Thou Art," by Elvis. Buried in the winter—Victor didn't know if he liked that idea. The ground would be frozen. The tomb would shift when the ground thawed and he could end up being buried at an angle *throughout eternity.* Assuming there was a body left to bury, that is.

The gas tank might explode when they crashed and he'd go up in a ball of flame, and Phyllis would be left with nothing but a pot full of ashes.

"Sprinkle me on a race track and let the horses shit on me," Victor whispered.

They shit on me in life, why shouldn't they shit on me in death?

The steering wheel spun in his hands and his head spun on his shoulders. He was getting dizzy. Tommy held on to the wheel just to keep from falling out of the Jeep.

The Avenue of the Americas was one big merry-go-round and Tommy Kosuri was sitting right in the middle of it. Lights and colors and buildings spun by. He was inside a spinning top, and Tommy realized for the first time that his thoughts of death could very well come true. For one brief second he felt remorse, then he saw nothing in life left for him and he resigned himself to accepting it. It was better this way. It was the only way out. His only regret: that he could not take that fool of a cab driver with him.

As the four Marines sailed around the intersection, Wainwright almost fell out of the Jeep. Better luck next time, McGovern thought.

To his surprise the ambulance quit spinning.

Victor didn't know what to make of it; they were going straight again. "I know, we crashed and we're dead and we're sailing toward heaven, right?"

No answer.

"Saint Peter? You hear me? I'm comin' home."

Miraculously, Tommy slid through the intersection without hitting the UPS truck. The truck, however, was not as lucky; it careened into the newsstand on the corner, sending a shower of paper exploding into the air.

Tommy's second target was the rear end of a delivery van whose timing was flawless: one second sooner or one second later and Tommy would have missed it completely. In fact, he did miss it, but it didn't miss him. Tommy never saw it. It came backing out of the alley and hit him on the right rear fender. However, as he had concluded earlier, the Jeep was of sturdy stock, and rather than send him sailing, to Tommy's surprise, the collision only succeeded in straightening him out. Before Tommy realized it, once again he was aimed north on the Avenue of the Americas, only this time there was no one in front of him. He had clear sailing. He took advantage of it by slamming the accelerator to the floor. He had to get out of here before those jackass Marines caught up to him.

$$$

"Marines? What the hell do you mean, Marines?"

Bill and Henry had managed to get back onto their feet again after being thrown to the floor when the ambulance started spinning. Bill steadied himself against the side of the ambulance and followed Henry's gaze out the back window. He gasped. Henry was right; there were four Marines in a Jeep right on their bumper. They looked angry.

Billy saw them in the rear view mirror. "Marines? Marines? Jesus, what the hell are they doing here? Is everybody in the whole goddam world after us?"

The Marines, in pursuit of Tommy, had come off 49th Street and hit The Avenue of the Americas two seconds and one vehicle behind the man who had stolen one of their Jeeps. The one vehicle just happened to be an ambulance driven by Billy Freely.

"Get that damned ambulance out of the way," Wainwright screamed.

That'll get them to move, McGovern thought. Nobody will want to screw with you.

"Jesus," Wainwright said. "What's the matter with that idiot? Can't he see we're in a damn hurry? Why doesn't he pull over?"

Ah, you got that assbackwards, chief, McGovern laughed to himself. We're supposed to pull over for ambulances; they're not supposed to pull over for us.

"Go around him, Corporal."

This time McGovern didn't laugh. Go around him? Are you nuts? There's no place to go around him. Sir. We could get killed trying to *go around him*. If you had an ounce of brains in that block of granite you call a head you'd see that, too.

McGovern looked over at Wainwright. His fearless leader was standing up in the Jeep doing his impression of George Washington crossing the Potomac.

McGovern glanced around at the two men in back. They just shook their heads.

Henry swallowed hard. "This—This is crazy. This is ridiculous. There's no way the Marines would be after us."

"Looks like they're after us to me, Henry," Bill said.

"They— They can't be."

Bill was sarcastic. "Tell *them* that. Tell it to the Marines, Henry."

Henry was too busy thinking to give Bill a dirty look. Why in the hell would the Marines be after them? He didn't come up with an answer, but he came up with a solution:

"Okay, that's it, Bill. This is the last straw. Whether they're after us or not, I don't care. All I know is, we've got to get out of this thing and we've got to get out now. We've got to dump and run; it's our only chance."

"What do you mean?"

"I mean we have to get the hell out of this goddammed ambulance. Every time we turn around somebody new jumps on the damned bandwagon. This whole thing is mushrooming; it's way out of control. We're in over our heads, Bill. City police, state cops, a crazy man with a gun. And now, the goddam Marines, for chrissake! I don't know how the hell the Marines got into this thing but it sure as shit looks like they're in it, so that means we have to get out. And we have to get out NOW!"

Bill wasn't arguing, he just didn't know what to do. "Hey, I'm with you, pal. I only have one question. How the hell do we do that? You got any ideas?"

Henry did. "Yeah, we dump everything. The ambulance, the manuscript, everything. We dump it all and run like a sonofabitch. I figure it this way: If we don't get caught with any of this on us, maybe, just maybe, we stand a chance of getting out with our asses still in one piece."

Bill liked the idea.

Billy didn't. He didn't like it at all. "Dump the manuscript? Now? After all we've gone through? No way, man. No way. The manuscript's ours. We earned it."

The word "manuscript" entered Victor's brain but it didn't register. Carmine Rico filled his brain to capacity.

Bill looked at Henry; Henry looked at Bill. Billy went on:

"Besides, what good will it do to dump the manuscript? It's the ambulance that everyone's after. We don't know for sure they even know we have the manuscript. The ambulance is the thing that we have to unload. Once they get that they won't be able to locate us anymore. We can take the manuscript and disappear into the crowd."

"But, son, with all those people after us. I think—"

"Dad, everyone will still be out there whether we have the manuscript or not, don't you see? Getting rid of the manuscript won't do any good. What do we gain by dumping it? I say we might as well—"

Henry jumped in. "Billy, if they have the manuscript, maybe they won't stay after us, that's the point. I mean, maybe if we give it back—give them everything back—they'll forget about us. Let us go. Let us—"

Billy shook his head. "Let us go? Are you kidding? No way. They're not going to forget about us. You think after all the shit we've put them through they're going to forgive and forget? Forget it, Mr. Nash. They won't stop until—"

Bill's turn to jump in. "No, Billy, Henry's right. It's our only chance of getting out of this mess. Everything's gotten too complicated. Too many people involved. We can't fight them all." He shook his head. "I think if we do what Henry says they just might take everything—the ambulance, the manuscript—and go home. At least it's worth a try. So we lose the manuscript, so what? If we stand a chance of getting out of this thing without getting caught, I say we take it. I say we go for it."

"But—"

"No buts," Henry said. "Look around; they're everywhere. We're surrounded. We don't have a prayer. Maybe we could have handled the city cops, but we've got the state guys after us, and the Marines—and, hell, maybe even the Federal guys. That man with the gun—maybe he's Federal. Who the hell knows? Frankly, he scares me the most because I don't know who he is. We have to cut our losses as best we can. The best we can hope for is to dump everything and hope they back off. Okay, maybe they won't forget about it, but maybe they won't care as much as they did before. Maybe The Nash-Freely Gang will get pushed to the back burner. That's all we can hope for, but that's more than we have now. We can pray that they all have more important things to keep them busy. It's worth the risk. Getting away is the only thing that's important now. The hell with the damned manuscript."

What a bunch of bullshit, Billy thought. He was running around with a bunch of chickenshits. He was the only man in the whole damn group. He stopped. *Live to fight another day* flashed across Billy's mind. Yeah, maybe that was the way to go. There would always be another day, another treasure some insurance company would be willing to buy back. But not in jail. They could do this again, *he* could do it again, another time, another place, but he couldn't do it if he was in jail.

Get away, that's what they had to do. Mr. Nash was right. His father was right. Hey, maybe they would back off a little if they got the manuscript back. Just an inch, that's all it might take for them to get away. Billy Freely knew one thing for sure. He did not like the sound of the slammer. He had his whole life ahead of him. A smart soldier knew when to retreat, and Billy Freely was a smart soldier. Fifty-fourth Street was on his right. He gunned the engine and said: "Okay, you win. But we gotta move. Hold on."

Billy jerked the wheel to the right, spun around the corner, raced his way to Fifth Avenue by winding his way between traffic that let him know with horns and shaking fists what they thought of his attitude problem, and then turned south. They had to get out of sight just long enough so they could stop the ambulance and get out, and it was up to Billy to get them out of sight long enough.

As they approached St. Patrick's Cathedral, Billy looked in the rear view mirror. Plenty of headlights, but nothing that appeared to be charging at him recklessly. Had he lost them? He watched for a set of headlights to break out of the pack. None did. Damn, he *had* lost them. He was just too quick for them. They never made the last turn. Piece-a-cake. Now all he had to do was find a place to pull over.

Out of the corner of his eye Stanley saw the gray Ford pulling up beside him, but he didn't pay any attention; he was too busy. The jackass in the ambulance was two blocks ahead. Stanley had lost ground when they turned south on Fifth. Bunch of goddam tourists on Fifth out for a fucking Sunday afternoon goddam drive, Stanley swore to himself.

Stanley was getting goddam tired of people crowding in front of him. First the state cop, then some dickhead in a limo. He'd been able to take care of the limo on 50th, but now there were seven or eight vehicles between them again—why the hell that Jeep full of Marines was in there he'd never understand—but with all the other traffic Stanley had to look out for, he had no time to spend dealing with the dumb gray Ford that had decided to pass him. He simply made sure he was right on top of the bumper in front so the asshole couldn't crowd in.

But the Ford tried to pull into his lane anyway.

There wasn't room and Stanley told him so.

"Hey, asshole," Stanley screamed.

The Ford kept coming. It was trying to force Stanley to slow down and let it in.

"Hey, can't you see there ain't enough room you stupid—"

Stanley quit screaming when he saw the man riding shotgun was motioning him to pull over.

He quit screaming because the man was motioning with a shotgun.

Billy turned right onto 47th Street. Then took another right on to the Avenue of the Americas.

"Jesus, Billy," Henry said. "We're back where we started. You're driving in circles."

"So? What does it matter where we are? As long as I lose them."

Henry couldn't argue with that. He looked out the back. Billy's plan appeared to have worked. "Well, hell, I guess you're right. I don't see them back there. Billy, I think you did it."

Bill smiled at his son.

"Okay, let's find a place to dump this thing and get the hell out of here."

"That's fine with me," Billy said. "Pick a spot."

Evans reached up, grabbed the door handle and swung open the door of the van with his left hand; his right was busy; it was filled with a shotgun. He expected to see more than just Stanley Kowalski sitting behind the steering wheel. He froze. Shock gripped his face. He looked into the back of the van. Empty.

Ferguson ran around to the right side of the van and jerked open the door. He, too, stopped in his tracks when he saw Stanley. Then he said, "Who the hell are you?"

"Who the hell am I?" Stanley repeated. "Who the hell are you?"

"Here's as good a place as any," Henry said.

"Right across the street from Radio City Music Hall?" It didn't seem like as good a place as any to Bill.

"Hell yes. Let the Rockettes worry about it."

Billy laughed. He liked that.

Bill didn't see any humor in any of this.

Billy pulled over to the side of the street, pulled the emergency brake handle and shut off the engine. They were about to climb out when Bill remembered that they had a passenger.

"What about ..?" Bill motioned with a nod at Victor.

Henry thought for a minute, then said, "Forget him. The police can let him go when they find the ambulance."

"He can identify us, Henry. Maybe we should let him go. He was in a pretty big hurry to get away from us earlier. Maybe he still is. If he took off on his own before the police got here, it might solve a big problem for us."

Henry shrugged. "Ask him."

Bill moved to the back and looked down at Victor. "Ride's over. You still want out of here?"

Victor's face was blank. Bill was about to repeat his question when Victor came to life. A switch clicked in his mind and his eyes came alive. Maybe there was still a chance after all. He could hope anyway. What did he have to lose? His words came out in short, quick bursts. "Hell yes, lemme outta here. Jesus—whaddaya think I've been trying to tell you all this time?"

Bill unhooked the straps and Victor was up and out the door before they could react. Henry expected to hear him scream for the police but instead he disappeared down the street.

"That guy sure is in a big hurry," Bill said.

Henry agreed. "Yeah, you'd think the police were after him."

Should he run? Should he even *try* to get away? Should he bother?

Tommy thought about that. His chances of finding the man in the van were next to impossible. Which meant his chances of finding out anything about the manuscript *were* impossible.

And his only regret minutes before had been the fact that he couldn't take that cab driver with him when he crashed.

And he couldn't, the cab driver was nowhere near—

Behind him. A Jeep full of Marines.

Hey, wait a minute. Why not? His forefathers before him had done it.

Tommy slowed down, pulled to the side of the street, and stopped. He thought about it. The more he thought about it, the more it appealed to him. It was a way out. It was an honorable way out. Tommy looked back over his shoulder.

Traffic was coming toward him.

The Marines were coming toward him. Perfect. He would not retreat, he was done retreating; he would charge. Charging south on a northbound street would certainly get the Americans' attention. Tommy made a U-turn. He was going back, back into traffic. Back into the jaws of death.

Tommy smiled to himself; he had a purpose again. Tommy Kosuri had a mission.

He was going hunting. Marine hunting.

If his forefathers could do it, why couldn't he? He had their courage, their faith. He would make his own Divine Wind.

Kamikaze!

A phone. Victor had to get to a pay phone. Maybe, for some reason, Samuelson didn't leave. Why the hell he wouldn't have left, Victor didn't know. But he was a desperate man, and desperate men hope. Gamblers are filled with hope.

He found a phone booth at the corner of 49th Street.

He'd call his office first. Maybe there was still a chance. Mrs. Copperman could call the airlines while he called the hotel. If Mrs. Copperman was still there. There was no reason she should be but—

After the first ring. "Carneby-Glenn."

She was. Victor exhaled.

"Edith, thank God, you're still there. I need—"

"Ah, Mr. Romaine; you finally called. I so hoped you'd call. That's why I'm here. I thought you might need me, as soon as you got to the airport and found out. What took you so—"

"I—" Victor stopped. Found out? "Found out? Found out what? I never got to the airport. I had an accident on the expressway and—"

"Oh, my. Are you all right? Are you—"

"Edith, I'm fine. What happened? What was I supposed to find out?"

"Oh, yes, ah, well, you see, I thought about it all day. I just couldn't get it out of my mind. I was concerned that I might have transposed one of Mr. Samuelson's flight numbers—I do that sometimes. I get in a rush and don't really think about what I'm doing and—"

"Edith, what are you trying to say?" Irritated.

"Oh, right. Well, I called the hotel to see if I got the flight number right, and they said that Mr. Samuelson had just returned. It turns out that he didn't go to London after all."

"What? What do you mean?"

"Well, she said he got to the airport all right, but he had to come back. His flight was canceled. The airport's closed."

"Closed?"

"Yes—the weather. Closed some time this morning."

"So you're telling me he's still at the hotel?"

"No. The receptionist said he went to Grand Central Station."

"Grand Central Station? Why?"

"She suggested that he might be able to take a train to Albany and then catch a flight to Atlanta, and then from there get a flight to London."

"What time was that."

"Around four."

Victor looked at his watch: 6:12.

Victor was silent. That was it. He was dead. By now Samuelson was definitely gone.

The irony: Victor had been wasting his time trying to get to La Guardia, and all the while Samuelson had been practically next door. Victor could have gotten to Grand Central Station without any problem at all if he'd only known.

"Mr. Romaine? Hello? Mr. Romaine are you—"
"Thanks, Edith."
Victor hung up the phone.

"Unit two-eleven, are you in the area?"
"Unit two-eleven, Roger. We're at Fifth and Fifty-first."
The dispatcher said:"*An ambulance has been reported empty and abandoned near Rockefeller Center, West Fifty and America corner. Verify.*"
"Roger."
Scotty's heart stopped as he waited for the rest.
There was no more.
"But what about the manuscript?" Scotty asked the radio. "You didn't say anything about the manuscript. Was it the robbers? Was it the guys I'm after?"
The radio did not answer.
Shit.
West 50th and The Avenue of the Americas—that was Radio City Music Hall. Somehow they'd gotten north of him, or he'd gotten south of them. Scotty made a U-turn, dodged a pedestrian, and drove as fast as he could toward Rockefeller Center.

Gorman had to swerve to get out of his way.
"Damn, now where is he going?" Gorman said. He pulled into the delivery alley beside The New York Public Library and stopped.
"I don't know, but it looks like he has a purpose to me," Michael answered.
Gorman gave him a stare.
Michael shrugged his shoulders and said, "Person usually doesn't go that fast unless he has a reason."
Gorman didn't have to think about that for very long. "You're right. He must know something."
Gorman checked behind him, then started to back out onto 5th Avenue. "He has a police scanner in his car; he must have heard something."
This whole ridiculous escapade was turning into a stupid Laurel and Hardy movie as far as Marcella was concerned. And she'd never liked Laurel and Hardy.
Only this wasn't a comedy, it was a tragedy. Children playing adult games, that's what it was. Dangerous adult games. Three people risking their lives because one man said let's do it. Was that how wars got started? Because one man somewhere said, "Let's do it?" Marcella would bet everything she had

that it certainly wasn't a woman who had uttered those infamous words. Women had more sense. Men had to be macho. Why fighting and killing and dying was macho was another thing that never made sense to Marcella. Men were such little boys—did they ever grow up? If it wasn't so sad it would be funny.

Gorman backed over the curb.

Make that a Three Stooges movie.

Which one was she: Moe, Larry, or Curly?

"Run the bastard off the road, Ralph," Lilith said, when she saw the Cadillac coming back their way. "I'm getting tired of this bullshit. Jerk keeps turning around all the time. Hell, he doesn't know where the hell he's going. Run him down. Let's get to the bottom of this."

Ralph ignored her; he knew she was kidding. Lilith didn't know she was kidding, but Ralph knew she was kidding.

They watched as Gorman drove by.

Ralph did not bother to ask Lilith if she wanted him to follow the black car. He took it upon himself to very calmly turn into the first alleyway he came to, stop, look both ways, then back out into the street and drive off in the direction of the man who was really irritating his wife. Ralph did not have look at her; he knew Lilith was wearing a face of stone.

This is it. It's payback time.

Tommy was beside himself with glee. It had hit him like a flash out of the blue. Revenge: that was the answer. Revenge for his ancestors; revenge against this country that had ruined him. That's how he would go down: with a smile of satisfaction on his lips. He may not be able to get the manuscript, but he could repay an old, long overdue debt. Hari Kari with a Jeep. The Marines were finally going to pay for Iowa Jima.

Chapter 26

"There's Scotty."

Michael looked, but didn't see him. "Where?"

Gorman pointed. "There, just in front of that red pick-up truck. Crossing Forty-ninth."

Michael saw the red pick-up, and there was a dark Mustang in front of it, but from this distance he couldn't tell for sure it was the same Mustang they had been following.

"That's his Mustang," Gorman said, sounding slightly irritated.

Michael took Gorman's word for it. Marcella didn't.

"How do you know it's Mr. Hunter's car?" she asked.

Michael wished Marcella would leave well enough alone once in a while. She'd questioned Gorman about one thing or another since she got here. Why couldn't she just take his word for it?

Gorman tried to sound confident. "I recognize it."

Marcella thought: There must be a lot of black Mustangs in New York. How can he be so sure it's the right black Mustang? And how can he tell from this distance it isn't dark blue?

As if he read her thoughts. "I'm sure. Take my word for it. I know *his* car." Of course he wasn't sure. It could have been anybody's black (or dark blue) Mustang. But Gorman needed to think he'd found Scotty.

"Now what?" Marcella asked.

There she goes again, Michael thought. Did she have to sound so challenging every time she asked a question? Everything she said, every inflection in her voice seemed to be questioning what Parker Gorman was doing. If it was as obvious to Gorman as it was to Michael, then there was no doubt in his mind that Marcella was doing her best to irritate him. Michael was on shaky enough ground as it was; he was in no position to irritate Parker Gorman, and he wished that his assistant would quit stirring the pot.

Roger Muldowney looked around. How the hell had he gotten here? He was in the middle of Manhattan for crying out loud.

Driving in New York City was like putting a gigantic jigsaw puzzle together with a blindfold on as far as Roger was concerned—even when he was paying attention to what he was doing, it was an impossible chore. Even when concern for his best friend didn't fill his mind it was a nerve-racking experience; a trip through the Twilight Zone. To Roger Muldowney, Manhattan was nothing but a series of one-way streets that forced you to go in circles, eight-lane highways infested with bumper-to-bumper traffic that sucked you into intersections that if you didn't know where you were going four blocks before you got there, you were out of luck by the time you did get there. Designed by the same lunatic who gave the world Rubic's Cube, it was a highway system that once you made a wrong turn you could not correct it; you were destined to wander forever with Rod Serling as your only companion.

Roger had apparently been driving around in a trance, because when he looked up he was right in the middle of Rockefeller Plaza. He checked his watch and found out he'd been in this semi-coma for the last hour. He remembered nothing of what happened in that time. He remembered leaving the hospital and driving south, after that: blank. It scared the hell out of him.

"Jesus, Rog," he said to himself. "You could have had an accident. You could have run into someone. You could have been killed. Pay attention, you big jerk."

Roger tried to regain his composure. Now that he was here, how the hell was he going to get out of here? Rockefeller Center was packed with people. Why was it so busy? He'd been to Radio City Music Hall before at Christmas and—

Then he saw the Christmas tree and it dawned on him—the Tree Lighting Ceremony at Rockefeller Plaza, that's why they were all here. It was more than just Christmas shoppers; he'd picked the second worst time of the year to be stuck in downtown New York. Maybe the worst, how could New Year's Eve be any worse than this? Damn, he was in a real mess now. Not only would he never find Henry, he might never get out of here himself. Traffic was barely moving.

Pierre couldn't believe his eyes. "*Mes amis*, do you see what I see?"
The men stared at the sight before them.
Jacques was the first to speak.
"*Mon Dieu*, is that our van? Can it be?"
"Quickly," Pierre said, pushing his confederates toward the side of the building. "Do not let them see you."

The cold that had built in the men over the past few hours quickly drained away in their excitement. They moved into the alleyway and watched as the two FBI agents leaned the big ugly man who had stolen their van up against the side of the vehicle and began to frisk him.

"Pierre, that is our van. That is the ugly one. Those two men, they must be the police."

"I think they are the Federal agents who have been following us for the past six weeks."

"But— They will find the explosive. What are we going to do?"

"We wait."

With that, L'Ange pulled a revolver out of his belt.

"No, I say we do not wait. It belongs to us," L'Ange said. "I say we take it back. Now."

L'Ange looked at Pierre. Challenge filled his eyes.

"Where'd you get the van?" Ferguson asked.

Stanley Kowalski was leaning forward with his hands against the van and his feet spread-eagled while Evans patted him down.

"Bought it," Stanley said.

"You bought it?"

"That's right."

"Where?"

"Used car lot."

"Used car lot?"

"Yep."

"What's the name of this used car lot?"

"I forget."

"You forget?"

"Right. All them lots sound the same. Joe's Used Cars. Or Al's. I don't know."

"You get this at the same lot?" Evans asked, pulling out Stanley's gun.

"I got a permit for that."

Evans handed the gun to Ferguson. "You don't say."

Ferguson said, "Where are the people who were in this van?"

"What people? I told you, I got it at a used car lot."

"You get a registration with it? Maybe a title?"

"Just picked it up. They're gonna send me that stuff."

The Christmas tree at Rockefeller Center would probably look beautiful once the lights were turned on, but Scotty Hunter was not here to absorb the season.

He'd spotted the ambulance, and the police car parked behind it. He'd pulled up behind the black-and-white and stopped. The only thing left to do was to find out what they could tell him.

"He's pulling over. He's stopping. What's he doing?"

Gorman didn't know what to make of Scotty's actions. Scotty had pulled his car into the alleyway beside Radio City Music Hall and was getting out.

"Why the hell is he stopping?" Gorman asked.

"Why the hell is he stopping?" Lilith asked.

The man in the black Cadillac was stopping and Lilith wanted to know why.

"I don't know," Ralph answered.

She gave him a look. "I know you don't know, Ralph. That was a restorical question; you weren't supposed to answer."

Ralph knew better than to correct his wife, especially in front of other people. Lilith always said restorical instead of rhetorical. Ralph had tried to help her as subtly as he could by saying the word correctly himself a number of times in the past, but she never caught on. Probably figures I'm saying it wrong, he concluded after a while.

"What do you want me to do, dear?" Ralph asked.

Lilith watched as three people quickly climbed out of the black Cadillac and headed north, in what Lilith defined as a real big hurry.

"Stop!" she exclaimed.

Ralph jumped. "But—There's no place to—"

"Stop the damned car, Ralph. We have to follow them."

"I—"

Lilith opened the door. "You better stop this car, Ralph, because I'm getting out."

Ralph jerked the steering wheel to the right and pulled over to the curb. The snow was piled high on the street and sidewalk, but Ralph managed to luck out and stop near a pathway that a merchant had shoveled. Lilith banged the car door against the snow and hit the sidewalk running.

"Lilith," Ralph called. "Wait. I can't stay here. There's no place to park. What do I do with the car?'"

Over her shoulder. "Leave it."

"What?"

"It's Avis' problem."

"But—"

Still walking. "Nobody will bother it, Ralph. It's a piece of crap. Come on."

Ralph turned and looked at the two people in the back seat. No help there.

Three people got out of the rental car and headed down the street following the crazy woman.

"There he is. Up there." Gorman pointed. "By that ambulance."

Michael saw him, too, just west of the skating rink.

Gorman could see that it would be a waste of time to try to fight the traffic, so he pulled his car over to the curb, turned off the engine and started to get out. Michael gave him a funny look.

"You're just going to leave it here? In the street?"

"What?"

"The car."

Gorman waved his hand. "Why not? Look around, there are cars double-parked all over the place."

"They won't tow it away?"

"How are they going to get a tow truck in here?"

Gorman had a point. They all got out.

Marcella and Michael followed Gorman as he muscled his way through the army of frigid bodies impatiently waiting for the speeches to end and the tree to be lit. The city had promised ten thousand lights. At least five people per light was Michael's guess.

Gorman couldn't wait until he got all the way through the crowd; fifty feet from the other side he hollered at Scotty. It took Scotty a second to locate him, but once he did he started walking Gorman's way. They met at the west edge of the rink, no more than fifty feet from the Christmas tree.

"Are you crazy? Put that gun away."

Pierre wished he had not used the word *crazy*. But he was frightened; he wasn't thinking.

He was frightened *and* shocked. He was not aware that L'Ange had a gun.

When in doubt, talk fast. "Wait, L'Ange. Give it a second. Calm down. We don't need to be shooting off fireworks right now. Let's see what they're up to."

L'Ange stared at their leader. It was obvious he did not feel compelled to follow orders anymore; the plan was out, so much for following a schedule. Time to improvise. Time to shoot from the hip, as the American cowboys were inclined to say. L'Ange liked the expression because shooting from the hip was one of his favorite things; actually, shooting from anywhere was one of Angel's favorite things.

Pierre waited.

After a minute L'Ange put the gun away.

Pierre exhaled.

Abandon all hope ye who enter here.

Dante said it and Victor Romaine felt it. He could now truly abandon all hope. He was finally free, but he didn't feel free; he felt trapped more now than when he was strapped in that ambulance. At least then he could hope.

But he had no hope of finding Samuelson now. Samuelson was on his way to Atlanta. Good-bye cruel world.

Victor leaned against the building and looked across the flood of people gathered around the skating rink. Faces red with cold, but filled with joy. Eight hours ago he was one of them, but not any more. Now he was just filled with cold. And the weight of the world was still with him, still boring down on his shoulders just as strong as it had been since the beginning, since that first dreadful instant when he picked up that telephone and found out that the manuscript had been stolen.

This time it was definitely over. This time he was definitely out of time. He looked again at the crowd gathered around the plaza—was his banker out there? Was the man who would cash in his chips standing there pretending to be one of the crowd?

Had Carmine Rico sent him yet? That's what weighed heaviest on Victor's mind. Was he out there right now watching him? Waiting for the right opportunity? Waiting to ...

Victor shivered. Would he see it coming? They say you don't hear the bullet that has your name on it.

Traffic came to a dead stop and Roger with it.

Roger let out a sigh. It was no use, he wasn't going anywhere. Nothing was moving.

As Roger sat there wondering if he'd ever get out of the city, he noticed that people all around him were turning off their engines, many were getting out of their cars. Drivers became pedestrians. "What the hell are they doing?" Roger asked aloud. He saw the exodus move toward the tree.

Well, hell, he thought, they're going to the ceremony. They're parking their cars in the street and going to watch them light the tree. This city is crazy.

Then he shrugged, what the hell? I might as well go, too. No reason to wait here; I'm not going anywhere until the ceremony is over. Always did want to watch them light that tree in person.

Roger moved the shift lever into PARK, turned off the engine and climbed out of his car. The cold air hit him. He turned up the collar of his coat, then pushed down the lock and slammed the door shut at precisely the same instant that he looked up at the sidewalk and saw the man that he had come all this way to find. He called to him.

"So, what do we do with it?"

The Rustlers Three were standing in an alcove of a book store on 49th Street wondering just how they should go about getting rid of the manuscript now that that was their new objective. Unloading the thing was turning out to be a more complicated problem than getting it in the first place. It was a hot potato, coated with glue. The sign over the book store door read: MURDER INC. It seemed appropriate.

Henry shifted the weight under his arm. The manuscript was getting heavier each second. "I don't know, maybe we should have left it in the ambulance."

"Yeah, right. Then someone else could have stolen it and the police would still be after us. No, we have to leave it someplace safe. Someplace where we're sure it will find its way to the police."

Henry looked up at the sign. "I suppose we could drop it off here; it's a book, and this is a book store."

Bill questioned that idea. "What are you going to do? Just walk in and hand it to the cashier? Say, 'Here, Merry Christmas,' and walk out?"

"No, we could leave it in the stacks. They'd find it sooner or later."

"Sooner or later? What if they find it later and *us* sooner? Isn't that the whole point? I thought the idea was to give them the manuscript so they'd leave us alone."

Billy tried his argument again. "I still say we should keep it. I mean, we dumped the ambulance, right? We got this far; why don't we just go on with the plan? He looked around. "No one's spotted us."

"*Yet*," Bill Sr. added. "No one has spotted us yet."

"Hey, I'm for holding on to it." Billy was determined. He hadn't seen the man with the gun for the last ten minutes and he was getting cocky again.

"We can still pull this thing off if we give it a chance. I mean it. All we have to do is give the insurance company a call, work out a deal and go from there."

"What insurance company is that, Billy?" Henry asked.

"What do you mean?"

"What insurance company do we call? What's the name of the company?"

"I— I don't know. Whoever we were going to call before."

"*Before,* we had time. Time to find out who was insuring the thing. Time to plan. Time to make a deal. Time to get away. We don't have that time anymore, Billy."

"Sure we do. We can find out. We can—"

"What about that guy with the gun? And that state trooper is still out there somewhere."

"Hey, look around, there are eight million people out here. What are the chances of anyone finding us?"

Henry said, "They found us before, they can find us again."

Bill added, "And what about the Marines? Have you forgotten about the Marines?"

Billy had a response ready; it matched his disgusted look. "What about Mom? Have you forgotten about Mom?"

Bill Freely just stared at his son, then turned and looked at Henry. "Henry? What do you think?"

And what about Gladys? Henry thought. He had a wife to think about as well. Then he shook his head no. "No, it's no good. We have to get rid of it, Bill."

Billy wanted a reason. "But why? Tell me—" A couple approached. The three nervous thieves moved out of the way and let them enter the book store. A bell over the door jingled. When it jingled a second time Billy finished his sentence:

"Tell me why."

"Your car, for one thing," Henry responded. "It's still back there."

Billy gave him a curious look.

Henry answered the look. "It's still sitting back on the expressway. They can trace it, you know? To you." He looked at Bill. "They can find us through the car, Bill. Once they have the car, they have us. And once they have us, they have the manuscript. And once they have the manuscript, we've had it. Face it, this whole thing has been a waste of time ever since the accident. We've been fooling ourselves and getting in deeper and deeper."

Billy thought for a second, then, "Hey, wait a minute. I don't buy that.

Okay, they can trace the car to us, but they can't trace the manuscript. They don't know we took it. The only thing they know for sure is that we were involved in an accident. Period."

"We stole an ambulance," Henry countered. "What about that?"

This time Billy was not so quick to respond. This time he didn't have a response.

Bill tried. "They don't know *we* took it."

Henry gave him an are-you-kidding look. "Bill, all they have to do is match the cars at the accident with the people at the hospital, whoever's missing are the thieves. Guess who's missing? Besides, the guy from the museum can ID us."

Bill didn't argue. But after a second, he had a question. "Well, hell, Henry, if that's the case, what's the use then? We're screwed either way, right? If they can trace the car to us, then how are we going to explain stealing the ambulance? Even if they can't tie us into the manuscript, they sure as hell can nail us for robbery—Grand Theft Auto, I believe is what they call it. We're sunk either way. Billy's right, we might as well just keep the manuscript now that we have it. What more do we have to lose? Maybe we can bargain with it, you know, give it back if they give us a break. Hold it for ransom. As least it's something; without it we have nothing. Frankly, I don't see any other way out."

Henry didn't know what to say. He had to admit, however, that he didn't see a lot of options either. He did, however, see a problem besides the manuscript that they had not yet discussed: How were they going to get out of here, with or without the manuscript? The last time he looked they didn't have a means of transportation. Maybe Bill was right. Maybe keeping it was the only thing they could do. Maybe—

Then, before he could say anything, he heard someone call his name.

"Do you see him, Ralph?"

"Not yet, dear. I think he went that way."

"Oh, hell, Ralph, you don't know which way he went. You can't see past your nose." Lilith turned to Louise. "Get up here, Dearie. You have to identify him for us—make the positive ID, as they say on TV. I didn't get a real good look at him in the car, so when we think we've got him in our sights we'll point him out to you and you can tell us whether or not to pull the trigger. Okay?" She grabbed Louise by the arm and jerked her forward. Louise slipped on the slick pavement but Lilith's grip of steel kept her from falling. "Watch your step, this ain't no corn field."

They pushed their way through the crowd of people, Lilith the battering ram. Suddenly, "There, is that him?" Ralph said.

Lilith leaned her head back and aimed with her nose in the direction that Ralph was pointing. "Where? I can't— Yes! That looks like him." She jerked Louise again. "That's him, isn't it?"

Louise strained her neck, but at five-feet-two, she was too short to see over the top of the crowd. "I— I can't really see. The people are too— Where do you want me to look?"

Lilith said shit and pushed Louise forward, toward the man she knew was the one she was after.

"Henry!"

Henry's eyes searched—where was that coming from? Who would be calling his name in this throng of people?

Again. "Henry!"

And then Henry saw him. What the hell was Roger Muldowney doing here?

"What did you find out from the police?"

There was a look of hope on Gorman's face. Scotty wiped it away with a word. "Nothing."

"But, what did they say? They must have said something."

Fog poured out of Scotty's mouth as he spoke. "They never heard of any manuscript. Didn't know a thing about the robbery; they just came on duty. They weren't even aware the ambulance had been stolen until they got here. They were just answering a routine call to check out an abandoned ambulance."

Gorman wasn't happy. "Shit. But the ambulance does have something to do with the robbery, right? With the manuscript?"

Scotty tried to explain. "Well, we—I—thought the thieves might have been involved in an accident on Ninety-five. A ten-car monster, wreckage all over the place, heard it over my police ban. One of the ambulances that responded to the scene was stolen as it pulled into St. Mary's. We—I—figured that maybe it was our bad guys."

"You *figured?* You didn't know?"

Scotty shrugged. "Not for sure. I was just playing a hunch. Figured it was as good a shot as any."

Gorman looked back at the ambulance. "But that's the ambulance, right? The one the thieves stole?"

"If it's the one that was stolen, and if the thieves were the ones who stole it." Gorman didn't like any of this. "When will we know?"

"The police are checking it out now." Scotty shook his head again. "Really doesn't make a whole hell of a lot of difference if it was or if it wasn't, actually. It's empty. No thieves; no manuscript; nobody—"

"You mean you've been leading us on a wild goose chase this whole time?"

Scotty didn't like the insinuation. "I haven't been leading you anywhere. I've been following a hunch. I don't know what the hell you were doing."

Gorman could see the look in Scotty's eyes. He didn't challenge it. "What about fingerprints? They must have left fingerprints."

Scotty calmed down. "Maybe, if they weren't wearing gloves. What do you think the chances of that are in this weather? Besides, even if they left prints, if there's not a set on file then there's nothing to match them to anyway."

Scotty looked at Michael and Marcella; he recognized them from the trips he'd made to the museum. He did not, however, understand why they were here. Gorman offered no explanation.

Instead, Gorman looked very upset. "Well, shit, that means we're right back where we started."

Just then the people behind them started to cheer. Marcella turned. The ceremonies at the tree were beginning.

Chapter 27

SO MUCH FOR CHARLIE BROWN'S CHRISTMAS.

Clifford Wiseman was mad at himself, he'd forgotten all about the tree-lighting ceremony. He looked at his watch. He'd never make it home in time now.

Jayne was going to be pissed. He had agreed with her that he should spend more time with the kids. They were supposed to have a mother *and* a father, not a mother and a police officer. She would not buy the fact that he got hung up in traffic. *Leave earlier*, she would say.

He came to a dead stop.

He'd be lucky if he made it home in time for Christmas in this traffic.

Wiseman cranked his window down a notch and lit a cigarette.

"Roger, I don't know what you're doing here, but thank God you're here."

"I've been looking for you, Henry. That's what I'm doing here."

Confused. "What? Why?"

Roger looked at Bill and Billy. He didn't know what to say. Did they know about Henry's crazy plan to steal the manuscript? Were they part of it? Or were they innocents? Maybe Henry and his friends were just on a shopping trip as Gladys had said. Finally Roger said:

"I talked to Gladys and she said, well, that you were Christmas shopping, and I thought, well, hell, I never heard of Henry Nash going Christmas shopping, so I—" His voice dropped a decibel. "Frankly, Henry, I was afraid you might try that," pause, "you know, that stupid stunt we talked about." Henry got a self-conscious look on his face that Roger read immediately. "Ah, shit, Henry, tell me it isn't true."

Henry rolled his eyes like a little kid who'd just been discovered lifting his hand out of a cookie jar and knew there was no use lying; his hand was filled with evidence. He lowered his eyes sheepishly to the package under his arm.

Roger looked down at it. "Jesus."

"Relax, Rog. We were just about ready to get rid of it. You were right—dumb idea."

Roger looked at Bill, then Billy. Then Henry. "What do you mean 'get rid of it?'"

"You won't believe this, Rog, but everybody in the whole damned state's after us. City cops, state troopers, a Federal guy, maybe. Even the dammed Marines."

"Marines?" Roger's face was frozen, nothing moved, he didn't even blink. He couldn't; he didn't remember how. Marines?

Henry shook his head. "Ever since we got this stupid thing the world's turned into a major toilet, and somebody keeps trying to yank the handle. I should have listened to you." Henry shook his head back and forth. "Big mistake, Rog. Big mistake. Big." He turned to Bill and Billy. "Don't worry, Roger knows all about it. He's on our side." Back to Roger. "We've decided this thing is too big for us so we're going to chuck it all and get the hell out."

Billy wanted to say, hey, wait a minute, *who* decided to chuck it all? It seemed to him that's what they were talking about when this guy came up. His father beat him to it.

"Well, Henry, I'm not sure that's exactly what we were talking—"

"But, Bill." Henry stopped him. "Don't you see? We have a way out now. We have a car."

Roger gulped. "A car? What do you mean?"

Henry: " Oh, ah, ours was in this little accident."

Roger looked around. "Where is it?"

"I-Ninety-five."

"I-Ninety-five? But how'd you get— Hey, wait a minute, I was right, that *was* you in that ambulance. They said someone stole— Henry, how did you get here?"

Henry's turn to gulp. "Ah, let's not get into that right now, okay? I'll tell you all about it later. Let's just get our butts out of here."

Roger didn't press it. He figured maybe he was better off not knowing. "Well, I have my Blazer, but it's not going to do any good. The traffic is stopped cold. We're stuck here until after the ceremony." Once again, he looked down at the package under Henry's arm. "And, when we do go, there's room for you, but there's no room for that."

Henry knew what Roger was saying. He looked at Bill. Henry could tell by the look on his face Bill knew what Roger was saying, too, and he didn't like it. They had a problem.

"You're a real smartass, aren't you?" Evans said, spinning Stanley around and pushing him toward their car. "Well, we'll see how smart you are in front of a judge."

"What the hell are you talking about? I didn't do a damned thing. I got a permit for that gun; all you have to do is look in my coat and you'll—"

"You got a permit for a stolen van?"

"Huh?"

"Gun's not the only thing—van's stolen."

Stanley stopped walking. "Bullshit." Stanley knew they had to be bluffing. No way were they around when he stole the van. They couldn't have seen him. "I didn't steal—"

"It was stolen in Chicago, last week," Ferguson said, smiling, knowingly.

Stanley stared. "Huh?"

"Yeah. We know it's stolen because we watched them steal it. *Them*—as in, the people you took it from."

Stanley said shiiiit.

Ferguson said, "You stole a real hot piece of property this time, my friend. The federal government's been after those guys for the last year. We've been on 'em for six weeks."

Evans couldn't wait to talk. "That's right, Cesspool Breath. You're in a shitload of hurt now, pal. You screwed up an operation that's been going on for a whole year. A federal operation. Taxpayers' money and all that. You realize how pissed Uncle Sam is gonna be when he finds out what you did?" Evans leaned closer. "They're gonna throw away the key."

"But—"

"But my butt," Evans said. "Come on. Move."

Evans and Ferguson led Stanley off to their vehicle, leaving the van unattended. They had no reason to suspect anyone would bother it.

"Look, Roger. I know that you—"

"Forget it, Henry. Save your breath. I told you once before I wouldn't have anything to do with this, and I meant it. I still do."

"But—"

"I came here to stop you, not to help you. You've got your choice: *That*, or a ride out of here."

Henry gave Roger a look, let out with a sigh, then turned to his partners. "Bill, I'm out of here with him. You want this," he looked down at the package, "it's all yours."

"Quickly, now is our chance. While their backs are turned."

Pierre was caught off guard. "What? What do you mean?"

"Our van," Jacques said. "Now is our chance to get it back. And the explosive."

Pierre didn't like that idea. "But, those two men are federal agents, Jacques. The same ones who have been hounding us for the past six weeks. We can not just run up there and take back the van. They will see us. And then they will have us as well as the van."

The group seemed convinced that Pierre was right. He breathed a sigh of relief. Damn, he thought, of all the bad luck. What were the chances that they would stumble across the van?

"Then let us take just the explosive."

L'Ange had spoken.

Pierre turned.

"We can get the explosive out without them even knowing, if we hurry," L'Ange said. "While they are taking care of the ugly one."

Pierre disagreed. "No. It's too dangerous."

L'Ange showed a sneer. "Too dangerous? This whole business is dangerous. *Mon ami*, I am beginning to wonder if we have chosen the right man as our leader. You do not want to steal our van back; you do not want to get the explosive; you do not want to do anything. All you want to do is walk the streets. Is this how we fight for our cause—by doing nothing? Is there no fight in you?"

This was not good. L'Ange sounded as though he was campaigning for Pierre's job. They would all die with L'Ange in charge. L'Ange was a madman.

"It— It is just that ..." and then Pierre stopped. They were all staring at him. He saw it in their eyes: Doubt. He was losing control. He had to hold on. "L'Ange is right," he blurted out, just like that.

It was the only response that would work and Pierre knew it. It was the only response the men wanted to hear, so he gave it to them. He didn't have time to think of some clever way out of this. He had to act. He had to give them action. He could see it in their faces. If they did not get satisfaction from Pierre they would get it from L'Ange, and no way could he let that happen, not if he was to get them back home alive. If Pierre wanted to stay in control—if he wanted to stay alive—he had to be the one who gave the orders. It could be Angel's *idea*, but it had to be Pedro's *way*.

Calmly, "L'Ange is right; we have to get the explosive. But we must go for the explosive only. Agreed? Trying to take the van is no good. Foolish. Those Federals can see the van; they can see it go, follow it, as they have been doing for the past six weeks. But they will not miss the explosive because they cannot see the explosive. They do not know it is even there." He looked at L'Ange. "I will go alone. One man does not stick out like four."

L'Ange said nothing.

$$$

Bill stood there staring at Henry. He didn't know what to do. He looked at Billy. Then he knew. He let out a sigh. "Let's get rid of it."

"Dad!"

Bill shook his head. "No. I've decided. It's over."

"But, why? What about Mom?"

"Two reasons, son. One is *because* of your mother. The other is you."

"Me? What do I—"

"It just hit me, this very second. Something has been bothering me about this thing from the beginning and I finally realized what it was. It wasn't what I was doing, it was what I was allowing you to do. No matter what happens I can't come out a winner. If we keep the manuscript and we get caught, it won't do your mother any good. If we keep the manuscript and we don't get caught, then it won't do my son any good. That's the point."

Billy didn't understand. "But I don't—"

"Either the two of us will be in jail, or I'll have raised a thief. Not much of a choice if you ask me. Either way I lose. No, we get rid of the manuscript and hope we can get back to where we started. We'll just have to think of another way to help your mother."

He would ram them. Head first. Plow into them like a divine wind. And then it would be over.

Tommy Kosuri aimed his Jeep at the Marines and pressed the accelerator to the floor. There they were, just on the other side of the intersection, waiting, staring at him stupidly, just as their ancestors had done fifty years before. He could taste the glory. Pride swelled up in him. This was to be his destiny. This was what he had been born for.

The man looked a lot like Scotty Hunter.

Clifford Wiseman looked closer. It was Hunter. What the hell was he doing here? Wasn't he supposed to be after some bad guys or something?

Wiseman flipped his cigarette through the crack in the window, rolled it up, opened his car door and got out.

His feet slid in the snow. Jayne would be mad about that, too. He would ruin his shoes. He was supposed to be wearing his Totes.

Totes? Totes were for sissies.

Faster.

One giant explosion and that would be the end of it. A ball of flame.

Faster.

It was too bad that Tommy didn't have a bigger target; it was too bad he couldn't take more of them with him. A destroyer maybe, a battleship, or an aircraft carrier.

Faster.

And it was too bad Tanaka was not here to see it. Tanaka-san would have been proud of the way his trusted servant had died.

"What the hell is he doing?"

McGovern wondered the same thing. "It looks like he's turned around and is coming back this way, Captain."

Wainwright didn't understand. "Why the hell would he do that? What is he, some kind of nut?"

I'd say that, McGovern thought.

Wainwright watched closely as the twin headlights of the Jeep charged toward him. His eyes grew bigger as the Jeep approached.

"Corporal, does it look to you like he's aiming that thing at us?"

McGovern didn't answer. He was too busy contemplating the possibility that his fearless leader may, for the first time in his life, be right.

"Do what with it?" Henry couldn't believe his ears.

"Put it under the tree," Roger repeated.

Henry had heard right. Roger was actually suggesting that they get rid of the manuscript by putting in under the Christmas tree at Rockefeller Plaza.

Bill Sr. and Billy stood stunned. Billy was still a little shaken by the fact that his father had agreed to get rid of the manuscript in the first place. He wasn't sure he completely bought the reasoning behind it—weren't they all thieves from the beginning? Wasn't that the plan? What had changed? But he'd been outvoted, so there wasn't anything he could do about it. Except sulk. Which he was doing. And live to fight another day, he told himself, next time without the old people.

"I mean it," Roger said. "Put it under the Christmas tree."

"Are you out of your gourd?"

"Henry, I'm serious. That's the perfect way to get rid of it. That way, the Marines will find it, give it to the police, and you'll be out of it."

"I— I don't know. I—"

"This is your chance, Henry." Roger's look was deadly serious. "Personally, I think it's a pretty good idea. This is the perfect way to not only get rid of it, but to make sure it gets back to the right people. You leave it any place else you'll never be sure. If the right people don't get it, they'll never call off the bloodhounds. Get out, now. Once and for all. Come on, Henry. Do it."

Henry thought for a minute. Then he stopped thinking. "Okay, you win. Who plays Santa Claus?"

Pierre slid in behind the back of the van, putting it between him and the gray Ford. He looked back at his men leaning against the side of the building. Fools. This was stupid. They should have gotten the hell out of there when they had the chance.

But our money and our airline tickets, as well as the explosive, are in the van, Pierre.

Right.

Pierre reached up and grabbed the handle on the back door and slowly began to ease it down.

Screeeeccccchhhh!

Damn, he'd forgotten the door handle squeaked when you opened the door.

Pierre stopped. Had they heard?

He eased his head around the side of the van.

They were still at their car, dealing with his almost-friend, the auto thief.

Jerk it quick. Maybe it won't make so much noise if you jerk it.

Pierre held his breath and jerked it.

It popped open.

Pierre pulled the door open all the way and looked inside. There, in the darkness, he spotted the canvas duffel bag that had all their money, their passports, and, most important, their airline tickets out of the country. Beside the duffel bag was the shiny aluminum container that Pierre swore would be the destruction of them all.

Chapter 28

"YEAH, RIGHT IN FRONT," Bill said, echoing Roger's words. "Put it right in front so they find it first."

Henry had already started walking away. He nodded his head yes, but didn't turn around.

Henry wasn't sure he liked Roger's idea after all. Putting ten million dollars worth of valuable property under a Christmas tree, out in the open, unprotected, seemed a little dangerous to him. Or was it the fact that he was the one who had to do it that made him nervous?

Or the fact that everywhere he looked he saw policemen. In patrol cars, on foot, on horseback. Crowd control, Henry concluded. Still, he didn't like it. Were they all looking at him suspiciously, or was it his imagination?

Just as he was about to bend over and duck under the railing he heard someone shout. "Hey, you!"

Henry turned. Damn, it was a cop.

"Okay, we have it," Pierre said. He was back at the building with his men. Getting the explosive and the duffel bag had gone without a hitch. "But now that we have the explosive, what are we going to do with it?"

L'Ange had an idea.

"Put it in front, Pierre, so we can see it go off."

Pierre couldn't believe it. "You are joking?"

L'Ange never joked.

They stood huddled in the alleyway looking down at the aluminum container, then up at each other. Pierre looked at L'Ange, then at the others. Pierre had hoped to convince them to dump the explosive, take their tickets and run. That did not look possible now. "Are you sure? Are we agreed? That is what everyone wants to do?"

Jacques thought out loud, "Well, the U.N., that was the best idea, to destroy the building as a symbol. *Oui*, that would have sent our message loud and clear to the entire world. But that is out now; we have no way to get to the U.N. because we have no transportation. So, *merde*, whatever we do, we must do here." He scratched the stubble on his chin. "I think— Yes, I think this is the best we can do now, under the circumstances."

Everyone seemed to agree. Everyone but Pierre.

He did it because it was the lesser of the two evils.

Pierre thought blowing up a Christmas tree was the dumbest idea he'd ever heard. It would send a message to no one. But it was better than alternative number two: give L'Ange time to think of something else.

No, as dumb as it was, as Jacques had said, it was the best solution under the circumstances.

So, here he was, standing in line with all the other people waiting his turn, waiting patiently until he got to the front of the line so he, too, could put his present under the tree. Forty pounds of the most dangerous explosive known to man and he was going to put it under a stupid evergreen.

What bothered him the most was the fact that he'd set the fuse to go off in ten minutes—at L'Ange's suggestion—and that was three minutes ago. That didn't look very smart now. He should have given himself more time. The line was moving slower than he'd anticipated. He didn't know for sure whether he could drop off the package and get out of there in seven minutes. Was this another way for L'Ange to get his job?

In the end Pierre knew he had no choice. L'Ange was right, they could not afford to wait around there forever. The longer they waited, the better chance they had of being spotted; who knows, maybe there was more than one car of Federal Agents following them. And he could hardly have waited until he got up to the tree before he set the fuse, for everyone to see, that was no good either. No, his only hope was to pray the people in front of him would hurry. He did not want to light up like a Christmas tree himself.

"Ah ... y-yes ... Off-officer?"

Henry's voice was quivering and he knew it.

The police officer walked up to him. "And where do you think you're going with that?"

He was looking at the manuscript.

"Ah, well, er ... I was just ..." Henry stopped. The policeman waited. Henry was dead and he knew it. Caught red-handed. He might as well surrender. "I— I guess you want—"

"You want to put that under the tree," the officer interrupted, "you have to get in that line over there like everyone else. You can't just crawl in wherever you want. This thing is organized, pal. Get with the program."

Henry looked. By God, there was a line.

He thanked the police officer and walked over and got in line behind the gentleman carrying a Christmas present in an aluminum container.

Marcella looked at the tree. And then she saw it. And she stopped breathing. My God, it can't be. This was impossible.

Marcella looked again. It couldn't be.

She took a deep breath and looked one more time.

That was it all right. She'd know that package anywhere. She'd wrapped it; she should recognize it.

But how in the world had the manuscript gotten under the Christmas tree in Rockefeller Center?

No, how the package had gotten under the Christmas tree was not the question. The question was: How could she get it? And, should she tell Michael, was the second question that crossed her mind. That one she didn't have to ponder long.

"Good God," Michael said. "Marcella, is that what I think it is?"

Marcella looked at Michael. He was looking at the same thing she'd been looking at. She did not respond.

Gorman did. "What did you say?"

Michael looked at Gorman and smiled for the first time that day. "The manuscript. You're not going to believe this, but I think that's it under the Christmas tree."

Lilith thanked God that she had not pounced on the man as soon as she got there.

She'd wanted to. She'd thought about it. As a matter fact, that was her plan. Grab the pinched-nosed little pecker by the scruff of his scrawny neck and show him what for. She ached to do it.

But just as she was about to do exactly that she heard the man beside him say something about the manuscript. That caused her to stop, and listen. They were whispering, but Lilith had very good hearing. Something about the manuscript being under the Christmas tree. Lilith looked at the tree. Jesus. How in the hell—

Who cares? The important thing was: Which one was it?

She had to be still. She had to listen. If she could get to it before them— hey, what did they say? *Possession was nine-tenths of the law?* Just let them try to get it once she had it in her hot little hands. If they touched her she'd sue.

This was the break she'd been waiting for. Lilith felt warm inside; she smiled a sinister smile. Finally things were beginning to go her way.

"Which one?"

"The white one."

"Which white one?"

"The white one with the big red bow."

Gorman stared. Scotty stared too.

Then a voice from behind, "Scotty, I thought that was you."

Scotty turned. "Cliff—Inspector, what are you doing here?"

Wiseman joined them at the guard rail. "Got stuck in traffic. I looked over here and saw you and thought to myself: Hey, isn't that the same guy who was in my office earlier today trying to convince me to jump on a case I didn't need? The same guy who I *thought* was out looking for a stolen manuscript or something? Doesn't look like you're working to me. Looks like you're waiting for them to light the tree."

Scotty introduced Wiseman to Gorman, Michael and Marcella, and then informed the inspector that he was, in fact, working, but that it looked as though his work may soon be over because it appeared that the manuscript had just been found.

Wiseman couldn't believe it when Scotty told him where they thought it was.

"Lilith, I think—"

"Shhhhhhh, be quiet, Ralph. I'm trying to hear."

Ralph was quiet.

Louise wasn't. "Oh, look, Raymond, over there's Mr. Parks, and that young lady from the museum. Let's go over and say Hi."

Lilith grabbed her. "You're not going anywhere. Shut up and be still."

"Under the tree? Where?"

"The white one with the big red bow." Michael pointed it out to the inspector. "It sure looks like the package."

Gorman spotted it, too. "You're sure that's it?"

"Positive," Michael responded. Then he had second thoughts and turned to Marcella. "That is the manuscript, isn't it, Marcella? I mean, that is the box."

Marcella hesitated, then said, "Well, I don't know. It certainly looks like the same box to me, but I ... well, I can't be sure," she lied.

"How the hell did it get under the tree?" Wiseman asked.

Michael shook his head.

Marcella was silent.

Gorman's look said he didn't care one way or another how it got there, just as long as it was there. If that was it then they had to get it, that was the point. "I don't give a damn how it got there. I only care how we can get it here. We have to get it. We can't just leave it sitting there." He looked at Scotty. "Scotty ..."

Oh, yeah, right, me, Scotty thought. Good old Scotty.

"And how on earth do you think he's going to do that, Mr. Gorman?" Marcella came to his rescue. "What would you have him do? Just walk right out there in the middle of everything and pick it up? They're about ready to throw the switch. I don't think that would be a good idea at all."

Gorman's look told Marcella he didn't care what she thought.

Marcella's look, however, didn't tell Gorman what she was really thinking. A good idea would be to have me go out there and get it, Marcella thought to herself. As a matter of fact, it's imperative that I be the one. After all, I'm the only one who really cares.

"Dad, did you hear what that man said?"

Bill shook his head no and leaned toward his son.

The man Billy was pointing to was Parker Gorman, but, of course, Billy didn't know that.

Billy said, "He said something about the manuscript being under the Christmas tree."

"What? Are you sure?"

Billy said he was. "Who is he? And how does he— Dad, that man standing beside him. Isn't he the guy from the museum? The guy we stole the manuscript from?"

Bill looked. Jesus, it was him. He turned to Roger and nodded yes.

Roger wanted to spit. They were practically shoulder to shoulder. They backed away.

"Where's Henry?" Roger said. "We've got to find him before he comes back this way. If they spot him we're dead."

"Ralph, get your butt out there and get that thing."

Lilith had spotted it along with Gorman. She pointed it out to Ralph.

"But, Lilith, I—"

"Don't but me, Ralph. It's right there in front of us for chrissake. There'll never be a better opportunity." She pushed at his shoulder. "Go. Go!"

"But, Lilith, I can't just go running out there. They're about ready to throw the switch and light the tree. Everyone's looking. I'd look like a fool."

"You are a fool, Ralph. Don't worry about it. Moooove."

"Lil—"

"Ralph, are you going to make me do it? Do I have to do everything?"

She gave Ralph another one of her looks.

"Lilith, I'll tell you what. As soon as they light the tree, and all the fuss is over, I'll go get it. Okay?"

Lilith's look said that was not okay.

"Okay, as soon as the mayor lights the tree, I'll go get it," Wiseman said.

Gorman looked at Michael. Michael looked at Marcella. Lilith, standing no more than three feet away, thought to herself: Bullshit, I'll have it by then.

The mayor threw the switch.

The lights came on and the crowd gasped in unison at the beauty.

It lasted only a split second, because then the Christmas tree exploded into a giant ball of flame, and the gasps of joy changed to screams of horror.

Chapter 29

Panic ensued.

People scrambled, ran for cover. The podium emptied. Dignitaries and peons alike intermingled in mass hysteria, proving, at least in an emergency, that all men are created equal.

The Marines went for their Jeeps, the police for their radios. Bodies were crushed against cars, buildings, other bodies. Bedlam.

Fire rained from the sky.

Roger did not have to worry about the man from the museum spotting Henry; the man from the museum was in a state of shock as he stood there and watched the white box with the big red bow go up in flame. They all stood there in disbelief and watched.

In the middle of the stampede Roger spotted Henry. He grabbed him and the four of them ran to the side of Radio City Music Hall and stopped. The spectacle was unbelievable.

The fifty-foot Wisconsin pine was a four-story steeple of angry red fire. Tongues of flame licked at the sky. It spit off balls of fire that spewed out for a hundred feet or more, a giant Roman candle. The sky glowed like a fireworks display on the Fourth of July. All the people, except for the thirteen who knew that a lot more than just a Christmas tree was going up in flame, were in a real big hurry to get away from Rockefeller Plaza as fast as they could.

Gorman, Wiseman, Michael, Marcella, and Scotty Hunter stared in disbelief. Lilith, Ralph, Mr. and Mrs. Bridges did likewise. As did Henry, Bill, Billy and Roger. No one said a word. It was enough that they remembered how to breathe.

The good news: It didn't last long. The sight was magnificent, but short-lived. The entire catastrophe took less than a minute. Like the carbide at the end of a match, a flashbulb going off, the tree exploded into a gigantic burst of white flame, which seemed to suck all the oxygen out of the air in one gigantic gulp, and then flickered and died almost as quickly as it started.

Everything under the tree was ash.

Police cars arrived on the scene in a few minutes. Ambulances followed. The crowd seemed to sense that the danger had passed and somehow gathered itself, and after a brief pause to reflect in disbelief, began to disperse in a surprisingly orderly fashion. The police shuffled them along quickly, just in case the first explosion was not the last. It would take a while to clean up the mess, but miraculously, it appeared that no one was seriously injured. It had been more show than substance.

Assuming it was over.

As it turned out, it was.

"Pierre, it was just a simple fire bomb."

Pierre was pleased. Naturally, he didn't let it show.

"We were ripped off," Jacques said. "The *Americain* bastards ripped us off."

Inside, Pierre was smiling. Now they had to quit; there was no more money. "Let's get out of here," he said.

"Jesus, it's gone. The manuscript's gone."

"Let's get out of here, Henry," Roger said.

"Shit, Rog. They'll never let us alone now. The damn thing is—"

"Relax, Henry. It's okay."

"No, it's not. They don't know it's been destroyed, don't you see? That's the point. We know it, but for all they know it's still—"

Roger grabbed Henry by the shoulders and looked him straight in the eye. "No, Henry, it's okay. They do know. That's what I'm saying."

"What do you mean?"

Roger looked at Bill. Bill picked up the ball. "Billy overheard the people next to us talking. They knew about the manuscript being under the tree. How, I don't know. One of them was the guy from the museum. They know it's been destroyed, Henry. It's over. It's all over."

Henry couldn't believe it. Roger shook his head. "Yeah, it's all over."

They led Henry back to Roger's Blazer. Henry knew he should feel better—now that they could never trace the robbery to them—but he didn't. They climbed inside.

"You okay, Henry?" Roger asked.

Henry sighed. "The whole goddam thing was a waste. All of it." Roger nodded. "I feel lower than whale shit, Rog, and that's at the bottom of the ocean."

Roger laughed. "Hey, that's better than feeling jail."

Henry looked at Bill and Billy. They looked equally depressed. They were all right back where they started. Life sucked. "Yeah, right," Henry said.

"What about my car?" Billy asked.

Roger answered. "We'll pick it up on the way out."

"How? It won't run."

"I can tow it. I have a tow bar rigged to the frame that I use to pull my boat. No problem."

"Maybe it's already been towed away."

Henry shook his head. "I doubt it. It was in the median strip, didn't affect the flow of traffic. Getting it out of there is the owner's problem."

"What about the police? Won't they be waiting for us?"

Henry held up crossed fingers. "Let's hope not. If we're lucky, maybe they haven't tied our car into the ambulance yet."

"What about that trooper? He must have figured it out."

Henry held his other hand with fingers crossed. "My guess is he assumed that whoever stole the ambulance, stole the manuscript. That doesn't mean they can put us with the car, with the manuscript, with the ambulance. Not until they account for everyone involved in the accident, or at the hospital. I'm counting on things being hectic enough that they couldn't have done that yet. I think we have a chance—with the storm, and all the other accidents that they must be involved in. If we can get to it quick enough maybe we can be in and out before they have a chance to figure it all out. If they ever do."

"What do you mean?"

"Hey, they've got their ambulance now, and the manuscript is gone. Right? If we can get the car out of there I don't think they can tie us to any of this, especially since we won't be leaving tracks by using a tow truck. And that guy from the museum—in the middle of a blizzard, in the middle of an accident—he couldn't identify us in a million years, even if he saw us again, which he never will. So, case closed. I don't think they're going to spend a lot of time trying to find the bad guys when it wouldn't do them any good even if they did. They got plenty of other things to keep them busy."

Should he call Phyllis or shouldn't he? Should he have her pick him up or should he take a cab home? Or should he say the hell with it and stay in the city overnight?

Or should he just go jump in the river and get it over with?

No, he might be swimming in the river soon enough as it was.

So close. He was so close to hitting it big. If it hadn't been for that—

"Mr. Romaine, fancy seeing you here."

Victor looked up. He'd died and gone to heaven. Coming toward him with his hand extended was an angel. "Mr.— Mr. Samuelson. What are you doing here? I thought— I thought you were going to London."

They shook hands.

"Ah, all the fool airports in this here town are closed. Can't believe they'd let a little thing like snow get them down. You people a bunch of sissies or what? Heck, even tried to take a train to Albany and catch a flight outta there." He shook his head and gave off with a frown. "The last connection I could get took off for Atlanta thirty minutes before I got here. Hell's fire, that was no good. So, here I am, stuck in New York." He gave Victor a sideways glance and winked. "You wouldn't reconsider selling my vase would you?"

"Well, it was a merry ride. But I have to admit, I'm glad it's over."

Marcella didn't say anything.

Michael walked her over to her car. It had started to snow again. The parking lot at Jefferson was empty now except for the two cars owned by the visitors from Connecticut. "Sure you want to drive back in this? We could try to find a couple of rooms and stay the night."

Was that a proposition? Marcella looked at Michael. No, it wasn't. Her smile was one of disappointment, not because she would have accepted, she knew that they were too far apart to ever get together, but because she was not offered the opportunity to decline. "No, I'll be fine," she said.

Michael opened her car door. "I'll follow you then. Just in case."

Marcella climbed in. "Thank you." The closing at the end of a business letter, polite but impersonal.

Michael sensed it. There was something wrong. He may not be the most observant man in the world, but he knew when something was bothering Marcella. He thought he knew what it was. "I'm sorry about the manuscript. I know how much it meant to you."

Marcella put her key in the ignition and started the engine.

He was so blind.

Michael waited for a response.

It never came.

$$$

The car was right where they left it, and it was not surrounded by the cavalry, but it was completely covered with snow. They would have to dig it out.

"I got a shovel in back," Roger said.

"Do you think they got my license number?" Billy asked, concerned.

Henry looked at the car. What he saw made him smile. "Not unless they got it before all this snow. The plate's covered."

Billy saw what Henry meant. The entire rear end of Billy's car was covered with snow.

"What if they got the number before the snow covered it?" Bill asked.

Henry walked up to the car and brushed the snow away from the plate. He smiled again. When he stepped back they all smiled. The accident had twisted the plate around so that none of the numbers were visible. The only way anyone could have gotten the number would have been to pry the plate flat again, and if anyone had done that it was unlikely that they would have bothered to double it back over. They were safe.

Roger backed his Blazer down to Billy's car. Henry hooked it up to the tow bar and they headed for Fort Lee. It was a long silent trip. They were home and in bed by midnight. No one slept well. They all wondered if they were going to awaken the next morning and find the police sitting on their door step.

That did not happen.

Sunday through Saturday
December 11-17

The Final Curtain

Chapter 30
Sunday

"I DON'T PLAN ON SPENDING ANY TIME TRYING TO FIND THE BAD GUYS, if you want me to be honest with you. I'll never admit that in public, but it's true." Inspector Wiseman leaned back in his chair, balancing the telephone on his shoulder. "I have too many other things to keep me busy."

That's why the hell he was in his office on a Sunday morning.

Wiseman glanced over at the corner office and lowered his voice, out of habit, because the man next door was not in. "Man next door doesn't think it's important enough—politically, that is—to waste any manpower on it. The manuscript is gone, what good would it do to catch the perps?" His voice went down to a whisper. "First thing he ever said I agreed with. I don't have a problem with that at all. I got New Year's Eve twenty-two days away. That means Dick Clark and three hundred thousand drunks in Times Square."

The inspector waited while Scotty put his boss on the line, then listened to Gorman argue his case. Wiseman was a patient man; he'd been through this kind of thing many times. After a few minutes he said, "I can appreciate that, Mr. Gorman. But not only don't I have the time or the manpower to allocate to this case, we don't have the prison space available even if we did catch them. We got 'em crammed in like sardines now. You want me to tell the governor to throw a couple of crack dealers, or killers, out onto the street so we can make room for your people?" He shook his head even though there was no one there to see it. "Doesn't work that way, Mr. Gorman. Sorry."

The conversation lasted another thirty seconds, then Inspector Wiseman hung up the phone. Parker Gorman did likewise on his end.

Parker looked at Scotty. "The case is closed as far as he's concerned."

Scotty nodded his head. He understood.

Lilith smiled. "Then you might just as well make out the check right now, Mr. Gorman. No reason for us to hang around any longer. If the police say it's shut, it's shut. We've already been here longer than I care to be anyway. Paperwork, bunch of crap if you ask me. Stall tactics, that's all it is."

Scotty looked at the woman sitting next to him. A karate chop to the throat would do perfectly. She hadn't shut her big yap since she'd entered Gorman's office at nine that morning.

Gorman looked for a escape route, but knew there was none. He picked up his phone and punched in three numbers, waited, then said, "Mr. Tilbury, would you come into my office for a minute please?" Pause. "Thanks."

Gorman looked at Lilith. "Mr. Tilbury is our chief financial officer, and the head of our Legal Department. I called him last night and asked him to be here today. He's the man who takes care of this kind of thing."

"Just make it quick. I don't want to stay in this gawdfersaken town any longer than I have to—one night's plenty. Like I said, we've been here too long already to suit me. A hundred and fifty bucks for a room, for one night—ridiculous. They ought to give you the damn room for that. And breakfast—who can afford to eat in this damn town?"

The room was silent.

The door opened and Mr. Tilbury stepped it.

Lilith swallowed a giggle; actually, a guffaw. He looks like a chief financial officer, she thought to herself. A cream puff in a blue suit ... if that's what you'd call that piece of cloth he was wearing. Had to be a holdover from his Robert Hall days. Lilith hid her mouth behind a cupped hand and took in the rest of the man. Head as bald as a billiard ball and twice as shiny; she snickered under her breath. Thick glasses cut out of the bottom of old Coke bottles squatted in the middle of a nose that was almost nonexistent. The pencils sticking out of the plastic pencil holder in his breast pocket—the one that had Jefferson printed in black ink across the flap—screamed ACCOUNTANT! Beancounter, that's what he is, Lilith thought. This guy was going to be a pushover. She wondered if he was wearing arm bands under his jacket.

Tilbury entered the room and shut the door behind him. "Yes, sir," he said, looking at Gorman.

Squeaky voice. Lilith wasn't surprised.

Gorman sighed. "About the Twain manuscript: Mrs. Bridges and her husband," he paused and looked at Lilith, "and their friends, are here to collect on the policy. The police just informed me that although the case is not officially closed, they don't see much hope of finding the people who stole it, since they have neither the manpower nor the finances to allocate to one case when they have so many 'more pressing' matters on their priority list. I have to admit that that doesn't really surprise me. I suppose it even makes sense on a Cost-Reward basis, at least from their standpoint, though certainly not ours." He let out another sigh. "Therefore, that being the case, I suspect that we should get on with it. Can we write the check now?"

Tilbury hesitated. He seemed confused. "But, excuse me, sir. I don't understand."

Lilith wanted to laugh out loud. His voice was hilarious.

Gorman hadn't liked saying it the first time. The second time through he knew it would taste a lot worse. "The Mark Twain manuscript, as you know, was destroyed. The policy Mrs. Bridges carried on it is—"

"—Is null and void, Sir," Mr. Tilbury interrupted.

A hush fell over the room. Even the heating system shut down at that precise moment. All of a sudden Lilith didn't think the beancounter's voice was that funny after all. All eyes were on Tilbury.

Gorman looked for his voice and found it. "What?"

"Yes, sir. That's why I was confused. I didn't understand what you were getting at. It's perfectly clear, sir, that policy is null and void; there will be no pay-out."

Lilith found her voice without looking, she always knew where she kept it. "What the hell do you mean: null and void? No pay out?"

Tilbury turned to Lilith. His eyes looked like BBs through the thick glass. "That's correct, Madam. That policy specifically states that if the covered property should be destroyed by an Act of God, an Act of War, or an Act of Terrorism—as do all our policies," he directed his gaze at Gorman for that one phrase, then returned it to Lilith, "then there will be no obligation on the part of the company. It was a terrorist bomb that destroyed the manuscript. Ergo: The policy is null and void." He looked at Gorman. "You did say that the police confirmed that it was terrorists who set the explosive, did you not?"

Gorman shook his head. "Ah, yes. That's correct."

Tilbury held up his hands in surrender. He looked at Mrs. Bridges. "I'm sorry. But that's the way it is."

That was not "the way it is" as far as Lilith was concerned. "And how in the hell do you know it was terrorists? How do the police know? It could have been anybody."

Mr. Tilbury looked at Gorman. Gorman said, "Apparently a state trooper spotted them. According to Inspector Wiseman, the trooper said they were wandering around Rockefeller Center looking suspicious, so, on a hunch, he called to them to stop. When he did, one of them pulled a gun. He had to shoot him. It was terrorists all right, there's no doubt. Some South Seas group, I believe. I don't remember the name."

If there was any glee in Mr. Tilbury's eyes it was hidden by his thick glasses. Gorman's relief, however, was obvious.

Louise didn't understand. "Does that mean we're out then?" she asked. Gorman didn't say a word.

Scotty thought he must be dreaming: Could they really be this lucky? Louise and Raymond waited.

Lilith said bullshit. Actually, Lilith screamed "Bullshit!"

Gorman wanted to tell her where to get off. He wanted to rub her nose in it, wanted to throw her out of his office in the same manner that she had barged in, wanted to bask in the glory of this victory, but he was so ecstatic about the good news that he was able to be the smooth business man he had been before all this happened. "I'm sorry, Mrs. Bright, Mr. and Mrs. Bridges. I really am. But there's nothing I can do. I'm sure you're very disappointed, but the policy did so state, as Mr. Tilbury reminded me—as do all our policies—that—"

"Bullshit. Bullshit, bullshit, bullshit—that's what I so state. If you think I'm buying that for a second you're as crazy as a loon. I—" Lilith looked at Louise, "—we—are not going to put up with this crap for a second. If you think you're dealing with a couple of country bumpkins fresh off the farm, you're out of your skull, mister. Not this time. Not. This. Time."

"Mrs. Bright, I know you're upset. But I think if you'll read the contract, you'll see that it specifically states that if there's—"

"—Horse—shit."

Gorman held his patience. "I'm afraid there's nothing either one of us can do."

Lilith shook her head. "Wronggggggggggggg. Not this time. There's a hell of a lot I can do. I can sue your sorry ass for one thing. I can sue you up one side and down the other. I can sue you black and blue. And that's just for starters. I plan to sue not only for the value of the manuscript, but for mental strain as well. You've caused me all kinds of anguish, pal. You've caused," she looked at Ralph, "and my husband, too. You've caused him all kinds of pain just worrying about me."

"Lilith, I—"

"Shut up, Ralph."

Ralph shut up.

Lilith turned toward Louise. Louise flinched, as if Lilith was about to threaten her.

"And poor Mrs. Bridges here. And her dear husband. A hundred million—that's what I'm going for. A hundred million big ones."

Gorman didn't even blink. Go ahead, waste your money, he thought. This kind of case had been tested time and time again in courts and the insurance company always won. We have as many attorneys as you do and we will fight this one forever if we have to. You don't know it little lady, but we have more to lose than you do. We have everything on the line.

Lilith stood up.

Ralph knew better than to remain seated, so he stood, too.

Louise and Raymond didn't move. Lilith noticed. "Well, why are you two just sitting there? Let's go. We have to find ourselves an attorney. We have to go shopping for Mr. Bad Ass."

Louise looked at Raymond. Raymond spoke:

"We started with nothin', and we end with nothin'. No big deal to me."

Louise smiled. "Hey, I was on the Jay Leno Show, that was something."

"What the hell's that supposed to mean?" Lilith asked.

"Means we're going home," Raymond announced. Louise's smile grew.

Ralph couldn't believe it: This couple had nothing, and yet they had everything. They had each other.

Lilith gritted her teeth. "You don't jump on the bandwagon now, don't expect any money later, sonny. You pass the hot potato, you pass the gravy."

"It's all yours," Raymond said, as he stood up. He helped Louise to her feet. "Come on, honey. Let's get out of here. We got a free trip to California out of it, look at it that way. Besides, we don't have no use for that kind of money anyway. All that kind of money does is let you find out you just inherited a whole bunch of relatives you didn't even know you had."

With that they nodded to Gorman and walked out of the office. The door closed behind them.

Lilith ran to the door and jerked it open. She screamed at them. "Hey, you can't walk out of this thing now. What do you think you're doing? Who the hell do you think you are? Get back here. You have to stay. I came all this way and now you want me to carry the whole damned load myself? Get back here, you deserters. Get—"

"Lilith." It was Ralph.

"—your sorry asses back—"

"Lilith!" It was Ralph, louder.

She turned. "— here! Ralph, will you—"

"—LILITH!" It was Ralph, very loud.

Lilith stopped cold. She stared at her husband. He was standing now. She'd never seen him look this way before. He seemed ... taller. And there was something about him, something ... strong ... something manly.

Ralph spoke in a calm tone. "Lilith, brain open, mouth shut. Try to stay with me on this. I'll go slow."

Lilith turned red. She was about to explode. Ralph put out the fuse. "We're leaving. It's over. I've decided. It's—"

"You've decided? Who the hell died and put you in—"

"I said it's over."

"Bullshit! It's not—"

"Lilith, it's over because I say it's over."

Lilith grinned, a sinister grin. "Ralph, don't push it. Don't push your—"

"I will push it. I'll push it all the way to the breaking point. I'll push it over the edge. I've had it, Lilith. I'm not going to put up with it any more. This stupid chase is over. We're done running around begging for table scraps. We're finished chasing rainbows. I say it's over and I mean what I say. I'm ending it, Lilith. I'm ending it now."

Lilith cooled off a degree. "Ralph, what the hell's gotten into you? You've never acted—"

"Like this before." He smiled. "No, I haven't. And it's high time I did. I've—*we've*—wasted too much time already. We have a life to live, and it's time we started living it. It's time we quit throwing it away on wild goose chases."

"Ralph, where in the hell did you come up with this dipshit idea?"

Ralph told her. "The Bridges. They just taught me a very valuable lesson. They know what life's all about. They live it, Lilith. We're just passing through, on our way to death."

"The Bridges? Ha! They don't know their asses from two holes in the—"

"They have it all."

"They have nothing."

"They have each other."

Lilith stopped to think.

Ralph didn't need to stop; he'd been thinking. "And that's exactly what we have, exactly what we've always had. All we ever will have. We have each other and we have to learn to live with that. We just never realized it before, Lilith. Don't you see? That's all we need. The only thing we don't have now is time. We've squandered that away over the years. But we're not going to squander it away anymore. We don't have enough time left; we can't afford to throw anymore of it away. Let it be, Lilith. Let it go. Let go of what we don't have so we can use both hands to hold on to what we do. There is no Twain manuscript. No relative. No inheritance. Face it. There's just us. The two of us. We have to be satisfied with that. I am. And you'll just have to be, too."

"But, Ralph, I—"

"Let it go, Lilith. We'll let it go and hold on to each other."

Lilith seemed to melt before their eyes. Sharp edges became rounded, corners disappeared. Granite changed to lace. A transformation: not to beauty, to subtle grace.

Ralph turned to the two men in the room. "Gentlemen, sorry we took up so much of your time. Have a nice day."

He walked to the doorway, took his wife of twenty-seven years by the arm and led her out. She went without another word.

"The first thing I'm gonna do when I get out of here is find that guy and break him in two."

Stanley's cell mate grunted. "Yeah, when's that gonna be? What year in the next century?"

Before Stanley could respond, a guard walked up to the door of the cell. "Kowalski," he said, "let's go. You're outta here."

Stanley grinned at his roomy. "Wha'd I tell ya?"

The guard opened the door. Stanley was about to walk through when the guard said, "Turn around."

"Huh?"

"I said, turn around."

Stanley turned around. This made no sense. Before Stanley could react the guard grabbed both of Stanley's wrists, jerked them behind his back and snapped on a pair of handcuffs.

"What the hell are those for?" Stanley asked. "Why are you puttin' on cuffs if you're lettin' me go?"

"Who said anything about letting you go?"

"But I thought—"

"You thought wrong. We're not letting you go. We're moving you to better accommodations."

"What the hell does that mean?"

"That gun the Feds took off you? Seems like it was the murder weapon used in a killing not too long ago. DA figured it might be a good idea to put you in something a little more secure until we figure this whole thing out."

Tommy groaned and tried to turn over.

He couldn't move. There was a weight on him, pressing down.

He opened his eyes. It was daylight. The sun was pouring in the window. His eyes cleared. What he saw made him wish they hadn't.

He blinked. His eyes had not lied. It was just that it was such a shock; Tommy had never seen a body cast before.

From head to toe, Tommy Kosuri was dressed in white. Hard white. Plaster white. He tried to move again and the pain that raced through his body suggested that that would not be a very good idea.

Jesus, what had happened to him? Where was he? He thought back. It came to him in a rush. He remembered stealing the Jeep. He remembered the Marines chasing him. He remembered turning around, sighting his target, and charging. He was about to scream *Banzai!* and ... he started to slide ... then spin ... then all at once a flash of red on his left. And then a million stars engulfed him, and after a second even the stars disappeared and he was swimming in a heaven of darkness.

"Well, I see you're finally awake."

Tommy's eyes shifted to the man in the white coat who had just appeared by his bed. A woman in a white dress stood beside him.

"I'm Doctor Shufelt. How do you feel?"

"Where— Where am I?"

"You were involved in a pretty bad accident, Mr. Kosuri. You've got a lot of broken pieces in what was once a very healthy body."

"What happened?"

"You had a run-in with a red station wagon. The station wagon won. You're very fortunate considering you weren't wearing a seat belt. You have a lot of broken bones, but none that won't mend. I think you're going to be fine, in time. The spine—and I still don't know how you managed it—was spared. You're lucky, Mr. Kosuri. Very lucky you're not paralyzed."

Paralyzed? Tommy's brain tried to sort through everything that was going on. "A station wagon? But—" What about the Jeep, and the Marines?

"There is, however," the doctor continued, "a little question about how you appropriated that Jeep you were driving. The police want to talk to you about that as soon as you're able. I told them that you wouldn't be able for at least forty-eight hours. But that's their problem. My job is to sew you back up and make you better so that they can talk to you."

The doctor turned and whispered something to the nurse. Then, as it appeared that he was about to leave, he paused and reached into the pocket of his white jacket. He turned back to Tommy. "Oh, by the way, the lady who ran into you asked me to give you this. She said she was terribly sorry, but she had a very sick child at home and could not wait until you regained consciousness. Said she'd call in a day or so. Nice lady, very worried about you." The doctor held out a white business card for Tommy to read. "She's apparently into remodeling, redecorating, that kind of thing. Has a rather unique name."

Tommy blinked. The card came into focus:

Ms. Pearl Harbour
Restorations
Call for an appointment
(812)465-Home

Chapter 31

It screamed like a banshee.

The bullet ripped through the hot August air catching the kid in the left side of his chest. The impact was like a sledge hammer; it threw him backwards, up into the air. He fell like a dead piece of meat onto the dusty street. THUD.

He heard footsteps. Madden was coming for him.

The kid tried to reach for his gun, but he didn't know where it was, and worse, he didn't know what he was reaching with, because he had no feeling in his hand. He had no feeling anywhere, except for the raging hell that burned in his chest.

A shadow over his face.

He looked up, tried to see, but Madden moved, and was now standing with the sun perched on his left shoulder. The kid squinted, but could only make out a coal-black shadow hovering over him. His chest was on fire; he could feel his heart pounding inside his head, fighting to hold on to life. "Go ahead. Finish it," he forced out. A small stream of blood trickled out of the right corner of his mouth.

"You are finished," was all that Madden had to say. Then he eased the deadly Colt .44 into his holster and turned and walked away—

Riiinnnnggggg!

Henry jumped. "Jesus, damned phone can scare the living hell out of a person." He closed the paperback novel and picked it up. "Hello."

"Henry? Bill."

"Hey, Bill." Great, all Henry needed was his ex-partner in crime calling to cheer him up with stories about how his life was turning to shit. Henry tried to sound cheerful. "What's up?"

"You'll never believe it."

"Hey, after yesterday, I'd believe anything."

Bill grunted an acknowledgment. "Tell me about it. But, anyway, Henry, listen to this: Jake Carpenter—my buddy, down at the fire station?—just called. This—this is unbelievable, Henry. You know that operation that Marge has to have?"

"Yeah?"

"Well, yesterday, while we were gone, the Union got together and—hey, wait 'til you hear this—they're going to sponsor a fund raising drive to pay for Marge's liver transplant. Can you believe it? Got the whole thing organized already. They're going to put canisters at every store in town telling people about Marge, and the operation she needs, and the fact that it's not covered by insurance. They're going to have bowl-a-thons, raffles, solicit funds from local charities, even campaign on the local TV station, do all kinds of things to raise money. Jake said they're going to try to convince the United Way to shift some of the money that it receives from the firefighters toward the operation. If they won't agree to do that, all the firefighters are going to pull out of the United Way for a year and make that same contribution to Marge. Can you believe that? They don't want to make any promises, naturally, but they think they'll be able to raise the whole thing. Henry, is that great or what?"

Henry was speechless. "Jesus, Bill. That's fantastic."

"You don't know how this makes me feel. I— Well, you know, I didn't know what I was going to do."

"Yeah, I know. This is great, Bill. Really great." *At least one of us has managed to get his tit out of the ringer.*

"I just wanted to call and let you know."

"Thanks, Bill. Appreciate that. I'm happy for you. I really am. I think it's wonderful. I'll tell Marge."

"Hey, I knew you'd probably be worried about me, you know, now that you don't have to worry about your problem anymore. So I just wanted you to know that it looks like everything is going go work out."

What the hell did that mean? "Ah, I don't understand. My problem?'"

"The strike. I just heard it on the radio."

"What about it?"

"You haven't heard?"

"No. Haven't had the radio on."

"According to the local news, the UAW and GM have reached a tentative agreement."

"What?"

"That's right. That's what they said anyway. Heard it not more than five minutes ago."

Henry tried to catch his breath. "Bill, I gotta hang up. You understand. I gotta make a call."

"Hey, if anyone understands, I do. Go get 'em, Tiger. Talk to you later."

Henry dialed Roger's number.

"Hello."

"Rog, is it true?"

"Henry, I've been trying to call you but your line's been busy. Guess you've heard. There's not gonna be a strike, my man. We got a settlement."

"You're kidding."

"Nope."

"You're sure?"

"I talked to Willie."

"Positive?"

"Just a matter of dotting the I's and crossing the T's."

"Don't shit me, Rog."

"Hey, would I shit you? You're my favorite turd."

"What happened? Why no strike?"

"The Japs."

"What the hell are you talking about?"

"The company and the union finally saw the light. They both agreed that the only ones who would win with a strike would be the Japs. They're already kicking our butts here, all they would need to take over the whole damned world is a shutdown in this country. This is World War Three, baby. Only this time they're dropping Toyotas on Pearl Harbor."

"I— I can't believe it."

"Me neither. When was the last time you heard of GM and the UAW agreeing on anything?"

Henry was silent. Then, "So, what happens now?"

"We go to work. Just like before."

"That's it?"

"That's it."

Henry was suspicious. "What about pay cuts?"

"No such animal. There's a bunch of Mickey Mouse crap in there, just like every contract, but nothing that amounts to anything more than triple-O shit. The biggies are a lock—the company agreed not to shut down any more plants for the length of the contract if the union agreed to a wage freeze. It did. We got wages and security for another three. Hell, I can live with that."

Henry said he could too.

They hung up without mentioning the little incident that had taken place the day before, even though they both knew it was on their minds.

Henry leaned back in his chair and reopened his paperback. Marge was going to be thrilled. Bill was right, maybe things were going to work out after all. As long as the guys in blue suits didn't come calling.

As Henry began to read he noticed that the print seemed smaller than usual, and just a tad bit out of focus. Did he need a new pair of reading glasses, something stronger?

Naw, he told himself, it was just the light.

Chapter 32
Saturday

THE TEAPOT WHISTLED JUST AS MARCELLA GOT TO IT.

She poured the boiling liquid over an herbal tea bag in her "Star Light, Star Bright; Where The Hell is Mister Right?" tea mug, then looked out her kitchen window at the—according to the last weather bulletin—beginning of what was projected to be "another five inches of the white fluffy stuff."

This time the forecast didn't bother Marcella at all. "Let it snow, let it snow, let it snow," she sang. It was Saturday morning, and she wasn't planning on going any farther than her own living room. A blazing fire in the fireplace, a hot cup of herbal tea and a good book—the perfect way to spend not only a Saturday morning but an entire weekend as far as Marcella was concerned. Especially after the hectic activities of last weekend.

While her tea brewed, Marcella got the toaster out from the cupboard under the silverware drawer, dropped two slices of whole wheat bread into the slots, checked the lever to make sure it was set to LIGHT, and pushed the handle down. While the bread toasted she took the tea bag out of the mug and put in a teaspoon of Coffeemate and two bags of Sweet-n-Low.

She stood by the sink almost trance-like, stirring the cream-colored liquid and staring out the window at the snow. So close, she thought. Her knees felt weak when she realized all that she'd gone through. It made her heart pound. It was not a pleasant recollection.

The toaster popped. She jumped.

Calm down, Marcella, she told herself. It's all over.

She put the two slices of toast on a paper plate, spread a generous path of Peter Pan Plain on one slice and a sticky swatch of Smuckers Grape Jam on the other, snatched her mug of tea off the counter and headed for the living room of the little one bedroom apartment she'd called home for the past three years.

The fire she'd started as soon as she'd crawled out of bed was blazing now. God, how she loved a fire in a fireplace. It cracked and snapped, filling her with joy. She set her breakfast on the coffee table in front of the sofa, grabbed the lapels of her white terry cloth bathrobe and pulled them tight around her chin. She swooned in the glow of the fire. It reminded her of her childhood in Iowa, and the warm fires her father used to build in their farmhouse every Saturday morning all winter long. She used to spend hours sitting in front of that fireplace reading and dreaming. There was nothing in the world like a cold winter day on the outside and a warm crackling fire on the inside.

She looked down at the sofa ... *and* a good book.

Marcella walked to the window and pulled back the sheers and looked across Broadmore Avenue at Collins Park. It was empty now, too early for ice skaters. But by noon the frozen pond would be crammed full of laughter and giggles and bruises patiently waiting to surface one slippery step away. Marcella wasn't much of an ice skater—skiing was her game—but she vowed that she just might give it a try a little later. If she was in the mood. If she could pull herself away from her reading.

Marcella turned from the window, walked over to the sofa and sat down. She took the afghan off the back of the sofa and wrapped it around her body from the waist down, making certain her feet were tucked in nice and snug. Even with slippers on, her toes were always cold—a minor circulation problem Dr. Yoder had told her not to worry about. She put her feet up on the sofa and leaned back against the arm. Her toast and tea were on the coffee table at her elbow, easily within reaching distance. She picked up the tea mug and tested her concoction. Perfect.

She grabbed a slice of toast (peanut butter always came first, jam second) in her left hand and her reading material in her right. She took a bite and started to read, continuing the adventure she'd been unable to put down until 4:00 AM that morning. It was a wonderful story; the author had outdone himself. She could have stayed up all night and finished it, but she wanted to prolong it as long as possible. She wanted to savor it, to stretch it out so it would never end. Good books should go on and on forever.

This one didn't go on forever, but it was extremely lengthy. She had to admit she'd peeked. Not to see how it ended—oh, no, she'd never do anything like that, that was sacrilege. She just peeked to see how long it was. The longer the better.

It was long—twelve hundred pages to be exact. Which seemed like a lot, but it wasn't really. Not when you considered the fact that it was written in longhand. The typed version would probably be no more than eight hundred pages, and the book form less than six hundred. She originally thought that she might have trouble reading longhand, but quickly found she had no problem at all; Mark Twain's penmanship was as beautiful as his prose.

Marcella shivered again when she thought how close she'd come to getting caught. The storm; the canceled flight. Trapped. Nowhere to run. The manuscript stolen. What on earth would she have done if they had opened her little Christmas present before she was tucked safely away at the ski lodge?

She looked at the floor. The white wrapping paper and the big red bow lying there by the fireplace so innocently; it had been such a simple scheme. Two packages: one, the Twain manuscript, the other, the complete works of Mark Twain, Michael's Christmas present. A simple mix-up. She didn't know how it could have happened; in her rush she must have gotten the two packages switched. Oh, how embarrassing! She was so sorry.

Marcella smiled. That would have taught all those money-grabbers a lesson. Talk about egg on your face. Talk about looking like the fool. The only downside was the fact that she would not have been there to see their faces when they opened the package and found the books, and not the manuscript ... and there was no way they could reach her. She was incommunicado for ten whole days. Ten whole days while they squirmed and wiggled, and looked for a place to hide. What would they say to all those eager buyers? How would they explain this to the media? Of course, Michael would be in deep weeds, but, then again, he never thought she was competent anyway, now his suspicions would be confirmed. He should feel good about that.

What a terrible thing to do to poor Michael. Marcella felt bad, even though it was little more than he deserved. Little more than they all deserved.

But that was all behind her now. She could relax. The manuscript was safe and she was safe. And now, thanks to the terrorists and the fire, it was in the hands of someone who could truly appreciate it. Someone who *cared*. Someone who would enjoy it over and over again ... and not just for ten days.

Of course she would give it back one day. She wasn't a thief, she was a ... a guardian, a protector. She was keeping it safe from fools who would buy it and horde it away from the world. It belonged to the world; she would keep it concealed until the time came when the world could accept it.

Marcella looked down at the manuscript and sighed. Mark Twain had outdone himself this time. This was his best novel ever. He could make a story come to life like no other author ever had, or ever would. What Mark Twain did with words was magnificent, marvelous. Magical.

She took another bite of her toast and started to read. Less than two pages into it Marcella realized that she would not have time to go ice skating today. She was only on page five-twenty-two of her journey.
She had miles to go.